End
Of
Days

Also by Aaron S. Jones

The Broken Gods
Flames of Rebellion

Paths of Chaos

A Long Way from Home - A collection of short stories from the world of The Broken Gods (available as an audiobook read by Mark Rice-Oxley)

Memories of Blood and Shadow (2022)

End
Of
Days

The Broken Gods:
Book Three

Aaron S. Jones

First edition 2022

Book cover by Mars Dorian

ISBN: 9798471498334

Imprint: Independently published

If you enjoyed this book, please leave a review on Amazon and Goodreads.

Visit **www.aaronsjones.com** for more information. You can sign up to the mailing list to be the first to find out about author events, interviews, and will always be the first to hear of new books from the author.

For you.

For being here at the end of days...

THE KID

'Fucking Barbarians,' muttered Sly, spitting the bitter taste of the word into the snow and keeping his growling to a low, inaudible volume for any who may be listening. Should've wiped the whole lot of them out cycles ago; would have prevented this shit from happening. He'd be sitting beside a fire at Cagen's having an ale or ten and moaning to the girlie and the big man. Raven would be chuckling along as old stories filled the tavern and Socket would be nodding off, his thin frame drifting as the warmth took its toll on the ageing archer. He smiled a wicked smile at the scene playing out in head.

A crock of shit.

Sly loved the fighting. He lived for the chaos and madness of bloody battles. Sinking his axe into his enemies was as essential for him as breathing. He knew it. Those who fought beside him knew it. Hells, the whole of Takaara probably knew it. If the Barbarians had been wiped out cycles ago then he would have just found another enemy to battle. No point denying it. Fighting was in his blood. His heart pumped fury through his veins and if he ever stopped, it would be the end of him.

Climbing up the steep slope of the hill, his eyes darted in every direction, scanning the landscape for any sign of the camp. The old town was nearby, he knew that. Even in the dark of the night he could see the tracks leading north to what had once been a small outpost, a dot on the map that sat amongst the white hell of the Borderlands. Too close to the Barbarian's land for most to venture there. Of course, now the whole place was Barbarian land. The thought brought bile rising to burn his throat. He swallowed the acidic liquid down and grimaced. Raven would be spinning in his grave if he could see what was happening. Redbeard might have been soft at times but the way Herick had gone about things would have brought that infamous fiery glare to the warrior's eyes. But Redbeard was just bones now. Same with Baldor. Socket, too. The old guard was dwindling. Even Kiras hadn't seemed herself since returning from the labour camp. Baldor's death had hit her harder than even Sly had expected. She smiled less and gripped her twin blades with such ferocity that her hands turned whiter than the snow at Sly's feet. She preferred her own company now, the shadow of Baldor's death lingering around her like a bad smell that just wouldn't leave.

The faint glow of firelight reached his eyes as he forced through a gap in a crumbled down wall. The remnants of the town had been charred by the flames. Still, most of the boundary wall still stood, though less effective than it should be. Sly slipped through a break in the wall as the icy wind carried the sound of men's voices. There wouldn't be too many in the camp. Danil had claimed no more than fifty. The leader of the red cloaks had offered the number with a shrug. Sly wanted to be certain.

He crept towards the sound of voices, keeping to the shadows, his hood raised and his boots dropping gently with each step, minimising the crunch against the snowy blanket beneath him.

The firelight shimmered against a shield in one of the men's hands. A single soldier on patrol watching the boundary. Careless. Not enough light to see him properly but Sly didn't care. Barbarian or Borderlander, they were part of Herick's rebellion and that meant they were fair game. Taking a deep breath, Sly slipped a dagger free from his boot, leaving his axes clasped to his belt. Dark work meant daggers. There would be a time for the axes to come out to play but not yet.

Sly snapped his back to the wall, waiting silently on the corner of one of the dilapidated houses. He dared a glance around the corner and counted six men sitting around a campfire. The flames offered him a chance to witness the young, grinning faces of the men wrapped in thick cloaks, shielding themselves from the wind. The light danced off a few tents that had been erected not far from the flames. Most likely the rest of the men were sheltering in what was left of the buildings, unaware that enemies could be nearby. He ran his dagger down the side of the wall, the scraping sound instantly alerting the patrol.

The soldier on patrol turned the corner and Sly was ready.

He pulled the surprised soldier in and smashed his head against the man's face. The shield fell to the ground with a soft thud, the snow cushioning the sound as Sly pressed a grubby hand against his mouth and ran his dagger across the throat with an experienced ease. The soldier clutched frantically at his throat as the blood poured from him like a waterfall of death. Sly watched the wordless struggle with a proud grin on his face. He forced a hand around the back of the soldier's neck and pulled the dying man's head into the wall with as much strength as he could

3

muster.

Sly relaxed and released the soldier. The body fell beside the shield, eyes closed and blood still pouring from the gaping wound in his neck, pooling around him and turning the snow a sickening shade of red. Nose looked broken too, twisted at odd angles, not that it mattered much now. He knelt beside the still body and thrust his dagger straight into the heart, ensuring that there was no chance of this bastard getting back up.

Pleased with his work, he grunted with pride and stood, wiping the blood that had somehow got onto his hands against his dirty cloak and peering once more around the wall. The others seemed none the wiser. Still chuckling around the flames and acting as though having Barbarians settle in the Borderlands was just the way of things. He counted them again.

Six.

Six men.

Six armed men.

He placed his dagger through an empty slot on his belt and whipped out his two axes. He caressed their handles, breathing in deeply and moaning like he had been returned into the arms of a long-lost lover. The axes had always felt like an extension of himself, extra limbs that he had been born to wield. He spun them in his hands and felt that old familiar yearning for battle and blood rise inside his chest. In the distance, the mountain of fire erupted, spewing its orange glow up into the night sky and making those around the campfire jump from their wooden seats. More stumbled in a sleepy haze from the surrounding buildings.

Sly didn't care.

Ignoring the volcano and its explosive song, he stalked forwards, axes in hand.

'Gentlemen!' he cried, smiling at the look of sheer confusion and shock on the men's faces. They all reached for their swords, blades singing in the wind and adding to the music of the volcano as it continued its fiery outburst. 'What a beautiful evening…'

One of the men, the oldest judging by the weary look on his face and grey streaks in his beard and hair, stepped forwards and frowned at Sly. 'I know that face. Sly Stormson,' the man said, still pointing his blade Sly's way. 'Well, I'll be damned…' The man chuckled and looked around at his fellows, their own frightened faces now mirroring their ally's smile. 'Never thought I'd see a goat fucker like you this far north. Heard you had grown soft and taken a love for the South. Too cold for you up here now since Raven's turned to bones.'

This brought a round of chuckles from the men, each guffawing like the dumb children they were.

'Too cold,' Sly repeated, spinning his axes round in his hands and nodding slowly, eyes fixed on his weapons. 'I can show you too cold…'

The smiles twisted into angry glares.

'Been told that if a traitor like you turns up, we'll get good coin for your body. Alive or dead,' the grey man said with a greedy glint in his eyes. The volcano erupted again and Sly was interested to see that the men were jumpy. Scared little shits who had not been forged in the bloody battles that had sharpened Sly into the weapon he was.

'Traitor. Funny word. You are the ones who betrayed us and got into bed with the Barbarians. Being called a goat fucker is nothing compared to being a Barbarian's little bitch,' Sly spat, all traces of humour leaving his voice. How dare this fucking worm call *him* a traitor. 'You are all traitors to the Borderlands. And as such,

5

you have been sentenced to fucking death.'

'And I suppose you are the one to carry out that judgement?' the greybeard asked, licking his lips and giving a small nod to his allies.

Sly glared at them each in turn. Only the greybeard could hold his gaze without pitifully turning away. 'Not just me. You see, I've been making some friends.'

Cray jumped into the firelight with a roar that joined another eruption, burying the sword deep into greybeard's back. He kicked at the body and pulled the sword free with a wild stare, picking out his next target as the greybeard slumped beside the flames.

Sly knew the signal.

He dashed forwards, using the confusion and chaos to his advantage and landing a clean blow of his axe straight into the skull of the nearest soldier. He twisted and pulled his weapon free, moving onto the next bastard.

The confusion only held sway over the camp for a moment. A sword stabbed his way but Sly dodged it with ease. He snapped an elbow up into the fool's jaw and whipped his axe across, aiming to take his opponent's throat. A lucky raise of the shield saved the man but Sly hadn't stopped. Bringing his left hand up, he raised his other axe and brought it down with a gleeful scream into the night, blood splattering over his face and painting him red as another soul was sent through the black gate.

Sly looked away from his fallen opponent and frowned.

Four more bodies lay beside the campfire. Cray grinned that dull grin that Sly hated so much.

'You've killed four?' he asked Cray incredulously, kicking at one of the bodies in frustration.

'And you've killed two,' Cray replied, grin growing wider.

'Three,' Sly bit back. 'There's another back there.' He jerked a thumb over his shoulder and scowled. 'I ain't losing this one, you bastard fuck.'

'I'll go easy this time.'

'Like fucking hells you will!' Sly growled and finally smiled at his ally. 'You know the plan.'

Cray nodded. 'Kill the fuckers.'

Sly danced through the crude attacks and gifted death to any who were foolish enough to step into his path. His axes blurred with an added intensity, ignoring Cray shouting numbers out with each kill, knowing the warrior was intending to wind him up. Wasn't gonna happen. He ducked under a wild swing of the sword that would have whipped his head off and came up with his deadly axes. One caught his attacker right in the nuts. The other swipe opened up the man's stomach and released a stream of guts onto the battlefield. All thoughts of attack left the soldier. His sword hit the ground with a thud as he screamed, his hands reaching uselessly to grab at the pile of shit flopping out of his wound. Sly ended the man's suffering with a single cut across his neck.

'That was nasty,' a familiar voice said beside him.

'The one to the nuts or the guts?'

Kiras paused, focusing on blocking an attack with her two blades. Her swords crossed one another, halting the potentially deadly strike coming her way. With an effortless ease, she dived under the swords and twisted her body, jabbing a blade behind her and straight through her shocked victim's chest.

'Both,' she answered Sly, not stopping. 'Nuts and guts. Fucking disgusting. Give me a clean strike across the neck when it's my time.'

'You're dying in your sleep as an old, nagging woman,' Sly responded with a laugh, taking the legs from beneath the soldier racing past him and towards the bastards who had stormed the camp following Cray's cry into the night. 'Too annoying to die young.'

'That a compliment?'

'Nah. I don't do those.'

Kiras knocked a strike high with one blade and thrust the other straight through the heart of her shocked attacker. He fell to his knees and Kiras showed no mercy. Crossing the swords over one another, she pulled the blades wide before bringing them together with a fury that would turn Gods into whimpering fools. The Borderlander's head dropped with a dull thud and Kiras moved onto her next intended victim.

Sly made for the north of the ruined town. He jumped over the rubble and debris that had been left when Herick's forces had sacked the place. This was one of the few places in the North that had fought against the new rule of Herick and the Barbarians. Accounts from the farmers and fishermen in the area who had survived all agreed what had happened. Rejgar had led a group of Barbarians and a few of Herick's soldiers into the town. They had blocked any exits and set fire to the place. As the flames had burned, the warriors had shown no mercy, slaughtering men, women, children. One of the farmers had wept as he told his story; claimed he still heard the screams when he closed his eyes at night.

The red cloaks were fighting well, shields side by side and spears picking off any who dared get close enough to them. The remaining warriors fighting, all Borderlanders, were panicked. Wild-eyed and frightened, searching for a way out of their predicament and focusing on their own survival. They knew that victory was no longer an option.

What they didn't realise yet was that retreat was no longer an option either.

Sly rushed past the tents, the decrepit buildings, and the fallen bodies. His axes sang the song of death as he passed the fleeing warriors, cutting them down with ease as he made for the broken, wooden archway signalling the northern exit. He ran twenty paces through the gate and turned, boots digging into the snow and eyes turned to the town. The sounds of battle lessened but he could still hear the clear ring of swords against shield, cries of pain cut off with single, fatal strikes, and the shouts of victory from the red cloaks under Danil's leadership. He glanced to his right and offered Danil a small nod of his head.

'A simple battle,' the red cloak declared through his dark, beaked mask. 'They weren't ready for us.'

'Why would they be?' Sly scoffed. 'The town is destroyed and there is no strategic value in holding it. Must have thought it was an easy place to hold up before Herick called for them.'

'Good to know that our scouts were correct. Master Arden will be pleased.'

Sly bowed his head and stared at his boots upon hearing the kid's name. He'd been happy to see the kid alive; shocked, but happy. In the time since the kid's return though, Sly had seen a big change in him. Killing Socket had just been the start. The old archer had played by his own rules long enough. As much as Sly had respected him, he couldn't argue much against Arden's revenge. Everyone becomes bones at some point. But Arden didn't seem himself in the days and weeks that had followed. He was cold, distant. He barked orders and threatened hell upon any who did not follow his commands to perfection. The only time he wore even the hint of a smile was when Sly or Kiras would speak to him. Even then it passed quicker than the eye of a storm. Made Sly feel uneasy, and that wasn't something that happened too often.

'Yeah, the kid will be pleased,' he snarled.

Danil shifted uncomfortably at the nickname. 'Don't think he is too fond of still being called the kid.'

'Then he can come and tell me himself, can't he?' Sly snapped, pissed that everyone was having to walk around on eggshells whenever Arden's name was brought up. He was still that little quivering rookie who threw up all over himself – he may have lost the gold in his eyes but that didn't change who he was.

Their conversation was interrupted by a small group of warriors stumbling out of the gate, chased by a marching line of shields held by the red cloaks. Sly growled and held his axes up, showing the fleeing warriors that this would be the end of the line. Danil twisted the spear in his hand and dropped into his own fighting stance as the red cloaks separated on cue, fanning out and circling around the fifteen or so warriors who had managed to leave the town's boundary.

Aware of their fate, the soldiers dropped their weapons. Just a couple of them at first, followed reluctantly by the rest. A few had worried looks on their faces, mainly the younger ones, but the more experienced had that knowing look of resignation that Sly had seen a thousand times before.

Kiras and Cray trudged through the snow and through the gate, walking around the circle of red cloaks until they reached Sly and Danil.

'This is the last of them,' Kiras said, gesturing at

10

the nervous men enclosed within the circle of shields and spears.

'We can take them as prisoners,' Danil suggested, turning his back to them so that the warriors would not be able to work out his words. 'They don't all need to die.'

Sly growled, recalling the farmer's tale. 'More mouths to feed. Times are tough enough for the rest of us. Too many of those working the land are in with Herick and his cowards.'

Cray grunted, agreeing with him.

The howling wind stopped unnaturally fast and Sly uttered a curse that only he could hear. He coughed and turned on the spot, frowning as he saw a dark-cloaked figure gliding across the snow, flanked by two armoured warriors who smelled of rot and decay. The volcano behind them lit up the night sky and illuminated Arden's pale face. Hundreds of pairs of eyes were reflected in the shadows by the sudden burst of light, sending a shiver down Sly's spine.

'You have done well. All of you,' Arden's voice danced through the still air. He flicked his hand and the red cloaks backed away, fading into the darkness of the night. His black eyes met Sly's for the briefest of moments and then turned to Kiras, the edge of a smile blossoming on cold lips. 'Though, we cannot have any speaking of our coming. I want to witness the shock and fear in Herick's eyes when he sees what I am capable of.'

The warriors no longer had the wall of shields to prevent their escape, yet none of them moved a muscle. One of the men, a young man with just the shadow of a beard on his face, began to whimper and cry. An older fellow placed a comforting hand on his shoulder but offered no words. There were none that would help now.

Still, one of them attempted to work a way out of

11

the predicament. 'Please, we can help. We don't like what Herick has done. Just had to go along with him as there was no one else to fight against him. Now we have you! That's why we stay here, no stinking Barbarians here. They're all holed up in Hillheim and the capital. Please…'

Arden clicked his fingers and uttered a single command. 'Feed.'

Sly stormed away but he could still hear the screams and the tearing of flesh as Arden's beasts ripped into the fifteen men, young and old. He stopped when he felt a gentle hand on his shoulder.

'What we are doing is cleansing Takaara,' a strange voice declared. 'I need to know that you are still going to fight by my side.'

Sly shrugged the hand off from his shoulder and turned to stare into Arden's starry eyes. 'I'll fight by your side.' He inclined his head towards the beasts as they continued with their demonic work. 'But not with them. You want to cleanse Takaara?' Arden nodded, face stern with determination, so entirely different to the young archer who had wanted to be accepted into Raven's tribe. The young archer who had come to Sly for advice. 'I heard another man talk of cleansing Takaara. My aim is to kill him. Don't let those fancy new eyes of yours blind you to what you're doing, kid. I'm here to take back the Borderlands and I'll die trying. You sure you know what you're doing?'

Arden paused and bit into his dark lips, thinking carefully. 'I'm getting my revenge.'

'On who?'

'Everyone.'

A LIGHT THAT BLINDS

aterina Kane raised an arm to shield her face from the midday sun's bright light. It was hotter than all the hells but Istari had wanted to press on. They were close to the city and delaying their arrival would help no one. So, thirsty and exhausted by the extremes of the eastern climate, Kane pushed the camel on across the golden sands and tried her best to ignore the sticky wetness of her shirt against her skin. She was a woman born and bred in the North. Nothing had prepared her for such heat. Even the air seemed against her. Each breath brought with it a choking heat that dried her throat. Istari seemed unperturbed. The old warrior cut a dashing figure as he bobbed up and down with ease on his own beast of burden, a navy scarf wrapped around his head and twisted to cover much of his face, leaving only those sparkling eyes. His forearms were a golden brown, darkened further by the sun's heat and he looked at complete ease on the sands. She wondered how she must look, struggling on the strange camel and soaked in sweat, each movement ending with a soft groan or grunt.

'Are we close?' she asked for what must have been the hundredth time.

'There is a small village that we will reach before sundown. You can rest and drink there,' Istari Vostor replied, eyes focused on the shimmering horizon.

Kane nodded, too weak to reply. She felt a nudge on her arm and looked up to see Istari holding his own water flask. He inclined his head, prodding her again with the bottle.

Usually, her pride would prevent her from taking the bottle from her companion but her pride had been whisked away like the grains of sand in the wind. She took the flask eagerly and leant her head back, pouring its contents down her throat and moaning with relief. Some of the water splashed onto her chin and down her shirt but she did not care.

She left a bit of the water at the bottom of the flask, remembering that Istari would need water too, perhaps before they reached this village.

'Thank you,' she said, thirst quenched for the time being.

'You are welcome,' Istari replied, grabbing the flask and placing it back into his bag. 'I remember the first time I travelled the sands. It is a harsh and unforgiving land. Capable of honing its inhabitants into hardened, resilient people.'

'Braego used to tell me the same of the Borderlands. He insisted that it was the most unforgiving piece of Takaara. He would tell me it is the landscape and climate that trained the men and women and forced them into being fighters, capable of doing anything to survive.'

'He sounds like a wise man.'

'He was. I miss him.'

14

An awkward silence hung in the air. Kane exhaled and fought back against the heat of tears struggling to force their way out at the memory of the warrior from the Borderlands.

'How did he die?'

'Killed,' she said bluntly. 'T'Chai. One of Mason D'Argio's hounds. Used magic to ensure it wasn't a fair fight.' The shadow passing over Istari's face at those names worried Kane. She swallowed hard and asked the difficult question.

'You know them?'

Istari scratched his beard beneath the scarf, his unease clear even with most of his face covered. 'I know them. Mason was a little brute even in his youth. Selfish. Greedy. Awful temper. And T'Chai...' Istari's face sunk further at the warrior's name. His mouth opened and closed as the warrior struggled to find the right words.

'What about T'Chai?' The pit of Kane's stomach dropped like a march from a cliff.

Istari cleared his throat and turned away, unable to look her in the eye. 'Quiet lad. Watched everything with an analytical eye. Keen to learn. Smarter than Mason, by a long shot. Skilled with any weapon pressed into his hands. He was my greatest student.'

The dizziness sweeping over Kane had nothing to do with her thirst. She swayed on the beast, catching herself at the last moment as Istari rushed to be at her side. Vomit lurched up into her chest and throat, threatening to overwhelm her. She choked and leaned forward, jerking away as Istari attempted to place an awkward reassuring hand on her back.

Kane winced and ran a shaking hand down her face. She turned when she felt capable to look at Istari, eyes burning with betrayal.

'You trained that monster?'

'My time spent in the East is a complicated one. There is good and bad in all armies. My role at the time meant that I had to do what was asked of me. I was asked to pick and train a selection of promising young soldiers. He was one of them.'

'You regret it?'

'No.' There was no hesitation in his answer. 'I did what was asked of me. I followed my orders and people are better off because of it.'

'Braego isn't better off.'

'You said he was a born warrior; he would have understood. He would have done the very same thing that I did.'

'Do you think he would have married the Empress of the East? A woman who has split Takaara in two and caused the deaths of thousands.'

Istari's face hardened, his sympathy leaving his face in an instant. 'You have no idea of what you speak.' His tongue rolled around his cheeks before he chose his next words. 'And did Braego not sleep with an enemy? A widowed enemy...'

The words were a slap across her face. Flames of shock and anger burned through her. Fists clenched, teeth grinding together, she did her best not to swing for the legendary swordsman. 'It would be best if we leave this conversation there.'

'I wholeheartedly concur.'

Istari clicked his heels against the camel and pushed forward, sand kicking back from the animal's feet. Kane cursed herself when he was out of earshot. She shouldn't have let the conversation get to her. It was true that she didn't know enough about Istari to judge him. Perhaps it was the heat, the thirst, the whole cursed situation that had her on edge. She would need to calm before they reached the capital, things weren't going to get any easier. Istari had warned her that they would be meeting the very empress that Kane had just badmouthed, the woman believed responsible for burnings across the whole of Takaara – a woman who many claimed believed herself to be a God.

Kane muttered a prayer to The Four and pushed on, followed the trail of dust left in Istari's wake.

*

Kane let Istari do the talking as they entered the village to curious looks from the inhabitants. He slipped effortlessly into the Eastern tongue, organising rooms and food for them as a couple of small, elderly women emerged from the small crowd that had gathered to greet the strange guests and take their animals to the stables.

The stone buildings scattered throughout the village were all the same kind of beige colour Kane had grown weary of as she traversed the sands of the desert. Flat roofs told her that it wasn't often that they would have to deal with a downpour of rain. The villagers all had dark skin and hair that was almost as black as the night sky. Some of the women wore dark, flowing dresses with thin scarves that pulled loosely over their heads. The men wore lighter clothing, whites and greys that hung loosely from their lean frames. All of the men had grown their beards out, though most were trimmed to various styles, much smarter than the wild northern style and not as pretentious as the thin or curled moustaches that had been growing in popularity in Archania.

Kane's eyes fell on a small group of children who had managed to meander their way through the crowd and were now staring at her in amazement. She wondered if they had ever seen someone as pale as her this far to the east. She smiled and waved at the children, a chorus of excited giggles greeting her in response. The adults around them instantly relaxed, smiling with the children and sharing laughter at the simple exchange.

Slowly, the crowd dispersed, leaving Kane with Istari and three women who were listening intently to his words. A farmer strode past with a goat, pulling the animal forward and giving Kane an embarrassed, pleading look as he passed. He said something in a tongue she did not understand but she smiled back and that brought a grin in return.

Istari gave the women some coin and they turned to speak with one another as Istari nodded and turned to speak with Kane.

'They will give us shelter and food. They will feed the animals and clean them. We can leave in the morning for the capital,' he informed her.

'Are they not curious as to why we are here?' Kane queried, unsure of how trusting she should be now that she was in enemy territory.

'It is not often that they have visitors from the West,' he explained. 'We are a curiosity and nothing more. They have more reason to be wary of people from Darakeche than they do of the West. Darakeche is the only nation that has fought against them in recent cycles. We have used Darakeche to fight a proxy war on our behalf. Consequently, these people see no reason to be suspicious of us.'

Kane accepted the explanation with little resistance. It made sense.

One of the women strode over to them and

pressed two fingers against her forehead before pointing up at the sun. Istari mirrored the greeting and so Kane copied it, not wanting to seem ignorant, though she had never seen the gesture previously.

The woman led them down the dusty path that ran between the low, stone buildings. Kane's attention was pulled in every direction as they passed a variety of animals Kane had never seen before; children running between the gaps of the buildings and ignoring cries from the adults they passed by; curious people either side of her waved and gestured to the sun, smiling at them on their journey. Fascinated by it all, Kane nodded to each and every person she passed, blessed to enjoy this shot of life that was so different to her own.

A group of men lounged in low chairs outside one of the buildings, embracing the shade offered by a low animal skin covering that had been erected alongside the roof with two wooden poles. They fanned themselves with long, thin, green plants as they chatted, stopping only when Kane's guide waved and pushed Istari forwards.

'Looks like I am in here,' he said to Kane as he saluted the men jumping up from their seats. 'The women's quarters will be farther along,' he explained to her.

Kane nodded as the woman guiding her took her hand and whisked her to a similar building just down the pathway, smiling at the clutch of children that had gathered to stare and point at Kane.

The guide playfully shooed the children away before leading Kane into the building. Stunning flowers of all colours stood in decorative vases that filled the spacious room. The sweet scent of the flowers took Kane back to her rides in the fields of Archania and she had a sudden longing to return home.

Two women draped in black rushed over, their

beautiful, dark hair falling in waves past their shoulders as they greeted Kane with short bows and took her hands in their own. Her guide smile and waved, leaving Kane to awkwardly cry a strained goodbye and her thanks.

'Don't worry. We will look after you,' the woman to her right said in broken Northern.

Kane started at words that she understood. 'Thank you,' she managed to utter in return, bringing laughter to the two women.

They brought her to a corridor with two open doors. The woman who had spoken pointed to the door to her right. 'Bath. For cleaning.' She mimed cleaning her body and Kane nodded with a small chuckle, letting her know that she understood. The woman pointed to the door to the left. 'Bed.' She closed her eyes and feigned snoring. The three of them laughed together and Kane squeezed their hands softly.

'Thank you. Thank you so much for your help.'

The women turned with more bows and left her to make the choice alone.

Both were needed. Both were longed for.

Kane smiled and took the door to the right.

'The water was so lovely and warm!' Kane recalled, grabbing Istari's arm and enjoying his look of unease at the familiarity. 'And that bed! I've never felt such comfort.'

'You are aware that we are currently staying in a village on the outskirts of the Empire?' he asked, looking down at his arm until she removed her hand. 'If you are impressed by anything in this hovel then you will pass out with joy when we arrive in the city…'

The woman who had spoken to her earlier returned

with small cups of tea. She had spoken with Kane after her short sleep, informing her that her name was Duaa.

Kane sipped the sweet tea and enjoyed the warmth trickling down her body and warming her. 'Thank you, again.'

'My pleasure,' Duaa replied with a broad grin, flashing her dazzling teeth and pushing her dark locks away from piercing brown eyes. 'I hope you are liking the dance,' she said, pointed past the large fire pit at the men and women dancing in colourful garb around the flames.

'It is beautiful,' Kane admitted. She leaned closer to Duaa and offered a cheeky grin and nodded towards Istari who seemed in a trance as he watched the elegant, rapid movements. 'I think he is enjoying it too.'

Duaa winked and laughed, a beautiful sound that carried across the night. Kane placed her cup on the ground beside her seat and clapped along with the beat of the drums playing out, lost in the rhythm of the simple, but joyous music.

'I must admit, this was not what I expected from a village on the edge of the Empire.'

Istari broke from his trance and smiled sadly. 'No one expects this. They think everyone lives in fear: no joy, no smiling, no life. They misunderstand the Empire and what it means to live in the light.'

The words sobered Kane, pulling the joy from her. She had not expected the famed Sword of Causrea to defend the Empire. 'The Empire has caused the deaths of so many. Burnings. I saw a young boy burned alive because he wished to speak to his late father one last time.'

'And would you say that your precious United Cities of Archania was not capable of evil before it joined with the Empire? No suffering, or torture?'

Kane thought about it for a moment. She recalled the dungeons beneath the palace. The labour camps farther south where violent criminals would be shipped away. These were things that existed generations before the light of the Empire shone upon Archania.

'Most people are quick to judge the Empire. They see them as evil. I am not defending them. I have seen the horrors of the Empire. But I have seen such horrors wherever my path has led me.' He stopped and looked Kane in the eyes and winked. 'Why do you think I live in the middle of nowhere?'

They laughed and Kane relaxed. 'Your daughter despises the Empire. How does that make you feel?'

The bones in Istari's neck cracked as he twisted his head from side to side. 'She is young. She has been through much. Too much for one still so bright with life. Hating the Empire makes her life easier. It also makes it easier for me to protect her. That is more important than her understanding the nuances of the Empire.'

'And what about me? Will I be able to take on such a burden?'

'You are old enough and weary enough to handle it I think,' Istari chuckled, allowing a soft punch on his arm as Kane feigned horror at his words. 'People are complex. Nations are complex. Empires even more so. I do not believe that anyone sets out with malicious intentions. We are all doing what we think is best, what we think is right. From where we stand, we think we are in the light, fighting against an oncoming darkness. The only problem is, stand too close, and that light blinds, and we cannot see the evils that we might bring into the world.'

A horn blew on the edge of the village, halting their conversation.

The dance stopped and the villagers shared nervous glances with one another. Kane made to stand as the worried looks eventually landed on the two outsiders sitting by the edge of the fire. Istari grabbed her wrist and pulled, forcing her back to her seat.

'Stay. We do not want any trouble,' he muttered.

Kane did as she was asked, staring at him with confusion.

A deep voice called through the village; Eastern words lost on Kane. She watched Istari's reaction, hoping to understand from his movements what was happening but the warrior just sat and sipped his tea with annoying calmness.

The dancers and villagers stepped back from the outsiders as the sounds of boots made their way towards the fire. Kane glanced up and saw the reason for their worry.

Five soldiers armed for battle marched together. Three women and two men – all with shields and swords drawn, the light of the flames flickering from their silver breastplates and shining on their long, flowing white cloaks.

The group stopped as they reached Kane and Istari. She spotted one of the men, the one standing farther back than the others, gaze at Istari, his jaw dropping. The others held their emotions in check, staring at the two of them with detached professionalism. One of the women stepped forward and stared straight at Istari.

'Istari Vostor. On behalf of the Empress of the Empire of Light, we are to escort you to the city of Yalaandi where you are to meet with a jury who will hear your defence regarding crimes committed in your time away from the Light.'

Kane stayed silent. All eyes were on Istari.

The man gave no indication that he was even listening. He chewed on his cheek, spitting at the floor between his boots and rolled his shoulders back, wincing as they cracked with the effort.

'You are to give up your weapons whilst we escort you to the city.' The woman did well to keep her voice from shaking but there was no hiding the nervous glance she gave to those beside her. The shields trembled in their hands as Istari rose from his seat and locked his eyes upon the poor woman.

'You all know me. Or have heard of me.' Istari said. 'The only way the five of you will touch my weapon is if I stab it through your heart.'

Kane hid her glee, biting her lip to stay from laughing at the clear looks of distress on the soldiers' faces.

'We are on our way to the city. You may join us on our journey if that is your wish,' Istari offered, throwing the rest of his tea into the fire and marching right through the middle of the soldiers, forcing them to move out of his way. He stopped as he reached the quaking boy at the back, glaring at the trembling soldier. 'These good people know where our bags and clothes are being kept. Make sure you get them all if you are to join us. Pay them well, they have cared for us as great hosts do when touched by the Light.'

The young soldier nodded, sweat pouring down his dark skin and pooling around his lips and beard.

'Now!' Istari growled. The soldier ran from Istari and searched wildly for any sign of where their belongings may be kept.

Kane stood and followed Istari, meeting the fearful eyes of the soldiers as she walked between them, still stifling her laughter. Eventually, she caught up with Istari, pleased to see the wide grin on the old warrior's face.

'You enjoyed that,' she claimed.

'Of course I did,' he admitted. 'Those soldiers have grown up with tales of my prowess with a blade. It is about time I had a bit of fun with it.'

A NEW ROLE

'The matters that you wished to be resolved have been resolved. You expressed the importance of haste, therefore we ensured that our teams were aware that they may act as they saw fit to capture those rioting against the changes in the kingdom. Thirty men and women were apprehended from the list you handed to us. Ten were killed in unfortunate circumstances when they refused to cooperate with our investigation. The other twenty are currently residing beneath the palace as you wished. Five others from your list remain elusive but our teams are working to ensure that if they are indeed still in Archania, that we find them and bring them to justice.'

Amana delivered the report with a proud glint in her eyes. *Currently residing beneath the palace.* Cypher had to admit, one of the perks of his new role was working with the young woman from the East. She followed orders to the letter with no hesitation. He remembered a young Zaif behaving in a similar way. Hopefully this new relationship didn't have to end the same way.

'Excellent,' Cypher said, rubbing his jawline and turning his attention to the nervous, young man beside Amana. Haadi was good at his job. He followed the orders and had the right amount of fear and respect for Cypher. But the man always looked as though he was just about to piss himself. Not the best look for one working for the new regime in the kingdom.

'And what about you, Haadi? How do you feel that the case is progressing?' he asked the poor fellow, boring his eyes into the sweating young man.

Haadi stood to attention, eyes flickering to Amana, searching for support as he swallowed and stuttered his way through his own findings. 'The citizens of the Lower City have fallen into line. Your advice on ensuring the punishments were public have struck fear into those who may have carried thoughts of rebellion. With the main culprits rounded up or dead, we can expect little resistance now from that area of the city.'

Cypher nodded and hummed a little tune as he stood from behind his brand new desk and strolled over to the quaking figure. He ran a gentle hand down Haadi's clammy cheek and locked his eyes upon the nervous fool.

'And what of the Upper City, Haadi? Should we be worried?'

'N-n-no sir. They have rallied to support Mason D'Argio. The citizens of the Upper City have made it clear that they support any path that will lead to ending the sparks of rebellion and defeating the savages of the Borderlands. General T'Chai is currently training the army in preparation to march north and we have the full backing of the great houses of Archania. Only Norland remains silent.'

27

Haadi breathed a long, slow sigh of relief as Cypher nodded and turned away, happy with the report.

Norland would not be joining them any time soon. That information wasn't new to Cypher. Ambassador Matthias had made it quite clear in his last letter that Norland was staying out of any conflict for the time being – they wanted freedom and that was it. However, it was good to know that the city was beginning to settle once again. Mason would never split the army whilst Archania stood on the edge of rebellion and without the army heading north, Cypher would not be able to carry out his task.

'This is all good news, Haadi. Like Amana, I am glad to have you in my service.' The young man broke into a relieved smile, shoulders relaxing as he finally fell from attention. Amana sighed with annoyance at her brother.

'There is one more person that I wish for you to find and bring to me,' Cypher said, taking a seat and staring at the two of them over his desk. 'This one is more personal for me. A character in the city who does not know the value of keeping his mouth shut. I wish for you to find Sir Dominic for me.'

Even Amana was unable to hide the surprise on her face. Unlike Haadi though, she was able to shift hastily back to that professional stare she had perfected in her time in the Empire.

'May I ask the reason for Sir Dominic's arrest, sir?' Amana asked.

'A knight,' Haadi grumbled, teeth tearing into his bottom lip so hard that Cypher spotted a trickle of blood.

'Dear Dominic is a highly valued knight who is known for his services in the war between the United Cities and the Borderlands,' Cypher explained, though they both knew his history. 'I am not wishing to arrest this great man.

28

With General Grey now retired and living on his estate by the coast, Sir Dominic is one of our most respected and experienced soldiers.' Cypher felt waves of pride just for managing to keep a straight face as the words effortlessly slipped from his mouth.

'War is coming, surely it is prudent for us to ensure that all of our best fighting minds are a part of the planning. Sir Dominic is a valuable asset. All I want is a short conversation, just to see where his head is currently. As always, I expect that he is willing to do whatever it takes to ensure that he serves the United Cities of Archania to the best of his abilities.'

Haadi had gone a strange ashen colour and looked as though he may collapse at any moment. Cypher grinned at Amana though, the soldier seemed to be holding back from laughter, obviously understanding the truth hiding behind Cypher's words.

'We will have him here before sundown, sir,' Amana promised, heels clapping together. 'Sir Dominic is not exactly a difficult man to find in this city.'

'Truer words have never been spoken, my dear Amana,' Cypher agreed. He smiled at her before giving Haadi a quick look over, trying his best not to roll his eyes. 'And please look after your brother, he has turned a strange colour. Something he has eaten, perhaps?'

Sir Dominic did his best to enter Cypher's office with his usual pomp and bluster. Loud voice. Big grin. Chest puffed out as far as possible. Yet his garish, expensive clothes were drenched in sweat and his eyes were darting in all directions, betraying his true feelings regarding the summons.

'Cypher Zellin, dear boy! A pleasure to see you as always! And looking very well, I see. I was most pleased when I heard that our esteemed leader had given you such a high position within the Empire, couldn't go to a better man. I would have brought one of my favourite wines to celebrate if I had been given time,' he scowled at Amana as she motioned for him to take a seat. 'Flarian Red. None better. None better!'

A gentle breeze eased in through the narrow window. Cypher stood and strolled over to close it, taking his time as he stared out across the city from the high vantage point of the tower. 'You have lived in Archania for all of your life, have you not?'

Dominic's face creased as he turned to face Cypher, stumbling over his words and obviously hoping that he was answering correctly. 'All of my life, Zellin. Parents were born in the Upper City. And their parents before them. Cut me and I bleed Archania, let me tell you!' He thumbed a fist against his chest, his pristine silk sky blue jacket shimmering in the low evening light creeping through the windows.

'And you have bled for us, have you not, good knight?' Cypher reminded him, turning around and sitting back into his seat opposite the old soldier. 'Your efforts in the Northern Wars are the stuff of legend.'

The flattery settled Dominic. He was more used to these lines of conversation. He relaxed back into his seat and held his hands out wide, blushing and raising his eyebrows in agreement before clapping his hands back together.

'Well, it has always been a view of mine, and that of my family,' he sat up and pulled his chair closer, his bloated, red face leaning forward towards Cypher, 'that we should never ask what can Archania do for us, but what can *we* do for Archania. An old nation built on honour and dignity. When the war broke out, it was my duty to enlist and fight

30

against those savages, those heathens.' He wagged a sausage of a finger at Cypher and nodded his head, jowls wriggling manically as though in agreement. 'Did you know that some of them still worship the Old Gods?' He barked a harsh laugh and fell back against his seat. 'Madness. They really are a backwards people. No, it was my duty, my honour to fight against them.'

'Any particular acts that you are most fond of recalling?' Cypher prodded. He pointed to his two companions standing silently behind the knight. 'Amana and Haadi here may not have heard such tales before. They are new to this region of Takaara.'

'It has been some time,' Dominic said with a nervous smile, pulling out a handkerchief from his breast pocket and wiping the beads of sweat that had popped up on his brow. 'Most people in the city enjoy the tale of when I held the Northern Gate almost single-handedly. Hundreds of the bastards died by my sword that day. A great pile of the bloody invaders. Most of my unit were dead or fleeing – scared of the odds against us you see – it was a surprise attack from the Borderlanders and most of our forces were elsewhere, unfortunately.'

'*Almost* single-handedly?' Cypher bristled. 'From how I've heard it told, you did it all yourself! In fact, there are claims that you screamed for Reaver Redbeard himself to step forward and taste the blood on your blade. You do yourself a disservice.'

Dominic wiped a hand across his thin moustache and breathed in harshly through his teeth. 'Humility is vital for a knight, Cypher Zellin. A war is won by the army, not by single soldiers. Whomever told you that tale was obviously embellishing it for the crowd! An entertainer to appease the masses no doubt. You will have heard of countless such stories over the cycles in the taverns and inns across this country.'

Cypher pouted and sat forward slowly in his chair. 'But *you* were the person who told me that tale.'

He delighted in the way Dominic pulled at his collar and squirmed in his seat at that comment.

To his credit, the knight managed to display a passable look of injured innocence, even as he stammered his response. 'W-w-w-well after a glass or two of wine, the stories may take on a fresh tint. It is not an enjoyable experience recalling events from the battlefield. You would not know,' Dominic's face tightened as he glared into Cypher's cold eyes. 'You were not there.'

Cypher nodded in agreement. 'No. I was not. War is such a messy thing. And sadly, it appears that we are on the brink of another. A chance to finish what we started, eh?'

'About damn time, I say!' Dominic agreed, punching a fist on Cypher's desk, glad to be back on more stable ground in the conversation.

'I am glad to see such enthusiasm. You see, Dustin Grey was recently relieved of his post as General.'

'A good decision if you ask me,' Dominic stepped in. 'He did well for this kingdom but seemed to lose the energy for it over the past few cycles. One of the old guard, unwilling to do what must be done. Unwilling to show the rest of Takaara how great we truly are!'

'I am glad that you see it that way, Sir Dominic. I have been tasked with forming a unit of trustworthy men who have experience of warfare. This unit will guide our forces, attend meetings of the utmost importance, and when the times comes – fight for the Empire and for our beloved Archania!'

From the corner of his eyes, Cypher caught the curl

of Amana's lips. Haadi just looked as confused and out of place as ever.

The knight though, had turned an odd shade of grey. The blood had drained from his face and his eyes were working overtime as they blinked faster than the wings of a hummingbird.

'I understand that such an honour may seem overwhelming for a man of your stature and patriotic fervour, Sir Dominic,' Cypher smirked, rising from his seat and offering a hand over the desk to the man. 'No words are necessary. Mason will be so pleased to hear that you have accepted.'

Dominic nearly fell back into his chair as he stood and limply shook Cypher's hand. His face was now a sickly shade of green.

Cypher nodded over to the siblings and they rushed forwards, taking an arm each and leading him to the door. 'Such a pleasure, Sir Dominic, as always!' he called out to the knight.

When Amana and Haadi returned, Cypher was sipping a victorious glass of whiskey, looking out once more over the city as the sun fell in the west.

'Place a pair of eyes on that fool,' he ordered the two of them. 'Inform me as soon as the coward leaves the Western Gate.'

'You expect him to flee the city?' Haadi asked, a naïve frown plastered all over his dark features.

'That man couldn't teach a fish to swim, let alone be given any responsibility regarding our soldiers. I wanted him out of the way. He will flee to Grey and grovel for shelter behind those high walls that the former general now lives behind.'

'So you scared him with the burden of

responsibility you knew he would not take, but would not turn down,' Amana stated smugly.

'He is someone else's problem now. We have enough of our own to deal with...'

Cypher slipped into the shadows with as much ease as he would a familiar pair of shoes. Speaking of which, his new ones were polished to an almost unnatural shine. The rest of his clothes matched – black trousers, black waistcoat, black jacket, and a black hat pulled low at the front to further conceal his face.

Taking a seat at the back of the room, he sat on a raised platform high enough to witness the thrilling butchery in the circle of roaring men and women. The crunch of bone on bone was met with louder roars and shaking fists; pandemonium amongst the revellers as they fed on the brutality of the bare knuckle fighting before them.

He loved every bit of it.

The blood. The sweat. The bruising.

Even the stench of desperation as the two men lunged at one another, not knowing whether the next blow would be the final one. Many citizens of Archania had died in this ring beneath the city, all hoping for a chance to earn a bit of coin or a reputation to stagger their way up the ladder of the United Cities. The ladder was dripping with blood though, and likely to cause a fall right back to where they were now. Cypher had seen it all before.

'This is where I first met our dearly departed friend, Zaif,' Cypher said, arm leaning over the back of his chair, still facing the brutal battle but head turned slightly to the side so that the newcomer would be able to hear him. 'Even as a boy he was a terrifying brute. So much potential.'

'A riveting tale, I am sure,' a voice drawled from the darkness. The orange glow of the lanterns failed to reach the shadows this far from the ring, but Cypher knew that voice anywhere.

'How do you think you would fare in such fights, T'Chai?' he asked. 'That one is almost twice your size.' He pointed down at the fighter obviously in command.

Dressed only in shorts, the sinewy fighter's ripped frame was clear for all in attendance. Blood had splattered over his broad chest and caught on his wild, blonde hair that fell almost to his waist. Borderlander most likely. Or a Barbarian. From somewhere north of the United Cities anyway. He stood over his fallen opponent, a lean, shorter fellow with olive toned skin. The shorter man had a hand raised and was pleading for mercy. There was no mercy in this room though.

'Such fights are beneath my people.'

'Fights like this happen in every part of Takaara, don't take me for a fool,' Cypher said, his chair creaking as he leaned forwards to witness the end of the contest. The crowd were at fever pitch now, jumping and dancing about like wild animals, holding their slips of paper displaying their bets and watching every movement of the Northerner as he roared, arms going wide.

Then he felt a kick to the nuts.

The shorter fighter leapt up and grabbed his opponent's neck in a chokehold and dropped back, dragging the body to the ground and placing as much pressure on the larger man's neck as he possibly could.

'I hear that you are heading north to destroy Herick's forces and wipe the Borderlands from the map,' Cypher said, laughing as the audience erupted in anger as the contest swayed in a direction not of their liking.

'Sheer numbers will overwhelm them this time. What they did to Mason's daughter cannot go unpunished. They killed an innocent priestess and burned a temple,' T'Chai answered, leaning forwards himself to watch the spectacle.

'I thought those who killed her were punished. Saw Mason kill a man with my own two eyes.'

T'Chai sucked his gums and cast a withering look towards Cypher. 'We both know that was a show. The culprits are still out there, in the Borderlands.'

'Makes sense,' Cypher nodded. He had already come to that conclusion. 'My people tell me that word is making the rounds that it was one of the Borderlanders who Mason freed from my dungeons…'

'*Your* dungeons?'

'You know what I mean.'

T'Chai sighed. 'Whomever it was, they will be dealt with.'

'And what am I to do when you go traipsing to the Borderlands, General T'Chai?'

'Wait with Mason. Inform him when you are contacted by either the Guardian or Osiron. Then we make our move.'

'Right…' Cypher chuckled as a bell rang through the grimy room, signalling the end of the fight. The olive-skinned warrior finally released the huge opponent who had turned an odd shade of purple. He stood to a chorus of boos, face impassive. He tied his long, night-black hair up into a knot at the top of his head and pushed through the crowd, offering the hateful audience a bloody smile as he made his way towards the bar at the side of the room where the victor's purse awaited him, along with a strong drink.

'I assume you are scouting fighters to add to your team,' T'Chai stated, eyes following the bloody winner.

'I am.'

'And you have chosen *this* man to be a part of it?' T'Chai gestured towards the fighter who was now somehow managing to enjoy his drink whilst ignoring the barrage of abuse being hurled his way from the upset members of the audience who would have lost on the fight.

Cypher grinned and scratched at his freshly shaved chin. He looked over at the defeated blonde fighter as he rose from the circle and glared at any who wished to cast an annoyed look his way.

'I have picked them both,' Cypher announced. 'They are very good at following orders.'

'You cannot afford both,' T'Chai snarled.

Cypher stood. He pulled his waistcoat down and shifted his jacket so it sat comfortably around his slender frame. He tipped a hat to T'Chai and winked. 'I can now. I rigged the fight. Made a bloody fortune. I am quite fond of this new role Mason has provided me,' he called over his shoulder, making his way down the steps. 'Plays to my strengths.'

AFTER WE'RE GONE

S itting around. That's what war was, really. Loads of sitting around and waiting. Waiting to fight. Waiting to eat. Waiting to rest. The young and eager loved to focus on the glory and honour of a war but in Sly's mind, there wasn't much of that. Just sitting around and waiting. Then there would be a wave of excitement as the two sides finally met but that didn't last too long. Then it was back to sitting around. And waiting.

So, here he was, sitting around and waiting.

'What's the hold up? Why ain't we moving?' he snarled, spitting into the flames heating up the small group of warriors.

'Too many sick,' Kiras answered, her cold stare looking through the dancing flames. 'Danil is starting to panic. Never seen anything like it before.' She wanted this all over with as much as Sly did; if she could be patient with it, then maybe he could too. No point in arguing with the girlie now, she was in no mood for such things.

'Happens in war. Too many folk crunched together side by side. Bound to happen sooner or later.'

'This is different,' Cray butted in, eyes closed. Sly had thought him asleep.

'And what's different about it?'

'Only the mages are getting the sickness.'

'Thought there weren't any mages anymore?' Sly scowled. The quake had seen to that. Levelled the playing field.

'Ex-mages then,' Kiras added. 'Some strange kind of fever and nasty nightmares. We can't move out if half of our force is shaking and constantly shitting themselves.'

'Then why don't the three of us head off without them? Sneak into the capital and cut the fucking head off the snake ourselves.'

That brought a smile to Cray's face. But Kiras was there to dampen expectations. 'I love the idea, but we all know that is a suicide mission. The might of the Borderlands mixed with the backing of the Barbarians. Even if we somehow managed to get through to Herick, we ain't getting out alive.'

The statement hung between the three of them as the flames spat and crackled. Sly's eyes darted between the two of them under raised eyebrows, questioning them silently. He could almost see the cogs turning in Cray's slab-like head and the shadow that passed over the girlie's eyes.

'We're three of the toughest cunts the Borderlands has ever dared to shit out of its filthy, blood-stained arse!' he growled, stabbing a dagger in the dirt and inching closer to his allies. 'Kiras, men shake in their boots when they hear your name. The songs of your dancing twin blades have been sung across this shitty land for cycles.'

'Too fucking right,' she agreed, nodding her head and running a hand through her growing blonde locks.

'And Cray,' he said, punching his fellow on the arm to no visible response. 'You fought with Saul's tribe and then headed south and carved through more fuckers than most during that night of flames. Then you had the chance to stay and play happy families but you didn't. You left because you know that there is something more important for us to do. For you to do.'

Cray grunted, watching Sly with half-opened eyes.

'And you, Sly Stormson,' Kiras said. 'The bloodiest bastard the Borderlands has seen in a generation. A name that puts the fear of death into folk and is whispered as a warning to children in their beds.'

Sly barked laughter and clapped his hands together, feeling the excitement rise from the pit of his stomach. 'Exactly! The three of us are going to live on long after we are bones in the mud. After we're gone, they will be singing songs about us in every fucking tavern across the North.'

'And you think that means that we should go on this mission. Kill Herick but know that we won't make it out alive.' Kiras put it plain and simple. No messing about.

Sly nodded. 'Yeah. That's right.'

'Well, you know that I'd love to tell you I'm in,' Kiras said, cracking the bones in her fingers and licking her lips. 'But Baldor is dead because of that fucking Empire. I'm ready to die but only after they pay for that. And Arden says that he can help me with it.' Her eyes were filled with pity as she turned to Sly. 'I'm sorry, Stormson. Really, I am.'

The fires of his excitement dampened at her words, but he couldn't honestly say that he hadn't expected it. Kiras was living for one reason only now; take down the

Empire. He could understand that. Hells, he wanted it too, truth be told.

'And my family are in Hillheim,' Cray sighed. 'I'd want them away from the Barbarians before we move on Herick. Too much to lose.'

Sly's shoulders sagged, defeated. 'Pisses me off. But I get it.'

'We just have to be patient,' Kiras urged. 'Arden says that he will wipe Herick and the Barbarians from the Borderlands. You've seen his army. We just need to wait and let him work his freaky magic.'

Sly scratched his itchy beard and groaned. The whole business with the kid's army made him uncomfortable and they all knew it. Didn't sit right with him. 'I wanna do this the old-fashioned way. Axe in hand, man to man. Those *things*—'

'I know.' Kiras cut him off with a shudder of her own.

As close as he was to the roaring fire, Sly felt a sudden chill run down his spine. 'We go down that path, then that is what people will remember after we're gone. They'll remember that we threw in with demons and fiends from the hells as we weren't strong enough to deal with the business ourselves.'

'You saw what they did to Baldor…' Kiras's voice was colder than the icy Far North.

Sly swallowed hard as the image of their friend flashed unbidden into his mind. Arms and legs cut away. His skin a patchwork of cuts and bruises. Big man didn't deserve to die like that. Not many folks did.

'I know. I know,' he said, defeated at last as he released a tremulous breath. 'You want your revenge. Baldor deserves revenge and we're the only ones around to dish it out.'

'I'll ally myself with any nasty fucker if it means that I can watch the bastards who did that burn in hells. After that, they can whisper curses whenever they hear my name on the wind if they like, or they can choose to never think of me again. Once I've avenged Baldor's death, I don't give two shits what happens.'

'Guess that's that, then,' Sly winced as he stood up. Been sitting around too long. 'We'll wait for the kid to pull his finger out of his arse and point us in whatever direction he wants us to go.'

'Where are you going?' Cray asked, frowning with suspicion as Sly stalked away from the fire.

'Need a fucking piss if that's alright with you! Don't need you holding it for me.'

Arden glided between the rows of men lying on makeshift beds in the ruined town. The victory had been hard-fought for but there weren't many wounded. Still, nearly half of the red cloaks now filled the eastern half of the town, kept away from the healthy soldiers in case this strange sickness spread. Sweating, sickness, hallucinations. The men were all at various stages of the fever-like state but Arden recalled a scrawny Barbarian telling him what such signs meant. A scrawny Barbarian who had left him alone in a castle with Korvus and Socket whilst he escaped to the Borderlands and allied with Herick the Late. He had known what this sickness was.

Vald Sickness.

The sickness of magic.

He brushed the back of his hand against one of the squirming men. Hot as hells and drenched in sweat.

42

He wiped his hand against his cloak and moved on as the sounds of the sick followed him. Medics in plague doctor masks rushed between the patients, doing what they could to ensure they were comfortable and praying that it would not lead them on the path to death.

Arden waved one of the medics towards him. 'How are they doing?'

The medic's beaked mask tilted slightly to the side as whoever was behind the mask sighed. Arden could sense the frustration emanating from the man. 'Not great. We have tried to feed them but everything that goes in comes straight back out. Not worth the effort at the moment. Just wasting good food that is needed elsewhere.'

'Have you seen such sickness before?'

'Only a few times. Vald Sickness. Doesn't make sense though. Vald Sickness only occurs when an individual is overwhelmed by the threads of magic they have used. Most often it is seen in inexperienced mages who attempt something beyond their reach. But all of these patients have been without magic since the quake.' The medic took off his black hat and scratched his head, perplexed with the whole situation. 'It makes no sense…'

Arden placed a reassuring hand on the medic's shoulder and squeezed. 'Do your best. Try not to worry. We will solve this issue.'

He continued to the edge of the town, away from the cries and groans of the sick. The light from the full moon lit up the cloud drifting across the starry sky. He closed his eyes and breathed deeply, feeling his chest slowly rise and fall. When he opened them, a tall, thin being cloaked in black stood before him.

Osiron gave a small smile with their purple lips and glided forwards, black eyes speckled with stars boring into

Arden's.

'You are burdened with worry, my prince.' Their strange voice drifted to Arden, sounding like two voices mixed as one, wrapping themselves around one another in a tight but gentle embrace.

'A sickness has fallen on my soldiers,' Arden stated, taking a moment to adjust as he found himself standing in the dark realm of Chaos. Blue flames flickered in the distance, but it was just the two of them standing there. 'I recognise the signs of Vald Sickness. These soldiers have not used magic since my death.'

Osiron ran a soft finger down Arden's face and sighed. 'The magic we have used to open the bridge between realms is powerful, overwhelming even. Magic flows through many paths in Takaara, both its land and its people. The pull of such magic sometimes has an undesired effect; a sickness.'

'Our actions are hurting these people who are still dealing with the loss of their magic?' Arden asked. He bit his lip, thinking about the frightened faces of the men and women convulsing in pain in that ruined town. Men and women who had fought for him, fought for a better Takaara.

'The burden of leadership means taking action and doing things that others cannot, that others will not. Remember,' Osiron said, pity lining their pale face, 'these people fight for you. The sacrifice they are making is so that we can live in a Takaara that will be welcoming for all. We are purifying the land of those who betrayed you, those who betrayed me. Once our work is done, Takaara will be better for it. There will be difficulties on the way, but this is the path that you have chosen.'

Still uncomfortable, Arden grimaced and nodded. He was meant to be a leader now, the Prince of Chaos.

Now he had to prove that he was strong enough to bear such heavy burdens. Raven Redbeard had lost men under his command, yet he never moped around. He was a strong leader, as Arden should be.

'You are right, of course. I am sorry for bothering you.'

'Do not be sorry, such actions prove that you are the right person to lead us into this new world, Arden Leifhand.'

'My forces are depleted. Do I wait before heading to Herick's in Torvield, or do we move now?' He had been torn between the two options. He wanted to press forwards and get the bloody business sorted so that the Borderlands could be free of Herick and the Barbarian's rule but leaving now would mean abandoning the sick and injured to their fate.

'Leave in two days' time,' Osiron advised. 'Your actions in Archania have poked the beast of the Empire of Light. They will be sending their own army to the Borderlands. We can use this chance to strike two beasts with one sword. I will ensure that you have enough forces to destroy all who stand in our way.

'This battle will be a signal to all of Takaara of what we are capable of. It will light a beacon for all to see. After this, they will attempt to put out the fires that we have started. Chaos will truly have come to this world.'

Arden set his jaw and fought back against his worries. 'Then we will be ready for it. We have promised that Chaos would arrive. Our time is now.'

'All of Takaara will remember what we do, my prince. After the filth and sludge of this world is gone, a new day will dawn for all in Takaara who is ready for it.'

*

Sly had somehow managed to leave the town without being sighted. The lax security on the walls would usually have pissed him off but now it was a stroke of luck. He stomped through the snow with boots he had taken from one of the unwatched tents in the town after stalking off for his piss. A horse would have meant a quicker journey but leaving the town undetected would have been near impossible with such a beast. Best to trust only himself anyway. Kiras and Cray were best out of it. They had their reasons and he understood that. Not much else he could do. Arden wouldn't have let him leave if Sly had given the strange kid the option. Leaving under darkness was best for everyone.

He knew that what he was doing was madness. Most likely it would end with a dagger in his back, or front. He'd be bones before long anyway, the way things were going. But he couldn't sit around and wait any longer. The Borderlands was his home, and he wasn't gonna wait around whilst scum Barbarians and that bastard Herick lorded it up in the capital. His skin itched every time he thought of those bastards drinking his ale, sitting on his benches, and running over his land. Weren't right.

There was only one thing for it. Kill Herick.

The night was quiet. A few owls hooting and birds getting startled from their nests as Sly loped downhill towards the capital. He could walk this trek with his damn eyes closed. This was the Borderlands that he loved. The wilderness. Snowy hills, tall trees, the gentle rhythm of a river running in the distance. The bastard volcano had finally stopped erupting the day before, bringing the Borderlands some level of peace. He enjoyed it out here. He was free. So different to the crushed cities to the south, that was certain. Out here, he could breathe.

Out here, he was alone.

'Enjoying yerself?'

Sly whipped around, axes slipping into his hands with experienced ease. He growled and readied himself for battle.

Cray just smiled.

'I'm actually slightly hurt that you thought we were dumb enough to let you slink away like that,' Kiras said to Cray's side. 'You can slip away from the rest of them, but not us.'

Sly spat on the snow and placed his axes back onto his belt. 'You two got too much to lose with this. I'm taking Herick out myself. No questions about it. So turn around and trudge back up that fucking hill before things get messy.'

'We've had a bit of time to think about your plan. This whole killing Herick thing, haven't we Cray?'

Cray grunted, still smiling that stupid smile that didn't seem to annoy Sly so much anymore.

'And all this thinking,' he said to the pair of them. 'Where did it get ya?'

'We liked the whole plan. We want Herick and the Barbarians dead as much as you do. There was just one part we didn't like about it.'

'Which was?'

'Dying,' Cray grumbled.

'And what has changed since we last spoke about it?'

Kiras marched over to Sly and placed her hands on his shoulders, eyes sparkling in the moonlight and a smile dancing on her lips. 'Well, we decided that there was only one way to make it out of there alive. Cray's idea.'

Sly turned his head to Cray, cheeks aching with the grin spreading across his face. 'Cray?'

The lump of a man winked. 'Kill the fuckers.'

Torvield stood at the centre of the Borderlands. The town had been the capital for the warriors of the North ever since Haggar the Decapitator ordered the building of the Great Hall following his brutal victory over the allied tribes in the War of Brothers. It was the first sign that the people of the Borderlands were willing to settle and keep to life in one area; a first sign that they were ready to set up in a place where they could grow together as a people instead of constant warring. Of course, as was often the way in the Borderlands, peace wasn't an option for long. More fights broke out, but now there was a target for the warriors. Torvield was the shining diamond in the Borderlands that everyone wanted a piece of.

Taking Torvield meant taking charge of the Borderlands. And for warriors who prided themselves on owning the biggest and best, Torvield meant everything.

'The place seems deserted...' Sly grumbled from his vantage point on the hilltop. From his position, the thatched wooden longhouses, open stables, and Great Hall itself were clear to see. There were a few farmers out tending to their animals, enjoying the sudden upturn in temperature that was unusual for this time of the cycle. The warmth of the night had melted much of the snow, leaving a muddy terrain behind that clung to Sly's new boots. Damn weather couldn't seem to make up its mind. The usually bustling town was quiet, unnervingly so.

'Herick is meant to be bolted up in Torvield with those Barbarian bastards,' Sly said as Kiras and Cray joined him to look out across the capital. 'All I've seen since the sun rose is a couple of farmers and some old women gone to fetch fresh water from the river. The place is empty. Never seen it like this in all my time. Raven or Bear tribes have always kept a unit of soldiers to guard the town and ensure the fires in the Great Hall kept burning. Can't even see any smoke rising from there right now. Something's up and it don't feel good.'

'We press forward,' Kiras suggested, eyes narrowed and fixed on the Great Hall. 'We find out what in the hells is going on. Herick is expecting us with Baldor. If he ain't here, then something damned important has dragged him away. Stay alert. Need to find out what has happened here.'

Sly kept his axes attached to his belt as he crouched low, keeping as close to the ground as he could. Down the hill, he was able to keep to the shadows offered by the trees but it would only take one pair of eyes fixed in his direction for this all to go tits up. He rushed ahead of the other two, scouting the land he had called his home and darting between two of the longhouses. Peering around the corner of the house, he spotted a couple of the farmers strolling down the main path away from the Great Hall. Even from this distance Sly recognised them. Two old boys, been in Torvield longer than most folk. They weren't going to put up a fuss with Herick arriving and taking over – they'd been through enough changes for it to affect them too much.

Ignoring the farmers, Sly made for the side door to the Great Hall, silently praying that nothing was blocking it. The door eased open without a problem and Sly slipped into the darkness.

It was odd seeing the room without the fire pits blazing. Set alight to remind all in Torvield that the flames of their ancestors continued to burn as they looked down from the heavens, the fire was an integral part of

Borderland life. Seeing the pits cold and empty made Sly feel the same way as an unexpected feeling of loss threatened to overwhelm him. With a growl and a shake of his shaggy hair, he brought himself back to reality, cursing himself for the momentary lapse in focus. They were just flames. Nothing more.

Still, he wanted revenge on the bastards who had allowed them to fail.

He ran a grubby finger along one of the many round shields that adorned the walls of the large room. Sly scowled at the layer of dust that came away from the revered item – shields of warriors who had fallen defending the Borderlands in cycles past. Two stag heads stared down at him from above one of the low hanging beams in the cold and lifeless room. The banners of the four great tribes had been taking down since he was last in the room – only Herick's now hung from the ceiling. He walked up to the banner and spat on it, smiling as his saliva dripped down the material.

There was no one else in the room. No cups of ale clattering together. No songs to be sung. No fights breaking out amongst warriors driven by pride and honour. Just an empty room. Herick and his tribe were gone, taking the Barbarians with them. There was nothing left.

Running a hand along the wooden benches where he had sat listening to Raven and his various speeches, his chest tightened, realising what he had lost in such a short amount of time. Raven. Bane. Socket. Baldor. Some would be missed more than others, but the Borderlands would never be the same again, that was certain.

He walked up the steps at the top of the Great Hall and stared at the empty seat in the centre of the platform. Without thinking about why, he sat down and eased himself onto the throne. It felt good sitting up there, looking down on the long rows of benches and tables, empty as they may be.

Perhaps, one day…

No. He shook his head and jumped from the seat. Without a backwards look, he stomped away. Before exiting the building, he grabbed a lit torch and flung it over his shoulder and straight into the fire pit. Some things may change, but not everything had to. Some things had to stay the same. That was just the way of things.

His mood worsened like the ominous grey clouds to the south as he glanced across the main path to a row of thatched longhouses. He spotted the not-so-subtle figures of Cray and Kiras standing amongst a group of nervous looking women, hoods pulled low over their long, wild hair.

'Like to tell me what you're doing?' he growled as he reached them, turning to look for any signs of life in the capital.

'Gathering information,' Kiras answered, following his cautious gaze. 'These brave women say that Herick has taken all the men and women who can fight, Borderlanders and Barbarians, and dragged them south.'

Sly snapped back to the four women, scaring them with his confused scowl. 'South? Why in the fucking hells are they heading south?'

'The final battle,' Cray grunted to him. The women nodded, looking at Cray and then back at Sly as he spat at his feet.

'What final battle?'

'There's a young Barbarian with Herick, son of the leader I heard,' one of the women stepped in. She was pretty. Not so young but eyes that sparkled with life and skin that shone in the morning light.

'He has convinced Herick that the United Cities are heading this way. Something about revenge for burning a temple.' Sly's eyes flickered to Cray at the woman's mention of the temple. 'Herick thinks that the best thing to do is to head out in full force and defeat the Southerners.'

'As much as I hate the guy, he's got a huge set of bastard balls on him,' Sly whistled at the thought. 'No wonder he is always late when he has to drag such things along with him. There's more Southerners than there are stars in the sky.'

'Still, he wants a win. The United Cities will be coming no matter what; Herick sees the value in choosing the field and laying out the battlefield. He's no fool,' Kiras admitted.

The girlie was right. Sly didn't like it but he couldn't do much more than grumble about it. 'So if the bastard is heading south, where do you reckon he is going to set the trap?'

'The one place designed for that very purpose.'

Out of the corner of his eye, Sly caught Cray's face dropping like a rock from the edge of a cliff.

'Hillheim,' the warrior muttered, a look of utter dread on his face as the blood drained from him. 'We need to go. Now!'

Cray twisted and marched away, not waiting for the others to follow.

'Why is he in such a rush?' the pretty woman asked, peering after the sullen warrior as he trudged farther into the distance.

Kiras grimaced. 'His family lives in Hillheim. He fears that they will be caught between two crashing waves. Stormson,' she said, turning to Sly, 'What do we do?'

Sly swore and glanced around the empty land of Torvield. 'Got any spare horses?'

DECISIONS

The king's room was vast and spacious. Filled with signs of status and stature – the many lamps lit shone on gold and silver statues and ornaments designed to display the wealth of the Kingdom of Zakaria and intimidate anyone new to the centre of Southern power. Five kingdoms sat south of the border, ignoring the battling islands and warring tribes who fought amidst the southern seas, each with their own king or queen. But all answered to the Boy King of Zakaria: the man who had invited all leaders to his domain in the city of Ad-Alum to speak of the war to come. None would dare ignore his summons.

The king had called the various rulers of the South for a specific reason. They each followed the rule of Zakaria, trusting the young king and acting on his word as though it were a bloody command that if disobeyed would lead to death. In this instance that could very well be the truth.

'He has power. A shocking amount for such a young king,' Aleister muttered to his sister, leaning towards her so that the rest of those sat at the long table would not be able to hear him.

'Young?' his sister scoffed, 'The king is older than the city itself – you heard what he said. Guardians have ensured that he is regenerated each time he has fallen to the dark slumber of death. Such age cannot be measured in cycles.'

A servant paced around the table, holding out a silver platter in one hand and offering drinks in tall, thin glasses to all in attendance. Each leader gratefully accepted, bowing in turn to the servant for his work. Aleister took the glass offered to him with a short nod of his head. The drink was sweet but stronger than he expected, bringing a sharp gasp as it swished around his mouth.

The Queen of Edrium snorted at Aleister's obvious discomfort and sipped her own drink, swallowing the liquid with ease.

'If the pale skin was not enough, he also cannot handle a light drink in our company,' the queen said to laughter from the other rulers.

'I assure you,' King Zeekial stepped in, eyes narrowing at the queen, 'Aleister can handle more than you would expect. He and his companions have travelled a great distance to meet with us. It is only right that we treat them with the utmost respect when they are under our care.'

The queen nodded. Her hand, gems shining in the torchlight, patted against her chest as she bowed her dark, bald head in remorse at her words. 'I am sorry, my king. I meant no disrespect.'

'It is not an issue, Queen Cebisa. It has been many a cycle since we have hosted Northern guests. Their being here is strange to us, but we must remember that how we behave towards them shines a light on who we are as Southern rulers.'

'Of course, my king,' Cebisa responded, eyes down at her empty plate, scolded like a dog who had disobeyed her owner.

'Perhaps it would be better for us if we knew why such guests were here with us, my king,' King Milani offered. His lips bore two huge silver rings on either end, shifting in the light as he spoke in his deep, calm voice. His ears were decorated with circular wooden plated plugs painted in the green and black to display the colours of his native Ruhkaru people. 'Such a meeting has not been permitted in our time. Knowledge and understanding will only be gained when you tell us why we have been summoned.'

'Milani speaks true,' the final ruler to Milani's side agreed. He was a rotund man. His large frame barely fit in the wide chair offered to him. 'We have travelled far to join you. Why are we here, my king?'

'A fitting question, King Solomus,' Zeek said, looking around at each person sat at the table. Three kings and a queen along with the three warriors from the Red Sons. At the back of the room, amongst the shadows, Aleister thought he spotted the weary figure of Harish, waiting and listening in the darkness. 'We have sheltered ourselves away from the intruders for some time. You are all aware of the dangers that The Wise Women spoke of. War is coming to Takaara. Whether we wish it to or not, it is to come to the South, just as it will to every other part of this world. The God of Chaos spills forth their sickness across the land and we must stand united if we are to defeat such evil.'

An awkward silence. The rulers of the Southern

Kingdoms gave one another nervous glances. Milani cleared his throat and called for another drink. Cebisa busied herself with a loose thread on her colourful dress and King Bthanda found an interesting ornament standing on a plinth in the corner of the room to stare at. They all at least had the decency to look guilty at ignoring the king's statement. Not a lot of good that did them though.

'War is coming to the South,' Aleister stated, unable to put up with the uncomfortable silence any longer. 'Whether you wish it to or not. And this will not be a normal war. The God of Chaos will be leading an undead army to destroy any in their path. We must stand and fight.'

He didn't miss the looks shared between the rulers of the Southern nations.

'What right does a boy from the North have to tell us what to do? We have not permitted such people this far south in some time, and yet you have the audacity to attend such a meeting and advise us and our preparations for a war we have been aware of for longer than you have been born. Stay seated and close that pale mouth of yours, Aleister of the Red Sons.'

Cebisa's words irked him but Aleister felt the light brush of his sister's hand on his own, warning him about responding in his usual way.

'Mouth closed, brother,' Ariel mumbled so that only he could hear.

'Queen Cebisa,' Zeek scowled, his tone leaving no room for interpretation. 'I would expect you to speak to guests in this room as you would speak to myself. Now is not the time for animosity.'

'Yes, my king…' Cebisa said, biting her lip and averting her gaze from Aleister.

'Aleister, Ariel, and Bathos have travelled far to sit

with us today and thrash out an agreement. They come from the Republic of Causrea, a nation wishing for us to understand that the Empire of Light is close to blinding the whole of the North. The United Cities has lost two of its kings and the Empress's brother is ruling now. The Heartlands is still a mess of nations fighting amongst themselves, caring not for the wider world. Darakeche stands against the Empire but as we know, the Sultan of Darakeche is poisoned with pride and will not stand with us. His mistrust of the South means that we cannot rely on Darakeche.

'And now we know that an army of Chaos is ready to blacken the skies and march across Takaara. All these petty arguments that we have fought must be pushed aside if we are to survive this.' Zeek thumped a fist on the table, a cold fury shining in his dark eyes. 'The South has stood together stronger than any other region of Takaara. We have known that this day was coming. Now we just need to decide what we are to do to defeat the evil heading this way.'

Another awkward silence. Some of the greatest rulers in the world ignored one another, averting their eyes and looking for any excuse to fade into the background. Aleister felt the rage building inside him. His sister's hand brought him back to himself, reminding him that this wasn't the time or place for his anger.

'You lead the biggest nations in the South,' Bathos said, his booming voice alerting the rulers from their reflections. 'We are three humble warriors from the North. We are not telling you what to do. We are just telling you what has been done. Young children burning in front of baying crowds. Innocents beaten and arrested just for being different.' Aleister's eyes darted to Harish standing silently in the shadows.

'This evil and worse is heading this way. We three will stand against it. We will fight for your people and do what we can to ensure that such darkness does not overwhelm the South. The question is, what will you do?'

Aleister had to give it to the big man, the words were good. Damned good. Ariel gave Bathos a loving look, beaming up at the big warrior as she gave his hand a gentle squeeze.

'Even if it just the three of us, we will fight,' Ariel agreed, eyes still on her lover.

'We've faced bad odds before,' Aleister added with a deep breath, leaning back in his seat. 'But it sure would be good if we could have you on our side.'

Bthanda exhaled slowly and pinched the bridge of his nose before speaking to the outsiders, his voice lined with steel. 'For countless cycles, we have been the ones searching for any sign of the Guardian who could open the bridge between the planes and unleash Chaos. A thankless task that drove us to cut ourselves away from the north of Takaara as tensions rose and leaders in the North ignored our warnings and dismissed our messages as the ranting of savages. We banded together in the South, setting aside our own trivial disagreements and understanding that it is only through unity that we would be about to defeat the darkness to come. We have sacrificed our people in a plan to prepare for the breaking of the world – taken the blood of *our* people that we can save all in Takaara, even those who shunned us and treated us like animals.

'And yet, here you are. Three travellers from the North who arrive unexpectedly to sit in our halls and lecture us on how best to tackle the threat coming our way. We do not sit in silence because we are ignorant or filled with cowardice. We sit in silence because we *know* what is about to happen. And it scares the living hells out of each and every one of us.'

Chastised, Aleister lowered his head, his eyes jumping to his sister and Bathos as they accepted the reprimand.

'There is only one way to weaken the forces of Chaos and prevent Takaara from falling into complete darkness,' Zeek informed them. 'We must use Soulsbane and cut away the four naïve magi who started this whole sorry business. Osiron may feel like a God, but we know the truth.'

'Are we certain that the weapon will do as intended?' Cebisa asked, brow creased with worry.

'It was created for that purpose alone.' Harish walked into the light of the lanterns and addressed those seated at the table. He looked weary, dark bags hanging low beneath his sad, tired eyes. 'For ordinary people, the blades trap souls – destined to stay trapped on a plane that we created.' Harish motioned to Zeek who sat motionless, his eyes staring into space as he listened to his old friend's words. 'But for the four of us, myself, Zeek, Osiron, and Elena it will cut the bonds that tie us to Takaara. Sever the ties that we created all those cycles again in the hope of immortality. Once the blades cut through our flesh, we will be as dead as any beings have ever been in this world. Though, there is only one way to test the theory…'

'You have sacrificed enough, my brother. This time, let me be the one to take the fall.'

All eyes turned to King Zeekial at the suggestion. His fellow leaders sat in silence, jaws dropped at the thought of the young man's death.

But Harish just smiled and shook his head. 'No brother. You have people to lead. I am ready for this. It is what I have craved ever since I understood the folly of our machinations. There are too many people left waiting for your guidance. Only you can lead people in the final battle. I am not built for such things. Let me do this for Takaara, one final act to atone for my sins. Perhaps then I will be granted access to the afterlife, at Mamoon's discretion.'

Zeek stood and walked over to his friend, placing a hand on the man's cheek and wiping away a solitary tear. 'You still believe in that God?' he chuckled, his words and tone humorous but not mocking.

'I must. I have seen too much beauty in my many lives to not believe in a creator.' Harish's face grew dark. 'And too much darkness to not hope for something more than *this*.'

'One week,' Zeek stated. After swallowing the lump in his throat. 'One week to enjoy the beauty of this world. Then we will use the blade and finish what we started all those cycles ago.'

Harish nodded, tears rolling down his face as he took his friend's hand and squeezed, keeping it on his cheek as his thin frame shook with sobs. 'One week,' he agreed. Blinking away the tears, he released Zeek and turned, leaving the rest of them to bow their heads in silence.

'He is a brave man,' Ariel said after some time.

'The bravest,' Zeek added, voice breaking with emotion. 'Smartest too. His blade will work.'

'Then the question is, how do we get close enough to Osiron and the Empress to succeed in this plan?' Milani queried, scanning the room for any who could answer.

'Osiron's plan has always been to cleanse this world of what they see as those who wronged them. They see humanity as a plague that must be wiped out for Takaara to start anew. We need bait,' the King of Zakaria simply stated.

'Then we march,' Bthanda said. 'We take what forces we have and we line them up by the Gods' Bridge. Osiron will arrive to wipe them from the face of Takaara.'

'And the Empress?' Bathos asked.

'She has dedicated her lives to searching for Osiron and preventing his war. Where Osiron goes, she will not be far behind,' Zeek spat, slumping into his seat with the look of a man resigned to a dark fate. 'I may hate her methods, but when the time comes, she will be there. That, I can guarantee.' The steel in his eyes and voice left no room for argument. Aleister wondered on the history between the King of Zakaria and the Empress of the East.

'This unholy army, any idea how we can defeat it? We are just men,' Aleister said.

'And women,' Ariel added with a wink and a thump on the table from Cebisa.

'And women,' the queen agreed with a smile.

Zeek cracked his knuckles and allowed the hint of a smile to break out on his young features. 'Leave that to me. This is what we have been preparing for, my friends. With the blade, and the blood of our people, we will ensure that Osiron will regret returning to this plane.'

The view from the balcony was one that he wished he could burn into his memory for all time. Moonlight reflected along the winding river as he weaved through the city, like a shining snake protecting Ad-Alum in its time of need. Lanterns shone throughout the city's buildings like stars, illuminating the city with an orange glow as the sound of crickets played music for those still awake.

'Can't sleep?'

He shook his head and looked down over the

balcony as Ariel joined him, resting her arms on the railing beside him.

'Nightmares?'

He nodded and turned so that his back rested against the railing. He turned to his sister and saw the pity and worry in her eyes.

'Ella. Always Ella,' he said with a short breath. 'Seems like every time I close my eyes, I see the light fade from hers.'

The quiet stretched out, crickets still playing in the background of the city. Aleister shifted forward and stretched the muscles in his neck, groaning as they made a cracking noise. He was too tense. Any fool could tell that.

'It wasn't your fault, brother.'

'But it was. I fought Matthias. Without such idiocy, that blade wouldn't have ended her life. She'd still be here.'

'Still be here to tell you what an idiot you are?' Ariel said with a sad smile.

'I'd do anything for that. Anything,' Aleister admitted. 'But you don't want to hear about my problems. How's the little one?' he asked, inclining his head towards his sister's stomach.

Ariel's hand instinctively dropped to her belly and she smiled. An honest, warm smile that managed to lift the gloomy cloud perched over Aleister for the moment.

'Good, I think,' she laughed. 'Ife said that I should be able to feel their kicks soon.'

'You'll be getting less sleep soon then.'

'I already don't get enough. Bathos snores like a bloody elephant.'

'That's because he is half elephant.'

'That's his good half.'

The siblings grinned at one another, enjoying the brief moment of levity. Not wanting to break such a feeling, Aleister hesitated with his next words, but his indecision was clear to see.

'Spit it out, brother,' Ariel commanded lightly, her smile fading momentarily.

'This battle…' he started, unable to think of the right words for what he wanted to say. Thankfully, his sister had them for him, as always.

'You don't think I should fight.' It wasn't a question.

'Well, you're going to be getting bigger and it's not just you, your son or daughter—'

'Will not survive in this world if we don't win this fight. I fight for them, Aleister. I can't just sit on the side lines and twiddle my thumbs whilst you and Bathos risk your own lives in a fight that we don't know we will make it out of.'

'All fights are like that.'

'You know exactly what I mean,' Ariel spat. She jabbed a finger against his chest. 'Would you sit it out? If I asked you to.'

Aleister swallowed and dropped his head, unable to meet his sister's gaze.

'No. I have to fight.'

'So do I. I understand why you asked me, Al. But know that if you ask again, you'll get a kick to the nuts so hard any chances of *you* having kids will be over.'

He grinned and raised his head, happy to see the smile back on his sister's face.

'I love you, sis.'

'I love you too, you big fool.' She pulled him in for a hug and squeezed tightly. 'So don't go doing anything stupid.'

'When have I ever done anything stupid?'

Ariel pushed him away, eyebrows raised in mockery. 'It would be easier to list the times you haven't been stupid.'

'Let's not do that.'

'Good decision. Time for sleep. Night, brother.'

'Night, sis.'

THE LIGHT OF THE EMPIRE

For an evil empire bent on destroying free will across the lands of Takaara, Kane had to give it credit – the capital was a jaw-dropping display of wonder and amazement. A red sun hung low in the clear sky as she rode alongside Istari, the nervous guards following at a respectable distance. The sunlight kissed the numerous towers and spires stabbing up at the sky. Golden domes shine beyond the stone walls of the city, minarets dotted around the huge spheres that gave the city its unique silhouette. The buildings glistened like sparkling diamonds, a marvel like no other standing before the Endless Sea. The city stood on the edge of the world, a final bastion of civilization in the East. She had heard sailors boast of intentions to cross the sea but none to her knowledge had managed the feat. Those who had the courage to attempt the task never returned to tell their tales. This was the last stop. The last chance to save Takaara.

'I thought Mughabir was the jewel in the east,' she said, eyes stuck on the dazzling city in the distance.

'A name given by the Darakechean leaders to their own land. Those who braved the journey to Yalaandi know that this is the *true* jewel. A dazzling city of light built with the purpose to worship the One God. They have come far since the first homes of dusty stone were erected,' Istari said, patting his camel on its back and gazing up at the city.

'This city is the home of those who wish to destroy the way of life for many in the West.'

'All nations believe that their way is the best way. Given the chance, the United Cities would have crushed the Borderlands, or even Darakeche. They only play nice when it is useful,' he sighed. 'There are many good people in this city, Katerina Kane. Just as there are many bad people in the United Cities. Keep your eyes open and you will find the spark of light amongst the darkness...'

She kept her eyes open. Wide open.

She watched as white-cloaked guards blew on long, curved horns signalling an arrival. She watched as they lifted the gate allowing access through the tall walls surrounding the city. She watched as the city welcomed her with a wide-open circle of stone decorated with fountains and perfectly placed hedges and exotic flowers which she had never seen before.

The brightest of colours adorned the stone ground at her feet, spiralling their way around the centre of the circle where the biggest fountain Kane had ever lain her eyes on stood as the prime monument to the entrance.

She casually made note of the soldiers marching along the walls as she passed them and gazed up at the fountain. At least three times the height of the statue of old King Borris from Archania, the fountain had a stone basin which water splashed into from the sword of the figure of a menacing but beautiful woman. The statue was dressed in armour ready for battle, mail covering most of her figure and a stern look in her eyes.

'I've never seen this woman before...' Kane said, studying it while ignoring the bustle of people passing around her, all eager to get on with their day and ignoring the newcomers to the city.

'Well, the West is not overly fond of her. In all honestly, it does not do her justice,' Istari replied, following Kane's gaze and smiling up at the majestic artwork. 'Yet she refused to pose for the artist, so it is her own fault for the inaccuracies.'

'This is the Empress?' Kane asked, putting two and two together.

Istari nodded. 'She is worshipped as a Goddess here. Know that, before you open your mouth before her people. You have seen what happens to blasphemous folk. Tread with care. Lips closed and eyes open. Nothing will serve you better than following that phrase.'

The warrior turned to their sheepish escort and lifted his arms wide, questioning their next steps. 'Well, we are here. What next?'

The five soldiers glanced at one another, none wanting to upset the famed warrior. Finally, one of the women cleared her throat and stepped forward, pushing out her chest and standing tall, doing her best to give off the air of confidence.

'A carriage will take you to the Eastern Quarter. The Empress has decreed that you must reside in the Sapphire Rooms until you are called for.'

Istari nodded and strolled over to one of the gleaming white benches that ran around the curved plaza. Ignoring the soldiers, he turned to Kane and patted the empty space next to him. 'Take a seat. There is no purpose in wearing your feet out waiting for the carriage.'

Kane joined him, seeing the wisdom in his words.
She took the chance to scan the plaza. Colourful bunting
swayed gently in the calm wind, tied to the tall buildings on
either side of the wide plaza. Three wide roads opened out
from the fountain, each immaculately kept and litter-free: a
far cry from similar places in Archania. She felt a shadow of
embarrassment when she thought of the town square in
both the Lower and Upper Cities, both were constantly in a
state of disrepair, only tidied up for events involving the
royal family or other events of great importance. Here, the
plaza shone. The white and cream materials used for the
buildings glistened in the low sun and gave her cause to
shield her eyes.

'How long did you live here for?' she asked Istari as
their escorting soldiers stood far enough away for them to
not overhear the conversation. They glanced over nervously
every now and then but they didn't seem certain of how to
behave around Istari, not knowing whether to treat him as a
respected guest or a prisoner.

'Long enough,' he answered rather unhelpfully.

'Did you like it here?'

'At times. Like anywhere, there were good times
and bad times.'

'Why did you leave?'

Istari didn't answer right away. He peered out
across the plaza, fiddling with a shining blue ring, spinning
it around one of his fingers.

'Now is not the time for that,' he eventually
offered.

Kane accepted that, not wanting to push the man
further. If anyone understood keeping secrets and not
wishing others to pry into personal events, it was her. The
thought brought the memory of her last meeting with

Drayke roaring back to her. She prayed that he would be safe, that whatever he was planning on doing with the Red Sons would not cost him his life. She had to speak to him, to ensure that the last memory she had of her son was not of him deciding that she should be arrested. Not enough of his father in him, that was the problem. But there was enough, enough to hold onto the hope that he would stop this madness.

A grey pigeon dropped from the sky and waddled over to Kane's feet, searching for food, no doubt. She watched it scan the area around her worn boots, clearly used to people dropping scraps for the birds in the plaza. Finally realising that there was nothing to gain from her, the pigeon made a noise that Kane imagined was a disgruntled cry as it flew off, hoping to find better pickings elsewhere.

As she followed the bird, her eyes caught on something heading their way down the eastern pathway. The sounds of hooves hitting the road and wheels turning over the stone had her on her feet. Istari just stayed seated, watching and waiting for the carriage to arrive.

'The Sapphire Rooms,' she said to him, remembering the name that the female had used. 'You know them?'

Istari looked up, shielding his eyes from the bright sun. 'Know them? I designed them.'

Peeking through the gap in the curtain, Kane eyed the busy streets of the city. She witnessed masses of robed men and women walking along the dusty streets, barely glancing at either the horses and carriage or the many white-cloaked soldiers scattered throughout the city. The people of Yalaandi chatted, argued, traded and behaved just as they would in any other region of the world Kane had been to. Merchants stood outside of shops, calling out their latest deals in the heat of the Eastern sun and doing their best to snare a new customer or two. Expensive looking seats and sofas sat outside in the shade of trees as a group of men lounged around, smoking a pipe attached to a burning golden item in the centre of their patch. She caught a whiff of an unusual but pleasant smell as the carriage passed by.

'It is not faze.' Istari must have noticed the sour look on her face as the scent caught in the carriage. 'The herbs from the Kerulean Forest are burned beneath coals. Inhaling is said to calm the mind but not destroy it in the way faze seems to.'

'Have you ever tried it?'

'Once. When I was younger.'

'Apple flavour is my favourite,' one of the two soldiers added, listening to the conversation. The grin on his face was soon replaced with a scowl as the woman beside him gave a short, swift elbow to his ribs and hissed in his direction.

Kane welcomed the silence in the carriage that followed. She listened instead for the sounds of the city: the arguments between traders, the laughter and cries of children, birdsong in the trees, the hustle and bustle of a living, vibrant city. Yalaandi had the beauty and structure of the Upper City of Archania mixed with the life and character of the Lower City. Flags waved from poles sticking out from buildings on either side of the road, the white sun of the Empire clear for all to witness. As with Mughabir, she had expected to visit the Eastern city and pity the citizens for living under the oppressive rule of leaders bent on their own selfish needs. What she had found so far was so vastly different from her expectations.

The mass of people faded as the carriage took a bend to the right, following the curve of the road to a quieter area. A few men sat on the edges of the street; dark,

71

sullen looks cast towards the carriage as it rode past, and one of the men stood and spat at the street, raising a middle finger as the carriage continued on its path.

The carriage slowed and stopped. The female soldier was the first to exit, motioning for Kane to follow.

'The Sapphire Rooms are old guest houses. A place for *honoured* guests of the Empire to reside,' the soldier informed Kane as her eyes searched her up and down. 'You are lucky to be allowed to stay in such a place.'

Kane watched two armoured soldiers nod at the woman as she left Kane and strode over to a white, spiked, iron gate that ran around the perimeter of the huge grounds before her.

'We have been expecting you, Baqara Adira,' one of the soldiers said to her, pressing a finger against his forehead and then chest in salute. His dark eyes sparkled as he looked past Kane and towards Istari as the old warrior stepped out of the carriage with a scowl darker than a thunderstorm. 'Is that him? Is that *really* him?'

He sounded like an excited boy receiving the toy he had been asking for all cycle.

'You have a role here, be professional,' Adira reprimanded the young soldier. Kane watched as she creeped forwards and said in a hushed tone. 'But yes, it is him.'

Past the white gate, Kane stared in astonishment at the beautiful scenery before her. A flat stone path ran between two perfectly manicured green lawns that stretched out either side. The pathway ran towards a ramp under a white archway sat between two sets of steps that led to a raised platform. The lawn continued up onto the platform until it reached a long, wide sparkling blue building that shone like the sky on a clear summer's day. The building was tall with flat rooves on the flanks in the style of the East and, in the centre, the building rose higher towards the sun with its deep, blue dome in the centre. Two minarets flanked the done, perfectly symmetrical. It had been designed well. If this was to be where she stayed at the Empress's discretion, Kane figured she could do worse.

'You designed this?'

'With some friends. Come on, I will show you around,' Istari grumbled, glaring at the soldiers as he walked through the gate. They didn't seem to care, smiles wider than the ocean as they fixed their eyes on the warrior.

Adira groaned. 'I must escort you in—'

Istari waved down her words. 'This place is as much mine as it is hers, Baqara Adira. I will escort Miss Kane into the Sapphire Rooms and show her where she is staying. If you have an issue with that, go and tell the Empress that I am more than willing for her to come and discuss any concerns that you have with my suggestion.'

He waited, eyes daring her to test him. The smiles faded from the faces of the soldiers as they stood either side of the gate, watching the tense exchange and not knowing how to respond.

Kane had met many soldiers in her life, she could always tell the experienced ones from the rookies. Rookies always had to be told what to do. Their actions were inevitably linked to another's command. The experienced ones worked on instinct, trusting their hard-earned natural responses to react to any given situation.

Adira blinked first. 'Stay inside the gates. Empress's orders. And your weapons…'

'The Empress knows where we are if she wants them. We are not a threat. However, if you are willing to attempt to take my weapon from me, you are more than welcome to try.'

Kane had to give the woman credit; she held Istari's gaze for a while, as though judging her next move and weighing up the consequences of her next action. At last, Adira spun on her heels with one last dark look and started yelling at the carriage driver, clearly eager to get away from the infuriating man.

'You really do have a way with people,' Kane scoffed, marching alongside him towards the dazzling building.

'One of my many skills.'

The Sapphire Rooms were a complex of lavishly decorated rooms that many nations would have considered worthy as a place for leaders to reside. Even when compared to the Summer House in Mughabir, Kane did not find her new abode wanting. She slipped reluctantly out of the warm bath water, sitting on the edge in the opulent room and taking the opportunity to take in her surroundings. Such bath houses were popular back in the Upper City, though none were as large and lavish as this one. The polychrome mosaic walls were similar to the rest of the building that she had seen, though in here, the sunlight beamed through an open archway at the back of the room and hit the rippling water, bouncing off against the various colours and adding a wondrous light to the whole place.

Once dry, she headed to the adjacent room and gasped at the rows of hanging clothes available to her. Istari had informed her that the place would be ready for them and housed all manner of things to make their stay comfortable. House arrest was starting to shine in a positive light.

She picked a few dresses to try on, thinking that

they would be more suitable in the heat of this city. The first couple were elegant, fair dresses but not quite to her taste. Eventually, she tried on a dress that fell past her knees in waves and was the same colour as the ocean. A beautiful, deep blue that she felt would be appropriate for her first evening in such a beautiful place.

Staring in the mirror, she realised that she had let her hair grow longer than usual. She liked it. Silver streaks worked with the lines on her face to display her strength and experience. She knew many who would wish to hide such features and cling on to their youth, but Kane saw them as battle scars; hard-earned and a warning to others that she had been through tough times and survived. She was tough, and beautiful. She smiled at her reflection – pleased with what she saw.

Happy with her look, she brushed down the dress and exhaled. Istari was waiting for her in the dining room. He had his back to her as she entered, busying himself with pouring drinks from the astonishing number of bottles and glasses that lined the whole western wall in the room. The familiar colourful mosaic pattern filled the other walls in the room. No paintings or statues favoured in the West. Simple, but elegant. Less pompous to her mind. The back of the room opened onto the opulent garden. Flat, green lawn; rows of flower beds and the odd, strange tree. The garden ran all the way up to the white fence that signalled the end of the estate.

Istari turned and Kane was pleased to see him stall in his movement as his eyes found her, widening as he held a glass and a bottle of red wine in his hands. He quickly composed himself, clearing his throat and greeting her. 'Kane. I hope you found the bathwater to be an appropriate temperature.'

'It was most pleasing,' she answered, mocking his

forced formality. 'You can call me Kat now, you know. We have travelled far enough for that at least.'

His pause allowed her to get a proper look at him. He was dressed in an elegant black jacket that stopped just above his knees. Two silver swords crossed over one another, stitched into the chest of his jacket. He had slicked his silver hair back and trimmed his beard close to the skin. Kane had to admit, she could now see why an Empress would be on board with a relationship with this man. Well, only if he was less prickly and sullen all the time.

'Kat,' Istari said, the name awkward escaping his lips. They shared a laugh and he looked more relaxed. 'Would you care for a drink?'

She took a seat at the side of the long table in the centre of the room so that she could look out at the beautiful grounds. 'What would you recommend?'

Istari looked back across the bottles, finger in the air as he scanned the rows available to him. He strolled back and forth along the wall, searching for one in particular. 'There was a drink we had smuggled out of the South a long time ago. Best thing I have ever had. Looks like it is not here anymore though.' He picked up a bottle and took a long hard look at it before spinning and setting it down on the table by Kane.

'Option one,' he said before darting back to the drinks and humming to himself. He was in a better mood than she had seen him in for some time.

'And… option two.' He set an oddly shaped fat bottle down, filled with dark liquid.

'And would you happen to know what is in each of these options?' Kane asked with a grin.

'Option one,' he explained, reaching for the bottle and holding it up with both hands so that she could clearly view the bottle of red. 'This is a red wine from the vineyards of the West. A small town called Sanici. It has quite a fruity taste, fresh and floral with quite the kick to it.'

Kane nodded, trying not to laugh at the warrior's attempts at hosting.

'And option number two,' he continued, picking up the other bottle. 'This is a rarity. Whiskey brewed in Oslar, a tiny town to the north-west of Torvield in the Borderlands. Best whiskey in the North.'

'Oslar,' Kane repeated, biting her lip as the name brought back memories of sitting in dark taverns and arguing with the weapons master about the best whiskey in the North. 'Braego used to speak about that town. He agreed with your assessment, though I never did get to taste the whiskey he loved so much. I had always claimed Firewhiskey from the Lower City to be the best.'

Istari stared at her with a new, devilish glint in his eyes and pushed a glass towards her, still holding the dark bottle. 'Then it is time to settle the debate.'

It was late when Katerina Kane stumbled to her room. The sun had gone to rest for the night and the lanterns in the myriad of corridors had not yet been lit, meaning each turn she made in the labyrinth of the Sapphire Rooms was more of an educated guess than anything else. Istari had offered to escort her but she had waved his polite offer away, wanting to find the way by herself.

At last, she recognised the sliding blue door adorned with pink and silver flowers painted from top to bottom. Sliding the door to the side, she stumbled forwards, glad to be close to the enormous bed that waited for her.

But it was not just the bed that was waiting for her.

Two guards stood at the foot of her bed. One man. One woman. She recognised the woman – Adira, the soldier who Istari had treated with such disdain as they had entered the estate, the same one who had ridden with them from the village. The man she did not recognise.

Neither were in their armour. Instead, they wore loose, grey robes that dropped to their ankles and Adira bore a black and white chequered kufiyah covering her head.

'I may be lost,' Kane said, all effects of the drink leaving her as she eyed the swords around the soldiers' waists, 'but I'm fairly certain that this is my room. If so, you should both leave now. I am unarmed and in a foreign country. But test me and I won't hold back.' She was proud to hear the strength in her voice, even though her hands trembled behind her back. Istari was too far away for help if she needed it, and her own sword lay on the floor on the other side of the bed. Stupid, really. When did she become so complacent that she had forgotten to always keep it within arm's reach?

'Katerina Kane,' Adira said, 'you have been summoned for a meeting with the Empress.'

Kane didn't manage to hide her shock, eyebrows raised as she released a little snort. 'Me? The Empress wants to speak to me, at this hour?' More likely the soldiers of the Empire had been informed that a former Inspector from the United Cities was in their homeland and must be killed. Braego's dead body in the docks flashed unwelcomingly into her head. T'Chai had been the one to kill the great warrior. The mage had used his trickery to assassinate the Borderlander, to stack the odds in his favour. She reminded herself of the depths these people would sink to.

Still, what else could she do?

'The Empress is a busy woman. She just wishes for

a moment of your time. To welcome our guest from the United Cities of Archania, a place where her own brother now sits on the throne…'

'That throne does not belong to him,' Kane growled, needing no reminder of the treachery of that silver haired bastard, Mason D'Argio.

Adira shrugged. 'Who it belongs to is of no importance to me. He sits on it. You do not. Come with us to see the Empress, I promise you that no harm shall befall you on the route.'

Kane's eyes flickered to her sword on the floor. Adira noticed the movement.

'Take the weapon if you wish. Change into more comfortable clothes. It is a short ride through the city, but you should be comfortable.'

The male soldier glanced down at Kane's exposed legs and the blood rushed to his dark face before he averted his eyes, staring instead at a particularly interesting spot of the mosaic pattern on the walls beside her.

She smirked.

'I am a guest in her city. So I will come,' Kane said, walking between the two soldiers and picking up her sword. 'May I have a moment of privacy to get changed?'

Adira nodded. 'We will be just outside. Be quick.'

As the door shut behind them, Kane slumped onto the bed, all courage and bravado failing her. She wondered if she should call for Istari; the warrior would know what was best. Still, she was curious to meet the Empress without the cranky warrior at her side. This was a chance to speak to one of the most powerful leaders in all Takaara, perhaps most powerful.

So she got changed and buckled her belt, enjoying

the familiar weight of her sword at her hip.

FACES OF EVIL

This carriage ride was a strange one. After a tense argument, Kane had finally agreed to wear the black bag over her head for the ride. Adira had insisted upon it, claiming that no one in the city could vouch for her trustworthiness and they would be heading right into the heart of the city.

Bumpy tracks jolted Kane at first but soon the carriage must have found smoother pathways to traverse as the horses pulled forwards towards wherever they were heading. She assumed they would be meeting in the palace. That is where she had often enjoyed a late night drink in Archania with Mikkael – a friendly ear to bend following a day of stressful negotiations with the council. Guilt washed over her as she realised that she had not thought of her old friend in some time. She promised herself that she would light a candle for him and Ella as soon as she could and spend a moment talking to them, whether they could hear her or not. She was not a religious woman – seen too much horror in the world for that – but remembering the dead meant something, she just didn't have the words for it.

The lack of sight was disorienting. At first, she had tried to count the turns and the route of the carriage but that was pointless. Even the time spent on the journey was too difficult to gauge. It could have been minutes or hours. The soldiers with her were silent the whole way.

It was a relief when the sound of the horses' hooves stopped and Kane lurched forwards and then back against her seat as the carriage came to a gentle halt.

'Keep quiet,' Adira muttered, grabbing Kane by the elbow and helping her from the carriage, bag still covering her head.

'It is pretty pointless carrying a blade if I have my head covered, don't you agree?' Kane said, frustrated at relying on the soldiers for guidance.

'I do. Tough.'

For once Kane was thankful for the covering, it hid the twitch of her lips. This Adira was stern, strong, more assertive than the others that she had seen.

She heard the opening of doors and hushed voices as she was led in the darkness. Adira helped guide her up steps, Kane's boots muffled by carpet beneath her feet so that they hardly made a sound. Another landing. Then more stairs. She stopped. A knock on a door. Then another. Then the sound of a door opening. She was pushed forwards, though not forcefully, and then she felt a hand on her shoulder, guiding her down into a comfortable seat.

Kane squinted as the bag was whipped from her head, flinging her hair into her face along with the stabbing glow of light that filled the room. Moonlight crept in through the four circular windows to her left, each placed between tall, hexagonal pillars that rose towards a ceiling painted with a large, white sun in the centre and surrounding by blue sky and four figures, men and women looking towards the sun with an adoring gaze. Heavy scarlet curtains with silver trim hung from the walls, closed for the night. They matched the large rug at her feet, a rug that ran all the way towards the end of the room and three steps. Above the steps, sat on a white throne, was a woman with a stern, searching gaze.

The Empress of the East.

'Leave us.' She dismissed the soldiers standing either side of Kane with a wave of her jewelled hand, silver bracelets jingling with the motion.

Kane studied the Empress as the doors closed behind. Her silver hair was elaborately bunched up at the top of head. A black flower contrasted with the silver and matched her dark eyes. Her smooth, dark brown skin only bore the lightest touches of age upon it, small lines around the eyes. Wisdom lines, Kane had heard them called. A long white dress patterned with thin black flowers running from its base was one of the most elegant outfits that Kane had laid eyes upon. It wrapped from left to right across her body, black bars twisting through white rope down the right side of her body. Moonlight glistened off long, elaborate earrings that drifted to her broad shoulders. Everything about this woman spoke of power.

It was clear to see that she was the sister of Mason D'Argio.

The thought brought a bitter taste to Kane's mouth that made her grimace.

'Katerina Kane.' The Empress shifted in her seat but her eyes remained fixed on Kane. 'Does it please you to know that I have heard much about you, even this far from the United Cities?'

'I suppose your brother and his dog report back often. We are not on the best of terms,' Kane spat, unable to keep the venom from her voice. 'I apologise, I forget what I should call you, I have never conversed with an empress before.'

'Call me Elena.' The Empress sat back and relaxed into her seat, fingers tapping on the armrest. 'This is not a formal engagement. I want to speak with you; woman-to-woman. I know that my brother and T'Chai can be heavy handed with their approach to spreading the word of the One God. Such devotion and methods can be abrasive and lead to discontent in new cities unaccustomed to such behaviour. So, I do understand your concern with meeting me.'

'Their approach involves burning innocent, young men and women and assassinating honourable warriors. And they do it not just in the name of their God, they do it in your name too.'

Elena sniffed and rolled her neck from side to side, mulling over the harsh, but true words. 'There are bigger things at play in Takaara than you know, Katerina. Believe me when I say that I wish the sacrifices we make were not needed, but I, more than any other in this world, know the importance of what we are doing. It is only in the Light of the One that we may get through the darkness that is coming for us.'

Kane scoffed, forgetting for a moment where she was and ignoring the dangers of her actions. 'Rhetoric I have heard slither between the forked tongue of your brother. Do not use religion to shield yourself from the anger of those whose lives you have destroyed.'

Elena nodded solemnly, pausing and allowing some of the anger building up in Kane to fade away.

'Now is not the time for such discussions. I invited you here to get a better measure of you. My brother tells me that you are rebellious and eager to stir up trouble for the

Empire. Now I see you arrive with Istari Vostor, the greatest swordsman in living memory, and if I am not mistaken, a man who is known as The Sword of Causrea. Why would you travel all this way with such a man, into a land full of your enemies?'

Kane sighed and stared back at the piercing gaze of the Empress. How much was she allowed to tell her?

'I want a Takaara that is not filled with hate and violence. I have a mission: stop the war that is to come. And I will do whatever is necessary to achieve my goal. Istari Vostor was assigned to me as a guide, a warrior tasked with looking after me as I travelled to the East.'

Elena's face gave nothing away other than a slight crease in her forehead as she leant forwards to get a better look at Kane. 'You toiled through much hardship to rise to your role in the United Cities. Even if my brother does not see your value, I certainly do. You speak of preventing a war – I can assure you, that is also my goal. It is a goal that this Empire has had since its inception. It is a goal *I* have had since before the first days of this Empire.' She dropped her head and exhaled before looking back up at her.

'However, it now seems that it is too late to stop the war from coming.'

'But, you are the *Empress of the East*,' Kane implored incredulously. '*You* can stop the war from happening.'

Elena offered only a look of pity as she spoke. 'The war you speak of is not the same. I thought we would have more time to prepare. But the Final War is coming. The battle against the forces of Chaos. It does not matter who we are now – the Empire, Darakeche, Archania, Causrea, Austrea, Ad-Alum – all will need to stand together if we are to defeat the darkness that is to come.'

Kane frowned, struggling to comprehend the

words escaping the lips of the Empress.

'What do you mean?'

'I brought you here, Katerina Kane, because I need to decide whether you can be trusted. You will have travelled through Darakeche, no doubt. Most who pass through that mindless nation and speak to their foolish Sultan end up with a worse opinion of me than before they went in.'

'I spoke with the Sultan. He is not exactly fond of you.'

'He is an oaf. The fool had a sword of dear importance to me. The only reason I did not crush him like an ant was because of that cursed sword. Even his family know that he is a snake and arrogant one at that. His son fled to join a mercenary band and his daughter married a princess in the Heartlands. She has some sense. From what my spies tell me, the Sultan's daughter escaped the city of Mughabir before the ceremony and meet with Princess Laria of the Heartlands and managed to take a ship East of the Emerald Sea. Apparently, the Sultan tells anyone who asks about her that she is dead. That is the kind of man I have been dealing with. The fool changes his name with the passing wind. I am told King Mikkael received a letter one day commanding that he refers to him as Sultan Mahara – *The Great One*. He is ten stalls short of a market as we say here.'

'His eldest son was certainly… interesting,' Kane said, deciding to withhold her true thoughts about the idiot prince.

Elena raised an eyebrow, clearly aware of the words that had not been spoken. 'Prince Naseem?' The Empress nearly choked on her laughter. 'I have seen pigs with more intellect than that prick.'

86

Kane was unable to hold back her own laughter, beginning to enjoy being in the presence of this regal figure. 'My whole world, everything I thought I knew, seems to be built on broken foundations. Tell me, what do you want of me?'

'I will be asking Istari to go on a mission of great importance. He will need to head south and meet with old friends. I need someone strong enough to stare into the face of Chaos and not even blink at the horrors that stare back. Someone to head to back towards her homeland with women I trust in the hope of saving Takaara. Can I trust you?'

Kane narrowed her eyes and bit her bottom lip. Too hard. Blood seeped into her mouth, bringing the taste of iron.

'What do you expect me to do?'

'You will find out tomorrow. I will call for Istari. It is time to speak with my husband.'

Sitting on the edge of the cliff, Arden had the perfect view of the coming storm. Clouds blacker than a kraken's ink blotted the horizon and lightning flashed and stabbed at the world, soon joined by the rumble of thunder.

The moon's light cast a ghostly glow as slivers of light peeked through the darkness suffocating the land. Seas swells rose, whipped by the chaotic winds as sheets of heavy rain fell from the heavens. He watched the rainfall with curious eyes, wondering why he could not feel their touch as they fell all around him.

Arden had seen only one such tempest previously. A night full of bedlam and chaos. He had been helping a few sailors staying in Oslar and they had claimed to feel the snap in the air that told of the coming of a great storm. The old, experienced, hardened sailors had shaken their heads and muttered prayers to the Old Gods, thankful to the deities that they were not to be caught out on the water when the storm hit. But some were not so fortunate.

They allowed Arden to sit with them and watch the storm, despairing at the furious bobbing of the two ships on the waves as the storm raged. Arden asked why no one was helping. The sailors had only responded with pitiful smiles.

He did not know what he was speaking about.

'There is no helping them now, child. Only the Gods have such power to calm the seas and protect those caught in the maelstrom. That is why we pray.'

The bodies washed up on the shore in the morning light. Dawn's gift for the sleepy village of Oslar. Arden had glimpsed a couple of the bodies and the splintered wood of the wreckage displaying what was left of the two unfortunate ships and their crews. Then he had been pulled away. He was just a child. He should not be a witness to such horror.

Arden had fought against the hands pulling him back to the village, away from the bloody shore but to no avail. Other boys his age had left to join the tribes and earn their name in battle. And yet here he stood, ushered away from the destruction of the seas and the deaths of a few sailors too greedy to head home following the ominous warning in the sky.

'I was shielded from storms and bloodshed from an early age,' Arden said, his tone even and controlled. He had not heard Osiron arrive, but he sensed the presence of the Chaos God, growing accustomed to the shimmer in the air and the sense that he was not alone. 'People would say that I was too young, or too innocent to be tainted by the horrors of the world around me.'

Arden twisted his head around and looked upon Osiron's face just as the lightning illuminated the dark lips and sunken black eyes of his ally, giving Osiron an almost skeletal look.

'They thought they were helping me. Shielding me from dark things that I should not involve myself in. I worked hard with my bow. They allowed me that. Hunting was necessary for survival. I remember Socket visiting my village and offering to take me hunting. He was kind. Gruff and moody,' he laughed, 'but kind. He taught me how to care for my bow. How to breathe with my strike, how to focus on the release and ignore any distractions in my mind.

'I cared for him like family. And yet, I still watched the light fade from his eyes as I stabbed that dagger through his heart.'

Waves crashed against the teeth-like rocks beneath him as he swung his feet slowly back and forth over the edge of the cliff. He licked his lips, tasting the salt in the air and feeling the rocking of thunder around him.

'Socket took advantage of your good nature,' Osiron said, caressing Arden's shoulder with their bony hand. 'He groomed you for his own needs and stabbed you in the back. Just as he did with Reaver Redbeard, the greatest leader the Borderlands had ever known.'

Arden knew that Osiron's words rang with truth but he could not push the image of the old archer's eyes gazing into his own, the sorrow and guilt etched on that withered face as the light faded. The rattle of his final breath woke Arden up sweating and breathing heavily in the middle of the night, ensuring that he walked through the day in a half slumber, stumbling his way through the illness-stricken camp and silently begging for a chance to rest.

'Guilt wraps around me like a thick cloak, threatening to cut my breath away,' he explained, wrapping his arms around him and grimacing. 'But I know that is the cloak worn by the old Arden. The innocent Arden they tried to stifle and keep from the horrors of the world.'

He peered down at the shore and thought he could see the bodies, broken and smashed by the unrelenting storm, surrounded by the carnage of a ship picked apart by the constant attack of the sea. The usually white sea spray caressing the edge of the waves was red, painted by the blood of those taken by the sea's maw. Arden blinked and stared up at the sky just as the black clouds cut off any remaining light persisting to strike through from the moon. Only flashes of lightning emblazoned the sky now, momentarily preventing the world from sitting in complete darkness.

'And what does this Arden feel that he should do? What should the Prince of Chaos do?' Osiron asked.

'Make a stone of his heart. Stone that is strong enough to withstand the relentless crush of the waves. Stone that can stay standing as the blood washes around it, unmoving and uncaring. I know my role. It is time I started to act as the Prince of Chaos.'

He stood and stared at Osiron, the black eyes flashing with the lightning, an eerie sight.

'You know, my prince, I was once weakened by a selfless heart. A young child confused by who they should be in a world telling me there was only one path. They tried to break me over and over again, hoping it would force me down their path instead of my own. They wanted me to be something I am not. I wanted to be more. Not man, woman, human, nor mage. I wanted more. I wanted to be everything. I wanted to be the greatest version of myself that I could be. That meant releasing the shackles they had placed on me, walking the path through the darkness where they had extinguished guiding lights. They place labels on us because it is easier for them. Everyone sits in a neat little box that they can understand.

'I was not born to be in a box, in a cage. And neither were you. They will tell you that you are mad, that you are a remorseless killer. These are just words they use to make themselves feel better. You must follow your own path, Arden Leifhand. Become who you are destined to be. The darkness around us is not evil, it is the unknown. People fear the unknown. But those of us with power, those of us with the curious mind, we know that the unknown is just something that people do not yet understand. It is an opportunity for us to grow.' Osiron smiled and rubbed their thumb against Arden's cheek in a fatherly way.

'We must trudge through the mud, through the darkness, in the knowledge that we will be the ones leading Takaara into a better age. There will be death, there will be suffering, there will be chaos, just as there always has been. But at the end, there will be a better world, one which we will create.'

Arden pursed his lips and exhaled softly through his nostrils. 'Sly, Kiras, and Cray have left to find Herick, haven't they?'

Osiron gave a curt, resigned nod.

'Ready the army. It is time I teach them a lesson. It is time I show them who I truly am.'

'And who is that, my friend Arden?'

Arden ran his tongue over his lips as the lightning lit up the world and then left again, leaving all in darkness as the thunder boomed, shaking the land. 'I am the Prince of Chaos. And I will not be taken for a fool.'

TORTURE

'Where did you say you found him?' Cypher asked, peering up at the terrified man. The Barbarian held the squirming man with one hand pushed up against his throat, pushing him against the brick wall. 'He seems to be going that funny shade of purple that identifies that his time of death is almost upon us. You might want to release your grip ever so slightly, Sigurd,' he said to the Barbarian who just grunted and lowered the man enough for his feet to touch the floor.

'Hangman's Hill,' the olive-skinned fighter responded, handing Cypher a thin blade housed in a scarlet scabbard. 'Creeping about with this out. Could have lost an eye if he had fallen in the dark. Did him a favour.' The fighter's voice was deep and clipped with an unusual accent, one that Cypher could not place. When asked where he was from, the strange fighter had just waved a hand and said, 'The Blood Islands. I won't say which one…' Cypher had been happy with that.

'And was he alone?'

'One other. Dead now. Braver or dumber than this one; put up a fight and Sigurd bashed his brains in. Buried in the mud on the hill. Didn't want any others to see if there are others.'

'Excellent work, Sanada. And you Sigurd. Place him in one of the cells and I will begin the interrogation at sunset. Inform T'Chai that we are hosting a guest caught on Hangman's Hill. He will be most pleased.' Cypher peered again at the scabbard and pulled the hilt of the blade free, spotting the red mark that he was looking for. 'Especially when he knows that we have caught one of the Red Sons in our beautiful land.'

He looked at the prisoner and thrilled at the sight of the fire dying in his eyes, fearing that he had given away too much just by being caught. Cypher flashed him a wicked smile. Little did he know, this was only the beginning.

This was the part of the job he enjoyed the most. True, he missed the skulking around in the shadows and the almost tangible fear of the possibility of being caught when he out on the streets taking care of his nasty business. But here, here he was able to create a masterpiece. Given the right tools, he could produce a work of art that would withstand even the most intense of scrutiny. He could take a man, any man, and have him singing any tune asked of him within a day. Less than a day, usually, but Cypher wasn't one for rushing the fun. Draw it out. Squeeze every last drop of enjoyment from it like the sweet taste of fruit on a hot summer's day in Lovers' Park.

His muse for the day was hanging from an iron contraption against the bloody wall of the cell. Chains hung from his wrists and ankles, leading off towards an iron fastening attached to the ceiling. With a few pulls on the chains available to him, Cypher could manipulate the man's body into any position imaginable. He could have him standing upright, easy for them to look one another in the eyes as the pain began. Or upside down, so that the blood rushed to his head and turned the face an interesting shade of purple as the swelling started. Or even face down towards the floor, a floor decorated with various instruments of pain, needles and spikes of differing sizes, some soaked in slow-acting poisons and others made purely for the visual delight of seeing what a man could face before shitting himself. The room really was an artist's dream. Cypher had the tools and the canvas to create a work that would be one for the ages, one that people would look upon and never forget. Their eyes would bulge and they would gasp, unable to comprehend the sheer skill needed to play with the human body in such ways.

Cypher stifled a giggle at the thought.

He was doing what he loved and, better than that, he was given a position high in the ranks of the Upper City and paid well for it. Those who sneered at him had to stifle their own looks of disgust now as he walked past them. They were the ones who lowered their chins and averted their gazes as he took in the sights of the Upper City. He wasn't just a killer. He wasn't just a torturer. He was an artist. And now he worked for Mason D'Argio as his lead questions master. He was the one tasked with finding enemies of the United Cities and bringing them to account.

'How is this any different to what you used to be doing?' Amana asked, looking from the tools laid out on the wooden bench and over at the dazed man hanging from the wall.

'Mikkael and his rotter of a son are no longer amongst the living,' Cypher answered, hand hovering over the hammer before drifting along the other weapons at his disposal. 'Two blockades standing in our way to true power have been removed. The task looks the same, but now the distance to the top is shorter. T'Chai is heading north to deal with the stinking Barbarians and Borderlanders who beat their chests like apes, and that means that I only answer to Mason D'Argio. One man who holds power greater than me in the city. That is progress.'

'He would kill you if he knew of such ideas.'

'If he knew of such ideas then I would know who informed him…' He let the wink and sneer speak for itself and tell its own story as Amana nodded her understanding to the not so veiled threat.

'No need to worry there. You picked me and Haadi out when others were treating us as vermin. Outsiders from the East drifting in the Lower City. Thieves and nothing more.'

Cypher sucked his gums and cracked his head to the side. 'Most people barely see anything further than the tip of their nose unless it shines day and night. Wipe away a bit of the murk and filth and the greatest treasures are there to be found. Head to the mines outside the town of Barnham, you will see my words for truth.'

'Want me to stay in on this one?' Amana asked, changing the subject and nodding towards the still dazed prisoner.

'Nah. I've got this one, child. I want T'Chai to see my fingerprints all over it. This isn't like the old days. No false testimonies shined up with spit and blood until it looks the way we want it to. This one needs to be the real thing. A true confession of why the fuck the Red Sons are scouting in lands a stone's throw from Archania. We have enough to deal with focusing on the Borderlands. If the Red Sons get involved, we would be stretched thing indeed.'

'Chaos would ensue.' Amana grinned that knowing slight slip of a grin that Cypher loved to see. 'And the Chaos will blind those around it, blurring vision and stinging eyes. When those eyes open, they will be witness to a new world. In chaos, there lies opportunity.'

'You have been listening…'

'Every word.'

'I shall choose them with more care from this moment onwards.'

'You have always chosen them carefully around me, Cypher Zellin. I am no fool.'

'And so I will not treat you as one. Though my mission may be shrouded in secrecy, know that I am being truthful when I say whatever happens, if you follow my tutelage, you will leave the Chaos in a better position than when you enter it.'

Amana shrugged and made to leave. 'My life has been filled with Chaos. It all looks the same to me.'

'Then begin to wipe away the filth. Look past what others see on the surface.' Cypher raised a serrated dagger and blew out from his cheeks in excitement, eyes sparkling with glee. 'Cut away if need be. Do what you must to find those sparks needed to keep living.'

Cypher watched the prisoner awake in dazed madness with eyes glaring like a predator peering through the bushes at its prey. He sat up in his simple seat, wanting a front row seat for that blissful moment when the captive comes to their senses and realises the true depths of horror they were trapped in. That flicker of fear that glosses over the eyes; the squirming in the unrelenting chains; the whimpering as they tried in vain to escape from their predicament. He had seen it all before. Never got old.

The captive fought against the chains, wincing as they offered nothing for him to work with. He twisted his head, looking around at up at his wrists, red from the effort, and then down his naked body – already bruised and marked from the scuffle with Sanada and Sigurd. The Islander and the Barbarian were not ones for pulling their punches – unless the money was right. His eyes widened in further horror as realisation finally dawned on him that this was not something he would be walking away from. This was not something that could be defeated with fists or barbed words. He was trapped in chains in a cell beneath the United Cities with a grinning madman enjoying every moment of his hell.

Cypher saw all of that from his small, wooden chair opposite and he revelled in it. You have to enjoy the little things.

'What are you going to do to me?' the man asked, peering nervously down at the dancing flames crackling and snapping between the two of them.

Cypher sniffed and sat further forward, rolling his shoulders back and groaning at the cracking noise they made as the muscles in his back stretched. Sitting still too long.

'There are many things that I could do to you,' Cypher explained. 'You will not be able to free yourself. You are alive because that is how I want you right now. Of course, that can change. I am quite the volatile fellow, or so I am told,' he said with a shrug and a wry smile. 'However, I am currently in a good mood. That bodes well for you. You see,' he stood and strolled around the flame until he stood close enough to smell the man's stale breath, 'we are going to play a little game. A fun game – for me at least. It is a game of questions. I ask them, you answer them. The correct answers will make me happy, and my happiness is

definitely the aim of the game for you. Incorrect answers…'
Cypher grabbed him by the throat and pressed his forehead
against the captive's sweat-drenched head, close enough to
kiss.

'Incorrect answers will not be in your best interests.
Do I make myself clear?'

A wince and a painful nod were the only answers
he received.

Cypher pulled back, hand tightening around the
throat as he scanned the man's face through narrowed eyes.
Dark skin spoke of birth away from the North. Not dark
enough to be from the Southern Kingdoms. Maybe the
East. Possibly the Heartlands. A small scar at the edge of
his lips said that this man was no stranger to a scrap.
Though Cypher could be wrong. A scar could be from an
unfortunate fall as much as a tavern fight. Dark eyes stared
back at Cypher, glaring – torn between hatred and fear. He
wondered if they had once been home to golden pupils.

Releasing the throat, he stepped back, humming
merrily as he edged towards the bench and the tools at his
disposal. Knives, daggers, needles, pliers, and pincers – all
shining with a hungry gleam in the firelight, craving action.

The prisoner's breath quickened as his eyes
followed Cypher's look towards the vicious, unforgiving
tools.

Cypher's fingers hovered over them each in turn,
his eyes studying the prisoner's reactions, an eager curl
rising on his lips as he caught the sheer despondency that
was almost tangible in the air around the poor bastard. He
walked back and forth beside the bench, running a tongue
over his lips and glaring at the whimpering captive.

'Question one,' he said, picking up the pliers and
turning them over in his hand, studying them with an

expert's gaze. 'What is your name?'

Those dark eyes turned to Cypher and flared in defiance. A small bite of the lip and then an answer. 'Marcus. Marcus Andorra.'

A Heartlands name. Born in one of those fallen nations then.

Cypher pushed out his bottom lip and nodded as he inched back over to Marcus, still twisting the pliers in his hand, rubbing his fingers over the harsh iron. 'That was an easy question. Not one that I really care for, but it is always good to have a name to add to the face. Even when the face becomes unrecognisable to the man who once held the name. You could have given any name; I would not have cared. Though, this time, I shall trust your words, Marcus Andorra.

'Now, question two. Do you work for the *criminal* mercenary group known as the Red Sons?'

Marcus swallowed, his throat bulging as he steadied himself. 'I have never worked with that group. I am a simple farmer. Please,' his eyes followed the pliers as Cypher pushed them towards the hand creeping out of the manacles, 'I will do what you ask. I will answer your questions.' The tears rolled freely, snot dripping from his nostrils as he blubbered and wheezed.

Cypher slapped his hand, not too hard, against the man's cheek, the shock halting the tears momentarily. 'Pull yourself together! I have barely started,' he said in disgust, annoyed at the way the game was being played. 'I *know* you will answer my questions. The briefest hint of losing a finger and you squeal. There are other things I could work on…'

Cypher smirked and flashed his eyes wide, lowering the pliers and giving a dark wink to ensure that Marcus knew exactly what he intended to do if things did not go as planned.

'You will give me more than your name before the sun rises, Marcus Andorra. I guarantee that. Give me false information, try to fuck with me, and I will ensure that your pain lasts longer than the wax and wane of a moon. This isn't my first dance, Marcus Andorra. I am well versed in ways of torture. I understand the boundaries and thresholds that must not be crossed. I will push your body to the limits and then we will work on creating new limits for you, new ways of handling the pain that I am more than willing to inflict on your pitiful form.' Cypher raised the pliers and growled, shaking his head. 'Not good enough.'

He rushed back to the bench and threw the pliers down, searching for another more effective tool as they clattered and shook amongst the other weapons. Cypher thought about it for a moment, studying each tool in turn, frustration growing as each moment passed him by. 'Not good enough,' he repeated to himself.

Sobs broke him from his thoughts, alerting him to the low burning flames in the centre of the room. He looked from the flames up at the iron bonds trapping Marcus and he smiled, a plan forming in his mind. He'd done something similar before, though not in some time, and certainly not in the dungeons beneath the palace. He chuckled, the sound unnerving the prisoner more than anything else up to that point. It would be almost poetic. It would be rude not to.

He raced over to the chains beside Marcus and pulled and twisted, watching Marcus's body react to the bonds as he lurched forward and rose, stuck, and cursed in response to Cypher's unhinged actions.

The torturer rubbed his hands together at last with glee, smirking with success as he studied the now horizontal body of the captive, wild eyes staring down at the flames directly beneath his face.

'Please,' Marcus pleaded, distressed as he tried to turn his head to speak to Cypher. 'Not burning. Anything but burning…'

'Question two,' Cypher muttered with an icy glare, arms folded as he watched the dancing bright flames do his dark work.

'Yes,' Marcus gasped fighting with every nerve in his body to escape the flames. At this distance, he would just begin to feel the warmth of the fire, the kiss of heat on his skin. Any closer, it would start getting significantly more uncomfortable for the captive. 'I am a soldier for the Red Sons.'

'The truth really is a beautiful thing. How long have you been with them?'

'Just under two cycles. Joined when they were aiding the rebels in the Heartlands.'

Cypher drew his breath slowly through his teeth and scratched at his head as he stepped past the captive, resting a hand on the iron chain hanging from the wall. A short, sharp pull brought with it the creaking of metal and a terrified scream as Marcus dropped a step lower, his face now barely two paces from the rising flames.

'I told the truth dammit! I told the truth!' he cried out, somewhat shocked by Cypher's callous and uncaring actions.

'You did,' Cypher admitted. 'I just wanted you to truly realise the predicament you are in. That grazing burn of the flames you feel that on your face. Lie to me, and those flames will burn the eyes from your skull. A horrifying punishment if I may say so myself. Sickening.' He creased his nose and crouched so that he could look up at Marcus. 'It is the smell that I dislike. A horrid, acrid smell that clogs at the back of the throat. Difficult to withstand for onlookers.'

'Then why do it?' Whimpering. No courage.

'Because I have a role to play. An important one. The United Cities of Archania stands on the edge of Chaos. One step back and we will fall. The Red Sons suddenly appearing on our border might just be the little push that sends us on our way. So, tell me: why are the Red Sons sending scouts this way? Speak honestly, or I will pull that chain once more and embrace that sickening smell of burning eyeballs. At least you will not be able to see what happens next…'

'I'll tell you what you need to know… please…'

Cypher pulled gently on the chain, teasing the action that would blind the tearful soldier. 'What are the Red Sons doing sending scouts so close to the United Cities of Archania? Speak the truth, or…' He pulled on the chain, lowering Marcus closer to the flames before sending him back up and away.

'We have a new leader. He wants us to take over the capital. The Sultan of Darakeche has pledged to help the fight against the United Cities. We have enough men to take the city in days.' Marcus spoke rapidly, pushing the words out as quickly as he could as his eyes flickered from the flames to Cypher and back again. He wasn't lying – that much Cypher could clearly see.

'A new leader? And who might this new leader be? Who is this man who would wish to destroy one of the greatest nations in all of Takaara?'

'That's the thing, he doesn't want to destroy it. He wants to rule it,' Marcus explained, tears dripping down towards the fire. 'He claims to be the lost prince. Prince

Drayke of Archania.'

'Drayke…' Cypher was unable to hide his shock at hearing the name. The young prince who Cypher had once held at sword point in the Lower City. A man liked by the people of Archania, much more so than his bastard brother, Asher. If Drayke was leading the Red Sons, he would have the backing of many within the city. This news had to be controlled and handled only by the right people unless all hells were to break out in Archania.

'Are you certain it is the prince?'

Marcus nodded, his skin an uncomfortable shade of red. 'Some woman from Archania backed up his claim. She was in the camp for a few days. Kane or something.'

'Katerina Kane,' Cypher said grinning at the madness of it all.

'That was it. Katerina Kane.'

Cypher bit his bottom lip, still grinning wide at the incredulous situation he found himself in. The woman had balls. She certainly wasn't one to tread the easy path.

'And where is Katerina Kane now?'

'No idea. We fought a battle with the Empire and she fled with some old soldier. A fighter with more skill than I've ever seen in all my cycles alive. Old guy was a living weapon. No one would stand a chance against him.'

He wracked his brain but could not think of any from Archania who would fit such a description. The few knights linked with the cities were mainly drunk fools living off their faded glory from the Northern Wars. Mikkael had been keen to reward those who had shown prowess in battle but the stories had been embellished and blown out of proportion in order to give the rabble at home the opportunity to bang their patriotic drums and talk to one another in taverns over a few glasses that the United Cities of Archania was the greatest military power in the land. Sir Dominic was living proof of that.

'You have done well, Marcus Andorra. This information is much appreciated,' Cypher said, much to the relief of the captive.

'Then, you will release me?'

'I will. You will return to the Red Sons,' Cypher added, the sparks of a plan flashing to life in his mind. 'You will tell them that the United Cities of Archania is ready when they are. You will tell *Prince* Drayke that Mason D'Argio is sitting on the throne and is aware of what is coming.'

Marcus nodded frantically, still peering at the flames from the corner of his eyes as he turned to Cypher, relief etched on his sweating, red face. 'I will. I will tell them everything.'

One side of Cypher's lips curled up as he slowly dropped the chain, watching the relief fade from the captive's face. 'Of course, we must show them that we mean business; that Archania is a place of hardened people who do not take lightly to such intrusions in our peaceful way of life. But I am merciful. It will just be the one eye that I burn away today…'

Marcus's mouth opened in horrified realisation of what Cypher meant to do to him. His face dropped closer to the flames, too fast for him to form a response other than piercing screams that echoed around the dark dungeons.

Cypher watched closely, glaring at the man as he attempted to turn his head away. He locked the chain in place and strolled over to him, pulling at the loosened strap and buckle and using it to keep the man's head in place. 'Just the one eye. Those who worship the Old Gods claim that giving an eye as a sacrifice means that you receive wisdom, a vision for the future. You may wish to pray to those Gods now if you are so inclined. Personally, I think it is a load of horseshit.'

The flames licked at the eye as the prisoner fought to no avail against his restraints.

Cypher just watched, motionless and impassive. Arms folded, he followed the dance of the flames and ignored the pungent smell filling the room as the flesh melted and began to turn a horrid shade of black.

When it was done, Cypher used the chain to pull the motionless body away from the fire and studied the damage with a keen eye.

The door opened behind him as he unbuckled the strap around Marcus's head. It drooped forward so Cypher pushed it back up and smiled at the damage.

'Master T'Chai has already left with the forces to head north and battle those who defy us in the Borderlands,' Amana said behind him.

'Good,' Cypher replied without turning as he licked his lips. 'Send your brother to check the tunnels. We need them in a good condition if we are to live out this moon.'

'And what do you want done with this one?'

'Send for Sigurd and Sanada. They will dump him at the top of Hangman's Hill. He will be the message we send to the Red Sons.'

'What message is that?'

'Waiting is torture. We are ready.' Cypher spun and headed for the door, offering the young woman a wink as he passed her. 'Let battle commence.'

THE ENEMY OF MY ENEMY

Where Torvield had been empty – a ghost town masquerading as the capital of the Borderlands – the land around Hillheim was transformed, covered in tents running all the way to the wooden boundary of the usually sleepy village on the edge of the Borderlands and filled with the signs of warriors preparing for battle.

'Think they know we are coming?' Kiras asked, scanning the campsite and folding her arms in frustration.

'Why else would they be forging weapons and gathering in such numbers?' Sly answered, but a worry gnawed at the back of his skull. 'Though, if they knew we were coming, why not gather in Torvield? Easier to defend. The place has the weapons, the defences, the land. Torvield makes sense. This don't.'

Both Kiras and Cray stayed silent, the same worry clearly playing on their minds. Something was wrong with the whole messed up situation.

'Changing the plan?' Kiras asked, the raised

eyebrow and smirk showing that she already knew his answer.

'Bah! Ain't changing nothing. We sneak in and kill the bastard. If we can, we fight our way out and take as many of the cunts as we can.' He shrugged. 'Simple. No need to complicate things.'

'Horses,' Cray muttered, lowering his chin towards the three beasts as they stood waiting in the shelter of the trees.

'Need to let 'em go,' Kiras answered. 'If we tie 'em up then we aren't certain that we'll make it back out. Not fair on the animals.'

'Aye,' Sly agreed, scratching his beard and exhaling long and slow. 'They know the way back to Torvield. True border horses; they'll be fine. Made of sturdy stuff.'

Kiras began taking the bags and saddles from the animals, freeing them from any kind of burden for their trek back north as Sly turned back to the campsite and studied the layout, planning their next move as the sun dipped to the west. It was a clear evening and the red sun cast a menacing glow over the village and its new inhabitants. Old farmers used to claim a red sun meant the Old Gods were promising blood in the night. Whether that was true or not Sly didn't know. But he knew that this night the red sun would fall below the horizon and when the stars shone above, blood would come to many in that small village. Borderlanders and Barbarians alike. Anyone who got in his damned way in fact.

'Herick will be in Hillheim – holed up. He'll be in the safest place he can find. That's always been his way. He's no fool. We'll need help. Enter from the south of the town and find your family, see what has been going on and why they have left Torvield,' Sly said. Both Cray and Kiras grunted their approval for his plan. 'Could be risky but if there's a way we can get a few extra hands on our side it could mean all the difference. Reckon Sofia will help if she knows that you're with us and tell her what happened to Baldor?'

Kiras stroked the mane of the horse closest to her and thought about it for a while. 'She'll help. Or at least, she won't hinder. She's not Herick's biggest fan. She just knows that picking her moment is vital. She won't risk playing a hand that may lead to her losing everything. Still, like you said before, Herick is waiting to hear from us about Baldor – that can be our way in without trouble. Just need to make sure he don't find out the big guy ain't with us before we find him.'

Sly nodded grimly at the reminder of their lost ally. The big man left a hole bigger than words could convey. A quiet warrior. A shield brother as they used to say in the wars. He'd put his own body on the line if it meant saving the one next to him. Not much more a man can do then that.

'That settles it then. Cray, you find your family and get whatever information you can. Kiras, me and you are heading for Sofia's. If we even have an understanding that her men and women aren't to move on us until the dark business it settled, that will give us enough of a chance to get through the night. Don't give a fuck about the Barbarians. I'll kill every last one of them if I have to. And enjoy it too…' he added with a wicked smile.

'Kill the fuckers,' Cray muttered, almost to himself as he pulled out a short yew bow and studied it closely, checking for any damage from their travels. Socket's death meant one of them would need to carry a ranged weapon. Cray had trained with the bow when he was in Saul's tribe so he was the best fit in everyone's mind. Sly had never liked using the weapon. Too far away. Difficult to see the light fade from that distance. He'd thrown a few daggers and axes in his time but always close enough to see that light fade or the listen to the final rattling breath escape the body. Better that way. More final.

He heard three slaps and watched as the horses trotted away from Kiras, heading back to the safety of the forest and away from Hillheim and the red sun. The last of the evening light faded and darkness cloaked the land with only the stars and the light from the crescent moon left to shine on the world.

'That's it then,' Sly sighed. 'Let's get to it.'

Hillheim was busier than usual. Cray slunk into the crowds – lost amidst the Barbarians and Borderlanders with his dark hood pulled up to hide his face from view as he made for his family's home. Out of the three of them, Sly knew that Cray would be the one least likely to be recognised. On his own, Cray would be safe from the odd looks of the town's inhabitants – only a few in Hillheim would know who he was and the company that he kept. Sly and Kiras did not have such luck, but the Borderlands was a big place. Their names may be infamous, but men would not be able to put faces to those names. Still, they kept their heads down and hoods up as they pushed through the crowded streets, Sly fighting the impulse to drive a bloodied dagger through any of the Barbarians within arm's reach.

'Should have tied my damned hands to my sides,' he growled, leaning into Kiras. 'Fingers are getting twitchy.'

'Then play with your fucking cock! Now is not the time, Sly,' Kiras hissed. 'We have a job to do. You'll get your hands bloody tonight and you know it.'

Sly grunted and left it at that, glaring at a group of the large bastards as they passed him by. 'Herick made a deal with the fucking devil when he aligned himself with those cunts.'

'Has Arden done much different?'

Sly broke his stride, pausing as the question hit him like a shield wall in battle. 'Not something I really like thinking about…' he admitted before continuing and matching her quick but casual pace.

'Well, think we might need to start thinking about it,' Kiras said, side-stepping an elderly woman begging for coin. Sly grimaced and pushed the woman away as she attempted to follow Kiras.

'What you saying?' he asked when he was sure that the woman was no longer following.

'The kid has made a pact with some being capable of Gods know what. He wants to wipe out most of Takaara and reshape what is left. Herick made friends with warriors who lived close to him in the hope of protecting himself from a future coup or a battle between the tribes. Can we condemn one and ignore the other?'

'Yeah,' Sly said without thinking, 'the kid is killing those we don't like. Herick allied himself with people who have killed our kind for centuries. That makes it simple enough for me.'

'But it's not, is it?' Kiras gave Sly a sad smile and turned, walking down an empty, narrow alleyway filed with the litter of the day. 'You like the kid but you're questioning him. I know you Sly. You left him because you don't want to argue against him. But you still left him. We're warriors. We do messed up things and always have. I suppose we're just starting to discover the lines that we don't want to cross.'

Sly bit his tongue, the words hitting closer to home than he would have liked. The girlie's smile was infuriating.

'We've been hanging out for too long,' he moaned.

'Not getting rid of me now,' Kiras said with a gentle elbow in his ribs. 'I've lost one friend, not gonna lose another.'

'We friends now? Thought we were always just two warriors on the same side.'

'We're friends. If I am gonna die tonight, I'd want to at least die acknowledging that.'

'Aye,' Sly agreed. 'I'm getting soft.'

'Don't worry, I won't tell anyone.'

'Better not. I'd only deny it.'

Sofia's place was one of the larger buildings in Hillheim. Four floors high, the playhouse was home to the various vices available in the Borderlands. Two floors of rooms in various sizes and furnishing for those who were willing to pay good coin to sleep with people of all genders, shapes, and sizes. One floor set aside for the faze smokers looking to take time to kick back and forget the difficulties of the world around them whilst racking up debt to the cunning landlady. Rumours around the Borderlands spoke of a basement floor where men and women from all corners of the North would meet and fight, sometimes to the death, in the hope of earning coin, honour, and respect. Some just loved a good fight. Sly hadn't seen it with his own eyes, there was enough fighting and killing above ground to quench his appetite.

Then there was the top floor.

This was Sofia's floor. Only her most esteemed guests were allowed on the top floor.

'You sure you wanna do this?' Sly asked Kiras, looking up at the tall, wooden building and then down the dark alleyway beside it. The warrior guarding the side entrance was alone, unlike the four camped out at the front of Sofia's. Their best bet was getting to Sofia without anyone else knowing about it. That meant going in with weapons out and glistening in the starlight wasn't the best option.

'Yeah. The corridors are dark for a reason in there. Get in through the side and we'll make it up to the top. Will need to clear out a few guards but if we do our best not to kill then Sofia won't bat an eyelid.'

'Good.' Sly moved to stand beside Sofia's, leaning against the wall and under the black and white awning hanging beneath the second floor windows of the cobbler's. He turned and busied himself with looking at the boots and shoes on display through the window as the pitter-patter of rain began to fall against the awning. His eyes flickered from the window and down the alleyway, watching Kiras as she strolled between the buildings, stopping as she met the guard at the side entrance to Sofia's. Even from here, Sly could see the man's face light up as Kiras grabbed him by his shirt and push him against the wall seductively.

He chuckled as Kiras snapped forwards, whipping one of her blades free and thumping the butt of her blade against the guard's bald head. He dropped instantly, slumped against the wall and beside the bags of rubbish that filled the alleyway.

Sly made to follow his ally. That's when he felt something sharp pressed against his back.

'For a famed warrior, you're pretty easy to catch,' a familiar voice whispered in his ear. 'That's twice now.'

'Must be 'cause I like you so much,' Sly said, licking his dry lips as he started to raise his hands in defeat. No waiting for another chance, he twisted his body and pulled away from the knife in his back, grabbing at Frida's wrist and pulling it to the side, away from his body at the same

112

time as pulling her close to him, as close as lovers.

He stared at her scarred face and looked into her fiery eyes. 'Well, isn't this cosy?'

'Probably the closest you've been to a woman in half a cycle or more,' Frida spat.

Sly's eyebrows flicked up and back down in amusement. 'No probably about it. What are you doing?'

'That's what I was about to ask you.'

Sly ripped the knife from her hand and placed it on his belt before guided her around the corner and into the alleyway, ignoring her protests. He pushed her forwards and she stumbled on the uneven ground, balancing herself just in time for Kiras's curved blade to meet the edge of her throat.

'Who the fuck is this?' Kiras snarled, looking from the defiant woman at the top of her weapon and then over her shoulder to Sly.

He just shrugged. 'Some bitch who works for Sofia *and* Herick. Decent fighter. No manners. I like her.'

'The name's Frida.'

'Where's your little playmate?' Sly asked, looking around as though expecting the small woman to jump out from the shadows.

'I could say the same to you,' Frida snarled, noticing that Cray wasn't with them.

'You could. But you are the one with beads of blood trickling down your throat. So I'd suggest you answer before Kiras gets bored. She ain't as nice as I am.'

He smirked at the first signs of fear flashing across the woman's face as she stared into Kiras's cold glare.

'Maybe it's best we go and see Sofia. She can

explain things,' Frida said, her words slow and carefully chosen as Kiras started to pull the weapon away from the pierced skin. 'Have to admit, I'm surprised to see you here without Baldor. Herick made it clear to his tribe that if they see you back in the Borderlands without the big man, you're free game. No coin for your capture; just straight killing. Bones and nothing more. He ain't gonna be happy to see you without him.'

Kiras pushed the blade back against her throat and edge forwards, her breathing intensifying as her nostrils flared at the mention of her dead friend. 'Herick ain't gonna like a lot of things. He's gonna have to swallow that shit and thank us for it if he is to keep breathing.'

Frida raised her hands and glanced back at Sly, eyes pleading for support that wasn't going to come. 'Like I said, we need to see Sofia. She's the only one that will help. Has a soft spot for you,' she said, inclining her head to Kiras. You saved some of her girls a while back from what I heard.'

'It was a long time ago.'

'She has a good memory.'

Sly sucked his teeth and stepped forward, placing a hand on Kiras's raised weapon and gently pulling it away from Frida's throat. Frida wiped a hand across her neck and looked at the blood that now stained her palm.

'We need to speak to Sofia. It would be best if no one else knew we were here,' he said to her.

'Follow me.'

The usual sounds of flesh slapping against flesh and the high screams, rumbling moans, and sharp grunts of a brothel pierced through the walls of Sofia's Den. Even on the ground floor, Sly could smell the smoke from the faze drifting down and filling the corridors. He pressed up the stairs, careful so that noise was kept to a minimum. It wasn't just Sofia's guards who cared for the place, Frida had warned them that Herick had placed men and women in every establishment in the Borderlands to ensure that none were disobeying his orders.

'If we bump into one of Sofia's people, I can handle that. If it is Herick's, I can't make the same promises,' she warned.

'I can handle Herick's men,' Kiras snarled.

'You okay with that?' Sly asked, frowning. 'Thought you were all for him and his rule?'

Frida shrugged. 'I was. But things haven't been great lately. Herick used to always put us women first, look after us and make sure we were ones on top. Now, he's listening more and more to the leader of the Barbarians and his rat of a son. There was an incident in here a week ago where a couple of the Barbarians tried getting with one of our women, Senua. She told them that if they laid a finger on her then she would chop their cocks off.'

'What happened?'

Frida laughed. 'They ignored her. She chopped their cocks off. But then when word got out, the Barbarians started smashing some of the places up around Hillheim. Herick came to calm things down. Punished the Barbarians with a slap on the wrist.'

'And Senua?' Kiras asked, the question bringing an acidic taste to her mouth that made her wince.

Frida returned the dark look with one of her own. 'The leader's son did it himself. Chopped her head clean off. Herick watched. Did nothing. Just let it play out and then moved on. He's not the same man who led us through the harsh times in the Far North.'

'I told you that,' Sly stated smugly. 'Power changes people.'

One of the doors was parted slightly, giving Sly a glimpse into the busy room beyond. Gaming tables had been set up, yet another amusing distraction for the people of Hillheim and visitors to Sofia's Den.

'Branching out,' Frida commented, sensing Sly's thoughts as he peeked through the gap. 'Drink, faze and sex will always be here, but gambling is where it is at in the big cities. Fools will give up anything at the glimmer of chance that they could win it all.'

'I'm guessing not many here will win it all,' Sly croaked, watching the well-dressed men and women shuffling cards and placing counters in stacked rows of various sizes. At the far end of the room, a thin moustached man was spinning a large wheel much to the enjoyment of those in the room if the hollering and laughter was anything to go by.

'Course not,' Frida snorted. 'What would be the point in that?'

They carried on up the stairs, the hum of the den keeping Sly on high alert as he followed the two women, keeping a cautious eye over his shoulder and looking out for any who may creep up behind. On the top floor, the noise of the den subsided to a low buzz beneath them.

'Wait here,' Frida told them, placing a hand on the handle of the door and a finger to her lips, warning Sly and Kiras as she edged the door open and slipped through the gap. A moment later, her head popped through and she ushered them through with a motion of her hand.

Kiras turned back to Sly and he offered a small nod, one hand dropping to his axe as he loosed his belt, preparing for trouble. He exhaled slowly, noticing Kiras's hand slip to her hip where he knew her fingers ran along the hilt of one of her twin blades. If there was to be a fight, he couldn't have asked for anyone better in the close spaces provided by Sofia's Den. Anyone wishing to hurt them would receive what they gave out tenfold.

He straightened and walked through the doorway, gripping the handle of his axe tightly, tense and ready for a fight. Instead, he found… nothing. Just an empty waiting room.

'This room is usually full of people waiting to speak to Lady Sofia,' Frida said, frowning at the empty chairs and glancing towards the closed door on the eastern wall.

Sly marched across the room and held his hand to Frida's throat, pushing her back against a wall and glaring at the frightened woman. 'If you've led us into some kind of trap…' he growled, warning clear for all to see.

'Sly, let her go. How could she know we would even be coming?' Kiras said, the voice of reason.

He let her go but kept his eyes on Frida, unwilling to let her out of his sight.

Then the door opened.

Lady Sofia sat beyond the doorway, arms out in front of her on the elegant table. Candlelight shimmered from the sparkling jewels on her slender figures and she wore a dark, blue dress that reminded Sly of the colour of the ocean as the sun falls. Red hair dropped in waves past her shoulders and she stared through the doorway with a look as intense as flames burning in the night sky. She licked her painted lips and called to them.

'It is good to see you again, Sly Stormson. And I see you have returned with our mutual friend,' she said, voice strong and powerful with a hint of humour edging the words. 'Frida, please do bring our friends through, I am not

117

overly fond of waiting.'

Frida stepped through first. Kiras made to follow but Sly grabbed her wrist and shook his head at the frown on the warrior's face. He walked ahead, hand still close to his trusty axe.

Past the doorway, he looked to the right, a curse almost passing his lips as a flash of light blinded him, joined by a sharp, burning pain on the back of his head.

He stumbled to the side, fumbling for his axe as a wave of sound crashed around him. Blades drawn. Shouting. Screams. Angry voices and some stern commands. He felt strong hands grab his shoulders and he threw himself back, landing with a crash against his assailant. Rolling back over his attacker, he stood just in time to raise an arm and block a wooden club swinging towards his face. His forearm softened the blow and shifted him back onto his heels with a grunt. He stomped on the Barbarian's face beneath him and then launched himself at the tall bastard holding the club in front of him. Head ducked, he dived under another strike and speared the Barbarian, shoulder thrusting into the brute's ribs as he pulled at the taller attacker's ankles, dragging him to the ground.

The club clattered to the ground with a dull thud and Sly reared up, dropping his elbow against a cheekbone with all his strength and a roar. He lowered his head and bit the bastard's nose. Pulling away, a piercing scream filled the air as blood and flesh soaked Sly's grinning mouth.

A forearm grabbed him around the neck and pulled. Sly clutched at the arm, digging his nails into the skin and attempting to pull away as the bastard dragged him away from the whimpering, bloodied mess at his feet.

From the corner of his eye, he could see Kiras fighting with another of the Barbarians, driving her knee into the man's nuts with a perfected precision that almost made Sly squirm and feel a pinch of pity for the bastard. Almost, because he had his own issues.

Tucking his chin, Sly slipped his boot back between his attacker's legs and hooked the ankle. He felt the grip loosen and he took the opportunity that presented itself. Twisting, he drove his elbow into the man's ribs and locked his arm around the Barbarian's neck that present itself. Sly dropped to the ground with all the strength he could muster, the Barbarian's neck caught in the chokehold.

Sly grinned as he heard the crack of the man's face hitting the hard floor but he didn't let go. He tightened his arm around the neck, locking his fingers together and pulling tight until the bastard's body fell limp.

Breathing hard, Sly turned and got up onto his knees. Just in time to see the point of a sword inches from his face.

'I thought I warned you to never step foot in my lands again, Stormson,' Herick mocked with a leering, lopsided smile. 'Baldor was to be sent here, and you were never to return...'

'Must've missed your ugly, bald head, Herick.' Sly turned from the sword pointed towards him and instead focused on a grim-looking Kiras, standing tall with a blade pressed hard against a kneeling barbarian covered in blood that was still dripping from a nasty cut on his temple.

'He's dead,' Sly said, eyes not leaving Kiras as he uttered the words with a long breath. 'Tortured and killed by the cunts down south. We were too late...'

He turned back to Herick to see the chief giving a grim nod.

'I know,' the chief croaked, voice close to breaking. 'And that's why I'm not gonna ram this sword straight down your stinking fucking throat.'

Sly's forehead creased at the words, surprised with the unexpected reprieve. Leaning against the unconscious Barbarian to his side, he pushed himself up, standing and looking around the room. Two Barbarians lay unmoving on the floor, one bleeding a pool of the red stuff that said that he would not be getting up again. Kiras held another whilst one whimpered against the wall, clutching at his missing nose, hand soaked in blood. Frida stood in the doorway, nervous eyes flittering between the warriors and then to Lady Sofia, who still sat calmly in her seat, face impassive and giving nothing away. Sly chuckled at the thought of her testing that face at the gaming tables on the floor below.

'Another deal?' Kiras asked, cutting through the tense silence.

'Another deal,' Herick repeated, running a hand over his sweaty, bald pate and sighing. 'For the sake of the Borderlands. What do you say, Stormson?' He lowered his sword, dark eyes boring a hole in Sly.

Sly spat the blood from his mouth and ran his tongue over his teeth, checking to see if any more were missing.

'I'm listening.'

THE CALM BEFORE

There was no joy in the city of Ad-Alum this night. No singing. No dancing. No music. No laughter. Just a silence stuffed with dread that covered the whole of the city. Even the stars were in hiding, the sky an inky black to fit the mood of the usually vibrant city. It unnerved Aleister. Made him want to grab his bags and flee to the wild, open lands to the north. Get away from whatever disturbing event was about to occur.

But he didn't.

He couldn't.

He had his best friend, Bathos.

He had his sister, Ariel.

He had his niece or nephew growing every day inside her.

There was no running away from this. The darkness of Ad-Alum was not only of that city. Chaos was coming, he knew that. It wasn't something that one could run from. They needed to stand together. To fight together.

Side by side. To the death if need be.

The words of The Wise Women echoed in his mind, as they had been fond of doing since the words had escaped the golden lips of those strange people in the caves by the God Falls.

'You must use any means necessary, Aleister of the Red Sons. Even at the cost of your life.'

He walked the dark streets, the warm night air of summer pressing all around him. Once busy streets were now empty but for the guards standing outside of the eastern pyramid. He had wandered farther than expected, lost in his own thoughts. He looked back to see that he had followed the bend of the river that flowed through the heart of the city like a watery vein. Flickers of light from the lamps lining the streets caught his eye but nothing more. The city was in mourning. They grieved for those who had willingly given their lives to face the darkness, to confront those who would bring the Great War – the Final Battle.

Over the last week, King Zeekial had sent messengers to all four corners of the Southern Kingdoms, informing them of what was to come and asking for all who were willing and able to unite and face the dreaded threat. The tension in the city could almost be tasted as Aleister sighed and edged around the curve of the bridge, walking down the bank and placing himself on one of the stone benches looking out across the river. The gentle flow of the water calmed him. Always had.

His thoughts drifted to late nights in the summer laughing with Ella in Lovers' Park by the lake. They would watch the ducks and listen to the sounds of the calm pocket within the city they loved. They would talk of the future, of heroism, and fame. Of life and love.

He swallowed the lump in his throat and wiped his eyes with the back of his hand.

He would give almost anything to see her face again. To tell her how important she was to him. To hold her close and tell her that he loved her.

But he could not.

'This really is a truly beautiful part of the city.'

Aleister spun, shocked to see King Solomus standing alone on the river's edge, looking out across the silent city with a look of sorrow edged on his lined face. 'Your Majesty.' He made to stand but Solomus waved away the gesture.

'Such formality is not needed when there is just the two of us, Aleister of the Red Sons. I hope you do not mind the company of an old king on this warm night.'

'Of course not. You are most welcome,' Aleister responded, making room on the bench as Solomus pulled up the bottom of his robes and sat beside him with a sigh.

'Do you have such a place in your homeland? I am not familiar with the cities in the North. My entire life has been spent travelling between the Southern Kingdoms, ensuring strong bonds between my neighbours. It is a shame that I have not been able to see more of the world.'

'There is beauty in my homeland. Pockets of beauty where one can sit and contemplate the world. Also, rivers in the North sometimes freeze in the harsher winters that we have, offering another scene of beauty for the world to enjoy. The way the light of the falling winter sun hits off a frozen lake is almost incomparable.' Green eyes flashed with golden pupils shot into his mind and he paused, his hand rubbing his sweating forehead.

'Are you well?' Solomus asked.

'Just tired,' Aleister lied, shaking his head and smiling weakly.

'Tired,' Solomus chuckled with his entire body. 'You do not know the meaning of the word. At your age I would go a week without sleep!'

'And why would a prince wish to go such a long time without sleep?' Aleister joined in the mirth as Solomus leaned closer and gave a cheeky wink.

'A young prince does not bear the same weight of responsibility as that of an old king. I spent those sleepless nights well, even if it would not be wise of me to give away details of such events to strangers from distant lands.'

Aleister found himself grinning, thinking of the nights he would sneak into Ella's family home and somehow keep from waking everyone as he crept around in the shadows, his eyes only for the woman holding his hand and giggling sheepishly.

'It is difficult to watch the young carry the burden of great responsibility. My role as king is to help ease the burdens of my people. I have grown a keen sense capable of spotting those who wish to carry the world on their shoulders before it is their time.' Solomus pointed a stabbing finger into Aleister's arm and peered up into his eyes. 'Tell me your burden, young one. Sharing the burden lightens the load. Even if it is just a little.'

'This Final Battle, the Great War. I have the weapon that can kill the four greatest magi in the history of Takaara. Magi who are damned near Gods themselves. I am expected to succeed in something that will shape the world to come and yet I struggle to take care of myself...' Aleister sighed and picked up a pebble at his feet. He flicked it into the water, watching the ripples dance away from the impact.

Solomus stood, groaning as his old knees creaked with the effort. 'I told you that I was not a young prince anymore,' he laughed. 'Come,' he said, motioning for Aleister to follow as he walked up the bank and back onto the street. 'There is something I wish to show you. Something that helped a young prince when he had lost his way in the darkness and could not find the light.'

Aleister frowned but he stood and followed the old king.

*

'I have never seen anything like this before…'

'If there is one thing we in the South know what to do, then it is to build temples,' Solomus admitted. 'The Gods may watch over us. Or they may not. Either way, we have the comfort of knowing that we have achieved great things with the gifts we were given, by the Gods or not.'

The main chamber of the temple was quiet. A few Chosen – men and women called to walk a spiritual path as Solomus had explained it – were walking around the temple with just a long, thick covering falling down from their waists. Their dark faces had been splashed with what looked like white chalk accentuated in different places with various sparks of colour – offering them each an otherworldly look. They each wore elaborate, unique coverings on their heads, mainly consisting of vibrant feathers pierced through a band. One particularly impressive man had managed to create a headdress using what looked like the broken and cleaned skull of a deer patched with the long feathers of some colourful bird. They cut striking figures as they ambled around the room, all carrying in their hands a circlet of beads that they rubbed between their fingers, muttering to themselves and then every so often breaking into short bursts of song.

But it was something else that drew Aleister's gaze.

The stone floor had been painted with colourful rings interlocking one another. Stone statues stood at the edges of the circles – three times the size of Aleister but carved with such authenticity that a shiver ran down his spine and he shook himself as he stared up at the sorrowful face etched on one of the statues.

'Famous Chosen,' Solomus explained. 'They are picked to defend our kingdoms from threats that we must face. They are always peaceful men and women but trained to fight for freedom and to defend our lands and people. It is said they will cross the planes of existence to defend us at the End of Days. They will stand watch as witnesses for our people at the end of it all.'

Aleister stood transfixed as he looked up, expecting tears to roll down from those sad eyes staring back at him.

'This is Kwedini the Brave, the king said, joining Aleister in studying the awe-inspiring art. 'It is said that he made a last stand in the Akami River Pass against five hundred soldiers who had attacked the village he had grown up in. He died that day, but the people of his village were given time to prepare and his sacrifice meant that his people lived on. That village grew into a great city and eventually a kingdom full of colour and life. It is one that I am proud to call my home; proud to rule over.'

'Your people have a history that many in my homeland would love to hear,' Aleister said, following the old king as he turned away from the statue and towards a raised wooden platform at the back of the room. 'It is a shame that there is such a divide between the peoples of Takaara.'

'It truly is a pity,' Solomus agreed. 'But soon we will be forced together to face the dreaded threat that comes our way. Not even the Chosen will be able to keep the horrors at bay.'

The king whispered something inaudible as he stepped up onto the platform and stood before a large pewter basin. Solomus reached into his robes and when his hand returned, Aleister glimpsed the glint of metal of a small dagger.

'Do not worry, I will explain. Trust me.'

Aleister nodded.

Solomus reached up and gently pulled Aleister's increasingly wild, dark hair. With a flick of the wrist, he cut a few strands and placed the hair into the basin before turning the blade once more in Aleister's direction.

'Some blood, if you please?' Solomus requested, motioning for his hand.

Aleister held it out, intrigued by the strange behaviour. Another quick slash and blood dripped slowly from a thin, precise wound across his left palm. Solomus held the dagger over the basin and allowed the blood to drip onto the strands of hair, eyes closed as he muttered in his own language, just as the Chosen were doing around him.

His eyes opened and he clicked his fingers, igniting a flame that hovered over his hand, casting an unnatural orange glow over his tired but grinning face.

Aleister stepped back, shocked by the sudden use of magic. Magic that had not been accessible in Takaara since the big quake. 'How…?'

'There are many strands of magic,' Solomus shrugged. 'Some do not pull from the world around us, but from our very being. Sacrifices must be made for such power.' He dropped the flame into the basin and the stench of burning hair filled the air, mixed with some other smell that reminded Aleister of blades being forged by a smith.

For a moment, the two of them stood there, watching the dancing flames as they grew and filled the basin. Aleister frowned, realising that the flames were not giving any heat.

'A small amount of blood is not enough to truly bring this fire to life. To give it the energy it needs, we need more blood. More sacrifice,' Solomus explained. 'Many in this kingdom have given their lives to support King Zeekial and his plan to defend us.' He inclined his head towards the Chosen who were now stood in a half circle around the platform, muttering and shaking, their convulsions growing more intense with each moment.

'I do not know if you are a good man.' The king shrugged, his bottom lip sticking out and his face creasing at the words. 'But I know that you have made sacrifices.' Solomus stepped down from the platform and stood before the Chosen, running the edge of his dagger across each of their palms and asking them to wring their hands together until they were covered in the red blood glistening in the low light.

Aleister stood frozen to the spot as the men and women walked forward as one, bloody palms outstretched until they blocked all light from his view. But he could still hear the king's words.

'You have a grave task ahead, you will need the power of the Chosen to defend us from darkness. We will stand with you, if you are willing to make the sacrifices necessary, Aleister of the Red Sons.'

The murmuring men and women shook further but their palms paused a hair's breadth away from his skin.

'I am willing.' The words drifted from his lips though he could not recall deciding upon them.

The hands rubbed over his face, his neck, his body, covering him in the blood of the Chosen.

'Do not stray from your path, Aleister of the Red Sons. You are one of us now. And we are bonded to you.

When the time comes, you will have the power to stand before the Gods…'

'Please tell me that is paint…'

The look on both Bathos and Ariel's faces was worth the whole, strange event.

'I've been making friends. You should be proud!' he said, crashing into one of the free chairs in the room.

Ariel peered up at him over the book that she was reading, the look of incredulity as familiar to her brother as her breathing. Bathos placed the spear down that he had been cleaning, a gift from a group of locals who had grown fond of the burly but sweet warrior.

'Don't worry. It was some kind of initiation – nothing violent. Just,' Aleister paused as he struggled to find the right words, 'odd. Their temples are like nothing I have ever seen.'

Ariel arched one eyebrow and placed the book at her feet before standing and marching over to her brother. She placed the back of her hand on his forehead and shook her head. 'You been drinking?'

'Nope. Just had a nice walk by the river and then King Solomus took me to the temple.'

'His lies are usually more elaborate,' Bathos called over with a wide grin on his kind face. 'I believe him.'

'Hmm…' Ariel groaned, giving him a gentle slap across the face as Aleister winked and smiled at the support of his friend. 'I'll give you the benefit of the doubt. This time.' She glanced at the blood on the back of her hand and grimaced. 'Now wipe that stuff from your face. You are not heading to bed covered in blood. If nothing else you'll give yourself a fright when you wake in the morning.'

Considering the strange events of his evening, Aleister didn't find it odd that his eyes were heavy and his muscles ached. Happy that he had cleansed the blood from his skin, he fell into the bed in the room next to his allies' and drifted into a deep sleep, exhausted and drained from the long day and night.

His eyes opened but found himself lost in darkness.

His sore eyes attempted to pierce the darkness to no avail. At first, his body felt as though it were suspended in water, floating gently and bobbing up and down. He strained and, eventually, a green dot appeared on the horizon. He willed his body forwards, frowning in uncertainty as he struggled to remember how to move his body. Grimacing, tiny pinpricks of pain pierced his skin as he pushed forwards, fighting back against his movement as he edged slowly towards the light.

The light grew as he neared, shifting from a dot on the horizon to waves of emerald green that danced across the skyline.

Aleister peered down and found his boots stepping across dark rock, smoke rising up from the blackness as an uncomfortable heat grew around him. The light grew brighter, a green glow bouncing out and hitting against the meandering walls either side of him as he trudged down the path of a canyon. There was no sun in the sky. No light from a full moon. Just the shimmering glow of the green light overhead to guide him on his path.

Stopping, he suddenly became aware of an old man dressed in broken, silver mail standing before him. His whole profile shone with that strange green light that lit up the sky as he peered at Aleister with piercingly bright eyes through moon-white strands of hair that fell past mail emblazoned with the image of a hammer and dagger.

'You are not the one for whom I am waiting for,'

his clear, strong voice said to Aleister as he sighed. He stepped aside and the light fell on a whole crowd of men and women dressed in various states of battle armour. All were looking his way as he crept forward towards them. They each scanned him, searching for something and each eventually turned away, satisfied that this Aleister was not the one they wished to see.

Time passed. He could not tell how long.

Finally, he stood before a young man with dark, cropped hair, wearing armour emblazoned with an Eastern symbol with crossed, curved swords on a golden background.

'I have been waiting for you,' the young man said with a wry smile.

Aleister frowned. 'Do I know you?' He could not place the man's face, though he recognised the armour and the shining spear in the man's hand.

A shake of the head. 'You do not. Though I have dreamt of nothing but you in the cycles since my death. With each closing of my eyes, I see yours staring back at me as that cursed blade ripped through my chest and buried itself in my heart.' The soldier's voice trembled and he clenched a gloved fist before pointing at the weapon hanging from Aleister's belt.

'Such a thing should have been destroyed cycles ago. Yet, here we are, cursed to wait and suffer until the time comes when its wielder has use of us. Finally, you have the power to see us. Finally, you can free us from this cursed hell.'

Aleister felt his face twist in confusion. He glanced out across the rows and rows of grim-faced men and women. Now he could see more than just their armour lit by the light. Wounds of all shapes and sizes appeared. Wide, open cuts across throats. Thin stab wounds in the ribs. One soldier – with the look of a Darakechean warrior with his dark beard and bright jewellery – glared at him, holding a spear before peering across at where his other arm should have been. Instead, there was just a stump sticking out from the man's right shoulder. Aleister's heart quickened. He remembered that battle. Remembered fearing for his life in the clutch of bodies hitting into one another before he swung his enchanted blade and cut the arm free of the warrior closest to him, spear flying wide along with it.

'You are all dead. Killed by the blade meant to kill beings much more powerful than you…' he muttered, swallowing the lump growing in his throat. He glanced around at the faces, searching for one in particular, and praying that he would not find her.

The one-armed warrior stepped forward, glaring at Aleister with a look of pure hatred. 'My soul is due to be with my family and blessed by the Gods I have worshipped. Instead, I stand here. I wait here. I *rot* here,' he spat. 'Each second feels like a cycle in this cursed hell. *You* are the only one who can free us. Let us die with the dignity that has not been granted us before. Let us pass on.'

'I-I-I… I don't know how…' Aleister admitted, biting his lip and pleading for forgiveness as he tried to look into the eyes of as many of the poor souls he had condemned to this hell.

'Then you must discover how. Before anyone else does,' the first warrior warned. 'If another is to find a way to free us, then know that we will be coming for you, Aleister of the Red Sons. Revenge will be sweet for those of us who have tasted nothing but the bitter torture of life in this forgotten realm. Find a way.'

'I will…' Aleister promised, nodding. 'I will. Please, do you know if there is a raven-haired woman here? A mage by the name of Ella. I must know.'

The warrior scowled back, forehead creased with annoyance. 'Find a way, Aleister.'

Aleister felt his body ripped from the strange realm and pulled far away, the green light fading in moments and replaced once again by the suffocating darkness.

His body slammed onto a hard surface, forcing all the breath from his lungs. He rolled over, straining to get air back into his lungs as he crawled onto his knees, coughing and wheezing with the effort. As he looked up, he saw a beautiful, unnaturally pale woman staring back at him. Her features were thin and slender, cheekbones sharp enough to pierce skin for any who may dare to get close. It was her eyes that drew his attention though. Black like the night sky and filled with the speckles of light from the stars.

'Who are you?' he managed to wheeze at the strange woman peering down at him.

She reached down and helped him to his feet, smiling sadly as he winced and groaned with the effort.

'I am anything you wish me to be.' An odd voice. Aleister heard it as though spoken by a man and a woman, layered and musical, cutting through his soul and sending another shiver down his spine.

He backed away slowly as the woman morphed into something else. A midnight purple cloak billowed behind a slender frame though there was no wind in the darkness. The being looked skeletal, staring out through dark, shadowed eyes sitting beneath a crown that looked carved from a deer's skull, antlers sticking out tall and menacing on top of a head that was beginning to bleed from the hairline. The black blood dripped down a ghostly white face and fell past an unnaturally wide, black-lipped smile.

'I am like nothing you have ever seen before, Aleister of the Red Sons,' the strange being whispered, running a bony finger across his cheek in a gesture that he assumed was meant to be reassuring, though it unnerved him even more than ever. 'However, I can take an easier form if that is what you wish…'

Aleister watched in horror and disbelief as a deep blue light shimmered across the being's form and shifted into one that was much more familiar. He lost his balance, legs weakened in shock as he looked into a face more beautiful than any other in living memory. Green rings circled golden pupils. Raven-black hair fell to her shoulders as it had when they rolled about on Hangman's Hill. She smiled and blushed, cheeks turning that soft shade of red that he so loved.

'Ella…' he muttered, tears streaming down his face.

A moment later, Ella was gone, replaced once more by the menacing figure of the being in the deer-skull crown. Cold, dark eyes stared down at him as he whimpered on his knees.

'Most call me Osiron. You know who I am,' the odd voice drifted down to Aleister as though through water 'You are helping those who wish to destroy me. Men and women who do not know what they are doing. Men and women who made grave mistakes cycles ago and will make the same mistakes once again. They left me to rot in a realm of Chaos with none for company and they did not even look for me. I was their friend. Their peer. They knew the hells I had been through and yet they did nothing to stop my continued suffering. They are filth, animals. Less than animals!' Osiron raged.

'I do not expect you to take my side over theirs. I am no fool,' they claimed. 'I have come to you on the edge of war. Stand in my way, and you will lose everything. Even if you succeed on the path you have chosen, you will lose everything dear to you. I can prevent that. I can give you what you wish for. *Only I* can give you what you wish for…'

'And what is that?'

Aleister watched as a mist swirled around him, transforming into familiar figures and shining with a blue light.

He saw Bathos sitting on a wooden chair on the edge of farmland, gazing out across open fields with an ale in hand as the sun fell below the horizon. Ariel strolled over to him, a small bundle in her arms and a beaming smile on her face that Aleister had never seen before. She looked so happy. So content. She leant down and Bathos reached up and took the bundle, muttering nonsensical words towards the baby and laughing as the tiny thing yawned, mouth stretching wide in an action Aleister found so cute his heart ached with love.

He saw himself walking over, grin as wide as the horizon.

And holding his hand was a woman he never thought he would see again. A woman he would have died for.

'You show me a mere illusion,' Aleister croaked, fury rising in his chest at the cheap trick. 'She is dead. I saw it with my own eyes.'

Osiron nodded. 'True. Though my powers give me dominion over the dead. If you wish for this *illusion* to become a reality, you must ignore those who tell you to fight against me. Use that blade for the others, but stay away from me. I will have the greatest power known to any in Takaara. I will be the most powerful being in the history of this world. And I will return her to you.'

'And if I don't?'

Osiron's smile slipped from their lips, leaving a look that could burn through the world and turn all to ash. 'Then all you love will perish in the war to come. You will be last. You can watch as their bodies rot and fade. You will taste the ashes of defeat in your mouth and there will be nothing to rid yourself of the horrors that you will witness.'

'This is just a dream,' Aleister said, more to himself than the tall being towering over him. 'Just a dream. I will wake up and forget it all.'

'Blood magic is powerful. Leaves a trace and opens paths that were not accessible previously. I have made it my mission to find such paths during my time in the darkness. The others will use blood magic, they know that they are too weak without it. When they do, I will come. And you will have to make your choice.'

Aleister felt the jolt as his body was ripped once more away from the strange realm.

He bolted upright in his bed, drenched in sweat. His breaths came in quick, short bursts as he struggled to calm his racing heart. He pushed his hair from his face and ran a hand across his forehead, groaning at the pool of sweat that came with it.

Breathing finally under control, he lay back down and stared at the ceiling, unable to get those eyes out of his mind.

POWERFUL ALLIES

'You know I don't like this one bit.'

'Sly, that is the tenth time this morning that you've said it,' Kiras moaned.

'Well I fucking mean it!'

'I knew you meant it the first time.'

Sly growled and knocked on the door. He glanced over his shoulder and spat on the street as he caught the eye of one of the smirking Barbarians casually strolling through the village – a reminder of the shit going on in the Borderlands and Sly's current inability to do anything about it.

He turned back to the small house and scanned the building. The thatched roof looked as though it needed a bit of work and the white paint on the walls had cracked and was in need of another coat or two.

The door opened and a short, tired-looking woman answered, deep bags sat under her brown eyes and her mousy hair was pulled up into a messy bun. She wore a grey, woollen dress and her feet were bare. By her knees, a young girl clutched nervously at her mother's legs, half hiding behind her as she poked her head out to get a better look at the two visitors.

'You must be friends of my husband,' the woman said, a sad smile finally appearing on her weary face. She moved from the doorway and playfully ruffled the hair on her daughter's head. 'Please, come in.'

Kiras entered the house first. Sly checked behind and watched the bustle of the streets before turning and following her in, nodding at the woman and giving his best smile to the kid as he passed. The girl jumped back, clutching tighter at her mother's dress.

'He's in the room at the end of the corridor,' Cray's wife said, pointing straight towards the back of the house. 'With our son.'

The room was stuffy and dark. No windows to allow light into the room and just a single candle burning to offer an orange glow to the simple room. A single bed, low to the floor filled most of the room so Sly and Kiras edged their way by the walls and looked down at the boy coughing and spluttering, his head resting against the pillow, hair stuck to his skin with sweat and a hand clutched tightly by his kneeling father.

'How is he?' Kiras asked.

Cray didn't even look up. His eyes stayed fixed on his son as he brought another hand to rest on his. 'Vald Sickness. That's what they say it is. A sickness brought on by magic use, usually.'

'But he ain't no mage, is he?' Sly said, looking at the sick boy lying in the darkness. Cray hadn't mentioned anything about having a mage for the son. Not that it meant much. He hadn't said much at all.

Cray shook his head. 'No. There is another reason but the doctors can't work it out. The sickness is the same as Vald Sickness; fever, sweating. Vision blurring and a sensitivity to light. Anya's father had it. She watched him die from the bastard thing. Now she watches the same thing happen to her son.' He rose from his position by the bed and bent over his son, kissing him softly on the forehead before turning to his guests and motioning for them to leave the room. He joined them and closed the door carefully shut behind him. He led them into the next room and nodded for them to take a seat as he walked over to the table at the side and grabbed a large jug. He poured three drinks into separate, wooden cups and handed them to Kiras and then Sly, keeping one for himself before taking his own seat.

'So,' he said, eyes focused on his cup as he swilled the ale around, not looking up at his guests as he spoke. 'What have you found out? Judging by the cuts and bruises, I'm thinking you haven't just been taking in the sights…'

'Found Herick but he was waiting for us,' Sly explained. He held the cup in his hand but did not drink. Instead, he watched Cray. The warrior looked drained, exhausted, like his wife. 'Your son gonna be okay?'

Cray finally looked up and sniffed. 'No idea. Folk all over the place have the sickness, just like those back at the camp. He hasn't moved much in the past three days according to Anya, my wife. She's had to deal with it and look after the little one whilst I've been…'

'Fighting against cunts,' Sly finished for him.

'Aye.' Cray sighed and sniffed, the crease on his forehead seeming to be a permanent addition to his hard features. 'Tell me about Herick.'

Sly sat back and took a swig of the ale, pleased to find it didn't taste like piss. He peered at Kiras and shrugged his shoulders at her patient look. 'Probably best if you tell him. I'll just get all pissed off.'

Kiras rolled her eyes as the shadow of a smile danced at the corner of her lips. 'He wanted us dead.'

'Past tense?'

'Kind of. He knows that Baldor is dead and he wants revenge. He knows that we want this bastard Empire dead too, for what they did to Baldor and Raven. Herick is offering a truce. We speak to Arden and convince him to join, alongside Herick and the Barbarians.'

Cray pursed his lips and scratched at the scraggly beard on his chin. 'Against the Empire? Think such a truce can hold for that long?'

'That's the thing,' Kiras smirked. 'He said that they are sending an army from Archania. That's why they are camped here and not in Torvield. Catch them unawares with a strong force before they are ready. And if Arden does join them…'

'Archania will stand no chance. Hells, the United Cities as a whole will stand no chance.' Cray blew his cheeks out and took another drink. 'It could work. But how will you be able to convince Arden?'

Kiras shared an uncomfortable look with Sly who just folded his arms and started tapping his foot rapidly under the table. 'Herick will give Arden the heads of the Barbarian chief and his son.'

'Why would Arden give two shits about them?'

Sly placed his elbows on the table and licked at his cracked lips. 'The son and Arden had a little meeting in the Far North. Apparently, Socket wasn't the only one to thrust a blade into the kid.'

Cray's short laugh sounded like the bark of dog.

140

His broad frame shook and a disbelieving grin broke out on his face as he looked from Kiras to Sly in turn. 'We really do live in a fucked up place. You ever think about what you must have done to deserve this shit?'

'I'm starting to think Takaara has always been this fucked up. We're just the idiots living through this era of fucked up,' Kiras said, running a hand through her short hair. Sly still wasn't used to it. 'Not our decision to live during this shitshow. But it is our decision on how best to deal with it. When we fight those heading north from Archania, are you in?'

'They're coming to my home. They're coming to wipe us from the map.' Cray tipped the rest of his drink down his throat and wiped a sleeve across his chin. 'I'll kill the Gods themselves before I see one of the bastards set foot in this town. There's only one thing on my mind. And Sly knows what it is.' He pointed at Sly with a stubby finger and grinned.

He hated to admit it, but Sly found himself grinning back, glad to be on the same page as the hardened warrior.

'Kill the fuckers.'

Arden sensed them waiting for him before he saw them creeping through the trees. He felt the fires of rage blazing within as he saw Sly and Kiras walk into the circle of stones. The monument was older than any cared to remember. The Sky Stones was the name they had been given by the farmers on the outskirts of Hillheim. The tall, black stones stood in a perfect circle, each carved to precise points and stabbing up at the night sky. Arden waited in the centre of the nine stones, standing and staring at his old friends, old friends who had left without telling him.

'I received your message,' he said, concentrating on steadying his breaths and pushing down the urge to tear into Sly for his betrayal. 'I supported you, I helped you when you needed my warriors to avenge Baldor's death. So why did you leave my camp when I commanded that you stay?'

He caught the flicker of annoyance flash across Sly's face even in the low light of the moon.

'Commanded?' Sly repeated, brushing off Kiras's calming hand and glaring at Arden. 'I am not one to be *commanded*,' he spat. 'I fought for Raven 'cause he made some kind of sense in the madness of the Borderlands. I'll fight side by side with people I trust.' His eyes turned to Cray and Kiras standing behind him before turning back to Arden, unable to hide his disgust. 'But I will not be *commanded* to do anything. Even if you do have some fancy new powers. Kill me if you'd like, but know that I will follow my own path, kid. That's always been the way.'

Arden nodded, impressed with the fire in his old friend's belly, even if he wasn't overly fond of the words escaping his cut lips.

'Listen, kid.' Sly's face softened, the fury fading to just a simmer. 'I have no idea what you've been through. But you have to know that we stand together because we have bonds forged in the fires of battle and we know that we can trust one another to protect our backs.' He narrowed his eyes and jabbed a dirty finger into Arden's chest. 'Can we still trust you?'

Sly's question cut through Arden's hardened exterior, a reminder that these warriors were the ones who had stood by him when he had nothing. A group of experienced fighters taking in a naïve, young fool who could loose an arrow or two.

'You can trust me, Stormson. There is a plan to
142

improve Takaara, to wipe away the filth and horror.'

'And replace it with what?' Kiras asked, marching to stand beside the grizzled axeman. 'A different kind of filth and horror?'

Arden frowned. The confidence that Osiron had gifted him faded for a moment, leaving a gaping hole of confusion and uncertainty.

'Herick's given us a choice,' she continued. 'And for once, he is speaking sense. The United Cites of Archania are nothing but a proxy for the Empire of Light now. They are sending an army this way to attack the Borderlands. If we stand united, we strike against the bastards who killed Raven and Baldor.'

'Herick has betrayed you before. He had you beaten. Both of you.' Arden peered over at Cray who was leaning against one of the dark stones, happiest amongst the shadows. 'He threatened your family. So why are you all willing to fight alongside him? What can he offer you? What can he offer me?'

'What can he offer us?' Osiron's voice blasted uninvited into Arden's head. He groaned and rubbed his temples, ignoring the concerned looks shot his way. *'Just kill them all. We warned them that we were coming. Prove to them that you are the Prince of Chaos, just as you promised…'*

Arden shook his head, freeing himself of the voice and feeling exhausted by the effort. Now wasn't the time for that. He had to think.

'Ragnar, chief of the Barbarians,' Kiras answered. 'And his son, Rejgar.'

Arden tasted the bile in his mouth and spat the offending saliva onto the ground. He rubbed at his throat, fighting against the images flashing through his mind. An emaciated Barbarian locked deep in the confines of that hellish castle. Arden had freed him and been attacked for the effort.

'Rejgar. He is alive because of me.'

'And Herick offers his head on a plate, along with his father. If that is what you wish?' Kiras said.

Arden didn't need to think about it. 'He has one hour. I will be waiting.'

One hour. Arden waited alone, sitting in the centre of the stones with his legs crossed and eyes closed. He listened to Osiron's advice, debating back and forth over what should be done. Though he was thankful for the advice, Arden had made his decision and Osiron had welcomed the archer's determination and resolve to go through with the plan.

'Whichever path is chosen tonight,' the God of Chaos had said, *'Takaara will be cleansed. It is all just a matter of time. I have seen it. North. South. East. West. All will be Chaos.'*

Arden opened his eyes as the hour passed, a harsh wind howling from the south, whipping around the hill as he stood.

Three men stood in front of him. The moon shone on the bald pate of the short but stocky warrior waiting in the middle, eyes scanning Arden up and down. It had been a while since Arden had seen Herick the Late, though the time since had been kind to the chief. He wore a thick cloak covered in bright fur around his shoulders. A ring shaped like a skull sparkled in the night's light on his hand as he wrapped his fingers around the hilt of his sheathed sword. The warrior was wary, and certainly no fool.

'Arden Leifhand,' Herick said, hand still on the blade. 'My friend here claims to have left you for dead. I'm sure you have a tale or two to tell.'

Herick tilted his head towards the Barbarian standing to his left. Though shorter than many of the huge warriors, Rejgar had filled out since Arden had last lain eyes upon him. He was no longer gaunt and with the look of one who straddled the paths of the living and dead. Instead, his dark hair had the shine of one who could look after themselves. His black beard had been trimmed close to his jawline and those dark eyes were wide open as they glared at Arden, as though testing them to see if he was truly seeing the person standing before him.

'Interesting tales are not what we have time for,' the Barbarian to Herick's right muttered. He was a tall bastard. He wore no cloak, just a thin shirt that must not have been able to keep the chill of the wind from his bones, though he did not look perturbed by it. If anything, he was the one who looked most at ease in the circle of the Sky Stones. He had the same dark, piercing eyes as his son, though his black beard was long enough to fall past his chest, twisted into two elaborate braids. His long hair fell wild and low and his pale face was littered with scars that spoke of the dark experience of battle.

'Then why have you come here, Ragnar?' Arden asked, focusing on the infamous chief of the Barbarians. Raven had often spoke of the great warrior. His tone had been one of respect, even if he was leading the warriors known to be mortal enemies of the Borderlands.

'Herick promised powerful allies. I have led my people away from the exploding mountain of fire. Now, I will lead them into the glory of battle.'

Rejgar scoffed at his father's words and he stepped between Arden and the warriors. 'You cannot be serious? *Powerful allies*? This boy is a nobody. I saw him in Korvus's domain. Almost killed himself unlocking a door.'

'Do you know what the Sky Stones have been used

as in the past?' Arden asked the petulant Barbarian.

'I suppose you will tell me.'

'A fighting circle. One on one battles between enemies to settle scores. If you believe me to be so weak, then I challenge you to combat in the Sky Stones.'

The bluster of the young son visibility drained as Rejgar struggled for his words, his attention turning to the still form of Arden and then to his father and Herick who waited patiently for a response.

'Our people have always honoured such combat,' Ragnar said, pulling thoughtfully on the braids of his beard as he mulled over Arden's request. 'I will accept on my son's behalf.'

Rejgar's face was a sight to behold. Arden smirked as he watched the blood fade from the Barbarian's face, unable to comprehend his father's words.

'Such a fight will be a waste of time!' he cried, waving his arms wildly at his father.

'Then I suggest you end it quickly.'

Ragnar and Herick stepped out of the circle, standing between the stones and watching, their faces impassive as Rejgar continued to spit and rage.

The Barbarian pulled a curved dagger from his belt and rushed Arden, finally eager to heed his father's advice.

Arden waited with a calm smile.

Rejgar slashed wildly at first, giving Arden an easy chance to step aside to dodge the attack. Annoyed with his failure, the Barbarian pushed forwards, stabbing for the stomach. But he was not fast enough. Arden darted back, peering down to see the point of the weapon less than an inch from his belly.

Arden darted to the side, his hands still empty as

Rejgar's face turned as red as a blood moon. He marvelled at how slow his opponent seemed to be moving. Each attack was obvious to Arden, giving him ample time to move from the path of defeat laid before him and out of the way of the shining dagger.

Furious with embarrassment, Rejgar dropped the dagger onto the grass beneath him and drew a long, steel sword.

'Time to stop playing,' the Barbarian said through ragged breaths, his eyes gleaming with an intense rage as he leapt towards Arden.

Arden remembered Raven speaking about how he had managed to stay alive after fighting in so many duels. Redbeard had claimed luck was the most important tool to wield. Following that, it was knowing when to strike. And striking without mercy.

Rejgar's next thrust came fatally fast, but Arden rolled to the side, his hand catching on something on the ground. He rolled back and jumped to his feet as he watched the Barbarian snarling and roaring through gritted teeth, the deadly sword glistening in the moonlight as he once again made his charge.

Rejgar forced Arden back with his strikes, hoping to catch him off balance and land the winning strike but the archer was too fast and nimble.

He ducked under a particularly high strike from the Barbarian and found himself smiling, enjoying the little game with the bastard who had left him for dead in that accursed place in the Far North.

Arden remembered the pride he had felt at freeing the tortured captive. He had pleaded with Arden to free him, cried as he recalled Korvus's emotionless torture and yet he had left Arden bleeding on the ground as he had escaped the place.

Sweat dripped down the warrior's face with the exertion. He must have known by now that he had no chance of besting Arden. Speed. Agility. Stamina. Arden had it all.

The weary, defeated expression on Rejgar's face told a story that no words could do justice.

Arden spun the dagger in his hand that Rejgar had dropped and the Barbarian's face dropped as he spotted the weapon.

Arden bolted forwards and skipped past a thrust meant for his heart. He jabbed the dagger straight up underneath the warrior's chin and released a fountain of blood that sprayed all over him. The next thrust landed straight in the heart, finishing the Barbarian off before his limp body fell to the floor along with the thud of his sword.

Arden peered over to the two waiting warriors watching.

Herick clapped his hands together slowly in admission of the respect he now held for him. But it was Ragnar's response that Arden was waiting for.

'What do you think of that, Ragnar? I just killed your son.'

Ragnar shrugged. 'I have many sons. Do you mean to kill me now? I will not fall so easily.'

Arden thought about it for the moment. 'No. As you said, there is a benefit in powerful allies. The Empire of Light must fall if Takaara is to be cleansed. You will lead your Barbarians into battle and sing a song for Chaos.'

'It will be a song for the ages.'

Arden licked his lips and the iron taste of blood filled his mouth, Rejgar's blood. 'Your son tastes weak. I hope your warriors can do better in the war to come. Or they shall fall as he did.'

'They will stand and fight until it is their time to fall. I will pray to the Old Gods who will choose the time of their passing.'

Arden shook his head. 'The Old Gods abandoned us. The God of Chaos is the only one listening to your prayers now. And I'm warning you, Osiron is in a foul mood…'

THE ETERNAL EMPRESS

The library stood on the banks of a river wide enough for Kane to mistake it for the sea. The colossal building was a collection of three separate housing areas. The two side buildings, white like the main building and shining in the brightness of the midday sun, were devoted to times of war and peace. The eastern building, according to Istari, was dedicated to peace. The texts, paintings, sculptures and everything else filling the huge building related to work that would benefit the Empire when battle and war had ended. The texts would teach those skilled enough to read them of how to improve a nation and further progress when resources could be channelled away from the soldiers and the army that defended the borders.

The western building was the opposite. Texts devoted to warfare and ancient tactics and strategies to succeed in battles on varying landscapes and with various armies filled the cavernous halls inside, informing those keen enough to pay attention of how to build a nation into a powerful beast capable of defeating any enemy.

But it was the building in the centre of the three that Istari led Kane towards, flanked by four soldiers. For their own safety apparently.

Impossibly tall with a curved roof that slanted from the eastern tip westwards, it was unlike anything Kane had seen before. Six massive round, white columns rose from the base and up to the roof and behind, the front side of the building had been mostly filled with glass running all the way up the library so that Kane could see the many people wandering around the spacious rooms inside. Some were pacing the labyrinths between the copious number of rows of books. Others were seated in groups and sharing warm smiles with one another. On the second floor, she could see a huge painting, bigger than any she had ever lain eyes on. The image was one of a desert landscape with four soldiers riding on camels across the waves of sand as a white sun beamed down from above.

'I have never seen the like...' she muttered, mostly to herself, though Istari caught her words and grunted.

'The main building is all about the history of Takaara. It was built to teach those who wished to learn about where we came from and where we are going. However, it is the gardens that I loved the most...'

Kane understood why. The grounds around the library were filled with luscious green grass and the splashing of water from numerous fountains that littered the beautiful gardens. Flowers and trees of all kinds had been cultivated and grown in patterns that followed the semi-circular entrance to the library. Families sat in the shade of trees shielding them from the oppressive heat of the sun and shared a story – mothers smiled wide at the happy faces on their children as fathers pulled their loved ones close and laughed together.

'Why would the Empress wish to meet here, in the library?' Kane asked as they reached the steps leading up to the entrance. Istari nodded back at the soldiers either side of the open archway inclining their heads his way.

'You are the one who spoke to her yesterday,' he said with a shrug of his shoulders. 'Though, if you were to hold a dagger to my throat, I would assume she wishes to show off. It is not often that outsiders are allowed to view her city.'

'*Her* city?'

'Yes. This whole place was just sand before she arrived. Nomadic travellers would pass across the dunes towards the river for fresh water but that was it. Elena changed everything.'

Kane frowned, doing the mental numbers necessary to attempt to understand Istari's words. 'How old is she?'

Istari Vostor's only response was a mischievous smile. 'That is an interesting question. And not one with an easy answer...'

The meeting room was at the back of the library on the floor in the centre of the building. To reach it, Kane passed more books than there were fish in the sea. Men and women smiled at her and bowed, pressing a hand to the heart as she waved and inclined her head. There were no suspicious looks from the citizens of the Empire. None seemed worried that a woman seen as their enemy was wondering freely in one of their greatest monuments to the progress of the Empire.

'They don't seem to be nervous at an outsider being here.'

Istari shrugged. 'Of course not. They have seen a
152

few outsiders. None have been given the chance to cause harm. The people trust their leaders. The Empress rules. Her four closest advisors are Imlari, or Elders in the common tongue. They each have four sworn to them who oversee protection in the city and warfare. These sworn are named Kh'alar. They are often found around their Imlari, ensuring no harm comes to the preachers.'

Kane thought of Mason and his dog, T'Chai. The Imlari and the Kh'alar. The Elder and his bodyguard. She recalled standing in the temple as T'Chai and his men cut down Elder Morgan and threw her into a dingy cell.

'There's so little we know about this place.' She gazed around at the floor to ceiling bookshelves. Given an entire lifetime, she doubted whether she would have managed to read everything in this astounding room. The dark wood shelves and furniture in the room reminded her of the smoking rooms in the Upper City. The colourful mosaic floor meshed well with the unique, abstract paintings that filled any space not occupied by the books.

'Are you sure I cannot sit?' she asked Istari, stretching the muscles in her back and staring at one of the three seats placed around the dark oak table standing in the centre of the room.

'She must be the first to sit. It would be disrespectful if we are not standing patiently as she arrives.'

As if on cue, the heavy doors at the back of the room opened, pushed by two guards dressed in golden robes and silver headdresses that shimmered with a blinding beauty. Between them, the Empress strode through, herself dressed in a low purple dress, diamonds sparkling from both her ears and her neck. Her silver hair had been intricately braided so that a circlet of her locks wrapped around her head on top of a thin white crown resting against her forehead.

153

Her beauty almost took Kane's breath away.

Elena marched forward, the doors closing behind her so that only the three of them were present. Ignoring Kane, she pressed past and stood before Istari, scanning him up and down with pursed lips, her breathing coming in even cycles though her flared nostrils.

The slap echoed around the room. Kane flinched, her jaw dropping and eyes wide as Istari accepted the blow with a simple turn of the head before returning his focus to the Empress.

'I deserved that,' he muttered, clearing his throat.

'I have not even started to deliver what you deserve...' the Empress warned. She walked back around the table and sat in one of the empty chairs opposite the two guests. 'Both of you. Sit.'

Kane did as she was instructed. Istari followed a moment later, his wary eyes never leaving his wife.

The Empress sat, her fingers drumming against the wood, glowering at the man many claimed to be the greatest swordsman in Takaara.

'You have some nerve returning here.' Her venomous tone told Kane that this conversation was not meant for her. She was only supposed to wait her turn. Still, the suffocating tension between the old lovers made Kane want to jump out from her seat and escape the room, to leave them to it.

'Nerve has never been an issue for me,' Istari replied calmly.

'What about loyalty?'

'You dare to question my loyalty?'

'You dared to leave when we were *so close* to achieving what we set out to achieve.'

Istari shook his head and scratched his scalp, running a hand slowly down the back of his neck before answering. 'We may have had the same goal. But our journeys to reach it were not one and the same. I could not just stand by and watch, Elena.'

'Stand by and watch?' Elena repeated his words, breathing increasing in speed as she glared at Istari. 'Do you know for how many cycles I have had to watch? Do you know how many cycles I watched my people suffer the torture and abuse of others? There was nothing I could do. Then, finally, I found a way. Not an easy way. And it would take sacrifice, as most things do. I was happy.' Her eyes lost the fire and the tension faded as she relaxed back into her chair, her dark eyes turning to Kane, reminding her that it was not just the two of them.

'I was happy for the first time in many miserable cycles. And then you left,' she chuckled darkly at the memory. 'After all we had done together.'

'I could not stand by and see such suffering.'

'A means to an end. More suffering will follow if I fail.'

'The burnings…' Istari said. Kane was surprised to hear a flicker of emotion in his voice.

The room fell silent following his words. Kane looked away from the two of them, doing her absolute best to combat the images forcing their way into her mind.

The young boy Tate. Burned for wishing to speak to his father one last time.

Lord Tamir. A good friend who had died for trying to save his city from the horrors taking over.

'We were all abandoned. Only one remains,' Elena said, her voice low and lacking the certainty and strength it previously held. 'Like it or not, the flames are the only way.

We need an army.'

Kane frowned, unable to follow the conversation's sudden change.

'There is always another way,' Istari implored.

Elena sadly shook her head. 'Not this time. I have seen so much, Iz. I have attempted to stay the darkness for so long. There is no more time. Chaos is coming. And we must be ready for its hellish embrace.'

Kane took a deep breath, readying herself for the role she had been sent all the way from Causrea to accomplish. 'Your Majesty, I'm sorry to interrupt.'

Elena turned her shrewd eyes to Kane but nodded for her to continue.

'I was sent from Causrea with one goal. To prevent the war between East and West so that we can focus on a greater one to come. I understand the value of that goal, but sitting here, I realise that there is an opportunity to learn something. I lived in the United Cities of Archania all my life. I befriended the late king, Mikkael, Gods watch over him.' Kane paused and swallowed, holding herself together and choosing each word carefully.

'I cared for the people in that kingdom. Still do. I watched innocent people, mages and non-mages alike, burn alive in front of a baying crowd because your brother decided it was best for the kingdom, a kingdom that he had no right to interfere with.' She shifted in her seat, growing in confidence. 'Now, I am assuming he was there to do your bidding. So I must ask, why would you choose to commit such a horrific act against the people of that wonderful city?'

The Empress sighed and glanced at Istari. Silently he nodded to her and she turned back to Kane.

'Katerina Kane,' she began, 'the decades that you

have been alive are mere drops in the ocean compared to what I have witnessed.'

Kane screwed up her face and looked at Istari but the swordsman was of no use. Instead, he just stared impassively at the Empress, as though his thoughts lay elsewhere.

'Along with three friends, I become one of the most powerful mages in the history of this world. Powerful enough to threaten the Gods themselves. If only The Four had been watching. We used our magic to create cities that would stand the onslaught of time but we were not ready for such power.' Her face hardened, turning to stone as she gritted her teeth.

'We played with magic that was not meant to be touched. We pushed limits that were not meant to even bend. Immortality, or the shadow of such a gift, was within our grasp. Who could stop us?' She laughed but there was no joy in her eyes as she spread her arms wide. 'We could only stop ourselves. We attempted things that no one else would even comprehend, but two of our number began their own experiments. That was the first time I saw true darkness.'

'The Breaking of Takaara…' Kane muttered, remembering its true name.

'The very same. Though, most do not know the true details. The four of us were blasted across the Sky Plane. Three of us escaped relatively unscathed. All I remember is crawling across a dirt road on my hands and knees, unable to open my eyes due to a blinding light assaulting my senses. The next time I could open them, it was cycles later, and I was not who I was meant to be. Two of my allies crawled through their own strange realms until I had enough power to search for them and pull them out. Our remaining friend was not so lucky.

'I searched everywhere for Osiron. The poor mage was lost in Chaos. By the time I found them, it was too late. I was convinced by others that if I had freed Osiron, it would have meant unleashing thousands of fiends across Takaara and the world was not ready so soon after the breaking. We needed to prepare.'

'So you left your friend, to suffer in the Chaos Plane?' Kane asked, hoping she had managed to keep up with the odd story.

'Osiron had been through so much already. The power the rest of us wielded came naturally – our hard work enhanced what was already there. Osiron did not have such a gift. They had to work every second at it. They grew up in a village that looked upon those who were different with fear and anger. And Osiron always felt different. They were not like the girls, or the boys. They were something else, something special. The village did not like that. Osiron slaughtered every last one of the bastards who had abused them. I arrived to see Osiron sitting in the middle of the village, flames burning high and bright. Most of the villagers were turned to ash and the smell of burning flesh clung to the air. The children had been left. They were made to watch, but were alive when I arrived. Such raw, explosive power...'

'Osiron suffered,' Istari said, eyes glazed over. 'Yet the only people they ever trusted turned their back on them. Zeekial and Harish tried to kill them. You left Osiron to the Chaos. No wonder they are hells-bent on Takaara's destruction.'

'Not destruction. Osiron wishes to cleanse Takaara as they did with that village. Kill those who deserve it, leave the few who know suffering as they did. Takaara will continue. Osiron is leaving a few seeds after cutting down the forest.'

Kane took a deep breath, her head rolling from side to side as she struggled to comprehend the story being told.

'What does this have with you allowing your brother to burn innocent people?' Kane asked bitterly.

'Magic requires a source. Since the Breaking, we understood that most mages were pulling the energy from the world itself. It always requires sacrifice. We found other ways. Harish and Zeek pulled theirs from blood and darkness. I chose to pull mine from the light of the flames. Those who died in the fire will be reborn when the time comes. They will fight for us before passing on.'

'Can you be certain of that?'

'No, she cannot,' Istari said, voice wound with steel as he glared at the Empress. She matched his intense glare and did not turn away. 'It is a theory and nothing more.'

'Zeek and Harish's blades trap souls. It is a similar magic,' she argued. 'I know what I am doing.'

'You are guessing.'

'An educated guess.'

'Is that good enough for you?'

'For me?' Elena hissed through her teeth. 'Yes.'

'If you are so certain then tell your followers, allow them to make the choice,' Istari pleaded.

'Like Zeek with his volatile blood magic? How many do you think will line up to burn in the flames?'

'It will be their choice.'

Elena turned away, eyes staring down at the floor. 'I am sorry. It must be this way. There is not time to prepare for anything else. Osiron's army grows. Zeek's methods will shatter the skies; Osiron's gifts will break the ground. Only the flames will ensure that Takaara does not fall.'

'And if you fall?' Istari asked, face growing darker as he grew more animated. 'What happens when you fall this time?'

'You know what will happen. The blade will be nearby. Zeek and Harish will ensure that, if nothing else.'

'And who will wield such a blade?' Istari stood and ran his hands down his face in frustration. He spun and marched over to the Empress, falling to his knees.

Kane looked away, feeling as though she was intruding on something she should not see.

'Who will wield the blade?' he asked again, taking Elena's left hand in his as she brought her left up to his face to wipe away the single tear rolling down his weary face.

'There is only one who I would allow to do such a thing, when my time comes. Only one.' She planted a kiss on his forehead, eyes closed.

'Will it work?'

'I have seen so much death. I am numb to it all, even to my own. This time though, it will be final. There is no returning from this. You promised me, all those cycles ago. And you never break a promise, Istari Vostor.'

'I do not wish to part from you,' Katerina Kane said to the grumpy face looking away from her. 'I must admit, I have grown fond of you.'

'Tell anyone that, and I will kill you,' Istari muttered, only the hint of humour lacing the threat. He took a deep breath and spoke quickly. 'You are not so bad yourself.'

Kane rushed forwards and wrapped her arms

around the warrior, enjoying the way Istari froze, unable to decide what to do. Then she felt his strong arms return the hug and she squeezed tighter, praying this was not the last time they would see one another. She almost laughed as she realised she had been doing that too often of late.

Drayke.

Aleister.

Now Istari.

'You sure you have to go south?' she asked for the hundredth time that morning as she finally released him.

He nodded. 'I need the blade. And Elena must speak with Harish and Zeekial before Osiron attacks. You will be safe heading to the United Cities. Your chosen guards are well-trained and honourable. Find your son, warn him about what is happening.'

Kane bit her bottom lip, wondering if she should speak her fears out loud. 'What if he is dead?'

'He is your son. He will be hard to kill. Check on Sara if you can. Tell her what I am doing. It is only right that she knows.' He swallowed and cleared his throat. 'You still owe me that duel by the way,' Istari added, lightening the mood, his eyes sparkling in the morning sunrise.

'You better not die then,' Kane said, punching him playfully on his chest. 'Can you promise me that?'

Istari smiled sadly. 'Goodbye Katerina Kane.'

'Goodbye Istari Vostor.'

THE STORM

C ypher leaned against the window, looking out across the bustling, nervous city as the first flash of lightning tore through the world and lit the dark clouds up momentarily. The thunder ripped across the city, shaking the glasses lined on the shelves of the palace's smoking room. He tapped against the window, smiling at the chaos of Takaara playing out before him.

He hummed a tune that he recalled hearing from some wastrel of a bard in a dingy Lower City tavern some cycles before. An absolute cretin, but he could hold a tune and the wordplay was passable. The tune played in Cypher's mind and he hummed along, at ease with the display beneath him.

Fools searching for an escape choked the Upper City. Most would flee to their estates in the lands around Archania to the west. They knew the North would be off limits due to Mason's scaremongering of late. The Borderlanders were, more than ever, the true enemy of the United Cities. To the East, a new army threatened the comfortable way of life of the city's elite citizens. The Red Sons were known throughout Archania, of course. Mercenaries who fought for no land and could be paid off by the highest bidder. Even now, some of the more foolish in the city were calling for carriages to clandestine meetings where they would propose a truce with the mercenary band. Coin. That's what they would want. Enough of it and the siege would be over before it even begins. Even Lord Balen and Lady Penton had advised throwing money at the problem at their gates.

Idiots.

They knew nothing.

Some were pleased with the army camped outside the Eastern Gate of the city. Their patriotism blinded them to the fact that this battle would not be an easy one to win. T'Chai had taken a considerable force to the Borderlands, leaving inexperienced fighters behind and a smattering of soldiers from the Empire who may or may not be useful in the days to come. They were eager for the opportunity to defend their kingdom and show these upstarts who was in charge in this region.

And then there were the defeatists in Archania. Those who were at this very moment locking themselves in their gated housing and praying to the Gods for protection from the battle to come.

Cypher struggled to work out which of the fools were the most idiotic.

The rain fell like arrows from the sky, covering the grand buildings of the Upper City and the cramped labyrinth that was the Lower City – there was no prejudice with the weather. There would be no prejudice in the battle. The same blood would pour out onto the cobbled streets of Archania – the rich and the poor, men and women, the young and the old.

But Cypher would not be one of them.

A knock at the door snapped him from his thoughts as lightning lit up the dark room.

'Come in.'

Amana peeked in and gave him the nod. 'He's here.'

'And the others?'

'In position.'

'Good. You best head off. I will speak to him alone.'

He watched as Amana followed his instructions and felt a warm sense of pride. The four warriors under his wing had worked spectacularly well so far, each playing their part admirably. It would be a shame to cut ties with them should the need arise. But just as he did with Zaif, Cypher knew that he could handle such dark tasks.

Often, he had enjoyed working alone. But this game was so much bigger than anything he had played before. More players were needed and he had to make certain they were playing on the correct team.

'The city is panicked.' Mason entered the room as though he owned it. Cypher guessed that he probably did. Still, it irked him as he watched the preacher waltz in, a fur cape flowing behind him, not a line of worry on his face. 'I believe you oversaw the organising of the city in T'Chai's absence. You know it better than most.'

'Indeed I do.' Cypher sniffed and pointed at a chair for Mason to sit upon. He scratched at an itch in his ear and wiped the wax on his old, black cloak. 'The gates are closed and we have enough food to ensure survival in the inevitable siege that is to come. Messages were sent as soon as possible to the farmers around the city advising them to burn the lands and flee down river. The Red Sons will get hungry, as all soldiers do. Their hunger for battle will not win over their need for actual food.'

'And you believe that to be enough?'

'You promised help from your big sister. They will arrive and destroy this pretend army,' Cypher promised, punching a fist into an open palm.

'Good. Good.'

The usually calm and collected preacher seemed out of sorts. He sat with his chin on his palm, staring out towards the window. He wasn't even looking for the chances to demean Cypher and ensure that it was clear that Mason D'Argio was the true power in the United Cities. It was unnerving.

'Are you well, preacher?' Cypher tentatively asked, unsure if he wanted an answer.

Lightning flashed and Cypher saw a weary man, drained of life sitting on the chair for that short moment.

'I need power to take on this army. My old power,' Mason said, his lips trembling as he spoke. He glanced at Cypher and smiled, a slow wicked smile like that of a bully planning a new torment for those beneath him. Cypher knew it well. It was a look he was fond of wearing. 'Round up two hundred of our citizens and bring them to the courtyard.'

The preacher leapt up from his seat with a renewed fire. He shot towards the door, pausing only as Cypher called out.

'Who do you want?'

'Anyone. Everyone. I just need them breathing, Cypher Zellin. I will call soldiers loyal to me and my sister. They will understand. It is time for a light to shine in the darkness!'

Cypher frowned. The preacher had finally lost it. Power madness.

'You got it, boss. Two hundred.'

'You have half an hour, Zellin. I will be waiting.'

*

It wasn't a difficult task. Cypher sent the message among The Watch and they told any who they passed that Mason D'Argio had a plan that would save them. Three hundred arrived in the courtyard, all eager to hear the great plan.

Cypher watched from the high wall around the courtyard as Mason stood at the long balcony, grinning wide at those below him. Cypher scanned the area and saw a large number of Eastern soldiers lining the roof, bows in hand and arrows loose and ready.

What do you have planned, madman?

'People of Archania!' Mason called to his sheep waiting patiently. They cheered and pumped their fists in delight at seeing their leader, their hero. Some climbed the tall tree in the centre of the courtyard, ignoring the raging storm overhead. Cypher rolled his eyes. Fools.

'I stand before you now with a gift. You have followed me and accepted me as one of your own. Your kindness and generosity are to be rewarded this night.' The rain continued to pour but the cramped inhabitants of the courtyard didn't seem to care. Cypher peered to his side to see two soldiers slowly closing the only gateway out of the courtyard.

'My people witness such greatness every moon. You have not had the honour of seeing such beauty, but tonight, that changes. Archania will see the beauty and majesty of the Empire of Light.'

Fervent muttering broke out at these words, all eager to see what amazing gift the preacher had waiting for them. Obviously it was something special considering the circumstances.

'Know that whatever happens this night, Archania will not fall into the hands of those monsters at the gate. Those children playing at being soldiers. They will be crushed by the might of the United Cities, by the greatness of the Empire of Light!'

The screams and cheers that erupted were only drowned out by the thunder booming around the land. None seemed concerned, though Cypher thought he saw a mother pull her young child closer to her breast, calming the child following the eruption of noise.

Mason closed his eyes and held his arms out wide, embracing the storm as two soldiers clad in the armour of the Empire, white cloaks billowing in the wind, stood either side of him. One of the soldiers dropped pulled a dagger from his belt and the crowds broke into screams once more, this time in horror.

Blood fountained from the soldier's wrist as he slashed across his veins. Cypher exhaled in confusion as he watched Mason raise the man's wrist and allow the blood to cover his head, sticking to his silver hair and painting his face scarlet. More screams as the other soldier followed suit, soaking Mason in red.

The preacher cackled and stepped forwards to the edge of the balcony as the soldiers stepped back into the shadows, their work seemingly over.

Mason D'argio called out to the heavens, arms raised wide. When he opened his eyes, even from Cypher's distance away on the walls of the courtyard, he could see the shining gold of the preacher's pupils.

'What in the four hells…?' Cypher cursed.

Lightning flashed and struck the tree, sending the few idiots who had climbed it to the ground and panicking the cramped crowd. The large tree burst into flame, the fire dancing wildly in the wind and spreading the tongues of flames across the tree's arm-like branches, striking fear into those trapped beneath it.

After a moment of hesitation, the crowd made for the gate, banging against it to no avail. Cypher could only look on in confusion as they crushed against the gate, choking the life from one another. He glanced over to Mason and saw that the man was running his blood-stained hands through his hair, a manic gleam in his eyes added to the golden circles. He reached out to the flames and balled his hands into fists. Then he pointed at the fleeing crowd and grinned that wicked grin.

Cypher jolted back at the sudden heat of the flames. Every single person in the courtyard – man, woman, and child – burst into flame. He raised his hand to protect his face from the sudden heat and bright light of the fire overwhelming the courtyard. Screams and the scent of burning flesh hit him like a wave and he turned away from the horror. The soldiers stood still, watching calmly as though this was something that happened every day.

Now Cypher could clearly see the horror of the Empire of Light.

Mason roared with laughter, breathing heavily and holding his hands towards the heat as though drawing power from the growing flames.

Cypher looked across to the Eastern Gate of Archania and wondered how quickly he would be able to get the message to his team.

It was time to open the gate.

It was time for the destruction of Archania.

Once again, Cypher found himself down in the dungeons beneath the palace. With the message relayed to those on the gate, it was time to get the hells out of there. Mason's offer meant nothing to him now. The chance to kill a God. That had been what was advertised. Glory and the chance for Cypher's name to live on in infamy. Finally, recognition for his greatness. His work would at last be appreciated as it should be.

That look in Mason's eyes had changed it all.

Cypher had planned to stab the bastard in the back once the preacher had delivered the goods. Kill a God. Then kill the preacher. That had been the plan. But Cypher had placed his bets on the fact that Mason would be able to hold things together in the city long enough for the battle with the forces of Chaos. The Red Sons complicated matters. And now the preacher had gone mind-blowingly insane, massacring Archanians in a way that brought a bitter taste to even Cypher's usually uncaring mouth.

Things were getting out of hand. Cypher was a survivor above all. When Kane had caught him all those years ago and dragged him down to these cells, he had survived. He had bided his time until the opportunity arose to serve another, to escape the dark, damp hell of the dungeons. He had thrived in his new role. Joining the rebellion, he had seen the chance to cause chaos and sow disorder. Still, he had turned his back on his new allies when he saw which way the wind was blowing.

Survival. One of his many talents.

Whimpers and screams from the cells he passed relaxed him, a soothing song to remind him of where he had come from. Some of the occupants battered against the

169

doors, pleading for anyone who would listen to help them escape their living hell. No one would listen. No one who gave a shit, anyway. He knew that. The loud ones were always the recent additions. Time was the true killer down here. The men and women unfortunate to call this place home would be lifelong inhabitants, Cypher being the exception to the rule. The only way out was at the end of a noose, the edge of a blade, or a chair of fire. He wondered for a moment how the invading forces would view those locked away in the shadows. Would they free the prisoners, believing they were doing something just and right? Or would they leave the bastards where they were? Caution was often the greatest ally to an invading force when taking over a city. Best to wipe away the filth and start again. A clean slate. It would leave less to clean up later.

The final cell to his right was an unused cell. Long abandoned following a spate of attacks from whomever had been occupying the single, small cell – it had been largely ignored since Cypher's time began down here.

But it had not been ignored by him.

Pushing open the cell door, he looked around the damp room. At the dark stains on the stone walls. Shit or blood. Difficult to tell after so long.

Amana narrowed her eyes as she turned from the gaping hole in the wall and found Cypher entering the room.

'You're early,' she simply stated, the confusion leaving as fast as it had arrived. She learned fast.

'Things have taken a slight turn for the worse. It appears that my arrangement with Mason is no longer tenable.'

Amana grimaced, her face shadowed with what looked like genuine sorrow. 'Shame, that.' She shrugged and moved from the tunnel entrance. 'He had such nice things to say about you…'

Cypher took a step back as Mason crept out from the tunnel, head stooped to not hit it against the low rockface. His pupils still gleamed with the golden glow of a mage. The blood had dried and stained his face and his infamous silver hair. He looked like a devil crawling out from the hells beneath the world.

For one of the very first times in his life, Cypher felt an overwhelming sense of regret. Not for any of the bad things he had done; the killings, the torture, the pain he had caused. That was all part of the human experience he had helped deliver. No, he felt regret for not realising that Mason would have been one step ahead. He felt regret for trusting Amana and the others. He felt regret for thinking that anyone other than himself could be relied on.

He glanced over at Amana but the young woman bore no similar signs of regret for herself.

'What can I say?' she said, understanding the accusatory look shooting her way. 'We were poor. And he paid so damned well.'

With that, she gave a wave of the hand and raced down the tunnel, lost to the shadows.

Now it was just Mason and Cypher, standing there staring at one another.

'We are not so different, you and I,' Mason said, his eyes dropping to some of the blood stains beneath his nails. He frowned and tried to fix the blemish. An odd sight, seeing that so much of the preacher was covered in the blood.

'You think so?' Cypher scoffed, waiting for the inevitable explanation. His eyes scanned the empty cell, instinctively searching for any way out of his predicament.

Nothing. Two exits. The tunnel entrance and the cell door. Fleeing using either wasn't worth the effort. Mason would catch him.

His hand slowly dropped to the hammer hanging from his belt and then to the dagger he always carried. Both plausible options but Mason had the power of a mage now. Would it be worth the risk trying to strike, or just another thing to regret?

'Definitely,' Mason said, nodding and grinning like they were two friends at a party. 'Even now I can tell you are working out the different ways that could get you out of this room alive. You are a survivor. Like me.'

'I'm nothing like you.' Cypher glowered at the blood-soaked maniac. 'What you did up there, that was madness. What I do is art. I do things that people in cycles to come will appreciate. They will see the beauty of my work.'

'I used blood magic to rip the weather to my bidding and then sucked in enough power from the flames to fuel my magic for the night,' Mason laughed, the sound echoing in the small space. 'That is true artistry. And I would hate you to miss the opening night, viewing my work.' The preacher twisted his fingers in a slow circle and a flame grew from the edges of his fingers, growing into a ball and floating less than an inch from his palm.

Cypher lunged, dagger in hand, deciding that if he was to die then he would do it in a blaze of glory taking out this cunt.

But Mason was prepared. The flames roared and leapt around Cypher, trapping him in a cage of light.

'More devilry!' Cypher hissed. 'We should have killed the lot of you mages when we had the chance.'

'And when did you have the chance, Cypher

Zellin?' Mason D'Argio's voice called through the flames. 'When you were locked down here starving to death? When your people failed in their wars against the Borderlands? Or when your king married into a line of powerful mages? Archania has always been bonded to my kind, you are merely one of the rats fortunate enough to have been allowed to fester in its shadows.'

Cypher watched through a gap in the dancing flames as Mason raised his eyebrows and pursed his lips for a moment, tilting his head to the side, thinking.

'A useful rat, at times, I must admit. And I have one last use for you…'

Cypher writhed and wriggled against the restraints around his wrists. He cursed. Mason wouldn't be so sloppy. The magical bonds holding his hands behind his back were unbreakable.

Instead, all he could do was watch and observe.

Trapped on the roof of the palace, he could only watch as the Red Sons marched into the city and slammed into the shield wall bravely placed in front of them by the meagre number of Archanian soldiers left in the city. Behind them, citizens from both the Lower and Upper City were standing united, crude weapons in hand and fear on their faces. Still, they stood together, offended that such an army would dare to take their home.

From his vantage point, Cypher could see that this was a battle that could not be won by the defending army. He scanned the city for any sign of the white cloaks of the Eastern Empire's army but there was nothing but the resilient stand of the Archanian soldiers and The Watch, the city's guard fighting against the might of the mercenary band.

'Something missing?' Mason mocked, leaning against the balcony beside Cypher and smirking.

'Your bastard kin are not in the city…' Cypher answered, realising that Archania had been left to fend for itself. 'Norland send none to help. Starik's forces are lesser than our farmers united, and the soldiers sent by the Empire of Light are nowhere to be seen. And you knew this would happen.'

It wasn't a question.

'Of course.'

The red-cloaked warriors ripped through the shield wall with unnerving skill and expertise. Blood soaked the city's streets as the screams of the dying filled the air. Cypher did not care a jot about the fools wasting their lives beneath him. He only cared about one life. His own.

'What do you want from me?' he asked, eager to get it out of the way.

'I want you to witness what I am capable of.' The battlefield was lit up by the lightning, reminding Cypher of the preacher's actions and the power he was capable of wielding. Thunder rocked the streets as the blood continued to flow. 'My soldiers have marched north in greater numbers than the Borderlanders anticipate. They will wipe the Northern scum from Takaara and send a warning to the God of Chaos. I wish to make that warning even more explicit…'

'By losing a battle against mercenaries?'

Mason inclined his head towards the destroyed city gate. Floods of green-robed warriors joined by those in gold swept into the city – the colours of Darakeche, the Eastern city famed for standing against the Empire of Light.

'Not just mercenaries.' Mason closed his eyes and the air around the preacher seemed to shimmer. 'I worship

174

the one true God. Not some pretender. You will be the one to warn the pretender. You will be the one to pass on my message.'

The preacher released his sword from his sheath and winked at Cypher.

'I want you to die knowing that I was the better man. I was always the better man, Cypher Zellin. And no one will remember your life, just as no one will care for your death…'

He stabbed the blade into Cypher's stomach, punching the wind from his body so that he could only sound a small grunt with the impact. The warmth of his blood soaked his skin though he felt suddenly cold. His head dropped forward, vision blurred and hazy.

Mason D'Argio turned to the chaos of battle and watched as the soldiers tore at one another, crowding the city streets and smashing into one another in a wild, deadly embrace. He raised his arms in the air and roared, a guttural scream that shook the air as his whole frame trembled. Light glimmered around him and Cypher muttered a curse through ragged breaths as the rain stopped.

Lightning flashed and thunder joined in the roar of the preacher as Archania erupted into flames. Every building, every road, every part of the city burned in a bright, wild fire. The heat of the flames tore at the palace and Cypher felt the heat licking at his skin.

He used the last of his strength to raise his head and stare straight into those evil, golden pupils.

'Tell Osiron that Archania is a mere steppingstone. One of the oldest kingdoms turned to ash at my feet. Tell Osiron I will welcome the war to come. Tell Osiron I have the guts to succeed where they failed. Tell Osiron, *I* am ready to kill a God…'

DREAMS OF THE DEAD

Trudging through the muddy fields, new boots caked in so much filth that the shiny buckles were no longer clear to see, Aleister remembered why he had wished to move to more exotic climates in Takaara. More dangerous? Of course. But there had to be more to life than marching through the dirt and staring out across lands that seemed forever caught in the shadows of the grey clouds warning of the deluge to come.

It was strange to wander through the farmlands south of the capital city. He could see Archania standing tall and proud in the distance beside Hangman's Hill. That place brought with it an onslaught of memories and emotions, a bittersweet explosion of feeling that he felt unprepared to handle. He turned to speak to his sister, to his friend Bathos.

But he found no one there.

He scratched his head, stopping his march to look all around him. He knew these lands. He had traversed the length of Archania from border-to-border countless times in his youth. Each blade of grass, each hedgerow, each oak and flower were family to him. He knew them as well as he knew his own sister.

Yet, there was something different about the world around him. Familiar, but not the same. The cut of the land, the faded colour of the fields – so very different to the lush green he remembered. Even the sea to the west that broke up the land of Archania and Norland seemed to slumber, gentle grey waves so very different to the crashing vibrant blue he could recall.

This was his home.

And it was not.

Pulse racing, he picked up the pace as he made his way towards the city. Legs heavy as they climbed the sloped land towards Archania, he ignored the farmers' looks of confusion as he passed them, stumbling his way towards his homeland.

Risking a glance up, he saw the clouds blacken before lightning brightened the world momentarily. Thunder rocked Archania and still Aleister sped towards the capital. Rain poured down from the heavens and he slipped, smashing his hands and face into the mud. Ignoring the dirt and filth that splattered across his blood-red cloak, he staggered up and stared in dismay at the scene before him.

An army stood at the gates of the city, hammering against the gates and chanting familiar words and songs that had once escaped his own lips. Flags waved wildly in the brewing storm but as they unfurled and opened, it was clear to him who was storming the city and laying siege to his homeland.

He spotted the waving flags and banners all crested with a fiery, red sun. His own design.

He halted his approach and frowned. The Red Sons. The mercenary group he had dreamt of creating since he was a little boy running around the cobbled streets of the Lower City in Archania with his little sister and their big friend. The company he had started and led into battle countless times. The one he had watched grow and become something known and respected the world over.

The Red Sons were attacking Archania.

Steeling himself, he rushed towards the army, praying he could convince them to halt their attack as he rooted out the issues with his friends.

He pushed himself forwards but his body was tired. His legs spasmed and he dropped to the ground, unable to move. He could only watch as the gate opened and the soldiers rushed into the city, weapons in hand and a bloody song on their lips. Shields pressed forwards and clattered into the front line of Archanian warriors nervously waiting to defend their homeland.

Blood painted the streets he had run across growing up. Streets he had recently walked upon with Ella, sharing stories and smiling, enjoying her company and basking in the happiness and sunshine that seemed to follow her. Breathing coming in ragged spurts, he forced himself towards the city, ignoring the rising frustration and confusion of what was holding him back, what oppressive force was keeping him from bearing witness to the battle and preventing it from worsening. If he could just reach Ben, reach Jax, reach anyone, he would be able to stop this all.

But he couldn't.

Inside the city, the familiar hellish sounds of battle filled the air. The clash of steel. The thud of the shield wall holding strong against the first moments of attack. The screaming. The roars. The chaos.

Aleister searched frantically for a familiar face but every time he got close to someone, he felt his body ripped back, pushed away by some invisible force. Gritting his teeth, he pressed against the world around him and roared.

Then it happened.

An almighty crack deafened Aleister and he fell to his knees. His ears rang, disorienting him as he pushed his hands up from the blood-drenched ground and looked up, staggering sideways as he struggled to regain his balance. Peering up, his vision dropping in and out of focus, he caught sight of an old foe.

Mason D'Argio seemed to be floating high in the air above the palace courtyard. His entire form shone with a blinding light that wrapped around him like a Sun God. But he could not keep his eyes on that odd sight. The screams were different now. High pitched wails erupted as his hearing finally returned. Soldiers on both sides of the battle wandered through the streets like lost children searching for their parents. All burned with bright flames, the stench of burning flesh choking Aleister and forcing him onto his knees as he vomited onto the broken street.

Gazing at the scenes around him through tear-streaked eyes, he watched as the soldiers attempted to put out the flames to no avail. The world seemed to twist and turn in front of him as he staggered between the armies. Both sides had forgotten the battle and dropped their shields, their weapons, everything, just to help one another and end the madness around them.

Aleister found one of the lucky few who had not been consumed in the magical flare attempting to take off his red cloak and throw it over a man who had only moments earlier been trying to kill him. The lines between the armies were blurred and the brightness of the flames blinded all to the reasons for why they were fighting.

Aleister fell to his knees once more and openly wept as he watched the flames tear through the city, burning every building in sight and casting a black smoke into the stormy sky. There was nothing else he could do.

Thinking his mind was playing tricks on him, he caught the look of horror on a man's face, a face that looked the spitting image of the young missing Prince Drayke of Archania. But this man was dressed in the armour of the Red Sons. An older soldier close by ripped his cloak away and wrapped it around a bleeding stump. The man who looked like Drayke wept and rocked back and forth, clutching at the part of his body where his arm used to be.

The scene drifted slowly away, the dying soldiers, the burning buildings, the horror of the battle all wiped away as though by a great tide.

In its place was only darkness.

'This is what happens when those who oppose me are left unchecked.' That same voice. The one from his dream. Now it made sense.

'This isn't real,' Aleister said, relief washing over him. But the scent of burning flesh still clung to the hairs on his nostrils. The grief-stricken faces of men watching their brothers and sisters die beside them still haunted the edge of his vision. He could still taste the vomit in his mouth.

'Unfortunately, this is very real,' the odd voice told him. 'Archania has fallen, burned to the ground by a man who wishes to be a God.'

'How do you know?' Aleister asked, hoping for even a slither of a chance that the events were not real, that this being was mistaken.

A figure crept forward in the darkness, a grim look

on his creased face.

Aleister scowled as he recognised the bald, smirking man walking his way.

'Cypher Zellin,' he spat, recognising the old murderer.

'It's all real,' Zellin said with grim resignation. 'I was there. That bastard Mason D'Argio has finally lost his marbles and is burning anything he can get his bloody hands on. I've seen some messed up things in my life – proud of most of them.' He stuck his tongue into his cheek and grinned, flashing his eyebrows up and down with pride. 'But this was something else. There will be nothing left. No one to remember…'

'And why should I trust the word of a killer?' Aleister asked, still glowering at the man who had killed Katerina Kane's husband all those cycles ago.

'Killer? Your hands all nice and clean are they?'

Aleister frowned, chastised by Zellin's taunt.

'I enjoy the pain, the suffering.' Cypher pointed at Aleister and licked his lips, smiling in a way that said he knew who Aleister really was. 'But you enjoy a part of it too. Why else would you start the Red Sons? Why else would you seek out glory at the edge of a blade? I remember you, back in the Lower City. Another thief running around dreaming of glory. Could have worked for me if Kane hadn't had got her grubby mitts on you…'

'I would never have worked for you,' Aleister contested furiously, offended at the mere notion.

Cypher shrugged. 'Maybe. Maybe not. Life has a funny way of spinning a coin and then blowing on it one way or another. A blow in a different direction and we could have worked side by side. Of course, means nothing now.' The killer's face dropped and all of the arrogance faded, leaving a weary, sad look that seemed out of place on the man's face. 'They will remember me, won't they?'

'They will remember you as a man who tortured and killed innocent people,' Aleister spat back.

Cypher smiled weakly. 'Good. They will remember me.' And he faded into nothing.

Aleister woke, jolting up in an increasingly familiar bolt from his nightmare.

The sun was beginning to rise over the Southern Kingdoms.

The temple gardens were soaked with the late morning light of the sun. Basking in the heat, Ife fanned herself and moaned with satisfaction.

'I have no idea how you pinks are able to stay in the colder climates of the North,' she said to Aleister. 'Give me the heat of a golden sun and as little clothing as possible and I am a happy woman. Grey clouds, freezing winds, uncomfortable rain and *snow*.' She scrunched up her face in disgust as though saying the words alone would bring their feel against her skin. 'Us Southerners are not meant for such a world.'

Gazing around at the stunning greenery of the gardens with the sound of running water from the various fountains dotted around the large enclosure filling his ears, he found it difficult to argue against her point.

'Did you not say that a friend of yours headed north? How did he cope?' Aleister asked, recalling the slither of a previous conversation.

'He loved it!' Ife shot up and flashed her bright smile. 'At first, he would send messages almost every moon complaining about the cold. Snow confused the big bastard.

Though it wasn't long before his messages changed in tone. He loved the die-by-the-sword attitude of the Borderlands. The strongest survive and, *boy*, was he strong. He told tales of how he had to work twice as hard as the pinks to gain their respect and recognition. He collected the ears of significant kills and wore them around his neck as a sign of his worth.' The animated woman pulled on her ear and grinned.

'He sounds like an interesting man,' Aleister said.

Her face dropped, the joy fading. 'He was. The first Southern chief of a Borderland tribe. That was one amazing feat.'

An uncomfortable feeling of dread washed over Aleister as memories of flames burning and swords clashing snapped into his mind. They weren't images from his dreams. They were memories from a recent battle. The rebellion in Archania. The night Ella was taken from him.

He groaned and squeezed the bridge of his nose as he watched a Southern warrior leap towards him, smiling maniacally as the flames ripped the Lower City apart.

The ears on the unusual necklace swung wildly as Aleister remembered forcing the experienced warrior briefly onto the backfoot.

'Aleister… are you well?' Ife asked, concern etched on her face.

Bile rose and choked him as her concerned words rang out and the memory played of two Borderland warriors killing the southerner and coming to Aleister's rescue. A southern chief in the Borderlands who wore the ears of his victims around his neck. How likely was it that Aleister had played a part in Ife's friend's death?

There was no doubt in his mind.

'Excuse me…' He stood hurriedly, staggering to his

feet and pushing his seat back, ignoring Ife's worried calls as he made for the exit.

Another death on his conscience. Ife did not know. How could she? Should he tell her? Was it his place to inform her of how her dear friend had died?

'Aleister!' Ife's tone was no longer concerned, she commanded him to halt his exit and speak to her, to explain his abrupt departure.

He did as commanded, shoulders sagging as he turned, eyes low as he was unable to stare at his friend in the eyes. He had not the courage for it.

'What is wrong?'

She deserved the truth. He swallowed, breath ragged. Scrunching his face and blowing out a long, slow breath, he began. 'Your friend. He sounds unique.'

'He was. One of a kind.'

'He was in Archania the night of the flames. The night of the rebellion.'

Finally, Aleister found the courage to look up and see the confusion on Ife's face, tears beginning to fill her eyes.

'That is where he died…' she muttered, forehead creasing, her eyes fixed on Aleister.

'I fought a Southerner with a necklace filled with the ears of his enemies. We fought, and he was killed by two other warriors whom he had betrayed. I played a part in the death of your friend…'

Aleister swallowed the lump in his throat and grimaced, looking away and busying himself with staring at one of the fountains, giving Ife time to process the development.

He rocked back as strong arms wrapped

themselves around him and he looked down to see Ife squeezing him tight, her head against his shoulder.

'If ever there was doubt in fate, surely that time has now passed,' she breathed into his shoulder. Pulling away, she looked up into Aleister's eyes and squeezed his arms. 'Ikemba was a strong warrior. He took the name Bane in the Borderlands as he saw himself as someone who would ruffle feathers in the cold lands. He was no longer the boy I had played with in my youth. He was a true warrior, and he died in battle, surrounded by flames and covered in blood. He died as a warrior should.'

'But…'

Ife pressed a finger to Aleister's lips and shook her head. 'You carry enough of a burden around with you, Aleister Soulsbane. The guilt for his death should not be another weight to be added to your shoulders. You fought in a battle. People died. That is the way of a warrior. Breathe in,' she took a deep, dramatic breath, 'and breathe out.' She released the breath and smiled a sad smile. 'Release the guilt. Release the regrets. You make your own choices, Aleister. Some good. Some bad. But you are not a bad person. I know, I have served bad people.'

'Many have died because of me,' Aleister admitted, feeling some of the tension leave his muscles as he followed Ife's instructions.

'And many more must die for this world to survive. You have seen the ways of our people. Of our king.'

'Ife,' Aleister frowned and bit his lip for a moment, choosing his words carefully. 'Do you trust Zeekial? Do you trust that what he is doing is right?'

Ife's eyes scanned his, a searching look that made Aleister feel like a small boy standing in front of his betters, waiting to be scolded.

'I do.' She shrugged her shoulders and sighed. 'What is the alternative? Either he is right, and many people will die, or he is wrong and many people will die.'

'So either way, we are probably going to die…' Aleister chuckled darkly, surprised at the sudden calmness that enveloped him as he said the words out loud.

'Looks that way. But there are worse things than death. We believe it is not the end. The sun may set on our lives but that is when the stars shine brightest, housing all of the dreams of the dead.'

'That is a nice way of looking at it.'

'There are worse ways to look upon death. We are fighters, Aleister, death is just a part of our cycle. But a cycle it is. There is no true end to the journey of life and death in Takaara. You will see that before this war is over.'

THE TASTE OF BLOOD

S ly wasn't one for fear. He disliked the dark, that he could admit. But time spent frightened was time spent wasted. That's what folk had told him growing up.

He gazed out at the approaching army of white cloaks and thought that if there was ever a time for a man to feel fear then this was probably it. Instead, he slapped the edges of his trusty axes together and wondered how red the day ahead would be. Double figures were expected. Triple figures would be impressive. Either way, he needed more than Cray to keep the bastard off his back.

He could feel the tension in the air, taste the nervous silence of the men and women lining the hill and defensive positions around Hillheim. Most wouldn't have fought in any major battles. A skirmish or two, perhaps. Fights over land or respect. This was a different beast entirely. Borderlanders, Barbarians, folk who usually hated each other's guts were standing side by side and offering one another nods of encouragement as they faced the incoming army from the South. The seemingly never-ending stream of white cloaks marched between the trees

187

that signalled the border of the lands they called home and stomped their immaculate boots onto ground that was not their own.

'Reckon we got a chance?' Danil asked, not even attempting to hide his nerves. That alone showed a measure of courage in Sly's books. Nothing wrong with fear, it's what you do with it. Fleeing from battle and leaving your comrades to deal with the mess left behind would mean an eternity in the dark hells of the Gods. Use it to fuel a battle-rage and take the fight to the enemy and Sly could see that as a man who deserved a drink. Raven used to say every single battle brought with it a different fear. In his youth it had been the fear of dying. Then it became the fear of shame in losing. Then it turned to a fear in failing his friends. Finally, the fear of letting down those who counted on him as tribe leader.

A lot of fear, but in Sly's eyes, Raven had nothing to fear. He had fought with bravery and honour in every single fight he was forced into, fear or not.

'Aye,' Sly said to Danil, deciding to not belittle the man. The soldier had earned his place alongside him, fought well in the battle to free Baldor, futile though it had seemed. Now he had led his own warriors here to stand tall in a battle the guy probably thought was again futile. 'We got a chance. A small one,' Sly admitted with a shrug. He slapped Danil on the back and offered a grim nod. 'But we got a chance. Stand tall. Trust those alongside you to do their bit,' he inched closer and lowered his voice, his lips almost caressing the soldier's ear, 'and kill every single fucker who gets in your way!'

Sly winked and left the soldier to mull over the advice. Good advice, if he did say so himself.

'You being a cunt again?' Kiras smirked, pausing from sharpening her blades as Sly ambled over to her. She was wearing that war paint, a thick black line running straight across her eyes and giving her the look of a demon. He was sure as hells glad that she was on his side.

'When am I ever a cunt?' Sly chuckled, taking a seat on the log beside his friend and pulling at his ragged beard. 'I'm the epitome of sunshine and joy.'

'You been learning some big words?'

'Frida taught me that one. Think she has taken a shine to me…'

'Must be that yellow smile.'

'Could be something else.' Sly winked again and grabbed at his crotch.

Kiras snorted and raised her eyebrows, trying to stifle her own laughter. 'Definitely the smile then.'

Sly allowed the conversation to drop to silence, listening to the sounds of preparation around him. The checking of shields and armour. The calls of unit leaders ensuring their men and women knew the commands needed when the battle hit. The marching boots as the late stragglers finally found their position amongst the motley band of an army.

'This is gonna be a big one, you know?' he said, no humour in his tone as he looked across at Kiras. The light of the evening was fading, giving way to night as she stared back at him.

'Biggest one yet. Bigger than back at the camp. Bigger than the Northern Wars,' Kiras agreed. Her voice lowered to almost a whisper. 'I wish he was still here. I hate fighting without him. Damn bastard was my rock. Feels strange without him.'

'Aye,' Sly said, not needing to ask who she was on about. He still struggled looking at her and not seeing

Baldor's shadow somewhere nearby. 'The big man would have done anything for you, girlie. Now it's time to do something for him. Let's soak the Borderlands in the blood of those who harmed him.'

'There will be no prisoners this time,' Kiras said, her voice cold, eyes staring out at the sounds of thousands of boots heading their way. 'If I am breathing, every last one of them will die.' Her eyes turned on Sly, unblinking and certain. He didn't feel soft for admitting that that look scared him, just a little.

'I promise you, Sly Stormson. I am not leaving this place until all of them lie dead at my feet. I swear on Baldor's soul.'

'Aye, I know girlie. I know.'

A familiar face walked through the crowd, alerting Sly of his arrival with a low grunt. Sly nodded back at Cray as the stern warrior took a seat on the ground beside him and began fiddling about with a couple of twigs on the ground, comfortable to just sit together in the silence.

After a while, Kiras sighed and gave Sly a weary smile.

'What?' He scrunched up his face in confusion.

'I remember when Saul said that Cray was going with us to the South. The two of you were staring daggers the whole time. Didn't think you'd make it past the border with both of you still breathing.'

Sly raised an eyebrow and turned to Cray who just shrugged in response, obviously not bothered by the revelation.

'Gave each other a good battering in Archania. That was enough.'

'Aye,' Cray agreed. 'Found others to kill.'

'Too right. Saul was the catalyst for this whole sorry mess. And Bane, that fucking traitor. Herick took advantage of a people divided.'

'That's always been the problem with us,' Kiras said, picking up a stick of her own and running it along the dirt. 'Every time we got closer to being united, something tore us all apart. Reaver almost did it, then Socket…'

'Bastard,' Sly spat, 'though could do with his arrows right about now.'

'Baldor used to say how he wanted everyone to get along.' Kiras rolled her eyes and threw a stick at Sly as he snorted. 'I know! Foolish notion… but maybe once all of this is said and done, that could be the aim. We can't just keep killing each other until there are none of us left.'

'Look Kiras, you know I loved the big guy. Biggest heart in the land but not fully equipped in the brains department.' Sly accepted the expected glare shooting his way and carried on. 'There ain't anywhere in Takaara that has all the folk working together. We spent one damn week across the border and watched the place blow apart. Burned their own people alive. And they claim that we are the savages. We will always just kill to survive and nothing more. That's just the way of things.'

'I wish it wasn't the way.'

'I guess we'll find out once all this is done. The kid wants to start something new. If we live through it, maybe we'll see if it actually works. Doubt it.'

A snap of wood turned Sly's attention to the broad-shouldered man to his right. The remains of the twigs were at Cray's feet, his eyes glaring at the mess he had created.

'I want my family to live somewhere with no fighting. Somewhere with no bloodshed,' he said, glancing up at the two of them. 'That's why I fight. So they don't have to.'

'Gonna have to move to the fucking Moon then, pal,' Sly scoffed. 'Takaara is soaked in blood and it is stained so much that there is no way it's getting cleaned any time soon. Just gotta do what we can.'

'The small victories,' Kiras said, nodding her head. 'That's what Redbeard used to say.'

'Aye,' Sly sniffed, thinking of his old leader. 'The small victories.'

The last light of day left as they sat there, finding comfort in those they fought beside in what could be their last moments alive. Torches were lit throughout the camp but Sly, Kiras, and Cray kept away from the flames, preferring the darkness of the edge of the village as they watched the movements of the Northern army.

'Think they will attack tonight?' Sly asked.

'Be stupid. Or brave. Just as likely to kill one of their own than us,' Kiras responded.

'Maybe that's why they wear white cloaks,' Cray added.

'We'll turn them red soon enough, night or day,' the deadly female promised.

Sly peered through the darkness as a huge, mountainous figure walked towards them, the crowds of soldiers parting for the tall warrior as he marched towards Sly and company. Almost as tall as Baldor had been, though not as broad, the warrior wore only a leather tunic to cover his torso, his bare arms were covered in dark blue tattoos and his long beard was braided with an intricate pattern that made Sly roll his eyes.

'Can we fucking help you? Need another plait in

your hair?'

The huge man smiled, clearly not offended by the words. 'You must be Stormson.' He pointed a finger at Sly and then turned to Kiras and Cray. 'Kiras Deathbringer, my tribe calls you. And Cray Shadowheart.'

'Do we get your name? Or are you happy with us calling you Tall Cunt all day?'

Kiras snorted and even Cray had the shadow of a smile on his lips. The newcomer smirked, taking the jibe in good humour. Sly was impressed.

'I am Ragnar, Chief of the Barbarians.'

The laughter stopped and Sly jumped to his feet, axe in hand as he looked up at the huge chief, his eyes barely at chest level. That was no reason to back away from a fight though. The big ones fell hard in Sly's experience.

'You come here to die, Ragnar?'

The chief took a step back and lowered his head, palms out in peace. 'I wish for no fighting between us,' he raised his face and his dark eyes sparkled as they landed on Sly, 'yet…'

'Then why are you here?

'Barbarians and your kind are ancestral enemies. But I respected Raven Redbeard, and his father. They were great warriors. You were close to him, and so you were also close to Baldor.'

Kiras's ears pricked at the mention of her friend, her back straightening as she listened closer to the chief.

'What about it?' Sly pressed, fighting the urge to bleed the bastard here and now.

'At only twelve winters old, Baldor bested my brother, Arog, in one-on-one combat,' Ragnar explained. 'Crushed his nose and cracked his skull. Baldor let him live, commanding that my brother took the few Barbarians left alive and left his village to be. My brother did as he was commanded, he was fond of living,' he smirked. 'This debt to Baldor has weighed heavily on my family.'

'Didn't stop you raiding our towns and villages,' Sly snarled. 'Or working with Herick to fuck us all.'

Ragnar blew out his cheeks and cocked his head to the side. 'We do what we must to survive. I am sure you would have done the same.'

Sly stayed silent. He would have done much worse and they all knew it.

'You knew Baldor well. I will repay my debt to him, though I must ask for your help in deciding how best to do such a thing now he is not among the living.'

Kiras stood with a groan and rubbed at her tired eyes, smudging the war paint. The effect it produced made her seem even more frightening than before.

'You want to settle a debt?' she said, walking through the enclosure and heading towards a cluster of soldiers waiting for the battle to begin. 'Avenge his death and kill as many of these fuckers as you can. Then, when the taste of blood overwhelms you and leaves nothing but a bitter taste that sickens you, lay down your weapons and tell your people to do the same. Build a world where people can live without knowing the taste of blood. *That,* is what Baldor would have wanted.'

She drew her twin blades and a horn sounded in the distance.

Sly grunted as Cray stood up, stretching and rolling his shoulders ready for the fight. He marched past Ragnar, slapping the chief on the back as he passed him.

'I have always hated you fucking cunty Barbarians. I promised not to kill any of you in the fight to come.

194

Afterwards… that's another thing entirely.'

He heard a growl from behind him that turned into a raucous belly laugh.

'You are just as they said, Sly Stormson!' Ragnar called out. 'When we collide, the Gods themselves will sit and watch, transfixed.'

'Usually I'd say you were a madman for such a thought,' Sly said, spinning so that he could keep his eye on the chief as Cray passed him by. 'But I happen to know a God. I can put in a good word or two.'

A second horn rang out across the camp, this one much closer.

Night had fallen.

And the battle had commenced.

Arden heard the first horn and waited. All eyes turned to him. Soldiers held their weapons, their shields, flags, all in sweaty palms as they looked out at the patient army staring out at them in their perfectly polished armour. Most of the Borderland warriors stood with a mismatch of chainmail and helmets, weapons procured from their homes: axes, hammers, swords, scythes, daggers. One man was even holding some kind of scythe, his nervous eyes glancing at the weapon every so often as though he expected it to turn on him. The Barbarians weren't much better. Most were dressed for comfort. Thick furs to fight the cold of the Borderlands.

Herick just stood in his own furs, weapon still sheathed at his hip and a look of contemplation on his face as he turned to Arden.

'That is the signal for us to send a messenger. They wish to speak to us,' the chief explained.

Arden nodded. 'If they wish to speak to us then they will speak to us. A waste of breath before the end, but if it is their dying wish to hear the sound of their own voice before death greets them, then I will not deny them that privilege.'

'Who shall we send?'

Arden grinned. 'I will go.'

Arden marched through the camp alone and without a weapon. He ignored the looks coming his way: frightened, nervous, confused. The soldiers parted for him and he nodded at a small unit to the left of the front line who had all placed plague doctor masks over their faces in acknowledgement of the cleansing he was about to begin in Takaara. They had begun to worship him as a God, just as they would Osiron.

A single soldier stood in the clearing between the forest and the town of Hillheim. Tall, elegant. The man had smooth, bronzed skin and short, dark hair. His eyes were piercing and looked at Arden without fear or confusion. He bore no weapon that Arden could see, though beside him there stood a tall spear stabbed into the dirt flying a flag bearing the symbol of the white sun. The sign of the Empire of Light.

'There are more of you than I imagined,' the man said, nodding his head, impressed. His Eastern accent was thick though he had no trouble with the words.

'Numbers count for nothing. We have Chaos on our side and if you stand before us, we will wipe you from the face of this world,' Arden answered simply. 'I am the Prince of Chaos, Arden Leifhand.'

'My name is T'Chai. I am a Kh'alar, sword to defend my Imlari, the keepers of the faith. We fight in service of the One, the God of Light. Whatever tricks you

196

think you have to fight us, know that they will not work. We have been preparing for this battle since before you were born.'

'T'Chai, my master Osiron will remember your name when you walk amongst the darkness of their realm. The God of Chaos is waiting,' Arden taunted.

The Eastern soldier sucked his teeth and smirked. '*God?* Osiron is a mere pretender. When you next speak to them, say that the Empress is coming, and she has seen the One True God, and he is not happy…'

Arden felt the confidence fade and he scowled, hating that this mere mortal was so at ease. 'Is there anything else you have come to say? Or are you ready to die?'

T'Chai just studied him patiently. 'I've seen all I have to. There has been a nasty habit of royalty dying in the North of late.' T'Chai turned and waved a hand over his shoulder. 'I would not be so keen to tell everyone I was a prince if I were you. Even if it does mean next to nothing…'

Arden's hands clenched into fists and, for a moment, he wished he had his old bow in hand. Fuming, he spun and raised a hand. A horn sounded from the camp as the ranks closed back around him. The world rumbled and a huge crack sounded behind the town of Hillheim.

'Destroy them!' Arden roared to his warriors. 'And bring me his head!'

Sly stalked along the arrow-pricked shield wall of the Borderlanders, hissing through gritted teeth and pacing like a caged animal. This was always the annoying part of warfare. The triple rows of Empire archers released their volleys of arrows on command as those standing opposite raised their shields and prayed that none would creep through any gaps. The first few volleys behaved as they always did; sticking into mud a safe distance away from the lines of anxious and eager warriors waiting. The next few began to land with more accuracy as the soldiers found their range. Fiery arrows arced through the air like shooting stars and landed with a thud against the round shields of the Borderlands force. A few managed to hit flesh judging by the groans, shrieks and the gaps that began to appear in the lines. Sly darted to fill one such gap, glad to be one step closer the enemy.

'Fucking cowards,' he spat, glaring at a scarred warrior to his right who looked to have had half of his hair burned from his head some time ago. 'Put the arrows down and we'll see who can really fight.'

'Won't be you,' a soft voice came from down the line. 'I've sneaked up on you enough times...'

Sly hocked up some thick phlegm from the back of his throat and launched it on the ground. He grinned as he peered down the line and found Frida's smiling face looking back, shield raised high.

'Still alive ain't I?' he growled as he pushed through the soldiers to take a place beside her. 'Anyways, can't sneak up on someone in a battle like this.'

'And we are now on the same side.'

'Aye, for once.'

The whoosh of air alerted Sly to another stream of arrows heading his way. He glanced up and followed their route, taking a casual step back and staring at the flaming arrow that landed at his feet. Frida wore a shocked but impressed look as she looked from him and then down at the arrow and back again.

'You're either a smart cunt or a lucky cunt.'

'Why can't I be both?' Sly said, licking his lips and winking at the shieldmaiden. Her braided hair bounced off her rusted armour as she cracked her neck, turning her head from side to side. He found himself wondering what might happen after the battle if they both survived…

With a grunt and a subtle shift of his trousers, he turned his attention to more pressing matters.

The Borderland archers returned the attack, arrows flying through the air towards the forest filed with white cloaks and shining armour that reflected the torchlight. The arrows flew at different times and with varying accuracy, a stark contrast to the uniform volley of the Empire forces.

Sly growled and looked for Herick in amongst the crowd behind him. The chief was nowhere to be seen. Herick had mentioned waiting at the back of the force, picking out any who dared flee the battle. There were always a few who could not face it. A few who tried to chance their luck at getting the hells out of there.

Sly didn't blame them.

War was not for everyone.

'Our archers are shit.' Sly craned his head to the side and saw the Barbarian Ragnar standing with a load of his big bastards beside him. 'We do not win with arrows.'

Sly shrugged and raised an axe. 'Then let's cut the fuckers down.'

Ragnar gave a vicious smile and drew a mighty sword longer than some of the shorter soldiers. 'May our ancestors watch over us,' the Barbarian said before raising the sword high in the air and facing his enemies. 'Victory or death!'

Sly liked the sound of that. He almost repeated the line but then realised he would have been admitting that he was starting to like a Barbarian so he held off for the moment. 'Death or victory!' he cried, winking once more at Frida who only rolled her eyes in response.

Seeing the Barbarians sound the horn and rush forwards, he pushed the soldier over in front of him and jumped over his fallen, crying body, eager to join the tall bastards who had a head start on him. Caught by surprise and swept up in the wave of roaring and excitement, the first line of Borderlanders joined in the press but none caught up with Sly. Arrows whipped past his head and he heard the dull thud as they found a new home, either in the body of an advancing soldier or the mud, he wasn't sure and he didn't care. All he cared for was the blood and battle.

The enemy soldiers were well-drilled. The lines of archers dropped back and allowed those with spears and curved swords to step forwards, weapons designed for close quarters combat. But Sly did not feel fear.

Instead, he tightened his grip on the axes he loved so dearly and uttered a guttural wordless cry into the night, revelling in the flicker of nerves and fear he caught in the eyes of those in front of him as they realised they would have to face the madman wielding the axes.

Slipping between two spears promising death, he ducked low and then sprang up, diving into the first line and dropping his axes across the helm of the closest soldier he could find. A helmet could be the difference between life and death. Unfortunately for this poor bastard, Sly's axes were able to tear through the metal and split open the man's skull, releasing a stream of blood into the air as a warning to all others who stood before Sly.

Barely noticing the hail of black arrows rushing overhead towards the alarmed enemy, Sly pressed on, using his axe as a battering ram and knocking another soldier aside, bringing his knee high before smashing his boot directly onto the bastard's nose with a sickening crunch. He swung wildly as he felt the crush of the lines against one another. Not waiting to discover how successful he had been, he rushed forwards through the gap left by the fallen soldier and screamed with a maddening glee, carving flesh open and bathing in the blood escaping from the dying bodies. He felt the nick of the edge of a spear rush past his bicep. Turning towards the fool who had caused the damage, he scowled and stalked forwards, twisting the weapons in his hands as blood dripped onto the muddy ground, the sounds of the dead echoing around the forest. Caught with nowhere else to go, his target trembled, bloody spear wobbling with the weak grip as Sly leered at him and edged forwards, enjoying the effect he had on the young, beardless soldier.

A short blade took the man's head clean off with one great strike. The head, encased in the silver helmet, flew into the air and landed on the ground with a disappointing thud, rolling awkwardly until the eyes were looking up at Sly. He turned to the newcomer and groaned.

'For fuck's sake, girlie,' he moaned at Kiras. 'That was my fucking kill!'

'Didn't see your name on it…' she shrugged back with an infuriating grin.

'Need time to carve my name.'

'It's three letters, be quicker.'

'Can't have that damn Cray beating me again!'

Kiras smirked and raced off, eager for more kills. 'Not my problem, Stormson!'

The Barbarians who had beaten their way through the shield wall were now enjoying themselves like wolves who had broken into the sheep's pen. Swords, spears and hammers tore through the Eastern warriors in a red dance that got the blood flowing in Sly. Using the confusion and chaos to his advantage, he leapt forwards, burying an axe into the back of the nearest enemy retreating from the bloodshed and slammed his boot against him, tearing the axe free before bringing its partner around to strike into the open neck. More blood spewed forth as he pulled his axe free, spraying him with the warmth of battle. He licked at the liquid around his mouth and yelled into the night, alert eyes darting in all directions as he scanned the battlefield for his next victim.

More white-cloaked soldiers flooded the forest, reinforcements battling forwards to put an end to the charge of the Barbarians. Sly eyed a particularly huge soldier ambling towards him. There was no rush in the soldier's movements. He wore no helmet and his armour covered his torso but kept his muscular arms free. In his hands there was the biggest mace Sly had ever laid eyes on, a spiked sphere swinging freely from the iron grip.

'Oh... this could be beautiful,' Sly moaned to himself. Tearing his eyes from the chaotic weapon, he glanced up at the dark-skinned face of the warrior. Those around him gave them a wide berth, rushing to combat the Barbarians, swept up in the disorder of battle. This one was different though. He stopped ten paces from Sly and nodded, piercing green eyes staring out beneath a thick, bushy brow before flashing a broken smile that was almost lost in a magnificent, flowing, black beard. Sly had to give him credit, this guy knew how to make an entrance.

'What name do I utter when I pray for forgiveness from the One God for your death?' the great brute asked in good enough Northern for Sly to be mildly impressed.

Sly stepped over a corpse without glancing down at the motionless body.

'Call me Lord Cockface for all I care. You'll be

dead before you get to say your prayers tonight.'

'Well, Lord Cockface, I shall remember that name.'

Sly snickered and glanced around for a sign of the girlie or Cray. Neither were to be found so he laughed on his own. 'I've fought bigger.' He pointed one of his bloody axes up at the bastard and sniffed. 'Killed bigger too.'

'Not this time, little warrior.'

'We'll see…'

A wide circle had opened between the two warriors standing their ground and staring at each other. Other than a few thin trees and the odd corpse, Sly and his next victim were alone. A separate battle caught in amongst the larger war. Happened from time to time; a sense of calm amongst the chaos and crush of the general battle as small pockets opened of warriors vying for glory and a name for the bards to sing. Sly could give no less fucks about all that shit.

He just liked killing bastards.

Thinking fast, Sly flung one of his axes into the air and pulled out a short dagger from his belt, flicking it with all haste towards the giant opponent and hoping that he had been distracted enough for the ploy to work.

The dagger buried itself into the man's torso, his mail guarding the flesh and catching the blade and trapping it before it could cause any damage.

Sly caught his falling axe and lunged forwards as the Eastern brute roared in defiance and swung his magnificent mace around his head.

Sly ducked, feeling the wind rush past as the mace missed his head by an inch, its speed shocking him. Such a heavy weapon should have been slow and cumbersome but in the hands of this warrior, it seemed as light as a feather but a thousand times more deadly. He dived to the side, evading the weapon as it pounded into the earth, dirt flailing all around it in a showcase of the destruction it could cause if it landed on Sly's skull.

The speed and ease with which the broad soldier wielded the weapon reminded Sly of Baldor and his mammoth Warhammer. The thought enraged Sly as he remembered why he was here, why he was fighting against these invading bastards.

He jumped back, knocking unexpectantly into an Empire soldier rushing past and knocking the unfortunate bastard to the ground. He stood and cursed, cutting the soldier's throat and shaking the cobwebs from his head as he stared up at the laughing mace-wielding maniac.

'Find that funny?' Sly seethed.

'Yes.' The brute casually swung his mace and it landed flush on a rushing Barbarian, throwing the lower half of his running body forwards whilst stopping his head and shoulders from any further movement forwards. The soldier stood on the Barbarian's body and ripped the mace away, leaving an incomprehensible mess at his feet.

Sly licked his lips and narrowed his eyes, searching for signs of weakness. No helmet, so a good strike to the head meant death. Still, getting that close with the death dealing mace would be the tough problem to overcome.

The mace swung slowly in circles, gathering speed.

Sly kept his eye on the weapon and feigned left before darting right. He struck true with his axe but the brute raised his left hand, catching the axe on his forearm where it bounced free with a juddering effort. Sly dropped back, moving away from the advancing mace.

His opponent peered down at the now bleeding forearm with a look of laughable confusion. Perplexed by the sight of his own blood, the bastard growled from the back of his throat, confusion turning to rage as he lifted his mace and rushed towards Sly.

Pleased with the effect, the Borderland warrior grinned and licked the edge of his weapon, tasting the blood of his enemy. Now on the defensive, Sly jumped backwards, escaping the oncoming wild lunges of the mace that threatened to knock his head free from his shoulders. He glanced back over his shoulder, eager to not make the same mistake as earlier and caught sight of one of the trees in his path. With a knowing smile, he flung one of his axes at the bastard rushing him.

The brute deflected the weapon with his, dipping his shoulder to escape its path. Now, he saw that Sly had only one weapon available. His pace quickened, a triumphant gleam in his eyes as he swung the mace with frightening ease.

Sly stood tall, carefully watching the rotations and hoping that his timing would be perfect.

The mace whipped across, and thudded with a sickening crunch, burying itself at head height… right into the tree.

Sly whipped up from beneath his surprised opponent, wanting to end the fight before the mace was free. A second sickening crunch informed Sly that his nose was broken. The bastard's elbow had snapped back at the wrong time for Sly and now his vision blurred as he staggered back, panic setting in. He hacked wildly with his one remaining axe and growled, shaking his head in the hope of regaining his focus.

His vision cleared as blood fell freely from his broken nose, pouring into his mouth with the familiar bitter taste of iron.

The mace was still caught in the wood of the tree.

Fragments of the tree lay scattered on the ground next to a motionless hand and a pool of blood.

The great brute didn't look so intimidating now. No mace. No hand.

Sly breathed heavily and stepped forwards. He pulled the dagger free from the soldier's armour with a grunt and lazily pushed it into the man's throat, twisting it for good measure without even giving him a last look.

He stumbled from his latest victim, ignoring the sound of the body dropping beside the tree. He picked up his axe from amongst the fallen leaves and winced, his eyes watering from the pain.

The battle had moved towards the city now. Up the hill, Danil's masked warriors fought valiantly alongside the Barbarians and Borderlanders but the immense press of the Empire's forces pushed them back with their greater numbers. The longer the battle went on, the better it would be for the more organised force in white.

Sly rolled his head around his shoulders and moaned as he felt the cracks of his tense muscles.

It was another sound that put him on full alert, snapping him back to the reality of the battle.

A loud rumble echoed throughout the forest, nearly knocking him off his feet. He stumbled but managed to catch himself before hitting the mud.

The flames of the torches across the battlefield and lining the walls of the city went out in one single moment as dark clouds blocked the light of the moon and stars. Hillheim and the forest were plunged into complete darkness.

Sly cursed and took a deep breath.

'What are you doing, kid?' he muttered, feeling his

stomach drop as he steadied himself for Arden's attack.

DAWN

Arden strolled amongst the bloodshed and carnage. He had seen battle before. He had unleashed his own unrestrained power to wipe out Barbarians and Borderlanders caught in the horrors of his discovered power in the Far North and that was once something that he thought he would never wish to see again.

But now he stepped past the swinging swords and swooping shields. Annoyed by the meagre attempts on his life by the Empire's soldiers, he longed for that old power to be unleashed once more, to wipe away these frustrating bugs who dared to threaten him with their puny weapons. A prince need not worry about the actions of such fools so beneath him. Just as a bear would not give time to the fly buzzing around its head.

It was the awful attempts at sending death through bow and arrow that first irked him with the battle. Give Socket and Arden a quiver full of arrows and a bow capable of withstanding a long draw and the two of them could have done more damage than the hundreds of rookies loosing upon the Empire's soldiers.

Then he witnessed the whimpering and the trembling of the younger warriors, the ones who had not experienced such bloodshed. They fled from the battle, tails between their legs. Arden watched on with satisfaction as Herick's women sliced down the traitors before they could reach the freedom of the lands beyond Hillheim. Such cowardice had no place here.

He wondered when the last time was when he had handled a bow and arrow. Archery had been the one thing keeping him sane in the cycles of his life as the boy with golden pupils but no apparent power. Folk could laugh and point all they liked about his eyes but they could never laugh at him for the way he could use a bow. Now though, there were bigger things for him to accomplish.

The voice of Osiron played in his mind.

The Empire of Light is weak. Its leader is careless and she does not wish to draw her main force into battle,' they urged. 'Send forth my legion. Destroy them all!'

Arden stepped aside a lazy strike from one of the soldiers draped in white and stabbed a thin dagger through the stumbling man's neck, spraying red and soaking the soldier's once pristine cloak. It wouldn't matter now. He was dead. And shame was for the living.

The Barbarians and Borderlanders fought valiantly against the greater forces of the Empire. Arden watched with pride as those covered in the plague masks who had sworn their allegiance to Chaos leapt into crowds of the Eastern soldiers and gave their lives for Arden and his cause. But there was no regret. Arden knew that this had to be done. To make Takaara anew, it must first be cleansed.

The Northern forces dropped back to the walls of

Hillheim, clustered together as the sheer number of the Eastern warriors seemed too much to handle. Retreat in the city would mean the deaths of hundreds of innocents, children included. It was a decision that Herick, Ragnar, and Arden had all reluctantly agreed that would be a last resort in the battle. However, Arden knew that there was another trick to be played from up his sleeve. More soldiers were available. More death at his beck and call.

He closed his eyes and searched the Sky Plane, wandering through Chaos and searching for the warriors eager for vengeance and justice. The scarred and grim warriors held their shields, swords, spears, hammers, and everything else they had fought with in a previous life and waved their weapons in the air as they watched Arden float past them. Osiron waited patiently on the edge of the front line, a crown of antlers on their pale head and that black-lipped smirk etched on a weary face.

'It is time?' Osiron asked, knowing the answer.

Arden nodded. Blue and green lights danced in waves across the black sky and he tightened his face as he looked out across his new army of the dead.

'Enough to wipe this piss-poor Eastern force from the Borderlands.' He paused and rolled his eyes up, sucking on his tongue as he thought about his next words carefully. 'And if you happen to kill any Barbarians on the way. There will be no problem in my eyes.'

The smile on Osiron's face grew unnervingly wide.

'You have heard the words of your prince.' Osiron's voice echoed out across the chasm of Chaos. 'Your time is now. A new dawn breaks in the world of Takaara. Take back what you lost, my brothers and sisters.'

The world spun and cracked open as Arden felt himself snap from one realm to another. He shook his head and fought to control his breathing.

When he managed to see clearly, he looked out upon a sea of corpses, the blood of the Empire and Borderlands staining the earth in a way he never thought he would ever see.

Trees had cracked and fallen, splintering and broken. The corpses were so mangled and destroyed that Arden struggled to recognise which side they had fought on. There was the glimmer of a white cloak here and a cracked plague doctor mask there but other than that, they all just looked the same to him. Just more corpses to add to the pile on the way to rebuilding the world.

Dark clouds shifted across the sky and the light of the half-moon creeped through the gaps.

Arden took a deep breath and smiled.

Sly struggled to comprehend what had happened. He rubbed his eyes and gave them a moment to refocus, wondering if they were deceiving him. Knocked to the ground by something out of the corner of his vision, he had spent the next few confusing moments just watching silently as a dark swarm covered the battlefield, sickening cries filling the forest and the edges of the village as men and women were ripped apart by the dark shadows tearing through the crack in the forest that had opened.

The bodies at his feet shows signs of deep scratches, the work of unnaturally long claws or some demonic beast. The wounds on both Empire soldiers and Northern warriors were too alike to be a coincidence. None had been made by swords or spears, or even that fucking mace he had come across earlier. They were the markings of something from another plane of existence. And there was only one person involved in the battle who was capable of such destruction.

'Has to be the kid…'

He stumbled through the aftermath of the battle, heading for the walls of the town of Hillheim where he could still see some faint signs of life. Rain hammered down and Sly could barely see the walls of the town at the top of the hill. He trudged on, still caught in a wave of disbelief over what had happened.

He felt like an idiot.

He had seen the destruction caused by Arden and the dark wave of unnatural creatures under his command. He had seen the steel in the kid's eyes as they spoke of the war to come, of the battles that must be fought for Takaara to change. But Sly had been so caught up in his own yearning for vengeance that he had chosen to ignore what it would look like standing side by side with this new dark force. He scanned the chaos of the battlefield and sighed. Was this the price for vengeance? Was this the price for a new world?

Not for the first time, he wondered what Raven would have done under such circumstances. *Follow your gut.* That was a favourite line of the chief.

But for the first time in a long time, Sly's gut was screaming at him to run.

Calves burning as he reached the top of the hill, he listened to the sounds of the soldiers scattered around the edge of the town. Weeping, wailing, cursing. Some just sat with their heads tucked between their knees, eyes wide open and staring off across the hellish battlefield.

One woman was just shaking her head repeatedly, lips trembling.

More bodies were stacked in piles against the walls of Hillheim, as if thrown against them and crushed by whatever dark force had emerged from the cracked earth. Skulls were shattered and mutilated in ways that Sly had never witnessed before and ripped apart leaving horrific gashes across the flesh. He caught the sight of a familiar face amongst the piles of dead. Frida's eyes were still open. A deep wound had leaked blood from her head and her shield lay forgotten beside her. Sly inched closer, swallowing the lump in his throat. He closed her eyes with his grubby, bloodied hand and pressed his forehead against hers, praying that she would make the journey to the hall of their ancestors. Finally satisfied that he had done enough for her, he wiped away some of the blood from her now peaceful face and stood, wondering what might have been. She had been a good one. Deserved better than this. But that's how things go in battle. It wasn't often the good ones that survived. Death wasn't picky.

Sly breathed and blew out his cheeks as he spotted a bloodied warrior sitting beside a pile of the corpses, ignoring the scenes of stumbling warriors around her as she stared at nothing in particular. The smoky paint across her face was smudged and decorated with the red of her enemies' blood. One of her arms was openly weeping blood from a nasty-looking wound and her twin blades lay in the mud either side of her.

Kiras glanced up at Sly as he approached and her whole body momentarily shook with a dark laughter. Sly took a seat beside her and joined her in staring out into nothing.

'Thought you were dead,' Kiras said after a while, her voice low and weak. 'Searched through the bodies. Difficult identifying folk at the moment.'

'It's fucking carnage,' Sly agreed. 'I might actually be exhausted for once. Might be too old for this.'

Kiras turned to him with a weak smile before

rubbing her tired eyes. 'It was worse than before.'

There was no need to explain. Sly knew exactly what she meant.

'Cray?' He asked, voice breaking slightly as he offered a silent prayer to something, anything, in the hope that his friend was still amongst the living.

'In the town. The *things* made it over the walls and tore through Hillheim. He's searching for his family.'

Sly felt a twisting in the pit of his stomach like a snake coiling deep inside him. 'They attacked people in the town?'

Kiras nodded softly, lips pressed tightly together.

'Shit…' Sly made to stand, to head into Hillheim and help his friend search for his family. A hand shot up and grabbed him before he could leave.

Kiras's eyes were shining in the low light of dawn. 'We cannot condone this,' she stated simply, voice quivering. 'I don't know how, but he's gotta be stopped. Baldor wouldn't have wanted this. Neither would Raven.'

'Shit, even I don't want this…' Sly muttered.

'The things they did… they are as bad as the fuckers who tortured Baldor.'

Sly dropped back beside his friend and placed an arm around her shoulder, dipping his head so that she could look into his eyes and know that he was being serious.

'This army of his, there's no fighting it. Not here. Not now. Only one thing we can do.' He swallowed and fought against the urge to bite his tongue. His whole body tensed, confused by the word trying to slither it was way past his lips. 'Run.'

The word tasted bitter. He spat a load of saliva, trying to clear the taste from his mouth.

'Where to?' Kiras asked.

Sly pushed himself up onto his feet and pulled the arm Kiras held out, dragging her up. She grabbed her blades and sheathed them before holding out her hands, palms up and to her side, frowning as Sly waited to answer.

'We grab Cray. See if his family is alive. Then we head south.' Kiras raised an eyebrow at that one but Sly was ready for the incredulous glare. He patted it away with his hands and grinned. 'Yes, yes, yes, I know. I hate the fucking place. But if we stand any chance of outliving this war, we need allies. The Borderlands will be nothing but blood and ash soon enough.'

'I wish Raven were here. He would know what to do…'

'Well, he ain't. Just us now. Gotta make the big decisions.'

Kiras cocked her head to the side and shrugged her shoulders. 'There'll be a lot more blood before all this is done with. Reckon we'll make it out alive?'

Sly shook his head without a moment's hesitation. 'Course not. We're dealing with magic, Gods, and the end of the fucking world as we know it. We'll die doing whatever we do. No issues with that. I just wanna make sure I die killing bastards who deserve it. Used to think I could just be pointed towards folk with my axes and that was it. Now, I wanna be pointed at the right folk. Cause this didn't feel right. Maybe I was wrong about the Barbarians before. But I was definitely wrong about siding with the kid. He's too far gone…'

'So we run.'

'Aye, we run.'

The town of Hillheim was decimated.

Rain battered the caved in buildings and hit against the shocked, wide-eyed looks of the inhabitants who had survived. Were they the lucky ones? Or was luck only for those who died quickly in the chaos of the battle? Those who had bled on the muddy paths or were smashed against the walls of their homes.

Parents held the unmoving bodies of their children, rocking back and forth in their grief and wailing into the stormy dawn sky. Sly cursed as he spotted one youngster – no more than ten cycles by the look of him – pushing against a corpse in the hope of waking the bloodied male. Tears streamed silently down the boy's red cheeks, bloodshot eyes fixed on the dead body.

He weaved through the mass of bodies and broken buildings with Kiras in silence.

To his surprise, Sly found himself pleased to see the huge form of Chief Ragnar. The Barbarian was helping pile the corpses of the dead and preparing a pyre. The chief carried the bodies of Barbarians, Borderlanders, and Easterners alike. He did not seem to care who it was, each deserved to rest.

This number of bodies would take too long to bury. Flames would be best. The smoke would carry their souls to their ancestors in the Great Hall.

'Ragnar,' Sly saluted the chief with a curt nod as the big man lowered another corpse onto the pile and wiped his bloody hands down his ripped shirt.

'Stormson. Deathbringer,' Ragnar nodded to them both, his face a mask of exhaustion. 'It is good to see strong warriors have survived to see the dawn.'

'Aye, though many have not made it through the night,' Sly spat, unable to comprehend the devastation before him.

'I brought my warriors south for a better life, to keep them alive,' Ragnar said, guilt clear to see on his weary face. 'Barely a hundred stand with me now. Some have already scattered with the wind, eager to depart from the madness. But I will stay, I must clean up the mess I helped create.' The chief banged his chest, rainwater splashing with each hit of his fist.

'We were blind to it. Now our eyes are wide open,' Kiras said with a groan. 'We're heading south. You're more than welcome to join us.'

The Barbarian smiled sadly, his eyes warmed slightly at the gesture. 'It would please me to say yes. But I have a duty to my people. I must wander the hills and mountains until the Barbarians are one again. Only then may I decide on what is next for my people. The Gods will guide me, and perhaps, one day, they will send me on the same path as Sly Stormson and Kiras Deathbringer.'

The Barbarian held out his great arm and Sly clutched his forearm and squeezed tightly, eyes glaring at one another with respect. They had fought and bled beside each other. Barbarian or not, that meant something.

Kiras did the same with the chief before bidding Ragnar farewell.

They found Cray standing back from a crowd of people with Borderlanders and Barbarians. All were staring into the flames of a large pyre that had been set up by the broken stables. The smell of burning flesh was difficult to handle but Sly pressed towards his friend who stood holding hands with his wife, one small child clutched in his other arm with head pushed against his broad chest.

Cray turned to Sly and Kiras, red eyes filled with tears and a tired smile to greet them.

'You made it,' he grunted.

'Aye. The boy?' Sly asked, not wanting his gut to be right.

Cray shook his head, lips pushed together to fight back the grief.

Kiras breathed in heavily, nostrils flaring. 'It wasn't…' she began, but Cray cut her off with a shake of his head.

'No,' his voice cracked with the word, 'the sickness was too much. Gone before the monsters reached the town.'

Kiras stepped forwards and placed a hand on Anya's shoulder. The distraught woman turned and sobbed, falling into Kiras's welcoming arms.

Seeing the grief on his friend's face and feeling a tightening within his own chest, Sly grabbed Cray round the back of his neck and brought him close, pressing his forehead against his and stared into his eyes.

'I am so sorry, my brother. We are here for you and your family. No matter what you need, we will do it.' The words left Sly's lips without a thought. They had saved one another enough times for the words to ring with truth and Sly knew that he meant what was being said.

Cray nodded as Sly pulled away. He looked down at his child and determination replaced the grief on his face. 'I have two requests.'

'Anything.'

Cray breathed slowly and steadied himself. 'Get the hells out of this cursed place. And make sure this doesn't happen again…' He motioned towards the sobbing crowds staring at the pyre – a reminder of the destruction in the town of Hillheim and the scars that would never fade.

'You don't think small do ya?' Sly chuckled.

'We leave. We regroup. And then we do what we always do.'

The two men grinned at one another, both glad for the opportunity to push aside their grief and sadness for a brief moment. They turned to the women. Anya bore a grim, resolute look on her soft features. She had been through the hells and survived. She was ready for the hardship to come.

Kiras just rolled her eyes as the rain continued to fall from the foreboding sky.

'Let me guess… kill the fuckers?'

RIVERS OF BLOOD

Morning arrived with no change in the weather. Arden didn't care. Rain lashed against what was left of the town of Hillheim as he ran an approving eye across the leftovers of the attack: the bodies, the blood, the skeletons of buildings still standing following the quake and the onslaught of Chaos.

He had watched the lost and forgotten warriors stream from the plane of Chaos and felt an overwhelming sense of guilt and regret as they tore through any warriors in their way. Barbarians, Borderlanders, Imperials, Archanians, and even those dressed in the plague doctor masks signalling that they truly accepted Arden as their leader. All fell to the mass of black shadows and claws that ripped through the battlefield.

Then they made it into the town itself.

Men. Women. Children. The devastating army cared not. Blood soaked the town and warned all that this was the way forwards now. Chaos had arrived and Takaara would be changed forever.

He had thought about stopping the bloodshed in the town, of pulling back. That was when he had heard the voice urging him against such foolishness.

They must all see what it means to reshape the world. They must understand that there is a price to be paid if we are to begin anew. Sacrifices must be offered if we are to build something great, Arden Leifhand. You know this. You accepted this.'

So Arden had kept his mouth shut and averted his eyes from the darkest of horrors. Instead, he had focused his efforts on finding the leader of the opposition force and sending a message of his own.

And here the man knelt in the wet street in front of the broken beams and splintered wood of Lady Sofia's popular house of pleasure and debauchery. Ironic, as there would be no pleasure for the people of Hillheim today. Only grief and loss. There would be pain as the rebuild started, but Arden had known that all along.

'I am surprised to find myself still alive,' an Eastern warrior said calmly as he gazed up into Arden's face. Herick stood behind the man, keeping his hand close to his blade just in case the prisoner attempted anything foolish. Desperate people did desperate things and Arden was in no mood for such idiocy.

'T'Chai, wasn't it?' Arden said, frowning down at the last of the Empire's forces. 'Before the battle, you claimed that you had prepared for us. That you had ways of stopping us.' He glanced around at the destruction and grinned, laughing mockingly at his fallen foe. 'It seems you were wrong.'

To his credit, T'Chai kept that smug look on his face, dark eyes twinkling in the dawn light as the rain splashed against his brown skin. 'Is this your first war?'

Arden struggled against the urge to hit that smirk

221

clear off the bastard's face. Did he not know when he was finished?

'You are the sole remaining warrior. Such arrogance feels misplaced. I may not be as battle-hardened as you, T'Chai, but even an idiot can see that *I* have won the day.'

T'Chai gazed around at the desolation of Hillheim, at the wailing widows and the smoke rising from the crude pyres. 'It doesn't look that way to me. These people will not follow you after what you have done. You may have won the battle, but the war, that is only just beginning.'

Arden bit his lip as the rage burned inside him. He didn't need people to follow him. His army would destroy anything that stood in his way. Takaara would be born again regardless of the thoughts of the people of Hillheim. The Borderlands were filled with ignorant people, he knew that from personal experience. People who would bully and torment a boy born differently. People who would kill others just because they looked at them the wrong way. Osiron's vision, Arden's vision, required people with more intelligence. With more understanding.

'This war has only one outcome. And that will be the rebirth of Takaara. There is no stopping it. You have seen what we are capable of. What can your Empire of Light offer that can withstand such an assault?' he scoffed at the kneeling man.

'We will have the support of the One True God. He will guide us against your charlatans and pretenders. You have great power, but it will be nothing in the face of what we are truly capable of. Takaara will be reborn, but you will not be a part of that.'

Arden felt a shiver of nerves crawl down his spine but it was quickly brushed off as Osiron reassured him.

'LIES! The man is a liar and a fool. You are the one who knows the truth. These are just the words of a dead man hoping to leave the world with one last act of malice.'

Arden nodded, feeling his confidence return. 'You have proven today that you are capable of dying. That is all.' He turned away from T'Chai and waved a hand in the air, signalling Herick. 'Deal with him, Herick. I have wasted enough time listening to the words of liars.'

Darkness. All was darkness.

Arden was used to it now. Time spent on the Sky Plane often blended with his time in Takaara. The darkness was all consuming but he was the Prince of Chaos, he knew this realm and he knew that he had nothing to fear. Taking one step at a time, he walked at a leisurely pace, wondering when Osiron would greet him and commend him on his actions in Hillheim. The sands of time fell but Osiron did not appear.

Arden pressed on, searching for any sign of the blue and purple lights that often shimmered across the horizon during his time on the Sky Plane. But there were none. He scanned the darkness for any sign of movement, any sign that the lost and forgotten of Takaara were waiting here to meet him, as they so often had. But they weren't there.

A sense of dread gnawed at the pit of his stomach as Arden continued on his path, unsettled by the lack of anything around him. The lack of sound. The lack of people. The lack of light. Just a complete lack of everything. Yet he placed one foot in front of the other and carried on. There would be an end to this. There always was. Perhaps it was a test sent by Osiron, a way of measuring his willingness to do what must be done without backing out. That sounded right.

Feeling slightly more at ease, he picked up the pace and was pleased to hear the sound of running water greet him in the distance. Relieved, he headed towards the comforting sound just as a deep, red glow pinched the horizon. The louder the noise, the wider the red horizon became.

A ringing noise grew louder and louder until Arden dropped to his knees, wincing with the overwhelming volume of the ringing in his head. He clutched at his ears and pressed his head to the ground, praying that it would stop, promising that he would do anything to be free of the pain. And it stopped.

Breathing heavily, his body rocked back and forth, face still scrunched up from the battle within. Satisfied that the ringing was over, Arden glanced up, opening his eyes to a world that was not there before.

The whole world was lit with the red glow he had seen on the edge of the horizon. It surrounded him, broken only by the meandering cliff face either side of him. He peered at the towering cliffs and shook his head as he saw the rock drift and move in waves, something rock should not be doing, in this plane or any other.

He stood and jerked back, nearly toppling over as he realised he was standing at the edge of a river, the water lapping against his knees. The river was red like the sky and unnervingly similar to the colour of blood, something Arden had seen much of over the last night. He closed his eyes and took a deep breath, wondering if this was just some hallucination brought on by the chaos of the battle.

Opening them, he frowned. The red liquid now splashed against his hips and the rocky banks rose to towering cliffs that were tall enough to block much of the light cast down from the unique sky. He waded forwards, eager to get past the strange place he found himself in. The river felt thick, but he forced his body through it, holding his arms high to avoid touching the water. A low moaning filled the air but he couldn't decipher its source. The moans came from all around him, choking the air with their ominous tone and adding to Arden's growing sense of dread.

He followed the bend of the river, hoping to see an escape route from whatever hell he had landed in, eager to free himself from the growing moans and the suffocating smell of iron and rotting flesh that surrounded him. But there was no end in sight. He cursed and splashed a fist against the river, worsening his mood as the liquid splashed against his face, the bitter taste landing in his mouth and proving his grim theory. A river of blood. But why here?

He edged closer to the banks of the river, hoping for a shallow path to follow. That was when he realised what the cliffs were made of. Scarred, burned and bloody hands reached out from the walls either side of the river, each aimed towards Arden as they fought one another to grab him and pull him towards their unholy wall of death. He jerked back, terrified as burned fingers caught the edge of his cloak and threatened to drag him towards the deadly embrace.

Falling backwards, his whole body fell beneath the blood, silencing the moaning as he fought back to his feet. With a deep breath, he strained futilely to wipe the blood from his eyes and face. It was not worth the effort. Every inch of him was drenched in the red stuff.

Heart pounding, he struggled forwards through the river, attempting to ignore the deafening moans now mixed with the dark intelligible mutterings. They grew with each panicked step until Arden could comprehend some of the voices as they shot into his mind unwanted and terrifying.

You are no prince! You are a petulant boy playing at God!

225

Heathen! Heretic!

So much death. And for what…

We should take him and be done with it. Keep him here for all eternity.

The villagers… did you see what they did to the villagers?

The blame lies with the mage. This one is a mere puppet acting with each pull of a string.

Blame? He *was the one who called those demons forth! Takaara is dying because he was unwilling to let go of life…*

Images flashed into Arden's mind. Shadowy creatures with claws like daggers tearing through the flesh of innocent men, women, and children. He saw Socket's face as he drove the dagger into his chest. He watched as Ovar's head hit the ground with a thud. Other moments forced themselves onto him – Raven's corpse lying in Archania; Baldor tied and beaten in a darkened room, alone and scared.

He stumbled forwards, vomit burning his throat as he attempted to ignore the voices in his mind and the burning in his muscles as he fought against the pull of the river. He shut his eyes, not wanting to see the hands reaching for him as he passed them, hoping that this would soon all be over. Tears fell freely down his cheeks as he whimpered, panicked by the overwhelming sounds and the feeling of foreboding that he knew could drag him back down beneath the blood at any moment.

Then a blast of wind knocked him backwards but his body hit what felt like hard rock, slamming the wind from his body. He stayed there for a while, eyes closed as he regained his breath, body aching from his efforts. Relieved to not be drowning in blood, he opened his eyes and pushed himself up onto his hands, squinting as he adjusted to a new world.

The red glow had disappeared, replaced by a deep green painted across the horizon. A single ash tree stood alone, but Arden could only make out its silhouette. The world shimmered and swayed as he pulled himself gingerly to his feet. This world was silent. There were no hands desperately clutching at him and trying to drag him to his death. There were no voices screeching out for his punishment. There were no images seared into his mind with enough clarity to give him nightmares for the rest of his existence.

It was just Arden Leifhand, and this single ash tree.

Cautiously, he made his way towards the tree, but with each step forwards, the tree fell back into the distance. Confused, Arden stopped, searching the world for some sign of what he needed to do.

'It has been many cycles since any have journeyed to this plane. Generations, in fact.'

Arden jumped at the voice echoing around him, searching for its source and finding nothing.

'In my slumber, I believed that my work was done. I believed that nothing would wake me until all had gone. Yet I find myself awakened. It seems Takaara once more has power enough to disturb my kind. Interesting…'

'Your kind?' Arden asked, confused by the peculiar choice of words.

'You will understand when the time comes. We will meet again, Arden Leifhand, when we are ready. Blood. Fire. Darkness. Chaos. All will call out to worlds above and below. Now, only two remain to answer that call. Soon, it will be time for you to make your choice, and the fate of Takaara will rest upon your words…'

Before Arden could respond, the ash tree erupted in wild green flames, burning brighter than the sun and forcing him to raise an arm to block his eyes from the sight.

He stepped backwards and watched the tree burn to ash.

Without knowing how, Arden realised that he was now back on the Sky Plane with his army of Chaos. The familiar, reassuring purple and blue lights glimmered throughout the world. He breathed a sigh of relief as Osiron rushed towards him, anxiety creasing their forehead.

'Where were you, Arden?' Osiron asked. Arden found it odd that Osiron seemed so panicked, so unnerved for once. The usually calm exterior had been stripped away and in its place was a frightened and worried being who suddenly didn't seem so powerful. 'Where were you?'

Arden sighed, not wanting to recall the events but knowing that he must. 'A river of blood. A dying tree. There were… bodies lining the banks, fingers clawing at me, wanting to pull me in. They blamed me. They blamed me for everything.'

Osiron's anxiety faded, only to be replaced with a look of complete rage. 'You knew what would come, Arden. This is what you agreed to. There is always sacrifice and the greatest changes require the greatest of wills. You must show an iron will if you are to succeed where others have failed. Others will tempt you and threaten to derail all of the work we have done, but you must ignore them, the path you walk on is the correct one if we are to save Takaara and create a world for all.'

'I know,' Arden moaned, breathing irregular as he spoke. 'But there were so many dead. So much blood and death… surely there is another way.'

'There is not!' Osiron snapped, a black shadow covering their pale features. 'Humans have been given the choice time after time and still they prove themselves worthless! We will start a world that is fresh, one not tainted by the sickening actions of men.

'You are a part of this, Arden Leifhand. You are the Prince of Chaos. Remember what your friends did to you. Even now, those closest to you plot and scheme. They fall away from our forces and depart the land we have in *our* control. They live only for themselves and wish not to aid their dear friend who cares for them so much. How does that make you feel?'

Blood rushed to Arden's cheeks, burning as he felt the tears sting his eyes. He had been so happy to see Sly and Kiras alive. Now, he felt the burn of embarrassment take over as he realised that yet again he had been fooled by those closest to him. Only Osiron knew what was best for him. Only Osiron would stand by his side and ensure he received what he deserved.

Osiron glided forwards, placing a bony, comforting hand on Arden's shoulder. 'Follow me. There is work to be done, and I will not have them stop me this time. It is time to send a message to old friends. This time, all that will be left, is Chaos…'

Arden made to follow but a voice stopped him, a voice he recognised from long walks through the woods and countless lessons regarding the ways of archery and how to be a valued member of a tribe in the Borderlands. The voice of Socket.

Do what you must, kid. I'm sorry for how things went. And know that I forgive you. Guilt is a bastard thing to carry around and you have enough of that to bear right now. You'll know what to do when the time comes, that's what I always told Korvus. I believe in you.'

The tears rolled down his cheeks, but Arden had wiped them away by the time Osiron looked his way. The Prince of Chaos could show no weakness.

THE BROKEN SHIELD

The howling of the wind whipping up the sands of the desert forced Katerina Kane to pull the scarf across her face and peer out over the dunes to the lights on the horizon. It was a cloudy evening but there was still a suffocating heat that she had not grown used to through her time in the East. Her mouth seemed constantly dry and she found herself licking at cracked lips and wiping sweat from her brow every few seconds. Her shirt was drenched in sweat day and night and clung to her skin. If her three chosen escorts cared about the sticky heat then they were good at hiding their lack of comfort. The three women had kept quiet since leaving the city, each obviously missing their homeland and all not capable of being subtle when attempting to hide their displeasure at having to travel with Kane back to the United Cities. Their Empress had commanded them to fulfil the task with honour, though she had not said anything about enjoying the journey and that was clear. At first Kane had attempted small talk, eager to break them down with kindness as she had with Istari. But the Eastern warriors seemed more like stone than that thick skinned warrior.

'Are we resting here or pushing past Mughabir?' she asked, not expecting a response.

'No rest. Keep moving,' came a reluctant grunt in reply. It came from the youngest of the three women tasked with guided Kane back home. She had the dark skin of the East but the dazzling blue eyes often found in those who lived in the cold North. Those dazzling eyes peered out towards Kane from between the creased scarf wrapped around her head and jaw, watching her carefully. 'We are not dressed as though we are one with the Empire. They will not bother us if we hold to the edge of the city.'

Kane shrugged, content with the reply. She had been concerned at marching through Darakeche, the country known as 'The Shield in the East'. The Sultan prided himself on being the barrier to the Empire of Light, working hard to defend Takaara from the horrors of the Empress. After spending time in the city she once viewed as the pinnacle of all that was wrong with Takaara, Kane had to re-evaluate the misconceptions she had once held. The Sultan – and his arrogant fool of a son – were not the most endearing of figures. Yet, the Empress had been pleasant and welcoming. An intelligent woman capable of articulating her thoughts to those around her and making sure that they understood where she was coming from.

Kane could not bring herself to agree with everything the woman had said, but now she felt as though she could understand why so many followed her, and why they behaved in the way that they did. Even if she could still not condone their violent actions.

She nodded and hitched her bag higher on her back and trudged forwards with a deep breath hoping that they would soon be able to rest for the night. Once they had passed the city, she figured the others would be less temperamental and more inclined to relax. Of course they were on edge right now, if the Sultan's infamous Greencoats or his famed Golden Army were to discover three women travelling from the empire in his lands then punishment would be swift and painful. Everyone in the group knew that.

Wiping the sweat from her face with a slow forearm, she lowered her head and pushed forwards, eager to pass the city as soon as possible.

It was only when they drew closer to the city that Kane noticed something was wrong.

In the low light of the desert night sky, a red glow burned a halo around the city of Mughabir and plumes of smoke twisted their way towards the heavens, joining the dark clouds hanging above the Shield in the East. Darakeche was a nation full of life, but at this hour, such light was a cause for concern, the smoke adding to the tremor of nerves running down Kane's spine.

'Something is amiss,' Kane said, turning to the others and pointing towards the great city. From this distance, she could just hear the warning horns sounding, confirming her fears. 'We must check and see what has happened.'

One of the older women spat and ignored Kane, moving on and away from the burning city. 'The Sultan will protect his people. He is a proud man. He will accept no help. So we shall offer him none.'

Kane lowered her brows and held back a scathing remark, choosing her words carefully. 'There are *children* in that city. Innocent boys and girls who may need our help. Are you saying that we just abandon them to their fate?'

'They would abandon us,' Sabha said, another old head who had begrudgingly accepted the chance to escort

232

Kane west.

'Is that a reason to behave in such a way?' Kane questioned, annoyed by the lack of compassion. 'If you so truly detest the way Darakeche is run, surely you would wish to behave differently, to set an example that others can follow. Not stoop to their level.'

That got through.

The three women looked at one another, defeated glances shared by all as Kane left little room to squirm away.

'We have a mission,' Abhia said, the younger one of the three who had spoken the most on the journey – not that it was much. 'To take a detour would be to go against the Empress's command.'

The other two nodded, eyes lighting up at the clever way out of the box Kane had attempted to place them in. But that would not be the end of it. Kane had never been one for giving up with ease. Rising to the rank of Inspector of the Watch meant perseverance and resilience, traits she still prided herself was on. Just ask Istari Vostor…

'Your mission is to escort me home safely. If I head to Mughabir, you must follow to ensure my safety and then my passage home. You can follow me into the city to find the reason for the disturbance, or you can wait here. Either way, I am entering that city.'

She delivered the ultimatum with what she hoped was confidence and strength but was unsure whether her nerves and uncertainty shone through. Truth was, looking across at the rising flames and cloud of black smoke above the city, all she could see was the events of that night back home. The Night of the Flames. The night the Lower City burned for wanting more from their lives. The night Ella died and before Tamir strode away, head held high, to his doom.

A part of her wished for one of the women to fight back, to insist that she dispel this foolish notion of helping their neighbours and just carry on their journey. But a larger part, the part she felt to be her true self, was pleased to hear that they would not.

'Ascertain what has occurred. Then we leave,' Abhia insisted, breathing heavily into her scarf as she trudged towards the burning city. 'No funny business. I will drag you out if needed.'

Smirking behind her own scarf, Kane raced forwards, praying to the gods that there would be a simple explanation for situation in the city but knowing in the pit of her stomach that it would not be the case. She had worked in the Lower City for too long to hang her hat on foolish ideas of hope and wishful thinking. There was no smoke without fire – and Mughabir was blanketed in the stuff.

Mughabir burned with a fierce light. Smoke clogged the air as the wind whipped the hungry flames from building to building. But it wasn't the flames that drew Kane's attention. It was the charred bodies fallen in the streets. The crying and shrieks of those still breathing. It reminded her of the horrors in her homeland. The young and innocent, old and weary who had been murdered using fire and for little reason. There was no anger in the air, not yet anyway. Instead, an overwhelming sense of shock and grief loomed large over the city with most inhabitants barely even looking her way as she staggered through the city's streets.

Abhia, Sabha, and Dina followed Kane with concerned glances around at the destruction. The soldiers of the Empire had no need to feel concern for their own welfare in their enemy's homeland – the citizens were too affected and consumed by their own grief to care who strolled through the city now. Kane reckoned the Empress of the East herself could walk through the streets and none would care.

'This destruction is nothing to do with the Empire,' the usually quiet Dina muttered. Kane turned to the diminutive warrior, shocked to hear her speak. 'The Empress has always sought to conquer. This is just sheer brutality. It is not her way.'

Kane instinctively made to retort as she recalled the burnings in Archania but she bit her tongue just in time. Now was not the time for such an argument. Sometimes the best thing to be said is nothing at all.

A woman knelt in the dust and dirt, the headdress askew with ash and blood covering much of her face. There were no tears. She just rocked on the spot, her hands cradling what looked like a small, severed arm. A pool of blood glistened with the light from the flames burning across the city and Kane thought she could see the rest of the mangled body in the bloody doorway to a crumbling building a few paces from the shocked woman.

It looked like a battlefield. Dozens of wide-eyed, mumbling citizens of Darakeche stumbled between the bodies and the leftovers of what had only moments earlier been a thriving and beautiful city. They shook the bodies of the dead, ignoring the signs that warned them that the effort would be futile. Grief had a horrible way of playing tricks on the mind. Kane had seen it all too often in her line of work.

She had been sent to a home in the Lower City near the start of her career after a complaint about the smell emanating from one of the small, cramped rooms in a makeshift, ramshackle building housing hundreds of occupants, all too poor for any other kind of living arrangement but happy enough with a roof over their head for when the inevitable rain fell. She had broken the door down to see a small, narrow room with one elderly woman rolling back and forth on her wooden chair. The stench was overwhelming in the small space and it didn't take long for Kane to discover the source of the smell.

The elderly woman stared wide-eyed at a single mound of wool and furs on which a rotting body lay. She had married her husband some sixty-five cycles earlier. He had died the previous month and the shock had splintered her mind, causing her to ignore the state of his body and the fact that he was, of course, no longer amongst the living.

Kane had called a team in to take the body away. The cries had deafened her as she left the room and she could still remember the wild look in the old woman's eyes as she finally ripped herself free from the chair and lunged for her dead partner, wailing and pleading for them to leave him be, that they were happy together.

There wasn't much in the world that was as powerful as grief.

'Who then?' she asked as they continued farther into the city. 'Who would do such a thing?'

The three warriors from the East shared an uncomfortable but stern look between one another. It was Sabha who finally answered.

'There is only one being I know who would have the power to destroy this city in one night. Only one who would wish to send those living in the East such a warning.'

Kane frowned at her, knowing what was coming.

'The one who believes themselves to be the God of Chaos. Osiron wants us to know that they are not dormant.

They are here in Takaara and they are ready for war.'

'And what exactly do they want?' Kane asked tentatively.

Abhia sighed and bit her lip. 'Complete annihilation. An empty canvas on which they can paint a new future without the blemishes of the past.'

'But their paint will be the blood of the people of Takaara,' Sabha warned. 'We have fought for so long to ensure such an eventuality does not come to pass.' She scanned the city and tears dripped down from her dark eyes. 'But now I fear that whatever efforts we have made will be futile. How can we stand against such careless destruction?'

Dina placed a reassuring hand around her friend's shoulder and pulled her close enough so that their lips were almost touching. 'We are the ones with a God on our side. We are the ones who stand in the light. The flames burn here but for a moment. For us, they will burn eternally. You know this, sister.'

Kane bowed her head and tried to ignore the spitting of the flames around her mixing with the sobbing of the Mughabir people. God or no God, they were in for a hell of a fight.

'Let's head to Archania. I've seen all I need to here.'

THE MESSAGE

I t had taken a day to travel through the jungle and arrive at the village of Ubomi. Unlike the city of Ad-Alum, Ubomi was a simple, slow village renowned for producing tough but intelligent soldiers with a determination to fight for their kingdom. Ife had informed Aleister that the village was small but strong. It had a proud history and each person in the kingdom felt as though they had a debt to the sleepy jungle village. They paid that debt with a pilgrimage to the simple temple in the heart of the village and offered food and drink to those living in Ubomi and shared stories and built friendships that would last a lifetime with the young and old who lived there.

And that was why the message sent from the village had been met with such outrage and shock when it had arrived in Ad-Alum.

Ubomi burns and its people bleed. Darkness and Chaos have overwhelmed our home and there are tears enough to drown the world of Takaara. In these trying times, we respect that our leaders must make difficult decisions. However, if it is at all possible, the people of Ubomi ask that their leader visit and pray with us to ensure the calm passing of the dead.

Signed: Chief Cwaka

There had been no discussion. Aleister marvelled at the simple gestures passed between the leaders of the South. The narrowed eyes of King Zeekial. The grim, determined nod from Queen Cebisa. The closed eyes of King Milani and the sigh and gentle pressing of fingertips against his forehead of King Solomus. Nothing needed to be decided between the rulers. They knew what must be done.

And that was why Aleister found himself lost in sorrow beside Ariel and Bathos as they walked through the jungle village of Ubomi, holding back the tears as he looked at mangled corpses and the still smoking ruins of the huts standing in a spiral pattern around the temple of Ubomi. Keeping a respectful distance behind King Zeekial, the three of them bowed their heads as the king greeted the grieving villagers, offering his prayers and holding his people close as they wept and told a dark tale of the night Chaos came to Ubomi.

Aleister didn't listen to the words. He wouldn't have understood them anyway. Instead, he glanced around at the carnage. The bodies were ripped and carved with wounds that spoke of the work of a rabid animal. Teeth and claw marks opened the dark flesh of the villagers and blood stained the dusty paths and foliage of Ubomi.

Ariel knelt beside one body and rested a gentle hand against the woman's shoulder. She glanced up at Bathos with tears in her eyes and a grimace. 'What monsters are capable of doing such a thing?'

Dark, shadowed creatures with teeth like daggers and deadly claws flashed into Aleister's mind and knocked him off balance for a moment. He steadied himself and was relieved to see that no one had caught his momentary lapse in focus.

'This will be no normal war,' Bathos replied to Ariel, stroking the back of her neck and then pulling her in close as she stood and moved away from the body. 'We must be prepared for anything.'

Aleister felt a tapping on his shoulder and he spun to find the source. A short, elderly woman with more lines on her face than the night sky had stars stood gazing up at him. She held out a necklace lined with what looked like long, curved, yellowing teeth. She pushed it silently forwards, holding it high and towards Aleister.

'She wishes for you to have the necklace.' A tall, lithe man approached, bowing in greeting and pressing his hands against his heart as Aleister faced him. 'Made from the teeth of crocodiles, it is a good omen, said to protect its wearer from an untimely death.'

Aleister turned back to the short woman and smiled warmly. He bowed and tapped his heart, hoping the gesture would mean something to her. He allowed her to place the strange necklace over his head and felt a measure of joy as she gave him a toothless grin that reached her sparkling eyes.

'Thank you. This is a beautiful gift.' Though the words might not mean anything to her, she obviously understood the message. She reached up and pulled Aleister close, planted a kiss on his forehead before shuffling away and following her king as he strode towards the temple.

'She was wearing it when they came…'

Aleister took a closer look at the tall man. A nasty

looking wound ran from beneath his ear and down the right side of his neck, its journey covered by the loose, colourful garment he wore. He seemed unconcerned with the angry wound, smiling politely as he caught Aleister's searching gaze.

'A mere scratch. I was not lucky enough to be wearing a charm to prevent my early demise. But I *was* fortunate to survive with only this.' He tapped the wound and winced.

'What are they like? These creatures?' Aleister asked, unsure if he wanted to hear a truthful answer but curious all the same.

A shadow crossed the man's face and his eyes grew cold. 'They are not of this world. Chaos beings fuelled by nothing but a desire to destroy. They are sent from whatever hell they dwell in to decimate the lives of the innocent. I would rather face a thousand dragons than witness that army march upon this village again. Our bravest warriors didn't stand a chance. And the women and children...'

He didn't need to finish the sentence.

Aleister could still see what had happened to the women and children caught up in the destruction. Already he knew that he would struggle to get the images out of his mind when he closed his eyes to sleep at night. They would dwell in his nightmares as did so many others.

'How many survived?'

'Twenty in total. A blessing. Chief Cwaka claims that we were left alive to send a message to others. He says that he has received a message from the thing responsible for this. We always believed that the war to come would be fought away from our homes, away from our families. Now, we know that there is no hiding from what is to come. The fate of Takaara will be fought in the North, South, East, and West.'

Aleister narrowed his eyes and took a step closer the villager. 'But it is a war that we will win. A war that we *must* win. No matter where it is fought.'

A dark, pitying smile reached the wounded man's lips as Ariel and Bathos joined them, their mood dark and sombre.

'You have not seen them so I shall not take you for a fool. This war is not one we will win. This war is one that we must simply *survive*. Take your necklace and run for the hills and the mountains. Place as much distance between you and them. There is no victory to be found in the jaws of such creatures. Only death. Run. Run and do not come back. Takaara is doomed.'

At night, Aleister sat alongside the other visitors under the sparkling stars and crescent moon. The circular, red, clay homes of the village had been cleaned throughout the day and the bodies of the dead had been washed and placed beneath thin, respectful coverings on an ancient burial site sacred to the villagers. Aleister had asked permission to visit but the villagers had instantly taken offence to even the notion that he would step foot close the resting place of their dead.

'These people take death seriously. It is not seen as an end, just the next step on the endless cycle of their spiritual journeys,' Ife explained to him once he had done his best to convey his embarrassment at having offended the locals. 'Upon death that next stage begins with the guidance of family and friends. Outsiders cannot muddy the waters they must sail on to reach the next stage of their journey.'

242

Aleister understood, or at least he thought he did. So instead of trudging over to the burial mound in the east of the village, he spent his time studying the curious geometric patterns painted on the buildings that had not been decimated in the annihilation. Both bright and dark colours covered the clay, with the strange intricate patterns becoming more and more complex the closer they got to the centre. The temple itself was a rainbow of odd patterns designed in an orderly way, beautiful and unique. Aleister had never seen such an eye for detail.

'Such care and attention to detail…' he had murmured to himself.

'The people of this village do everything as though it is the last thing they will ever do,' Ife said with a weary nod towards a passing villager covered in cuts and bruises from the battle. 'It carries a great sense of pride.'

Aleister marvelled at the artwork, wondering if he ever took such time to complete a task to the best of his ability. The question brought an answer that he wasn't entirely happy with.

Now he sat beside his sister in the light of a tall fire twenty paces from the front of the temple of Ubomi. A group of villagers twisted and turned their bodies in a pleasing and engaging display, dancing in the light of the moon and flames for their honoured guests. Even after such grief, they wished to greet their king and his allies with a traditional celebration, a celebration that could also encompass the lives of those who had recently passed. He caught the eyes of the old woman who had handed him the necklace. She smiled at him and he touched the jagged teeth around his neck, raising a hand in greeting to the woman before turning back to the vigorous display.

The dancing increased in tempo, following the beat of the drums in the background. Elegant twists of the legs and arms and stomping of feet had Aleister mesmerised. Eventually, the drums built to a fast-paced crescendo, ending with the dancers standing in a line with arms raised to the heavens and painted eyes closed. The grateful audience thumped their chest in gratitude for the wonderful display. Aleister copied the response, honoured to have been welcomed in such a way following the aftermath of such a horrific event.

'Quite the day,' Ariel said once the guests and villagers stood from their seats and the general conversation erupted once again. 'These people are hardened. They are handling this better than most.'

Aleister raised an eyebrow.

'That wasn't meant for you!' his sister responded, turning an embarrassed shade of red at the insinuation. 'This village is proud and they are coping with a devastating event. You know what it was like in Archania following the flames. Madness and chaos.'

Aleister had to agree with that. 'Ubomi isn't divided like the North. It is a village united. Ironic, really. The United Cities is as far from united as any place we have been. That night was proof of the divide in our homeland.'

'Those dancers were all widows from the attack,' Bathos said, his weary voice drifting over as his eyes stayed fixed on King Zeekial who stood talking to the entertainers. 'Zeek told me earlier. How can they get up and drag themselves here just to perform for us?'

'Resilience. Courage,' Ariel said, stroking the big warrior's arm. 'They are an inspiration.'

Aleister felt suddenly small. When faced with such adversity, he had been found wanting. Drink. Drugs. Women. Anything to take the edge off his grief or sadness. He was astonished at how these people could pull themselves together so soon after the murder of their loved ones.

He could run into battle alone with nothing but his trusted sword, Soulsbane, but this took a different kind of strength. He envied those who were able to pick themselves up and dust off after such a fall. It was something he knew that he needed to work on and it made him crave a bed and a quiet night away from all of this.

'You okay brother?' Ariel asked, genuine concern on show.

He nodded. 'Yeah, just a long day,' he said wearily.

It was a while before the king made his way over to them, looking exhausted by the events of the day. Dark circles ringed his eyes and he looked older than Aleister had yet seen him. Not quite the Boy King he had once envisioned.

'Thank you for coming,' Zeekial said, tapping his chest softly and sighing. 'I thought we would be marching to face these horrors face on – not marching in the wake of their destruction.'

'It is not a choice you were given,' Ariel said, comforting the ruler.

'But I should have done something before. I was too comfortable with allowing Osiron to sit and stew. My guilt led me down the wrong path. A stronger ruler would have done what needed to be done. Instead, I have wallowed in my grief and guilt and many have lost their lives due to my hesitance.'

'A leader makes bad decisions from time to time,' Aleister reminded him. 'It is how they react that is important. We cannot change the past, only learn from it.'

'Your words ring with truth,' the king said, scratching at his thick bicep as he gazed into the distance.

'Yet I feel that my guilt will go with me to the grave and beyond. Takaara is facing the hells because of the errors made in my youth. What I thought was wisdom was just hubris and the arrogance of a fool with too much power. This village has suffered because of my actions. I must ensure there is no more suffering in Takaara.'

'And how do we do that?' Bathos queried.

'First, we speak with the chief. I am led to believe that he has some news.'

Chief Cwaka was a short, balding man with one of those smiles where his eyes closed, as though trying to keep himself from exploding. A wrinkled, dark face with wide eyes greeted Aleister as he took a seat in the temple. There were no guards, no other villagers. Just the chief, the king, Aleister, and his sister and ally.

'We came as soon as we received the letter,' the king said to his subject, voice filled with respect. 'I am so sorry that our visit is under such a shadow of darkness.'

Cwaka waved the worries away and made a dismissive sound with the back of his throat. He leaned on a thin stick and responded. 'Our village has bred the finest warriors in the South for generations. Most visits are under some shadow or another. Otherwise, why would we have the need for such soldiers?'

A pertinent question and one that made Aleister respect the elderly chief in an instant.

'Of course,' Zeek said, smiling despite the grief around him.

'The events of the other night were upsetting and will leave scars on our village for cycles to come,' the chief said. 'But that is not why I requested your presence.'

Zeek frowned at the chief, body tensing with confusion. 'Then why did you ask us here?'

The chief winked, eyes dazzling with mischief. He leaned forward and spoke with a conspiratorial tone, soaking in the mood of the room with a storyteller's flair. 'We caught one…'

Aleister backed off in shock, blinking as King Zeekial clapped his hands together and pushed towards the chief, his excitement clear for all to see.

'You caught one? Take us to it.'

Chief Cwaka chuckled. 'Of course, Your Majesty. That is why you are here.'

Aleister had seen much in his travels throughout Takaara. Nothing prepared him for the monster shackled to the wall in the grimy cellar beneath the temple.

Red eyes flashed out from charred, cracked skin. An iron shackle wrapped around its neck, pulling the thing back as it attempted to thrust forwards towards the newcomers, slashing wildly with claws sharpened to a deadly point. Spit flew from its dark mouth, between razor sharp yellow teeth and those red eyes glared with a dark fury at those just standing there and watching in mute horror.

'This truly is a creature of Chaos,' Zeek said, shaking his head and running a hand through his short hair. 'It is amazing that you were able to capture such a beast.'

The best snarled and flashed its blood-red eyes at Zeek, pulling to the end of its tether before grabbing uselessly at the chain and growling in frustration.

'How did you do such a thing?' Aleister asked, unable to avert his gaze from the strange creature.

'I would love to say that I was touched by divinity,' the chief said sadly. 'Though I fear it is a matter much graver than I ever thought I would care to speak of. You see, to trap this fiend and prevent loss of further life in the village, I did the one thing that I am asked not to do…'

'Blood magic…' Zeek muttered, the words sounding like a curse as they passed his lips.

Aleister squinted at the chief and paused, trying to find the right words to portray his confusion without seeming a fool. 'But *you* have used blood magic, Your Majesty. Why is this so different?'

The chief sighed and answered on behalf of the king who paced the room in silence.

'Blood magic tears the seams of Takaara apart. It is something that must be used sparingly,' he explained. 'Using it freely has caused Takaara to fall apart, earthquakes and the like are happening more often than people believe. Though useful in a tight spot, it is not a branch of magic that people are accustomed to.'

'And you thought you were capable?' Aleister butted in, addressing the standing chief.

'Magic is chaotic right now. The more we know about it, the better the chance we have of implementing these strategies,' Cwaka answered.

'We know that your allegiances are…complicated,' Zeek said to the elder chief. 'But I trust that this is proof that we can continue to count on you in the war to come.'

Cwaka enjoyed the moment. He stroked his large beard and the held a finger in the air, eyes flashing as though he was the first human to have discovered fire. 'My allegiances lie with the safety of these people. *My* people. No matter what happens, it is imperative that these people survive. They have been through enough.'

The tribal leader closed his eyes and frowned sorrowfully. The chief exhaled softly, his face bearing the remarkable range of lines and worries that one would expect from an elderly man working his ass off. He had led the people of the village during their darkest era, and now he stood at the edge of disaster, speaking of the war to come for Takaara. Things would have been much easier for him had this happened in a decade or so. Instead, he was forced to act during the turbulent time.

'How many of them were there?' Aleister asked, nodding at the pile of the dead.

'Hundreds,' Cwaka whispered, 'I believe. We stood no chance. This village has built the finest of swordsmen across this continent. They were not able to fend them off. Now though, it is time we move forwards. It is time we lead by example.'

Aleister nodded grimly at those around the table, glad to see that the others stood resolute and unblinking. 'And you wish to fight them again, but on a battlefield of our choosing?'

Cwaka nodded, booting the bloodthirsty creature at his feet and shedding a single, solitary tear.

'This blood magic, did it work?' Aleister asked, eager to find out more about the mysteries of the world. He remembered the chamber in the temple back in Ad-Alum, the pool of blood King Zeekial had used to bring his friend back from death.

'Only one way to find out…' Cwaka's eyes glowed red as the light faded from the room.

Aleister motioned for his sister to stay by his side, blocking her from the convulsions of the shadow creature writhing at the chief's feet. Ariel obeyed the silent command, fingers twitching for her weapon. Everyone was on edge. The heat, the battle, the chaos. All took their toll on those involved.

Cwaka cackled and pulled a small, golden dagger from his waist. He held the blade against the neck of the creature, instantly putting an end to the wretched thing's movement. 'Blood magic tears at the heart of Takaara. A blemish, though it can be fixed. But Chaos magic does nothing but destroy. It uses death as a source of power instead of letting those who have passed on rest. It stabs at the heart and doesn't relent until its job is done.'

'If blood magic is so dangerous, then why use it?' Aleister asked.

Cwaka looked at him as though he were a child. When he spoke, he ensured that every word was chosen carefully.

'Because we are desperate. Because we sit at the edge of a spewing volcano. Because the end of the world draws closer with every passing day and all I care for is to leave this world in a place that is better than when I found it.'

'We are all desperate, my friend. There is nothing wrong with that,' Aleister said, smiling as best he could. 'You have shown us that these creatures have a difficulty with those who have magic power. That is something we must test.'

'But using blood magic is forbidden for those who have not trained in this art,' Cwaka uttered, face horrified at the thought. 'It can overwhelm the user or send them through another plane, lost for all time. We may be desperate, but we are not foolish. We have one shot at fighting Chaos with our blood magic. If we mess up this one chance, Takaara will fall.'

ESCAPE

The steady rainfall was familiar but not much else. Sly knew the Northern lands were different to the Borderlands – full of rolling hills and farming land all the way to the coast. Not much snow but it was just as wet as the land he called his home. Five days of marching south and he had yet to see a clear shot of the sun. That didn't bother him. He'd been moons without seeing the bright bastard in the sky. What bothered him the most was that he had barely seen a man or woman on his journey from Hillheim. It was as though the people of the North were running scared, fleeing the arm of Chaos before they could dig their claws into United Cities.

And Sly couldn't blame them.

It hurt to leave the Borderlands. His last voyage south from his homeland hadn't exactly gone to plan and he knew that leaving again was taking a risk. But staying would be an even bigger one and the kid had shown that he was in no mood for negotiation. Sly was up for a fight, always had been, but what he had witnessed at Hillheim was

251

more than fighting. It was the complete annihilation of men, women, and children. For once, Sly found himself feeling that an army had gone too far.

Sly knelt at the top of a hill, scanning the land below and watching the work of a farmer with his dog herding a group of sheep. Finally, some sign of life.

'Should we say hi?' Kiras asked, creeping up beside him and following his gaze.

Sly shook his head. 'Nah. What's the point? We head past. Keep moving. Need to keep going south if we are to get some distance between us and the kid. No point wandering this far and then slowing down. Makes the whole thing pointless.'

He sighed and trudged down the hill without another word, knowing that his friend would follow without complaint.

Night fell and he didn't stop as the darkness deepened around him. He wove easily through the trees of a forest and came to a small river. Once his flask was filled, he leapt from wet stone to wet stone, keeping his balance and making it across to the other side without issue. Kiras joined him, followed closely by Cray. Danil hung back, waiting for the remaining villagers who had been convinced to join them in their escape to the South. Not that they needed much convincing. Arden had done that work for them.

In the distance, Sly spotted the light of a campfire. He signalled for Danil to stay his side of the river, wanting to scout the camp before risking any fight with a potential enemy. His time in these lands had taught him that caution was an ally. Even if he hated the bitter taste it brought to his mouth.

Across a small dell, and through a thick copse of

trees, Sly found himself close enough to spot a single silhouette beside the flames. Drawing his axes, he crept closer, eager to get the drop on whomever was awake at this late hour in the valley. The hunched figure poked and prodded the logs at the bottom of the flames, shuffling as they danced and rose, sparks flying with the motion. There was no weapon in sight, at least none that Sly could see.

He circled the dark figure, hoping to catch it unawares from behind before asking about their business. Edging forwards, Sly had the sudden, uncomfortable feeling that he was being watched. Trusting his gut, he spun to his left, just in time to catch another shadow leaping towards him from the shelter of the trees, glistening sword in hand.

His axe caught the blade just in time to deflect a fatal blow. Sly grunted and followed the path of his attacker, growling in anger and raising both axes in defiance. The next attack was more measured, precise. The thin sword snapped forward with a frightening ferocity but Sly was ready for it.

He knocked the jab high and wide but rapped his knuckles with the effort. Whoever this bastard was, they were no novice with the blade. But Sly had trained with Kiras for cycles and had faith in his own skill fighting a swordsman. This hooded bastard would get what was coming for him, make no mistake of it.

It was Sly's turn to launch an offensive. He rushed forwards, cutting across with his left hand and swinging high with his right. The first attack was blocked with ease but the second only barely avoided taking the man's head off, nicking his shoulder instead and drawing a shocked moan from him.

Sly enjoyed that.

He smirked at the bastard and licked at the blood dripping from his axe.

253

'You taste just like all the others. You'll die like them too…' he warned.

The hood dropped from his opponent as he raced forwards, the moonlight shining on a dark face with thin eyes and dark hair tied tightly at the top of his head. He didn't look like most of the Southerners Sly had come into contact with but that didn't matter – the bastard was attacking him with something more than a knife and that meant he would need to be taught a lesson, stranger or not.

He dodged the thrust meant for his heart and slashed with an axe, grimacing as his opponent rolled away, narrowly avoiding the attack. Sly kept up the attack, jumping forwards, only to feel his feet knocked out from beneath him by what felt like a horse slamming into his legs. He cried out and dropped to the wet ground, face splashing into the filthy puddle as one of the axes slipped from his grasp, sliding across the mud and out of reach.

He twisted and looked up, fearing the deadly blow. A long-haired brute stared down at him, colossal hammer in hand and a wicked grin on his face. He raised the mighty weapon with a roar and for a moment, Sly thought that it was the end of the road at last. The final moment of his life. A fitting end for the mad warrior who had lived a life of blood and war. Skull smashed to pieces in a foreign land that he couldn't give two shits about.

'I wouldn't do that if I were you.' A reprieve.

The shock on the bastard's face was beautiful. Sly laughed, not wasting a moment as he lifted his leg straight up and caught the brute in the nuts, rolling away from the falling hammer and jumping to his feet, single remaining axe in hand.

He stood, breathing heavily and glancing between the hopping fool clutching himself between the legs and the smaller, faster warrior pointing his sword past Sly in the direction he knew Kiras would be waiting, her own blades in hand and ready.

'What do you reckon, girlie?' he asked, chest rising and falling with each breath as he struggled to regain his composure. It had been a close call. Closer than he cared to admit. 'Kill the fuckers?'

'That wouldn't be the best idea…' Another figure crept out from the shadows of the trees, a young woman holding a dark, wooden bow with arrow notched and ready to fly. Opposite her, a man who shared her dark features who Sly guessed must be her brother by their similar sharp eyes and knife-edge cheekbones, wandered across, his trembling hands clutching at a sword that seemed too heavy for him to carry.

'Four on two,' the young woman said joyfully. 'It would be best for all involved if you placed your weapons on the ground.'

Sly cleared his throat and frowned mockingly, holding a thumb out and then raising each finger on his left hand before shaking his head in defeat. 'Now, numbers ain't ever been a strong point of mine. But I think you've made a mistake…'

He grinned as the woman gasped, her frantic eyes dropping to the sword held across her throat. She dropped the bow and arrow to the wet earth beneath her as Sly nodded a greeting at Cray.

'Nice of you to join us big man.'

'Thought you might need some assistance,' Cray said merrily, or as merrily as he ever sounded.

'Now,' Sly said, marching over to his fallen axe and reaching down to pick it up. 'Four on three ain't too good. But personally, this shitstick here don't look like much of a problem.' He pointed one of his weapons towards the shaking young fellow who glanced at his sister in apology. 'So let's call it three on three. Could be deaths on both sides if we lose our heads. So why don't we work on doing something that means we all get to keep breathing and this bastard here gets to rest his nuts…' He winked at the tall, Barbarian looking man who was still rubbing himself awkwardly and wincing.

'Drop the weapons and we promise you we will let you live. All of you,' Kiras offered, glancing at the four warriors as rain splashed on their muddied cloaks. None of them looked like Southerners. Could be that they had nothing to do with the United Cities at all.

Still, the four gave one knowing look to each other and did as commanded, the fast bastard with the weird hair doing so last, his eyes fixed on Sly as he dropped his sword.

'That weren't too difficult,' Sly said with a big smile. He winked at the trembling youngster and snorted as the fool jerked back like he had been attacked. 'Now, what are four weird looking cunts like you lot doing out in the middle of a storm in this valley? Don't you know that times ain't too good here right now?'

The woman eyed him fiercely as Cray lowered the sword from her throat. She rubbed at her neck but kept her gaze fixed on Sly. 'My name is Amana. This is my brother Haadi.' She pointed at the frightened fellow, and then to the Barbarian and the quick warrior. 'And this here is Sigurd, and Sanada. We are fleeing Archania following the battle with the Red Sons. The city has fallen, so we were heading to pastures new.'

'And where might that be?' Sly asked, frowning at the mention of the fallen city. He wondered if Arden had played a part in yet another battle. There would be time to find out the information.

Amana sighed and pointed to the west, just past the

rolling hills and dark clouds. 'There is an estate to the west owned by a former general of the Archanian army. High walls. A plethora of weapons. And men and women trained to fight. There is no safer place in the United Cities right now. Sigurd and Sanada will be offering their blades in return for food and shelter. My brother and I will be heading farther west to the island of Norland. The people there have vowed to keep from the battle to come. Seems like as good a place as any.'

Kiras raised her eyebrows questioningly at Sly who shrugged and tilted his head, looking back at Amana. 'If you're right, then it looks like we're heading in the same direction.' He glanced over his shoulder to see a stream of the Hillheim refugees heading down the hill towards them, fronted by a waving Danil. 'This place better be big. We're bringing some guests for this infamous general…'

The Southerners sure loved their walls. The estate looked bigger than some towns Sly had wandered in. The high stone walls ran around the estate, even on the side looking out to the sea to the west. Sly listened to the crashing of the waves against the rocks and then gazed up at the wall in front. Five guards dressed in rusting mail and fur lined cloaks peered down, spears in hand as they watched on with caution. The people of Hillheim joined Sly and the others at the gate, waiting patiently and praying that this would be their salvation as a small group splintered off towards the coast and the chance at crossing the sea to Norland.

Sly ignored the sound of coughing and worried whispers amongst the crowd that warned of more people suffering from Vald Sickness. These people had been through enough without more of them dropping like flies. Morale was low and Sly had seen enough battles decided before a sword was drawn to know of the importance of morale.

'They're opening the gate…' Danil said, drawing a wince from Sly as he turned to face the warrior and caught sight of the yellowing bruise around his right eye. Still, most folk had come off worse in the battle. Sly still fought to hide a limp from his twisted ankle.

'No shit. Glad that eye is still working,' Sly snapped, not in the best of moods. He didn't fancy heading behind walls, but he knew it was the only option for them now.

'I got two, anyway.'

'One's enough. Socket managed well enough for countless cycles. That one-eyed bastard saw better than most.'

'Still,' Danil said, rubbing his eye gingerly, 'I'd be happier with the two.'

Kiras was the first to march silently through the gate. Back straight, head held high, she stepped into the estate like she owned the place. Sly spat and slapped Danil on the back, nearly knocking the smaller warrior over, before following her. Cray was next, then the motley group by the river. Danil waved to the people of Hillheim, gesturing to them to follow and so they did. The horde of Hillheim citizens ambled as one, muttering to one another and giving worried glances up at the battlements of the high walls and the grim faces that stared back down.

'Damn place looks like a fucking town from the Borderlands,' Sly muttered to Cray as they walked forwards along the stone path that wound its way towards the centre of the estate. 'You think one person owns all of this?'

His friend shrugged, keeping a watchful eye on the soldiers either side of the refugees. 'Why not? We've seen stranger things.'

Sly had to admit that was true enough. Seen far too much over the last cycle, that was certain.

Inside the walls, Sly scanned the stone statues of muscular, nude men in various poses, and armoured men and women striking heroic poses. He glanced at the perfectly trimmed hedges running a labyrinth to his right beyond the watching soldiers. There were a few workers out, even in the constant rain. They gave the passing people a quick glance before continuing with their work, watching the various animals – the cows, sheep, and pigs. They whistled for dogs to come back when distracted and one woman waved out with a beaming smile as she tended to the horses housed in what looked like newly built stables judging by the lack of paint. A few of the group waved back but Sly just grunted and moved on, uneasy with the flanking guards.

The ground suddenly shook, frightening all of the people in the estate. Just a mild tremor. Sly thought they would be used to it by now but maybe that was just a fool's hope. Panicked looks crossed the group and women dragged their children closer to them, as though clutching desperately would keep them from harm. He saw Cray cast a nervous glance over his shoulder towards his wife and daughter, nodding at them as if to say, *it is okay. You are safe.* Sly didn't have anyone to check up on. Unbidden, Frida's cold, pale, blood-speckled face shot into his mind. He shook the cold feeling seeping through him away and blew out his cheeks. Instead, he focused on what was before him.

With a nudge, he signalled the strange-haired warrior he had almost killed. 'So, what's a general doing out here when the United Cities of Archania is fighting a war?'

Sanada smiled wryly and edged closer, keeping his voice low so as not to be heard by the others. 'General Grey served with distinction when leading under King

Mikkael. King Asher wasn't much a fan of the old guy, however. Mason D'Argio even less so. The general was sent packing following his useless handling of the rebellion.

'Still, not many folks would mind being sent to retire to this estate. Workers to look after the place. Your own land and a view of the sea. Some people claim that this is the oldest building in the United Cities other than a couple in the centre of Archania. King Borris himself used to host parties here.'

Sly hadn't a fucking clue who King Borris was and he didn't give a shit. 'Sounds interesting,' he replied, unable to keep the sarcasm from his voice.

'Hey, you asked,' Sanada laughed, raising his palms in defence. 'This is a strange place with strange rules. There is no place like the North.'

Sly growled. 'This ain't the North. Not really.' He inclined his head towards Sanada, grabbing his attention with the gesture. 'What about you, where you from? Never seen someone with your…' he struggled to find the right words, 'look.'

Sanada smirked. 'East. Very east…'

'Like the Empire?'

The warrior sucked his teeth and shook his head. 'Farther than the Empire. Their shadow has yet to fall upon my people, though that may only be a matter of time.'

'Then why are you here?'

Sanada's face dropped, the playful humour dripping away with Sly's question. His mouth opened but no words came, as though he wished to answer but didn't have the words. A moment later, he finally managed to reply. 'I am in exile from my home and my people. I can only return once I am confident that I will not be a disgrace to those I care for.'

'How you gonna do that?'

'I have yet to find an answer to that question…'

'No need to ask where he is from,' Sly chuckled, motioning to the Barbarian deep in conversation with one Danil who had to crane his neck to look into the man's eyes.

'Sigurd was born beyond the Borderlands but he was raised in Starik. A loyal man. And a great warrior,' Sanada claimed.

'Aye, I'm sure he'll come in handy in the days to come.'

The building in the centre of the estate was covered in creeper and lush greenery. The balconies pulled out from various windows across the wide building were filled to the brim with a myriad of colourful plants and flowers. The building itself rose at least five levels, tall enough for Sly to wonder what made this any different to a palace other than the fact a king or queen did not live there. Out front, the stone path widened and transitioned to a large semi-circular collection of small salmon pink stones that crushed under his muddy boots. The rainwater splashed down the angled roof and fell to purposely built gutters that led the water away and down what looked like two large holes either side of the building, carrying the water away out of sight. Sly's head hurt as he struggled to take in all of what his eyes attempted to show him. Grey gargoyles perched on the middle level of the building, mouths wide open and wings spread ready for action.

'You sure this is just a house for a general?' he asked Sanada.

'Some of the decoration and small details are the work of Lord Tamir, a council member recently deceased. A traitor, some claimed. It is odd that General Grey has decided to keep such features following the man's disgrace.'

'Perhaps the general doesn't see it as disgrace,' Sly shrugged. 'Each man has his reasons for doing what he does. What did this Lord Tamir do?'

Sanada narrowed his eyes. 'Apparently he was the one who incited the rebellion.'

Sly scoffed and nodded appreciatively. 'That guy must have had some balls the size of the moon! I was there when it happened. Bunch of peasants starting fires and waiting to be killed by the soldiers. That wasn't a rebellion. Just a bunch of disgruntled folks getting angry – like a dog barking at its master.'

'Perhaps Tamir thought the dog would have more of a bite.'

Sly entered the mammoth house flanked only by Kiras and Cray. The others had agreed to wait outside, allowing time for the warriors to discuss their current circumstances with the reclusive general. At first, it had seemed like a good idea. Then Sly saw the broad, ageing soldier marching down the winding, wide stairs to the east of the house, his magnificent moustache twitching with displeasure as his dull, grey eyes landed on the filthy warriors waiting at the foot of the stairs. He paused half-way down, bristling and turning an embarrassed shade of red.

'Which fool allowed passage through *my* estate to warriors who fought against the crown?' he cried, spit flying in his rage. 'If the Gods were just you would have died in the blaze!'

Sly took the outburst surprisingly well. As did the two Borderland warriors either side of him. Kiras barely twitched. Cray might even have fallen asleep.

'Calm yourself, Whiskers,' Sly said, raising a hand

smirking as he recognised the old fool he had seen in Archania. 'We're not here to fight. We want the same thing as you.'

'And what might that be?'

Kiras breathed heavily and stepped forward, drawing the old warrior's gaze. 'Not to die. And, perhaps, save some people while we're doing it.'

The general peered down from the stairs, the blood slowly draining from his cheeks as he calmed down, the bluster fading away as he looked at the weary warriors standing at the bottom of his stairs.

'Look, Whiskers,' Sly said, sniffing and running a hand across his mouth. 'Whatever shit your people and ours have had in the past, it's nothing compared to what's coming. You're a fighter. We're fighters. The people waiting outside are not. Let's sort them out, then we can work out a plan where the least people die. Or at least those who don't deserve it. What d'you say?' he shrugged, too tired to think of any fancy words for the old general.

He could see the conflict on Grey's face as the old soldier mulled over the words and the possibilities before him. 'I think that sounds like a decent idea. Tell your people they can enter. I'll have rooms prepared and food brought to them – though things are scarce and they may wish for the comforts of their home.'

Sly scanned the posh, ornate furnishings of the mansion and held back a mocking laugh. The people of Hillheim would feel as though they had died and gone to the halls of their ancestors just by entering this lavish reception. Discomfort would not be the issue, no matter how crowded it became.

'Sounds like a plan, Whiskers. Now, where do I go for piss?'

HOME

Home.

A word that meant different things to different people.

To some it was the building they were raised in. To others it was a land they were proud of, somewhere they felt they belonged. Some would claim it was more than that, a people they were connected to that had no link to a physical domain. But as Katerina Kane stood atop Hangman's Hill and peered down at the ruins of Archania, she knew that she was looking down at the death of what she knew as her home.

The walls were broken, no longer offering any kind of resistance to any outsiders hoping to gain entry into the capital.

There were no soldiers standing on battlements to greet her as she made her way across the fields and the shell-shocked Archanians were sheltering in makeshift homes outside of the crumbling city walls. Their eyes stared but Kane could tell they were unseeing as she passed them, their vision lost in the past and focused on something so horrific that Kane could walk right up to them and hit them in the face and she doubted they would flinch. There were bruises, cuts, and many other indicators that the people of Archania had been involved in recent conflict. A few of the men and women wore torn and ragged red cloaks that she recognised all too well – the cloaks of the Red Sons. She frantically scanned the battered people caught outside of the city, unsure if she wished to find her son or not. Rows of red cloaks had been used to cover bodies of the dead that had not yet been buried or burned. Unbidden, a thought flashed into her mind that one of the bodies could be that of her only son, Drayke. The last link between her and Braego. She shoved the thought from her mind but knew that its shadow would linger at the back like an unwanted guest refusing to leave a home it had no right to be inside.

She knelt beside the mounds of red and pulled a cloak slowly aside. She jerked back, covering her nose and mouth as her eyes caught sight of the charred body beneath. She had seen such work before, of course. Mason and his men and women had burned those deemed to have offended their God of Light, offering their souls to the heavens by lighting up the poor, unfortunate bastards they had caught. Lord Tamir had died in such a way. The proud councillor had fought for a better future for the United Cities of Archania, a future where people could be free to think and act as they wished without constantly glancing over their shoulders and trembling at every shadow in the street, wondering if that night would be their last before being hauled down to the dungeons.

When Kane had worked, she had been proud to defend the weak and prevent those who broke the law from causing any harm. Time had twisted her views on justice. She wondered if some looked upon her in the same way she had looked at Mason D'Argio and his sickening methods.

No. They wouldn't. She had acted in the best interests of the kingdom. Mason was cruel and enjoyed the suffering of others. That was something Kane would never accept.

'It's the same as Darakeche.' Kane stood upon hearing Dina's words. The woman stared off into the smoking ruins of the city, pointing at the destruction. 'Could it be the same army that did this?'

Kane rubbed her hands together and headed towards the city, holding back the nausea threatening to overwhelm her. Her stomach twisted in knots as she walked under the crumbling archway where the city's name and flag had once been as much a part of the city as the royal family themselves. She glanced down at the flag, its colours almost unrecognisable other than a small patch in the corner. It was soaked and dampened by the rainfall, turned a dark shade of brown by the filth of the city and ripped in numerous places. A fitting image for the once proud nation she thought as she stepped over the flag and continued farther into the capital.

It was like walking through a nightmare. There were just enough landmarks and fragments that she recognised for her to know that this was indeed her home, the place she had worked so hard for so long to defend and improve. But it was as though the details were now all blurred, her vision tainted. She recognised statues in the streets but their faces were now soaked in red with pieces missing for some. A building she could have sworn was once a theatre was now completely left open to the elements, its roof somehow blown off with most of the wood splintered and stone smashed to pieces and lying in the street. Not all of the bodies had been moved, she noticed. Some were left to wither and decay on their own, proof of the battle that had taken place in the heart of the United Cities, the heart of the North.

As she progressed through the destruction, her three companions keeping silent with their scarves pulled high over their heads to avoid any confrontation, she found the presence of living soldiers increased. Soldiers aligned with the Empire judging by their white cloaks that turned a muddy colour as they trailed through the dirty puddles scattered throughout the streets.

'Kat...' a voice muttered from the shadows of the city. She twisted towards the call of her name, eager to greet a friend, or even just a familiar face in the place she had once called home. 'Katerina Kane, as I live and breathe...'

Kane bolted towards a short, weak figure holding his right arm as though it had been knocked from its shoulder socket. She was gentle as she placed an arm around Inspector Marlin and smiled fondly at her old colleague.

'Marlin, my dear friend,' she said, unable to keep a smile from her face, even considering the grim surroundings. She had given the man up for dead a long time ago. He had taken over her role at the most difficult of times and she had believed him to be long gone following the changes in regime in the United Cities. 'I am embarrassed to say that it is a shock to see you amongst the living.' Her cheeks felt hot as the blood rushed to them, turning them a deep shade of red.

Marlin smiled weakly and ran a hand over his balding head. 'There have been times when I struggled to decide if being amongst the living was a good thing or not for a man in my position. Archania is not the place you left, Kat. Even in such a short time, the world has gripped tightly and shook the kingdom with all its might before placing it down and leaving the pieces scattered and confused.'

'But alive. It is a good sign that you are alive, dear Marlin,' Kane uttered defiantly. She watched the light fade from his eyes and felt her own joy drain at the slow shake of his head. 'Your family…' she said, catching on at last.

'Vald Sickness, apparently. Never used a drop of magic in their lives. Wife and the two kids.' His voice cracked but he waved away Kane's supportive hand. 'They are at peace now. I will see my three beautiful darlings in the next life, whenever the Gods deem it time.'

'Gods? As in plural,' Kane murmured, glancing warily over her shoulder for any who may be listening. 'So I assume you are not on board with Mason and his teachings.'

A dark shadow crossed Marlin's face at the mention of Mason. He leaned closer to Kane, tears glistening in his eyes as he spat back his response, a fire lighting in his belly. 'Gods. Nothing would make me follow that madman. He is a devil sent from the hells to test us all. I saw it myself Kat. He set everything aflame, used cursed magic to destroy this city and the army wishing to liberate us all. Prince Drayke, he had promised to guide us to freedom.'

'Drayke,' Kane echoed, chest tight at the mention of her son. 'What happened with him?'

Marlin shrugged. 'I'm sorry Kat, I know you were close. Lost his arm in the battle. Saw him clutching it in agony myself. Some have claimed he died of the blood loss. I didn't see him again though so I can't give credence to those claims. Didn't look in a good way though. Pale as a ghost. I heard rumours though…'

Kane rocked back on her heels, stumbling and struggling to regain her composure. She breathed out rapidly through her dry lips, not feeling the supportive hand against her shoulder as she thought of her son in the heat and chaos of battle.

'Are you okay? Need a sit down?' Marlin, for the first time in their conversation, seemed to spot the three shadowy figures waiting patiently for Kane. 'Perhaps you and your new friends would wish for somewhere to rest for the moment. Mason won't find you here. He is locked up in the palace, waiting for something apparently. He sits on that throne all day, every day. The servants said that he hasn't moved. Just laughs like a maniac and speaks to himself.'

Marlin led them through twisted alleyways towards the edge of the city, away from what had once been the more populated areas of Archania and to the areas of The Upper City that Kane had preferred. Peaceful, quiet, serene places where people called out to one another with a smile on their faces and where everyone knew their neighbours' names. The buildings here were mainly untouched. The low, mudbrick homes were inspired by those found farther to the south in the lands by the Inland Sea closer to the Heartlands. They had their own character and had always felt separate to the exuberant architecture seen in the heart of the Upper City. The outskirts of the city had a slower pace and less of the hubris found in the centre and Kane thought it was all the better for it. Less chaotic than the Lower City and humbler than much of the Upper City, it was a place that suited the understated Marlin.

'You'll have to excuse the mess,' he said to his guests as he pushed open his unlocked front door, leading them into a wide, open room with a low ceiling. Copious amounts of books littered the room, covering the mosaic

269

floor and lying open over the simple, brown sofa and armchair. He hurriedly cleared some clothes and books from the furniture and gave an embarrassed smile to the four women, motioning for them to take a seat as he rushed away with the items and out of sight through an open door leading to another room in the back.

Abhia and Sabha took a seat, scowling as they scanned the room, searching for any sign of danger. Dina circled the room with a predator's gaze, running a finger along the wooden shelves and peering from beneath her heavy brows as she inspected her host's room.

Kane sighed, letting the woman get on with her inspection as she dropped into the armchair, coughing as a wave of dust shot up into the air around her.

'Can we trust this, Marlin?' Sabha asked, face wrinkled in disgust as she watched Kane cough and wave the dust away.

Kane cleared her throat and nodded, attempting to rid herself of the itch at the back of her throat. 'He is a good man. I have known him for many cycles and he has never done anything to suggest that he cannot be trusted. Though, as always, we will stay on guard, just in case. A lot has happened since I was last in this city.'

'A good plan,' Dina agreed, finally sitting alongside her fellow soldiers. 'We must stay sharp as the sword of justice and not get distracted whilst we stay here. Though,' she glanced around the room, evidently displeased with her surroundings, 'I doubt we will get too comfortable.'

Marlin rushed back into the room with a forced smile on his panicked, red face. He carried a simple wooden chair in his hands and placed it opposite Kane so that he could see all four of the women. It was just like him to take the most uncomfortable seat in the room and care for his guests.

270

'Erm… where are my manners?' he wondered aloud, slapping his forehead. 'Would any of you ladies like a drink?'

'Just water for the three of us please,' Dina answered crisply, not attempting to hide her suspicion.

'Same,' Kane added with a reassuring nod as Marlin escaped the room once more.

He returned soon after with four glasses of water on a tray and placed it down on the table before the women, having to nudge more dusty books away before the space could be found.

'What happened here?' Dina asked, straight to the point, not even waiting for Marlin to fall back into his seat.

The nervous inspector paused halfway between sitting and standing, caught off guard by the question. He finally dropped into his seat and sighed, pulling his spectacles off his face and giving them a quick wipe over with his shirt. Pleased that they were clean enough, he placed them back on the bridge of his nose and glanced over at the four women staring at him. He looked at Kane last, eyes questioning her silently.

'This is Dina, Sabha, and Abhia,' Kane informed him, gesturing to the three warriors glaring at him. 'They have been escorting me home from the East. They are friends tasked with ensuring that no harm comes my way.'

Marin frowned. 'The East? Darakeche? The Empire? You don't look like you are from the islands if you pardon my assumption.'

'The Empire,' came Dina's confident and proud response, her chin rising slightly with her answer.

Marlin shrugged. 'Borders and lines in the sand have never meant much to me. If the honourable Katerina Kane can vouch for you then that is good enough for me.'

Kane nodded, touched by the man's complete confidence in her.

'It was odd standing behind the walls. Half of the soldiers were willing to defend the city against any kind of invasion. The other half had heard it was Prince Drayke leading the Red Sons and they were ready to open the gates wide and let the rightful ruler of this kingdom enter his home with a guard of honour.' Marlin rubbed his hands nervously together and looked at the three Eastern women on his sofa. 'But it wasn't just Archanians here. The Empire's forces have been in the city for some time. Mason had them under his thumb and rumours were that he had commanded them to kill without hesitation if any soldiers even looked like aiding the Red Sons.

'The confusion, the chaos. I've never seen anything like it. Three armies fought within the walls and most didn't seem to even know what they were fighting for. Brothers and sisters torn with indecision, swords and spears stabbing in backs and disorder of the kind that I never thought I would see in my day. I thought the Night of the Flames had been bad enough but that was a mere appetiser to what happened in the Upper City.'

'The destruction in the city, Marlin…' Kane started, struggling to find the words to convey the loss and horror she had felt as she wandered through the decimated streets. 'I've never seen damage on that scale. How long did the battle last?'

Marlin scoffed, biting his bottom lip as tears welled up in his tired eyes. 'Half a day. If that.'

Kane shook her head. 'What devilry could do such a thing?'

Marlin raised an eyebrow and notably looked at the three women who suddenly seemed uncomfortable in his presence. 'Mason D'Argio.'

'How?'

'I have no idea. I was shepherding the injured away to shelter, trying my best to calm the madness. I glanced up and Mason was glowing as though on fire. Next thing I know, the whole place lit up. I was blown to the ground, hit my head pretty hard too.' He rubbed at the back of his head and winced. 'When I sat up, it was madness. Most folk were aflame, still alive and crying out in pain as they struggling to survive. Men, women…' he gulped painfully. 'Even children. The flames were not picky. Red Sons. Eastern soldiers. Archanian soldiers and civilians. All burned. I was one of the lucky few not caught up in it. Fire everywhere.' His eyes stared at something in the distance as he focused on the horrors of the battle. Eventually, he lowered his head and pulled his spectacles away once more, wiping his sleeve across his glistening eyes.

'So much death. I have never liked the man; he never understood our way of doing things and the ease with which he could witness death and torture was uncomfortable from the beginning. Now he sits on the throne of my homeland and calls himself a king. He sent T'Chai to the Borderlands to claim them and I'm sure that won't be much of a struggle with such power. The madman will soon hold most of the North. I dread to think what is to come.'

'A resistance against something darker,' Kane said with conviction, leaning forwards towards her old ally. 'Against something more powerful than Mason D'Argio.'

Marlin shook his head in despair. 'You didn't see him, Kat. He wielded the power of the Gods. Whatever I have said about the Empire, it seems that they truly have power and it is a power we cannot resist.'

'We must be a beacon of light, Marlin. We must show people how to stand up and fight.'

'I'm tired, Kat. My family fled to Causrea under my orders to get them away from King Asher's madness before the sickness took hold. I thought he was a problem. He was a mere inconvenience when compared to this monster,' Marlin spat, rubbing his forehead gently. 'I don't want to be a beacon. These old eyes have seen enough. For once, I want the comforting blanket of darkness. I am not a fighter like you. I have done what I can to make this city safe but I have failed miserably. I don't have the energy for anything more. I just want to hide away in the shadows and pray that I never see anything again like the horrors that bastard inflicted on my home.'

Kane couldn't blame him. It was enough to push anyone to the brink. Out of the corner of her eye, she caught her three companions huddled together and whispering in their home dialect. Ignoring them for a moment, she looked back at the shaken Marlin.

'I am sorry for what you have been through my friend. I must ask you to remember one last thing. Prince Drayke, you said you had heard rumours?' She prepared herself for the answer, hardening her heart to stone in case Marlin's response was ready to break it and chuck it out into the decaying city around her. But there was a flicker of hope, a small spear of light shining through the canopy of darkness.

'The prince? Drayke did not fare well in the battle, I am afraid.' Marlin pursed his thin lips and sighed. 'But he made it out of the immediate devastation, well, was dragged out by those around him.'

Kane shot up from her seat, causing the nervous man to jump. 'Where is he Marlin? Where is Drayke?'

'The only place left to go. Causrea. The Republic of Causrea is known for having a strong stance against the Empire. All the survivors are heading there. Well, except the ones heading to Dustin Grey's estate.'

Kane hesitated and ran over that last comment, lost in confusion. 'Dustin? Why are people heading to Grey's estate?'

'High walls. Trained soldiers acting on his command. And a leader who actually has experience in battle. They see Dustin Grey as the last hope for Archania. Mason exiled him when Asher was still in charge and Grey has spent the time out of the city building his defences and preparing for war. Makes sense that folk want to head his way.'

Kane had always liked the general. A bit pompous and arrogant at times, but he was a man of honour. He was someone who could be relied on when the shit hit the wind and that was rare in these times.

'And what battle are they preparing for?'

'Once T'Chai heads back from the Borderlands with the rest of the soldiers, they'll head to Causrea and wipe that nation from the map. Grey is no fool. He knows that Mason won't let him sit there and live out the rest of his life by the sea with a bunch of followers who despise Mason and the Empire. They'll come for him and he will do his darndest to make sure he can put up a fight, even if it means accepting that the best he can gain is an honourable death.'

Kane mulled over Marlin's words. Her aim was to find her son and the chances were he was residing back in Causrea licking his wounds. Now it seemed that Causrea was next on Mason D'Argio's personal hit list. Her path was growing clearer.

'Looks like we have a choice,' Dina said, standing and pacing around the room, a determined look on her face as she turned to Kane. 'Causrea. Or Grey.'

'Grey will be small fry compared to Causrea. He can wait. Mason won't march on him yet and they need to wait for the army to return from the Borderlands. Anything you can do to hold him back? Thought you were meant to be on the same side?'

The shadow on Dina's face grew at the reminder. 'Mason and our Empress's relationship is…' She looked to her friends on the sofa for support.

'Complicated,' Abhia offered in support after a few moments silence.

'That is an understatement,' Sabha added with a roll of her eyes. 'Mason is acting outside of the boundaries set by the Empress. Since his daughter died, their strained relationship has only worsened.'

'That's a no then.' Kane tapped her fingers on her thigh and wracked her mind for any other options. 'What will she do once she finds out what he has done?'

The three Eastern warriors exchanged a dismissive glance before Dina spoke up. 'Honestly, there are bigger issues at play here. Mason will be dealt with when the time comes. Osiron is the true problem.'

'The Empress and Istari have their plan to deal with Osiron. We need to deal with Mason, otherwise more places will end up like Archania. Marlin,' she turned to the inspector and ran a tongue over her lips as a plan popped into her mind. 'Got a ship and crew ready to sail to Causrea?'

Marlin scratched his weak chin and thought about it for a moment before blowing out his cheeks and smiling. 'I reckon I can sort something out for tomorrow.'

'Today will be better. You ready for a little trip to the Republic of Causrea ladies?'

The Eastern warriors flashed their eyes. Sabha

cracked her knuckles whilst Abhia smashed a fist into her palm. Dina took a while to respond, watching as Kane walked over to her.

'We were tasked with helping you to find your son. If he is in Causrea, then that is our next destination.'

As the sun set in the west, dipping over the horizon line, Kane turned and looked back at the crumbling ruins of the place she called home. She promised herself that she would be back. She would return with her son and she would right the wrongs inflicted on Archania. Either that, or she would die trying.

It was mad to think that the home she had left only a few moons before had changed so much. A vibrant city burned to ashes and left to rot as a madman sat on the same throne that Mikkael had spent so many cycles on attempting to improve the United Cities of Archania. Time could be cruel. Mason D'Argio it seemed was crueller.

She walked down the steps below deck and found the corner that the slightly confused captain had shown her before leaving the city. Lying on the makeshift covers as light snoring from the other passengers filled the air around her, she wondered where Istari Vostor was sleeping tonight and if the grumpy warrior had made it to the South yet.

ECHOES OF THE PAST

The stench of decaying and burning flesh clung to Arden's nostrils and refused to let go. Sitting in the lake sheltered by the jagged black rocks of the cave, he attempted to forget about the destruction of Mughabir. The capital of Darakeche had been destroyed in mere moments. There was nothing that its soldiers, its citizens, or even its Sultan could have done to prevent the chaos. Arden had watched from afar as the warriors of Chaos overwhelmed the city, rushing forwards like a tsunami of blood and shadow and tearing into anything in its path. Fires had broken out across the city in the horrifying confusion of the battle and the beauty of Mughabir was now nothing but ash and dust. A ruined city of grief.

Osiron had stood close to Arden, keeping a close eye on proceedings with a reassuring hand on his shoulder when Arden felt as though it was all too much.

The screams had almost broken him. Just like back in the Borderlands, it wasn't killing soldiers. There were innocent people down there, men women, and children who could have gone on to live honest, eventful lives. But Arden knew Osiron's thoughts on the matter. To start again, to begin anew, Takaara needed a cleansing. Sacrifices had to be made.

Back in the cave, he lay back in the water and listened to the gentle lapping of the water against the rocks. With a long, slow breath, he pushed out the tension from his body and struggled to fall into nothingness, to numb himself from the visions flashing across his mind.

'You are struggling with the price to be paid, are you not?'

Arden opened his eyes but did not otherwise move at the sound of Osiron's voice. 'I've never enjoyed hurting people. In Mughabir, in the Borderlands, I watched so many people burn and die. I saw our army rip through flesh and leave bodies twitching, their guts spilled out onto the filthy streets.' Arden dropped his head beneath the water and for the briefest of moments, everything was peaceful as the steady rhythm of the gentle waves brought some relief. He returned to the surface and swallowed. 'Yeah,' he admitted, 'I'm struggling.'

He waded backwards through the water and then pushed himself upright, leaning back against the rocks and running his hands through his long, wet hair with a sigh.

Osiron lowered into the water and glided towards him. 'There has been something that I have been meaning to show you. You were lucky enough to live a different life to me, as difficult as it was in places. Let me show you the reasons for my decisions. Let me show you what happened, all those cycles ago. It is not pretty. But it will give you the backbone needed to carry this burden, Arden Leifhand.'

Arden studied those strange, black eyes and mulled over the offer. There was so much he did not know about

Osiron. So much that was missing. Perhaps this was what he needed to start seeing things like the God of Chaos. He nodded.

The room was dark. A single candle shone in the corner, casting light from its thin halo, offering just enough for a short, hunched figure to see the writing on the pages of a thick, dusty book in their hands. Arden moved forwards, each movement feeling as though he was wading through an avalanche of snow. He peered over the shoulder of the small figure and glanced at the strange writing in the book. The language was one that he couldn't read, though the pictures were clear enough. He could see an image of a glowing flame, rising higher and higher.

A moment later, the short reader placed the book open on the stone ground and stood, rubbing their hands together, their golden pupils glowing in the narrow light.

A mage. Just like Arden.

He watched as the child murmured something inaudible and waved their hands in the air. The frown on the child's face and the stomp of a foot against the ground informed Arden that something had not gone quite to plan.

The child took another steadying breath and calmed down, eyes closing. They flicked their long, dark hair out of their face and opened their shining eyes, staring intently with determination at the flame. Arden leapt back as best he could as the flame exploded, nearly blinding him as the child flew across the room, sliding across the ground and hitting a wall with a thud.

Eyebrows singed, hair all over the place and eyes wide open in shock, the child stared at the glowing flame that now lit up the cramped and empty room. Arden could see a narrow ladder running to the floor above but not much else. A crooked tower of strange books stood in the corner of the room but the child had no interest in that. Instead, they just focused on the colossal flame now lighting up the room.

'Gods be damned!' a voice screamed from above. The child spun in horror, staring with panic up at the hole in the ceiling where the ladder ran and shuffling back into the shadows of the corner.

A thin, wiry, tall figure dropped down the ladder and planted their bare feet on the floor, staring at the cowering child in the corner. The newcomer crept forward, tapping their long fingers against their hip and groaning.

'What. Have. I. Said?' he muttered menacingly, breathing heavily through his nostrils and cracking his head to the side. 'Magic is forbidden in this house. It is for the weak. I have made that abundantly clear to you in the past. So why in the hells are you spitting on my generosity by using the foul thing in my basement? Did you think I would not find out? I always find out...'

The child shook their head and wrapped their arms around their chest, attempting to look as small as possible.

'We took you in, we clothed you. We fed you. Only cowards and devils use magic. You know this. You have listened to my sermons each week. It seems another lesson must be taught...'

The tall man pulled out a sharp knife that glistened in the candlelight. 'Another scar to remind you of my message. Another scar to keep you on the right track. Remember, I do not enjoy this. I do this, as I know you can be better. You will thank me one day...'

Arden tried to move, to stand in the way and protect the child. He attempted to call out, to force the man to stop. But he couldn't.

The scene shifted with a scream into complete darkness and Arden felt a sense of despair and guilt for not being able to save the poor, defenceless child.

This time, Arden spotted a cloaked figure walking through the rain. It was warm, despite the weather, but the figure kept their hood pulled up and wrapped tight against their thin frame.

'Hey! Look who it is!' a voice called out from somewhere to the side. A heavy mist obscured Arden's view but he could see the fear on the person's face in front as they turned their bright, golden eyes in the same direction, fear and panic clearly on display.

With a thud, Arden spotted rocks flying through the air before hitting against the scared mage. They stumbled with the impact but kept on their feet, quickening their pace to escape the blows. But then Arden saw a huge, leering figure standing before the mage, blocking any escape route with their wide frame and leering at them with a face promising pain.

'Where do you think you are going, weirdo?' the brute asked, cracking his knuckles. Four other figures surrounding the mage, two men and two women, each holding some form of crude weapon. Rocks. Sticks. Even an axe.

The mage looked at them each in turn, fists clenched in defiance, but their eyes told the real story. Fear. They knew what was about to happen. This wasn't the first time.

'You deserve this, freak. You know that,' the big guy said to the mage, as though he were doing something helpful. Arden had seen this all before. He had been in that position. The odd one out. The different one. The one who stood out for all the wrong reasons. He knew the struggles associated with that pain. He knew the difficulties of the path that would send someone on. He knew the heartache ahead.

Again, he tried to step in to prevent the inevitable from happening, but it was as though an invisible wall had been erected in front of him, preventing him from moving.

He heard the crack as the first fist made contact with a jaw. He growled but could do nothing as the blows rained down, knocking the mage to the ground. Hit after hit followed, mixed in with laughter like the sound of barking dogs as the strikes pummelled the curled up victim on the ground.

'Rumours around the village say you wanna be a girl now. I can help you with that. My friend here has a sharp knife. It'll be quick! We can chop those parts right off...'

The mage's head glanced up, defiant and angry. 'I'm not a girl!'

The brute bristled and laughed at the futile response. 'Well, you're not a man, look at you... Not a woman either. What the fuck are you?'

'Something more…'

A boot to the face cut off anything else the mage wished to say.

It was as though he were watching scenes from his past. But this wasn't Arden's past. Osiron had wanted to show him something. Osiron had wanted to show Arden why they were so convinced that their actions were right and just, that their actions were in the best interests of Takaara.

Rage burst inside Arden and he roared uselessly. These were the people who need to be taught a lesson. They needed to be taught that people like him should not be messed with, people like this poor mage should not be messed with.

'Any of you scumbags in need of some light?'

Arden followed the confused gazes of the attackers as they turned to see a grinning woman heading their way. She checked her long, manicured nails and flicked her wavy hair back before offering a sparkling smile that shone in the pouring rain.

'What did you say?' the big attacker asked, marching towards her, rock in hand, his intent clear for all to see.

The woman just rolled her eyes and sighed. 'Never mind.' She clicked her fingers and each of the attackers erupted in flame, waving their arms and flailing wildly. They dropped to the ground, searching for puddles of filthy water in the hope of extinguishing the fire.

'What did we say about the fire, Elena?' an exasperated voice asked, entering the field of vision available for Arden; a young, attractive, dark-skinned male with a shaved head and rippling *muscles.*

'I can't remember, sometimes I zone out when you get into your lecture mode,' the woman responded feigning a yawn, clearly not bothered by the reprimand.

'Seriously Zeek, she knows what she is doing,' a third person added. This one had glowing brown skin and the shadow of a dark beard on his young face. 'They won't die.'

'I know Harish, but we can be more careful,' Zeek warned. He knelt and checked on the trembling mage. 'Come on, Osiron. Those bastards won't hurt you anymore.'

Arden watched the fiery attackers flee with their tails clearly between their legs, racing away without a backwards glance. He felt a measure of satisfaction at their pain. Justice had been done.

The mage stood gingerly, bruises clear on their jawline and eyes. They pushed away the helping hands of Zeek and trudged away. 'I told you before. I don't need your help.'

'Si…' Elena called after the mage. 'Osiron! You just had the shit kicked out of you again. Sooner or later, that power is going to explode and a lot of people will get hurt. We can help you. We have to help you. Lives depend on it.'

Osiron turned and threw their hands up in the air in exasperation, frustration clear on their young face. 'You don't get it. I've been fending these hateful idiots off all my life. I can control it. I have been controlling it.'

'There is a lot of power being bottled up in there, Osiron…' Harish warned. 'How much longer can you control it?'

'As long as I have to. Magic is for cowards and devils. I'm neither. If that means taking a beating every once in a while, then so be it. I'm not stooping to your levels. So, why don't you just all leave me alone!'

Harish made to follow as Osiron stomped away but Zeek grabbed his shoulder, shaking his head. 'Leave them. They will come when the time is right. We cannot ask too much.'

'But we need a fourth…'

'When the time is right…' Elena agreed, much to Harish's dismay.

The world changed again and Arden stumbled into a rocky valley soaked in the light of the midday sun. Four figures in cloaks stood together a short distance away, young mages grinning at one another as they reached out and grabbed each other's hands to form a small circle.

'You sure about this?' Osiron asked, looking more nervous than the other three.

'When is he ever sure about anything?' Elena chuckled, winking at the playful jibe towards the handsome Zeek.

'We have each other. That makes me certain this will work.'

'That doesn't exactly fill me with confidence…' Harish said with a nudge to Zeek.

'It'll work,' Elena added, the playful tone leaving her voice which was instead filled with a strength and determination that coursed through the friends. 'I know it will work.'

They exchanged nervous but determined glances, squeezing the hands of the people on either side of them. Arden could see the fear in Osiron's eyes as they landed on Elena, pleading with her for support. She squeezed his hand gently once more and offered a grim nod. There was no turning back now.

'We have spoken the words. We have pulled the magic from the land,' Zeek reminded them. The sky blackened, forks of lightning flashing wild and manic as if on cue. 'If this works, we will have all the time in the world to reshape this world, to burn away the imperfections and to bring order to what is too chaotic to exist. We can rule Takaara and with the power we wield, we can make this entire world a better place.' He turned to Osiron, eyes tightening. 'A world where being different doesn't mean a fight every day. This is what we *have dreamed of. We can become Gods…'*

Arden could clearly see the nerves on the faces of the three friends listening to Zeek's heretical words. Whatever power they had, they had still been raised in a world taught to fear blasphemy, a world that warned against defying the Gods. Now, Zeek was claiming they could put themselves on that level, stand tall on that pedestal and shape an entire world in their image.

Thunder boomed and Osiron jumped, their hand caught tight in Elena and Harish's grips. Arden felt the rumble beneath his feet as vibrations worked their way through his feet and up his body like a snake twisting to the top of a tree.

'It is time…' Harish murmured, dark eyes glancing up at the sky as ash fell from the heavens as if in warning against what they were attempting to do. Warnings from above and below.

Forks of lightning cracked the sky in an endless display of fury as the thunder deafened the four mages clutching one another, their golden pupils glancing around in trepidation at the madness of the crying world. Even Arden felt his heart skip as he volume of the screaming world increased, his teeth chattering with the trembling world.

He watched in amazement as he four mages jerked, their bodies tensing and their faces forced up to stare into the blazing heavens, mouths wide open in screams of agony.

'Hold!' Zeek screamed through the pain. 'We are stronger than this!'

'It is too much, Zeek,' Elena argued, the skin tearing from her cheekbones as the energy of Takaara threatened to rip her apart.

Arden turned in horror to the others and saw that they too were being ripped piece by piece away from their human shell. Osiron had it the worst. The skin was peeling freely, leaving a bloody mess as the young mage wept, tears flying away with the deafening howl of the wind whipping past. Harish fared little better. Flesh and blood flew from the bone as he clenched his teeth and roared through the pain.

286

Elena focused on holding Osiron's hand, keeping her friend close as they wept.

But it was Zeek that Arden kept his eyes on. The mage's panicked eyes flickered from person to person and then down at the fingernails ripped away from his skin and tossed into the night. Zeek gave Harish a frantic look and a tilt of the head in apology. His friend caught the look and shook his head violently.

'No. No, no, no, no, no! Don't you dare, Zeek. Not now!'

Arden's mouth hung open as Zeek pulled away from his friends, escaping their clutches and breaking the link between them.

'Nooo!' Elena cried, futilely attempting to grab at Zeek as he left the circle.

A sound louder than anything Arden had ever heard erupted around them, an intense light blasted forth, blinding the mages so that he couldn't see or hear anything.

Eyes shut tight and ears ringing, Arden felt a painful pulsing in his mind, as though his brain was threatening to burst out from his skull.

'It will pass.' Osiron. The voice Arden knew so well. 'This is the last thing I wish for you to see.'

Arden kept his eyes shut for some time, even as the ringing died down and the flashing lights of reds, blues and greens faded behind his eyelids. His body was trembling with whatever he had just experienced. Eventually, he opened one eye with caution, fearful of what he might find.

But there was only darkness.

Opening his eyes fully, he searched for something, anything. But there was nothing.

A sobbing noise started to his right. He followed the noise, not knowing what else he could do. A gentle light burst forth. Blue and glowing. It lit up a monstrous face. The skin had torn away from the skull leaving a bloody mess. The scared eyes were a panicked, bloodshot red and the gold had faded from the pupils to leave a blackness darker than the night sky.

Osiron wept, rocking back and forth in the pale blue light.

'*Zeek. Harish. Elena…' they muttered like a mantra in the darkness. 'Please. Somebody. I'm all alone. Please help me…'*

Arden wished he could help the young mage. He wished he could clean their wounds and hold them close, to tell them that he would get them out of here, that he would be able to return them to their friends. But he couldn't. Osiron was alone and would be for some time. This had all happened so very long ago and there was no escaping from the past.

'How long did you sit in the darkness?' he asked, fearing the answer.

'Centuries. The first few cycles were the most difficult. My mind still thought my body needed healing. And food. And drink. And air. The pain was relentless. My body crying out for what it felt I needed. I choked. I starved. I withered. Every second was agony.'

'What changed?'

'Nothing. I still feel that pain. But now, I have a reason to move on past it. I have the others who are lost on that plane to help. They must not suffer in the way that I did. They must return to Takaara before they can rest. That is why what we do is so important, Arden Leifhand. That is why I push so hard.'

Osiron wiped the tears rolling down Arden's cheeks with the back of their hand. Their beautiful, dark eyes looked on with pity as Arden sniffed and wrapped his arms around his own body.

'Why did Zeek let go? Why did he break the hold?'

Osiron licked their dark lips and puffed out their

cheeks gently. 'I'm not sure. I spent countless cycles pondering that very mystery. He had convinced us all that we would become Gods, that he could lead us to a new world. But when the time arrived to be brave and be strong, he fled, and I ended up here, lost, frightened and alone. The others landed elsewhere and made it back to Takaara.'

'Why didn't you make it back?'

Osiron's eyes hardened. 'They prevented me from returning.'

Arden frowned. 'Why? They were your friends.'

'They feared retribution. I had time to think about their betrayal, and time to grow in power. They worried that I would seek revenge.'

'Were they right?'

'At first, no. But now...' Osiron's eyes burned with a frightening fury. 'I will shred the flesh from their bones and place them on a plane to wither away for eons to come. They will regret what they did to me. Will you help me?'

Arden thought of the sobbing, mutilated, young mage. He didn't need long to think about it. 'Until the very end. We cannot change the past. But we will make a better future.'

'You can pity them. You can wish that there was another way. But there is not. I have had more time than any other to decide what must be done – to work out a thousand different ways to accomplish my goals, but every time I land on just this one. Annihilation and rebirth. Like the phoenix of legend. The old cities and kingdoms must be taken down. They must be razed to the ground before we begin again.'

Arden nodded. 'It is the only way...'

LOYALTY

Returning to Hillheim left Arden disoriented. The clarity of the world was higher than the murky past that Osiron had guided him through. The flames burned brighter, the small cracks of night sky not obscured by cloud bore stunning stars twinkling high above, and the river of blood running down the streets shone redder than he remembered.

Dazed, he staggered down the streets, one hand holding his head as though it may fall from his shoulders at any moment. The remaining soldiers cast concerned looks his way but he just ignored them as he made his way through the ruins of the city, past the broken buildings and the pyres of the dead. Past the judging faces and glares from bloodshot eyes. Past the corpses left lying forgotten like litter in the streets.

He slammed into the door to what was formerly a faze den and pleasure house. Now it acted as the base for Arden's forces. The leaders of the Barbarians and Borderland soldiers who had not fled like cowards sat amongst the decadent furnishings and lounged around on long, wide sofas with a bottle of drink in their hands as they struggled to speak of anything other than the destruction of Hillheim. Arden had heard them talking. They thought he was a God come to life – an avatar sent to judge those who had not been behaving as they should. They spoke in whispered tones whenever he marched past and averted their eyes as if looking upon him would blind them.

Arden had been intrigued by it all at first. Now it was just irritating.

'Where is Herick?' he asked, pointing at one of the wild-haired Barbarians who had proudly claimed to lead his own unit of warriors from Strengheim, north-east of Torvield. The fool stuttered, eyes searching for another who may jump in and save him from answering. No luck. 'Tell me now or I will relieve you of your head and place it on a spike for all to see.'

That worked.

'Upstairs,' the idiot pointed towards the staircase. 'I think…'

'For your sake, I hope you are right. I have yet to meet someone capable of living without a head…'

He waited until he was out of sight of the warriors before wincing and running a hand down his face. He was hot. Sweat poured down the back of his neck as he trudged up the steps. Arden hadn't seen Herick for a few days now and that worried him. The leaders of each unit within his army should be reporting in daily. More even. They were on the edge of all-out war in Takaara and now was not the time for warriors to become loose arrows flying where they may in the middle of a crowded battle. Anyone could get hurt.

Herick was alone in the room once used as an office by the previous owner. His eyes were bloodshot and unfocused. A bottle of what smelled like whiskey rested lazily in his hand and a collection of maps curled up at the edges and held in place by various bottles lay sprawled out in whatever space was left on the desk in front of him. Candles in each corner of the room flickered in their sconces and a single lantern stood next to the leader of the Borderlands' bald head, casting his weary face in an orange glow.

His dark eyes peered up slowly as Arden entered the room.

'Your Majesty, what an honour to see you,' Herick slurred, puffing out some spit in thinly veiled disgust at his ruler.

Arden shielded his rage, holding it back until the time was right. 'Your Highness is the appropriate greeting. I am no king.'

Herick spluttered and leant back in his chair, the wood creaking with the movement. The whiskey bottle stayed attached to his hand and he took a wild swig, some of the liquid dropping down his beaded chin and onto his already stained shirt.

'Of course. I am not familiar with greeting princes or kings.'

'You seem overly familiar with that whiskey bottle.'

'This,' Herick said, raising the bottle and chuckling with glee, 'this bottle is my new best friend. Never lets me down.'

'Even best friends can let you down. That drink will be spewing from your guts come the dawn,' Arden warned.

'Perhaps…' Herick stroked the bottle with a gentle hand, staring at it with his wicked eyes like a lover. The sparkle faded as he placed the bottle onto one of the many maps and turned to face Arden. 'I wanted a stronger Borderlands. I wanted my boy back, my Baldor. By my side, we would have ruled over all of the North and no one would have been able to stand in our way. It would be our slice of the world, nothing more. A slice of land where men and women could live, fight, fuck, and die in whatever way they wished and then their spirits would enter the Hall of Ancestors with a jug raised in salute and a song in our hearts.'

Arden scoffed and licked his lips, eyes dropping to the maps.

'What are you on about Herick? You sound like any other drunkard sitting in a tavern in the warmth of his own piss, moaning as it slowly turns cold in his lap and looking for someone else to blame. If there is something you wish to say, spit it out.' Arden had no time for such foolery. He had a war to win.

Herick smirked darkly, his eyes narrowed as the candlelight shone on his bald pate. 'That T'Chai... he was an interesting fellow. He showed me things. The bastard was bleeding. Bleeding a lot, as a matter of fact...' He scratched his beard, his lips curling. 'I wanted to do as you asked, I really did. But then he showed me something. The bastard Easterner showed me something interesting indeed.'

It was time for Arden's eyes to narrow as he marched forward and took a seat at last, scraping the legs of the wooden chair across the floor and falling into it, all whilst his eyes stayed fixed on the leering Herick.

'What did he show you?' Regret lashed at him. He should have killed the Easterner himself and be done with it. It seemed leaving even the smallest tasks to others was a waste of time now.

'The end. He showed me the end.' Herick's eyes bore no trace of a lie. His pupils kept still and his voice even as he said the words.

'The end of what?'

'The end of days. The end of this world. He showed me fires sweeping the entirety of the North, melting the ice and drowning the people of my blood. He showed me nations in sand crumbling into dust and falling into nothing. He showed me great mountains breaking and dropping into oceans that swallowed them whole and he showed me the final fire that would dance across the world in a sickening display of destruction leaving nothing but ash and decay in its wake.'

'And what did you do once this prisoner was done with his *cheap tricks*?' Arden spat, a piercing pain building between his eyes.

'Poor bastard bled out. Would have let him go otherwise.'

Arden slammed a fist on the table, the bottles ringing with the impact. Herick seemed unconcerned, he just sat there, unflinching.

'What madness crept into that tiny mind of yours to disobey me? I commanded you to deal with him, not listen to his lies.'

Herick frowned, confused. 'It won't make no difference, *Your Highness…*' he chuckled darkly. 'What I saw was truth.' His eyes gleamed with the light of a madman wholly invested in his delirium. 'You and Osiron aren't going to build a world for anyone. You are just out here to end this one. You couldn't live in Takaara anymore so you are lighting the whole place up in spite like a child in the hope that no one else will be able to get what you crave so much.'

'Lies,' Arden whispered, fighting to keep his rage from spilling over.

'You both lived your lives and they ended. Yet you come back here for more when no one wants you. You've even managed to drive away the few people who actually wished to stand beside you.'

'Guard that forked tongue, Herick the Late or I will cut it from your mouth…'

Herick stood from his seat, cheeks red with drink and emotion. 'You and that Mason fella are gonna burn everything and leave nothing for the rest of us. Everything I worked for, everything that I sacrificed to get here. It is all just ash and smoke now. The north has died a harsh death and there will be no one left to pick up the pieces and put it back together again. You face defiance by killing those who speak out against you. Look at Sofia,' Herick cried, eyes glistening with tears. 'She could have been a useful ally but because she said no to using her people for your war, you sliced her head off and stuck it on a pole. You are no leader, *Your Highness*. You are just a kid playing at prince. And whether you win or lose, you will be left with nothing, just like the rest of us.'

Arden clenched his fists and felt the fires burning in his gut, rising wildly to the back of his throat.

'Hells, I'd rather be sitting here with Saul and that cunt was th—'

Herick's head flew across the room and landed with a thud that made Arden shudder.

He couldn't remember standing from his seat. Or grabbing the bloody sword in his hand.

'He was not loyal. He let that prisoner go and would have betrayed you had you not killed them,' Osiron said, voice echoing in Arden's mind. 'It is time for the others to make a choice. We do not need them. We have our own army. I am done with petty battles for scraps of land. It is time to burn the old world.'

Arden walked grimly over to the fallen head, blood still dripping from the wound. He picked the head up, ignoring the blood staining his clothes as he carried it out of the room. They all needed to learn a lesson.

And there was only one way to do it.

BAD DREAMS

Aleister grimaced and rolled his tongue across the back of his teeth, pushing against the bit of apple skin that had found itself jabbed next to a canine. Discovering the culprit, he pushed harder and stabbed a fingernail along his gum, pushing up until it was free from its toothy prison. He spat the skin onto the ground and soothed his sore gum with his tongue as he watched the men and women of the South move forwards in their lines patiently, waiting for their turn to grab the equipment available to them.

He glanced down at his hand and saw the wet, pink blood dripping on his finger.

'You need to look after yourself more,' his sister said with her all-knowing smirk as she marched over to him. He glanced down at her growing stomach and felt a sense of dread about what was to come. There was no hiding her condition now. It was both beautiful and terrifying.

'And you need to look after yourself *and* the little

one,' Aleister said as he embraced her, pulling her in tight with one arm and planting a kiss on her head. 'You stink of sweat.' He crinkled his nose and allowed the playful hit his sister shot him. 'Been sparring with Bathos this morning?'

'Of course I have.' She pulled away from her brother and joined him in casting an appraising look over the growing Southern forces marching through Ad-Alum. 'Can't expect anyone else to save us. This is one impressive army but we've always relied on our skill and wits. Thankfully, I was granted the wits in the family so I only need to hone my skill with a blade in the mornings.'

'Very funny, sis. Seriously, though,' he started, peering down at her belly and steeling himself as Ariel frowned, knowing what he was about to say and not liking it already. 'You need to take things slowly.' Instantly, he cut off her protests with calming sounds and raised palms, making it clear that he did not want this to descend into a fight. 'I'm just saying, women during pregnancy can be the strongest things on the planet and the most fragile. Taking care of that life inside you is important.'

'And saving the world from a hellish darkness is not?'

Aleister had no response to that. He stuttered and stammered, puffing out his cheeks before eventually admitting defeat.

'Look,' he finally said, trying a different angle and hoping for more success. 'I get that. Saving the world means saving the place where your little one will grow up and thrive and become as annoying as you are and pig-headed as Bathos.'

Ariel chuckled, her eyes lighting up at the thought.

'But this is unlike anything we've done before.' He hated seeing the light fade from his sister's eyes but it had to be done. 'We're stabbing in the dark and hoping we don't get hit ourselves. There are so many moving pieces of the puzzle that we can't tell what the picture is anymore. All we know is that there are some bad people out there that have to be stopped. And there are other ways you can help to do that. You don't have to dive headfirst towards the monster's jaw like the rest of us.'

Ariel wasn't angry as he had expected. He'd prepared for rage, for fury. Instead, wet eyes full of pity looked up at him with a sad smile as she raised a hand and cupped his face. She rubbed his cheek with her thumb and sniffed, wiping away the tears beginning to flow.

'How can I raise my child in a world where I stood back and let those I cared for risk their lives as I twiddled my thumbs and wondered if I would ever see them again? What example am I setting if I let others sacrifice themselves so that I can live out my happy, little life away from danger?'

'It's about staying alive, Ariel.'

'I know, Aleister. But alive means nothing if I'm not true to myself.' She dropped her hand from his face and sniffed, taking a deep breath and exhaling slowly. 'When my child enters this world, I want it to be the one which I have fought for.'

'How does Bathos feel about your decision?'

'He trusts me and loves me enough to know that this is what I will do, what I must do. Of course he would be happy if I stayed away from the battles, if I holed myself up somewhere away from danger. But he fell in love with the stubborn woman who ran towards danger when she knew it was the right thing to do. He understands me. I thought you did too...'

Aleister sighed and lowered his head, unable to

meet his sister's gaze. 'I understand.' He looked up and smiled weakly at his sister's piercing eyes. 'Truly. It just scares me.'

'Me too.' Ariel placed a protective hand on her belly. 'This whole situation scares the hells out of me. But we're not alone.' She swept a hand over the steadily moving forces of the South and grinned. 'It would be arrogant to assume that we are the only ones left to decide the fate of Takaara. And don't get me wrong, there have been times when your arrogance has rivalled the size of the stars, but this time, we are just one of the moving parts.'

Aleister raised a single eyebrow and scoffed, feeling playful enough to lighten the mood. 'Have you heard of the importance of the sword I wield? I think now is the perfect time to be arrogant…'

'Of course you do,' Ariel rolled her eyes and turned away. 'Get some rest brother, we leave at dawn.'

There was no rest for Aleister.

His dreams were lucid, running through the burning Lower City of Archania in a panic, searching for someone, for something and growing more agitated by the second as the flames rose higher and higher. Familiar buildings from his youth crumbled and fell around him. He raised a hand to block the blazing light from his eyes and he caught the writhing figure of Elder Morgan, trapped beneath burning, wooden beams, his agonised cries piercing through the sounds of the dying city.

Aleister rushed to save him but it was too late. The temple fell, crushing the old preacher who could only look at Aleister with eyes full of horror and betrayal. He jerked back as the ash and smoke choked the tight city streets, running along the cobbled street in the hope of finding what he was looking for. Squinting through the smoke, he thought he could see Katerina Kane guiding a group of kids away from the orphanage, heading towards the docks and safety. He followed but his legs were lead, each step feeling heavy and painful. He tried to cry out but his throat was raw and felt as though he had swallowed a thousand pins.

Coughing, he pushed on, almost blind with the smoke now covering the city. He closed his eyes, trusting his steps and the memory of his home in the hope of escaping the hell.

When he opened them, the sky was an odd, shimmering green as far as the eye could see. He found himself sitting on Hangman's Hill beneath a familiar tree. Peering down towards Archania, he could see that the city was still ablaze, the flames showing no signs of dying.

'A pity, isn't it? Not the greatest city, but there was beauty to be found in Archania.'

Aleister choked on his reply as he turned to the speaker and saw Ella casually sitting back with her hands behind her on the grass, her dark hair falling in waves down her pale face and those sparkling eyes staring down at the city. It was painful, physically painful to see her sitting there in all her beauty as their homeland burned away. His heart ached for her. He was slightly ashamed to admit that he cared not one jot for his home as those stunning eyes turned to him. She was his world and that was all that mattered right now. Everything else could burn if he could have just one more moment with her.

'Ella…'

She laughed, such a beautiful laugh that Aleister felt his heart heal and soar to new heights.

'This was always one of my favourite places in the world. A place to sit back and relax and realise that the bustling, crazy world down there was smaller than you'd think. Whenever times got too tough, I could always go for a ride and head here to clear the cobwebs from my mind. It never failed to work.'

'Ella, there is so much I need to talk to you about…'

'I know.' She took his hand in her own and he felt as though his body would fall apart into a dribbling mess of goo. 'You blame yourself for my death.'

He nodded, a thick lump growing in his throat. It was what had been playing on his mind ever since the Night of the Flames. Those around him, the people who he cared for, were dying and he wasn't able to do a damned thing about it.

'I shouldn't have fought Matthias. I shouldn't have done what I did.'

'But you did,' Ella replied, harsher than necessary but Aleister couldn't blame her for that. 'And there are no words that can change the past. There isn't enough power in apologies to take back what has happened. Even the gods themselves aren't capable of it.'

'So what can I do?' Aleister pleaded, growing desperate. 'How can I make things better?'

Ella shuffled closer to him and took his face in her hands, lowering his head so that she could kiss him gently before pushing him away again. 'You can't. But there may be a way to honour me, to continue what I started back in Archania.'

'Anything.'

'You will be leading the scouts out from the South tomorrow.' Aleister nodded and Ella continued. 'There will be a battle. Some will wish to use blood magic. Encourage them. It is vital that mages return the glory days of old. For too long have we waited in the shadows, treated as second-class citizens. Now we must step into the light and take what is rightfully ours.'

Aleister frowned. Such a simple task.

'That will be easy enough. I'm sorry that I can't do more, my love.'

Ella ran a hand through his hair. 'It's getting long again. Do me proud, Aleister. The fate of Takaara may depend on it.'

She kissed his cheek just as the green sky shifted to a deep blue and then back again. He thought nothing of it. This was a dream. Strange things happened in dreams, and here he was having one final conversation with his one, true love. He could put up with a little strange in return.

He woke covered in sweat, his shirt sticking tightly to his skin.

Dawn came and he was ready, waiting for the others to meet him at the gates of Ad-Alum.

'You not get much sleep?' Ife asked, yawning herself as she greeted him.

'I got enough.'

'Good, we have a long road ahead of us, and we'll need all the energy we can gather.'

*

'You seem more quiet than usual,' Bathos said, leaving Ariel to speak to some of the recruits she had befriended already on the journey as he easily met Aleister's pace. 'Anything you wanna talk about?'

'Just tired,' Aleister answered with a dash of honesty. 'Bad dreams.'

'I get that. Strange times. I never used to sleep well before battle. Too nervous. Still, should be a while before we see battle.'

'Mmm…' Aleister agreed, biting his tongue as Ella's warning popped into his mind.

Ife's knowing glance placed him on guard, her dark eyes piercing through his defences. 'Is there anything you wish to speak about?' She tilted her head and squinted at him, as though hoping she could see into his mind and pluck the information required for herself.

'I'm fine.' Aleister shook off the concern and pushed his hair back from his face. 'We have a big day ahead of us. You know, saving the world and all that…'

Bathos laughed and slammed him on the back, almost knocking him over. 'Just that small matter. Small steps. That's what we need to take. We'll be fine, as long as we are together.'

Aleister watched as Bathos winked and left, heading over to his pregnant wife and picking her up, swinging her in the air before planting a soft kiss on her lips. He took her hand and they walked together, side by side, smiling as though the world was good and safe. No one looking at the happy couple would have guessed that the world was being seriously threatened by a powerful being capable of complete destruction.

'Bathos may be easily brushed off with an empty smile and words, but that will not work with me,' Ife warned. 'Tell me, what is troubling you.'

'I wasn't lying,' Aleister argued. 'I have been having bad dreams.'

'So, tell me about these dreams then.'

Aleister chewed the inside of his cheek, observing the steady movement of the rows of soldiers marching away from Ad-Alum, a sombre cloud hanging over every person heading away from the comforts of the South and their home.

'I'm visited in dreams by someone close to me who I lost the Night of the Flames. I have seen people whose deaths are my fault. It feels that every time I close my eyes, I see the dead wishing to speak to me and remind me of everything I have done wrong, and to tell me of everything I must do to right those wrongs.

'Pretty dumb for a man who has spent his life fighting to start to worry about the ramifications of such actions. If I spent an hour of each day thinking about the people that I have wronged, then there would be nothing left for me to do with my life.'

Ife clicked her tongue against the roof of her mouth and smiled at him in a way that said she understood and that she knew what he was going though. 'Aleister Soulsbane. You have wronged many people in this life. The nature of being a warrior means that there will be more people you piss off than help. Or at least, it will seem that way. The people you have helped often don't even realise that it has happened. Whereas the people you fight against will remember your name until the day they die, or beyond as in some cases…'

'How does that help me?'

Ife shrugged. 'I'm not here to help you. You're a grown man who chose to fight to better the world. The burden of leadership and the burden of being a strong warrior means that you need broad shoulders capable of carrying the load. What I can do is tell you that there have been thousands of people who are alive today in better conditions because of you. You fight for what you believe is right, and that is more important than you realise. So many people fight for honour, for riches, for a name. You fight because you don't want people to grow up facing the difficulties you and your sister had to face. That should mean something.'

Aleister saluted some of the passing soldiers as they smiled and bowed their heads his way, tapping their hearts in greeting.

'You cannot right the wrongs of the past, if wrongs are what you truly believe they are. The past has happened and there is no escaping it. Don't you feel that Zeek and Harish wish for some power where they could travel back in time and prevent all of this madness from occurring? Of course, but even with the power they wield, they cannot do such a thing. We must learn from mistakes and grow, but to wallow in a pool of self-pity and regret will lead to drowning in it and that will mean that you are of no use to anyone.

'There are thousands of people who will suffer if we do not do what it right. Distractions from the past and feeling guilty will not help the people of the present, and the future of Takaara.'

'And are you sure that we are the people standing on the right side of history with this one?'

Ife's forehead creased, confusion clear in her eyes. 'Osiron wishes to burn this world and start a new one. If that doesn't give you an indication of right and wrong, then I don't know how else to explain it to you…'

Aleister exhaled and grimaced. 'That's not what I mean. It's just, I've yet to see a war where there is one side that is good and one side that is bad. Even with the Red Sons, there were some bastards on our side and there were good people that we killed, people who fought with honour. I just want to be clear about what is happening here.'

'There are good and bad on both sides,' Ife agreed. 'As always. But if Osiron and their Chaos army win the day, then Takaara is done for as we know it. If we defeat Osiron, then those who make it out alive can find a way to build a better world.'

'Isn't that just what Osiron has claimed they want?'

Ife paused, clearly knocked by the question. 'Our way doesn't involve the slaughtering of innocents.'

'But Zeek has sacrificed many of his people. How is it different?'

The former mage's face darkened, her brow furrowed in anger at the question. 'You know how that is different, Aleister. You spoke to those who willingly made that heroic sacrifice. It is a sacrifice that will shape the world for generations to come.'

'Look, I get it. I just don't want to be making the same mistakes as in the past. I want to do *better*.'

'Then do what must be done. Listen to those who are more experienced.' Ife knocked him on the head three times with her knuckles and smiled. 'And keep focused on the battles to come, not the ones in the past. You are a good guy. Know that and fight as though the lives of everyone in Takaara depend on you.'

Aleister nodded, throat tight with nerves. He could still see Ella's glistening eyes in his mind and hear her melodic voice playing out around him. 'Make sure Zeek stays in the city. I'll make sure the land is clear for the march. Just focus on keeping him in the city, I've no idea why, but it was important to the wise women and I trust their judgement.'

'They are usually right. I will speak with him. Time to go, Aleister Soulsbane. I know that you will do what is right.'

Ife kissed him on the forehead, standing on her tiptoes before pushing him away.

'I'll do what needs to be done here.'

'I know you will.'

PENANCE FOR MY SINS

The Republic of Causrea shone in the midday sun. White stone buildings glistened with the light streaming between the few clouds drifting across a stunning blue sky. The Republic sat in the enclosed bay to the west of Takaara, over four-hundred bridges across a multitude of islands and canals that made up the wondrous and unique republic. Ruled by the Council of Ten, Causrea was special in Takaara in that it was ruled by a group of peers and not a single man or woman. Katerina Kane smiled as the warm breeze hit her, a reminder of the good times she had spent there following the dark times of the Night of the Flames.

'I have to admit, I thought it would be some time before we saw each other again…'

Kane winked and offered a warm smile to Sara Guidice as the young, beautiful woman strolled towards her.

'It is as much a surprise to myself as it is to you.'

Sara's eyes roved across the group of women, her face darkening. 'My father...'

'Is safe,' Kane responded quickly, welcoming the relief on the younger woman's face. 'He has taken the decision to head south, believing it to be the best course of action for us all.'

'That stubborn fool is rarely wrong, I must trust him this time, even if I will be praying every day until he returns. Still, it is good to hear that he is still alive. I feared the worst when you both headed to the East.'

'The East is not as terrifying as you my imagine,' Dina said, prickly and annoyed.

'You can inform all of the innocent people who have burned due to the Empire's teachings that that is the case, then. I am sure they will disagree...'

'Now is perhaps not the best time to have such a discussion,' Kane said, wishing to cut off the boiling argument. 'Is there somewhere better we can go to discuss our next moves? The United Cities have been decimated. Causrea is in serious trouble if we sit here and argue amongst ourselves.'

Sara nodded but her face was stern and the shadow had not yet passed. 'Istari Vostor will know what he is doing. I might not like it, but he will know what he's doing.'

'He does. Trust him. In the meantime, Causrea needs to be prepared. The United Cities of Archania have been destroyed by Mason D'Argio, Osiron has decimated the Borderlands, and Causrea is next on the list of places to face the wrath of either of them. You have to get the army ready and move those who cannot fight away from the Republic.'

'And where will they go?'

Kane thought for a moment. Causrea sat on the

edge of the West. Farther west would mean taking a ship across the sea. South would mean hitting the volatile region of the Heartlands. North meant hitting the war bound region of the United Cities and the East had never been an option.

She sighed. 'I'm not sure. But war will come to Causrea. That is certain. Plans must be made.'

'They will be,' Sara assured her. 'We just need a bit more time.'

'Time that you don't have,' Dina butted in. 'Death will come to this republic. The quicker you move the people out of the city, the better it will be for your people. Soldiers, warriors, anyone who can hold a weapon, these are the people who must be allowed to stay in this strange water city. All others must be cleared away before war arrives.'

Sara looked for a moment as though she would argue with the Eastern warrior, but the shadow passed, much to Kane's relief. 'You are right, of course. We knew that we would not be able to just sit here and let the war pass us by. We have trained warriors for cycles to defend this place and they will be ready when the time comes.'

'And you think they will be able to withstand the forces of Chaos?' Abhia asked.

'They will have to, won't they?' Sara asked.

Kane could understand the fear in the woman's voice. How would anyone be able to be sure that they would withstand such a frightening army? She had seen the destruction caused by Mason D'Argio and his forces and from what Istari Vostor had said, Osiron's minions would be much more deadly than that.

'There is hope, Sara. Your father knows that. We just need to hold them back until the time comes that we can take the fight to them.'

311

Kane walked across the wooden boards of the Republic, taking in the fresh salt air and wondering what would be left after the battle that was sure to come. She studied the laughing faces of the men and women walking across the boards and joking with one another, grabbing some food or a drink with friends and lovers and enjoying he bright sunshine that always seemed to land on the fair Republic. She had not been able to protect her homeland, but she prayed that she would be able to do something for this beautiful land instead. It did not deserve to suffer the same fate.

'You like it here, don't you?' Dina said, more of a statement than a question. 'I can see it in the way you smile at the people you pass, the way your eyes sparkle in the sunlight.'

'I am happy here,' Kane admitted. 'The sunshine, the water, the smiles on the faces of those who live here. What is not to like?'

'Less sand than back in my homeland. But I can see why you like it here. There is a positivity here which was absent in the United Cities of Archania.'

Kane's face scrunched up as she thought of that last comment. 'The United Cities had been destroyed by your Empress's brother…'

Dina shrugged. 'Still, it was grim and grey. Nothing fun about that. Even if the whole land had been thriving, I doubt I would have enjoyed it there.'

Kane bit back a retort and swallowed back the automatic response, instead choosing a more diplomatic version. 'It is very grey in Archania. Out here, the world feels brighter. It seems like there is more hope than back in my homeland.'

'The sun does that. It brightens moods as well as

the world. It is strange, but it is true. The brighter the day, the brighter the mood. I have always found it to be true.'

'Perhaps you are right, Dina. Whatever the reason, I feel content in this land. And the people seem nice enough. How do Sabha and Abhia feel?'

Dina shook her head. 'Not keen on water. Neither can swim so this whole place feels like a death trap. They will be happier once we are back on the sands, or at least hard earth.'

Kane pondered that strange nugget of information. Back home, her grandfather would laugh and tell her how people would chuck their babes into the rivers and watch as their legs thrashed before pulling them back up. Archanian life was one surrounded by rivers, lakes and the sea, not an island but with a similar feel. To not be able to swim would be a death sentence. Many of her warmest memories were of splashing about in the lakes and rivers of her homeland.

Causrea had a small, but well-drilled army. Situated away from the volatile Heartlands and far enough from the Northern territories. Their army had rarely been used for anything more than minor issues in the few hundred cycles since the Republic of Causrea had formed. Kane had been fortunate enough to spend time early in her career studying their training. Each member of the army trained with ranged and close combat weapons. They also spent three moons of each cycle at sea, honing their sea warfare skills on sleek, fast ships to ensure that they would be prepared if any nation threatened them from their western flank. It was an army that had trained hard and consistently though it was also one which lacked the experience of being in the heat of battle.

The United Cities had an army that was constantly ready for battle. They were sent out on peacekeeping tasks throughout Norland and Starik and used to quell any disturbances in Archania herself. Some of the more daring soldiers were also given leave to travel into the Borderlands or to the Heartlands to gain more of an insight into the lands around them and the way they work. The soldiers that had done so had always returned to the capital with a tough skin and nerves of steel.

Though, Kane had to admit, not all of them did return. That was the risk of being a soldier.

The narrow streets were packed with joyous spectators watching a group of people rowing boats along the wide canal and under the elaborately decorated white, arched bridges the Republic was famous for. They cheered and hollered for their favourites as one woman dressed in a black and white striped shirt and dark trousers pushed her way into the lead, her beaming smile clear for all to see beneath her wide-brimmed hat.

Kane scanned the crowd instinctively, searching for any sign of trouble. The locals were happy enough, enjoying the bright sunshine and the attraction of the race. But there were others amongst the joyous faces who stood out. Others who, like her, seemed to be recently arrived in Causrea. She saw tired faces with dark yellow and green bruises. She saw black eyes and men and women limping as they eased themselves through the crowd to get a better look at the display. Finally, she saw one woman dressed in a thin, red cloak, the colour of blood.

The cloak of the Red Sons.

She found herself wildly looking across the crowd, hoping for some sign of her son. The cheers of the crowd as the race neared its conclusion were now distracting, pounding her head and forcing her to attempt to block out the loud noise. A soft hand touched her and she turned to see Sara peering at her with concern.

'Katerina, is there something amiss?'

Kat shook her head. 'I know there are many soldiers here who fought in the battle back home. I was wondering, have you seen Drayke? Prince Drayke.'

Sara nodded slowly. 'Follow me. I will take you to him.'

The hospital was a domed structure built near the centre of the city. It was a tall, white, stone building with coloured windows depicting scenes from the proud Republic's past. On any other day, Kane would have spent time admiring the beautiful, careful, and loving work that had been put into the stunning designs and the architecture of such a creation. But today, she was focused on only one thing. Seeing her son.

Dina, Abhia, and Sabha had chosen to wander through the glorious city and take in the sights as Sara led Kane away. There would be time to catch up with them later. Now, it was all about her son.

Sara led her through the wide corridors and tall, spacious rooms filled with beds. Kane noticed that many lying in the white beds were sweating as if with a fever. Some were convulsing wildly as plague doctors dressed in all white with black masks rushed around the room and tended to their patients.

'What kind of sickness is this?' she asked Sara.

'Vald Sickness is what most claim. A sickness often brought on by overuse of magic, or the use of magic by those who are not skilled enough to wield it.'

'But I thought that magic had fled the land following that infamous quake. How can this be Vald Sickness?'

Sara shrugged and sucked her teeth in defeat. 'No clue. Some feel that there is an imbalance in magic across

Takaara and that has led to this illness plaguing the land. We're not too sure yet, but we are looking at all of our options. The Council meet on it every day to discuss the next steps.'

'And what are the next steps?'

'Currently? Make those who are sick as comfortable as possible. Make a note of those who die and check to see if they were once magic users. We want to do more but we just aren't sure what the best thing is yet.'

Helpless. Kane could see how helpless Sara felt in that moment as she passed the sick and dying, leaving them to their strangely dressed doctors.

'Can it spread so easily that we must use plague doctors?' she asked.

'We do not wish to take any risks. The last time we had a deadly disease in Takaara it led to riots in the North and even more chaos in the Heartlands. We were lucky out here, but we wish to learn from the mistakes of others, as all great nations should.'

Kane couldn't argue with such logic. She remembered the terrible days of the plague. The sickness was one thing to contend with, but the mistrust and lack of love between the peoples of Archania is what almost ripped it apart. She recalled having to head out with teams of soldiers and members of the Archanian Watch. They would be tasked with putting down disturbances each night as the lack of faith in leadership grew. Pride in the Archanian royal family fell to an all-time low and it was only with the death of the queen and the slowing of the plague that the people of Archania once again felt united.

But the city never truly got over those dark days, she realised. Lines had been drawn. A divide was clear to see in all of the city. The rich and powerful had been able to

spread out amongst the spacious Upper City and stay in
their homes to shield themselves from the relentless march
of the disease. Those in the Lower City weren't as lucky.
Some claimed that over half of its population had fallen to
the plague. The rest hated the people across the wall and
those living on the hill. Some had even celebrated the
queen's death, a horrid thing for anyone to do.

Perhaps if Archania had taken precautions sooner
when the plague had first been identified in Takaara, then
maybe things would have turned out differently. She
wondered what her home would have looked like now if
that had happened. Would Mason have been able to creep
his way in from the shadows and whisper in a grieving
Mikkael's ear? Perhaps. Perhaps not. Such questions were as
useless as screaming at the sun to stop it shining. Futile
things that would only bring more pain and misery to those
who asked the questions.

The two women walked up a curving staircase to
the floor above, Kane sweating in the heat of the midday
sun. It was not quite as stifling as in the East, but still
exhausting for one who had been raised in the colder
climate of the North.

The next floor was quiet. Sara spoke briefly with a
woman dressed in a boxed, white hat tied around her neck
before nodding and marching down the corridor. Kane
followed. They stopped outside a black door, Sara's hand
on the handle as she stared intently at Kane.

'I will wait out here. Take as much time as you
need.'

Kane swallowed the growing lump in her throat
and nodded, unable to say anything. She stepped through
the door into a darkened room. Floor-to-ceiling curtains
blocked out the sun's light, leaving only a shard of it to
creep through a small gap where the curtains could not

reach. The red of the curtains filtered the light, giving the room and its single occupant an eerie look as Kane stepped farther into it.

'What do you want now?' a weary voice slurred. 'I thought I told you not to come here again. I thought I told you to leave me alone.'

Kane raised a hand to her mouth to cover the urge to gasp as she looked at her son. He turned, standing from his position on the bed, the effects of the battle in Archania clear for her to see.

'Drayke…' she croaked, staring at the stump below his left shoulder where his left arm was missing. 'What happened?'

Drayke chuckled darkly and glanced down at the space where his arm had once hung. 'Pretty easy to work that one out. A fierce battle. One swing of the sword and there it was, my arm spraying blood on the ground as the fires raged around me. I thought I was invincible,' he murmured. 'I thought that what I was doing was right and just. I thought that the Gods would be behind me, that they would back me and lead the Red Sons to victory so that I would sit on the throne that my father once ruled from. But it was not to be. Just the thoughts of a fool…'

Kane walked over to him, tears falling down her cheeks as she looked from the stump of his arm to his bloodshot eyes. The poor, young warrior looked lost and defeated. He had aged cycles since she had last fixed her eyes upon him, since she had been sent away from the Red Sons.

She slapped his face as hard as she could, catching him clean on the cheek and wiping away those weary puppy dog eyes in an instant.

She glared at her son and he stared back at her in

shock, holding his red cheek with his good hand.

'What was that for?' he screamed at her in disbelief.

'For being a fool and an idiot!' Kane shot back, feeling the rage inside her wipe away any feeling of pity for her son. 'Attempting to lock me up. Attacking Archania with those idiots. You're lucky you made it out in the state you are in. So many more people lost more than an arm, do you know that?'

Drayke dropped his head, clearly ashamed, his dark hair falling and covering his pale face. 'I know that. Do you know how many died because I attempted to take the city? They believed in me, they wanted me to take the throne.' He glanced up at Kane, tears in his red eyes. 'But I could never have prepared for what was to happen. Honestly, the flames came from nowhere. Mason, he is a devil incarnate and the Gods know it. We were winning the battle, they were retreating farther into the city. Then everything changed in an instant. I looked around me and friend and foe alike were ablaze. I don't even remember when I lost the arm…'

'That is what it is like in a battle, Drayke!' Kane cried, letting her emotions get the better of her. 'There is confusion and uncertainty. There are things that you cannot plan for. This is why it was foolish for you to rush in without more experienced fighters. Istari would have been a great help.'

'But he left,' Drayke spat, turning away.

Kane grabbed his shoulder and yanked him back, making sure he could see the rage in her eyes. 'He left because you made him, after he had won a battle for you. One that you may have very well lost!'

The anger and youthful defiance faded from the youngster as he slumped back onto the bed, shaking his head. 'I made mistakes.' He looked again at the stump on his shoulder and then back at Kane. 'Don't you think I realise that?'

The simmering rage drifted away from Kane as she took a seat beside her son. 'You live to fight another day. That makes you luckier than so many who stood beside you in Archania. You have the opportunity to right the wrongs of the past. That is rare, trust me.'

'What should I do?' Drayke asked, looking more like the young boy that Kane had watched grow in the palace than ever before. 'How do I make things right?'

Kane smiled and grabbed his face, staring intently into the eyes that were so like his father's. 'You keep fighting. You fight until your last breath. You set an example to others and you prove that you are the leader that they always wanted.'

'But the Red Sons are scattered now,' Drayke moaned. 'Their soldiers have fled to the four corners. They wish to find Aleister, Ariel and Bathos, their true leaders. The founders who gave them hope. They don't want me.'

'Then fuck them!' Kane screeched, laughing at the shocked expression on her son's face. 'Don't think about them. Think about what *you* can do. Takaara stands on the brink of annihilation. Do you think I give a shit if you have an army behind you? At some point every living being on this continent will have to make a choice. They can either help Takaara survive or doom it to oblivion. Your actions may affect them. Or they may not. The only thing you are in control of is what you can do. People spend so much of their time thinking about how others perceive them that they forget that they need to do things that make themselves feel pride. There is only so much you can do, my son. Make yourself proud and do what *you* think is right. In time, others will follow. That is what it means to be a good leader.'

Drayke stood and stretched his remaining arm, wincing with the effort. He stumbled, almost falling to the ground as a rumble rippled through the room.

Kane jumped to her feet, alert at the sudden disruption to the equilibrium. She caught her son on the second hit, ensuring that he did not fall to the ground as they each shared a dark, foreboding look. They had felt such tremors before. It was similar to the one that had ripped apart the Halls of Justice back in Archania.

'We need to head down,' Kane commanded. Drayke didn't need another moment to think on it. They raced from the room as the third tremor hit, Kane slamming into the frame of the door. She grabbed a concerned Drayke by the shoulder and shoved him in front of her, silently urging him to move forwards. She followed as best she could as the world lurched around her.

She took the stairs two at a time during a moment of peace, blocking out the screams from the hospital as she followed her son towards the exit. Drayke dropped to the floor as the hospital seemed to twist to the left. Kane grabbed at him and pulled him to his feet frantically.

'Come on' she yelled, holding him close as chaos reigned around her, patients and doctors all racing for the exit. The building began to collapse around them, stone breaking and dropping as the world cracked and opened.

The roar of the breaking of Causrea deafened her but she kept on with her goal, dragging a screaming Drayke away from the hospital. Cautiously, she glanced to her right and witnessed wooden planks crack and fall, swallowed by the blue sea. Her eyes widened as she caught a colossal wave on the horizon heading their way, clearly arching towards the doomed republic.

'Quickly Drayke,' she urged, not allowed him to see the danger heading their way. She turned away from the wave and pushed him towards the edge of the city, hoping that they would be protected in some way by the large buildings around them.

A roaring louder than anything Kane had ever heard filled the air, blocking out the frightened screams of the residents racing across the bridges and attempting to make it to higher ground in their panicked state.

'Run!' she heard a woman scream amongst the terror.

Without looking back, Kane rushed forwards, shoving Drayke and praying that they would be able to escape the impending horror.

Then the waves hit her.

She felt as though someone had slammed her against a brick wall, knocking all of the breath from her body, her ribs breaking instantly. She looked for Drayke who had been torn from her grasp but her vision darkened and filled with spots of light as she gasped for air, pulled beneath the raging waters that had overwhelmed the city. The water rose above her, pushing all around and fighting her as she tried to make it up to the surface for some air.

In amongst the clear water, she could see broken bits of wood and stone, the remains of buildings and planks shattered on impact by the brutality of the tidal wave. Bodies floated in the water, their arms hanging low without fight as Kane tried to move towards them and wake them from their slumber. But it was useless. The pull of the water was too strong. It ripped her away and blasted any life from her as she held a futile hand out to pull at the closest body to her. She felt caught in a whirlwind, body spinning with the rage of the water as it twisted and pulled her every way possible, disorientating her as she tried desperately to make

322

it to the surface and breathe the much-needed air.

She slammed against a wall with a thud and felt the air rush from her body, her bones feeling like jelly as they rattled and shook with the impact. Her head finally pushed above the surface and she breathed in, air pouring into her lungs in a last attempt at keeping her alive. She scanned the destruction for any sign of Drayke but it was a worthless task. Bloated bodies floated on the surface of the still rushing water. Some people were frantically keeping their head above water, tears in their eyes as they gulped the air around them. Others screamed in horror at the destruction around them, desperately searching for loved ones.

Next to her, Kane caught the rushing body of a local Causrean man. She grabbed at him, pulling him to the surface and marvelling as he spat out a stream of water and coughed, his body fighting against the horrors as he breathed in, trying his very best to stay alive.

'Thank you,' the man croaked. 'My son. Where is my son?' he asked, desperately looking around at the still streaming water covering the debris and destruction of what was once such a beautiful city.

Kane had nothing to offer the man. Her mouth opened and closed uselessly as she surveyed the sudden change to Causrea. Only moments before, she had marvelled at the beauty of the Republic. Now, all she could see was the blood filling the clear waters and the broken wood and stone of the city floating amongst the corpses. A lucky few men and women stood on some of the taller buildings, looking down at the horror and doing their best to drop ropes to the small number who had survived the attack from the sea.

With the slowing of the waves, Kane managed to drag herself up a broken window and up onto an abandoned staircase, trudging up the steps and out onto a roof that had been only slightly affected by the tsunami. Tearful men and women greeted her, all strangers. They hugged her and she embraced them like family, crying into their shoulders and staring into their eyes with joy that they had indeed survived the sudden attack.

Her eyes finally landed on a young man in the destruction.

Lying on the ground, Drayke coughed, shooting water out like a fountain from his lips as an elderly woman watched over him with a cautious hand on his chest, checking his heartbeat. Kane knelt beside her and placed a hand around her shoulder.

'I am his mother,' she said, accepting the hug from the woman and the frantic prayer of thanks offered.

She held his clammy face in her hands, ignoring the pain shooting throughout her old body and focused only her injured son. 'Drayke! Drayke! Please don't do this to me...'

He coughed and shook, chest shooting up with the effort. His breath came in shallow rasps as he spoke to her. 'I deserve this. This is punishment from the Gods. You know it. And I know it. A tidal wave of retribution for the sins I have committed.'

'Speak of the foolish Gods again and I will drown you myself, boy,' Kane scolded, trembling hands resting on her son. 'Rest now and we will make it out of here. You are alive, and that is all that matters.'

It took most of the day for Kane to wade through the chaotic scenes in the ruins of the once beautiful city. The waves were calm now, mocking her and making her question her sanity as she recalled the anger with which they had recently battered Causrea. She found Abhia sitting alone on the coast as panicked men and women continued the frantic search for loved ones and fought to free some of the survivors from the ruins. There was a stillness in the way Abhia sat and stared with ghostly eyes that unnerved Kane and caused her to pause before she rested a gentle hand on the poor woman's shoulder.

'Abhia...' she searched for the right words but each time she felt close, they escaped her grasp like water draining through her fingers.

'I watched them both die,' Abhia said after some time. Her voice was lifeless and her eyes unblinking as she spoke. 'I saw the fear in their eyes as they realised what was about to happen. We have followed the One God our entire lives. Is this how we are repaid?'

Kane sat down and wrapped an arm around Abhia. 'Words can't heal the pain you are going through. I wish I could explain things but I can't.' She felt useless for not being able to offer something more helpful but she was too exhausted and drained for anything other than honesty. 'I wish I could say the pain fades away and things get easier but I can't lie. All I can say is that this pain will make you appreciate the beauty around you, the good moments that you have. Such moments are fleeting, I try to claw onto them as much as I can now, because I know how much worse things can get.'

Abhia rested her head against Kane's shoulders and started to sob quietly as the sun set on Causrea.

NUMBERS COUNT FOR NOTHING

The group of twelve warriors Aleister led had the Gods' Bridge in their sights when he made the decision to rest for the night. The scouting party had made good time since pressing ahead of the main body of the army heading north but even the most determined warriors needed rest once in a while. If anything were to happen, then they would need to be thinking clearly if they were to survive.

Crossing the damned bridge was another reason for stopping here and pitching up for the night. The narrow stone bridge was sturdy and he had seen a whole caravan of merchants and travellers cross on his way south, but that meant nothing when peering over the edge of the cliff and looking down at what would be certain death if he were to fall. Common sense told him that it would be fine. There were just the twelve warriors, along with Ife and himself, to cross. A short scouting mission and then they would wait for the others as they marched adjacent to the Heartlands where bigger numbers would stave off any daring bandits tempted to rob or attack the group. Peering over the side, Aleister found that common sense deserted him.

'You want to jump?' Ife snickered over his shoulder, almost knocking him off balance. She clapped her hands together and shook with poorly concealed joy at his dramatic reaction, eyes sparkling with mischief. 'It is just a bridge. Thousands have crossed it. *You* have crossed it. There is nothing to fear.'

Pacing away from the edge, Aleister turned to Ife with a disbelieving gleam in his own eye. 'Tell that to those who were knocked from the edge or stumbled down to their deaths. What would they have to say of the matter?'

She raised her shoulders and sniffed, letting them drop as she pursed her lips. 'Nothing, I suppose. They are dead. And the dead have nothing to fear anymore.'

Aleister wished he could believe that last bit but he had still been greeted in his sleep by the dead, by the faces and voices of those who should have moved onto the next life and left him alone. There was only one voice which he longed to hear and face he yearned to see, but Ella had not visited him since their last meeting and he felt guilty for wishing to wake her from her rest just for one more conversation.

'Well, I don't want to join them then,' he said eventually as Ife followed him towards the soldiers pitching their tents up for the night. A fire was already raging and the scent of cooked meat wafted over to him with the soft breeze.

'We will all have to join them at some point. But I doubt your end is here and now, Aleister Soulsbane. You have too much to do yet.'

'And is that meant to comfort me?'

'I am not sure. Does it comfort you?'

He thought about it for a moment, torn between the answers he could give. 'I'm not sure, either.'

'Many quiver and tremble in fear when thinking of their own mortality. But it is the fact that we are mortal that gives us such a thirst for life, a thirst to *do* something. To live,' Ife argued with passion. 'We should not be fearful of death. Even if it would be wise to attempt to do our best to prevent an untimely one.'

'And what about Zeek and the four mages? They were not keen on mortality.'

Ife raised a dark eyebrow and flashed her beautiful eyes. 'And look how that has turned out. The very fate of the world lies in the balance because of the powers they sought to control. That should be a warning to all who wish to test the boundaries and limits of life and death. Never again should we allow such a thing to happen.'

He wondered what he would be willing to do to break such boundaries and limits, to spend more time with the woman he loved. He shook away the dark thoughts and focused on the present. A lack of focus would only aid the enemy now, he had to concentrate and be ready for anything if he were to make it through the battles to come. Experience had taught him that. Hard-earned experience.

He took a seat in the circle created by the pyramid tents. There was no need to sit close to the fire in the centre, it was hot enough this far south, the flames were merely used for cooking and nothing else. One of the soldiers, a stern-faced woman with braided hair that fell from a circle on the back of her head all the way down past the lower of her back, handed a cup to him and nodded.

'Drink,' she insisted with a grunt, pushing the cup into his hands. 'It will keep you awake. You watch first.'

'Delightful,' Aleister muttered with a roll of his eyes, taking the cup and sipping its contents suspiciously as the woman watched him curiously. He winced and forced the spicy liquid down his throat, blowing out of his mouth and panting like a dog. The warriors around the circle stopped whatever thy had been doing at the noise and turned to Aleister, pointing and laughing and speaking to one another in their own tongue.

'What are they saying?' he managed to finally ask Ife, smiling along against his wishes as the woman beside him dropped from her seat, banging her fist on the earth in an attempt to staunch her own laughter. Ife just grinned.

'They placed bets on how you would handle it. Pinks aren't too good with such drinks. Can't handle the heat.'

Aleister could only nod his head in agreement, his mouth continuing to rage and burn. Every breath felt like he was a dragon breathing fire along his tongue and the roof of his mouth. His saliva betrayed him, carrying the unwanted spice around as he struggled to work out what was best to combat such a thing.

'Here, take this,' a thin, giggling soldier said, his tattooed hand holding a smaller cup of what looked like milk. Aleister gave it a concerned look, his suspicion growing. 'No worries, my friend. This milk will soothe the heat.'

Needing no further encouragement, he knocked back the small dose and breathed a sigh of relief as the heat finally faded from his mouth. His lips still stung as though attacked by bees, a reminder of the practical joke played on him.

'Thank you,' he said to the thin warrior, who just waved away the thanks as he shuffled away, laughter still bursting through from time to time.

329

Aleister twisted his head to look at Ife who still had a broad smile stretched on her delicate features. 'That *was* milk wasn't it?'

Ife stood and placed a reassuring hand on his shoulder, giving it a gentle squeeze. 'Best not to ask.' She had a dark chuckle and sauntered over to the pot of food perched above the flames, taking the bowl offered by another sniggering compatriot. 'You should be proud. Such an initiation shows that they trust you. You are a part of the band now, Aleister Soulsbane. We will spill blood together as brothers and sisters.'

Recalling all the initiations the Red Sons used to be a part of and how they would traumatise newcomers with their antics, he began to feel as though he had perhaps been let off lightly. Jax particularly used to get up to the oddest of things and falling asleep around the trickster often meant waking up with no eyebrows or even a shaved head for some. There were more interesting initiations that he had heard of but those he had put a stop to. Joining a mercenary band was difficult enough without having to keep one eye open at all times in case those beside you were up to no good.

The others were now taking their seats around the circle, grabbing food and sharing a drink with their friends. He noticed that they would often look his way with a smile; a warm smile that spoke of friendship and trust. They were not mocking him because they too had done things that he had done. Been through things that he had been through. They each knew what was to come and they were happy to have Aleister fighting beside them. He felt a distinct sense of pride at having been accepted.

'They heard about your talk with those who sacrificed their lives for our people. They know that you understand why we are the way we are,' Ife said, squatting next to him and offering him a bowl of stew that smelt delightful, sending wafts of the meaty smell up his nose that made his stomach growl in hunger. 'They like you.'

'That is good,' Aleister said, gratefully accepted the food and taking the wooden spoon offered. 'We will soon be risking our lives for one another. I'd rather do that with people I like.'

'I've fought a few times with people I detest,' Ife said, taking a mouthful of the food and wiping a bit from her mouth that had dripped with the back of her hand. 'Hated them. But I knew as soon as the ugly business started we were on the same page. Make it out alive. That was the most important thing. Still, can't hurt, being liked. Did all of your people like you, back when you were fighting?'

'Honestly, I'm not sure.' Aleister chewed the tender meat, savouring the explosion of taste from the variety of sauces, meat and vegetables in the meal. He groaned, eager for more. 'This is good stuff.' He pointed at the bowl with his spoon before returning to the conversation. 'I think I was liked. Didn't think about it too much. I always had Ariel to my left and Bathos to my right. In my mind, that was all that mattered. Together, the three of us could overcome anything. We trained others, taught them what we had learned, befriended some, but that was all. It was all about us three.'

'Were they okay with waiting back with the main army?'

'They understand why. Scouting is more dangerous. It is a slim possibility we will be attacked but we could be overwhelmed easily. We needed to split up to ensure all is okay, and Bathos isn't going to be leaving Ariel on her own any time soon and that goes both ways. How do you think King Zeekial is feeling now that his army is on the move?'

Ife sighed and stirred the stew thoughtfully. 'Nervous. He hates having to wait and stay by the temple but all we have worked for over these cycles relies on him being able to use the blood we have given to defend our people. If everything else fails, his act will be what saves Takaara. Now, more than ever, he knows that to be a true leader means sacrifice, and for now, that means staying behind and trusting that his army can get the job done. The other kings and queens are joining the army to show the strength of the South to any who fight against us. That is enough. That is what must be enough.'

Aleister allowed the talk to fade into silence, using the time to enjoy the hot meal as he listened to the melodic tones of his fellow warriors. Though he could not understand their words, he loved to listen to the sound of their joyful voices as they shared conversation with brothers and sisters who they had fought alongside for cycles. Unlike much of Takaara, they had prepared for this war all their lives. They were the only warriors in all Takaara who had known what was to come.

'Did you ever think about running away?' Aleister asked Ife after some time. The sun was long gone below the horizon and the stars were out in force to cast their sparkling light on the open land. 'You knew this war was coming.'

Ife chewed her lip for a moment before shaking her head. 'I ran away in my youth. I travelled. I learned. I enjoyed myself. But I always knew that I would be back here when the time came. We all have a calling from the Gods, whichever Gods they are. Perhaps we don't even know which are the true ones, but we have a calling from them all the same. I know that mine is to guide, to help those arrive in the right place at the right time when the battle begins. There will be devastation, there will be mayhem, there will be chaos. But I think, if I play my part correctly, there is a chance that people will make it out of this mess alive. And then we can build something beautiful.'

'Do you honestly believe that? That there is some kind of force playing their hand in all of this?' Aleister had always been sceptical of the idea of fate. He was in control of his destiny. Anything else would lessen his actions and the choices that he made. 'Surely that means I should have no guilt if I choose the wrong path. If indeed, I was guided there by some God.'

'Not every action is God-chosen,' Ife suggested. 'I see them as being lights at the end of a dark, forked path. They place things in our way to guide us to what they believe is right, but we can still choose to ignore it. It doesn't make it wrong or right, it just makes it our decision. We all do good things, we all do bad things. How we feel afterwards and how it shapes us in the future, that is what I feel is important.'

'So our future actions can absolve us of our wrongdoings?'

Ife sucked her teeth and sighed, frowning as she tried to explain herself. 'Not quite. Tell me. What do you regret? One thing only.'

Aleister didn't have to think. 'I regret not taking Ella away and living with her for the rest of my life. I regret not doing everything possible to be by her side.'

'And given the chance again, would you let the opportunity slip? Would you behave in the same way?'

Aleister's face creased with thought. 'No. Never. I would do *anything* to change that.'

'Then you have grown. Your mistakes chisel you and shape you into what you have become. The path you have taken may be dark and there may have been difficulties along the way, but you have learned more about yourself.

That is a good thing. That is always a good thing. Though it can be painful.'

Two of the warriors strode over with bowls of food cupped in their dark hands. A broad-shoulder main with silver rings in his nose and all down his right ear and a short, nervous-looking woman with a golden ring pierced into her left eyebrow.

The man bowed and then spoke to Aleister, voice deep and rich. 'Aleister Soulsbane. My name is Felize. This is Akhona. It would do us both a great honour if we could sit with you and share our food.'

Aleister raised his eyebrows, taken aback at the idea anyone would be honoured to sit with him. He saw the lopsided grin of Ife's face and nodded, motioning for the space beside him.

'Of course, my friends. Though the honour is all mine, seeing as I am in your land and eating with such great warriors.'

The man sat but the woman still stood, glistening eyes transfixed on Aleister.

'Akhona,' the man said, gently grabbing her hand and guiding her to a seat next to him before looking sheepishly at Aleister. 'I am sorry for Akhona, she has wanted to meet you for many days.'

'And why is that?' Aleister asked with confusion. 'I am no one special.'

The woman flinched and scratched at her hair standing on top of her head from the bun like two tall daggers. 'You were with my brother the night before he died. You sat and shared laughter with Mathusi and his friends.'

'Mathusi…' Aleister muttered, remembering the brave man who had willingly sacrificed himself for his people. The man who had helped Aleister understand the strange ways of these people so far from his homeland. 'Your brother was a great man. I was sorry that I could not spend more time with him, though what little time I spent with him was an honour that I will take to my grave.'

Aleister knelt and bowed his head respectfully. When he looked up, tears were rolling silently down Akhona's dark skin as Felize wrapped a great arm around her.

'My brother has guided you here to be with us, Aleister Soulsbane. I know that in my heart to be true. It will be an honour to fight beside you.'

Aleister took his seat and raised his bowl of food in the air. 'To Mathusi, and to all who gave their lives so that we may live ours.'

'To Mathusi.' The others echoed around the fire. The other warriors farther away heard the call and looked over, seeing the four of them raising their bowls. Without question, they mimicked the action and made their own prayers as dark clouds drifted across the night sky.

*

Aleister woke with a start, heart thumping. There had been no dreams this night so he searched his tent frantically for any sign of the disturbance that had halted his rest. Nothing. Just the same room he had fallen into alone after a long evening chatting to his new friends. Still, he had survived this long by trusting his gut and he wasn't going to drift off to sleep any time soon.

He pulled his shirt and trousers on and wearily stepped into his boots. He tightened his belt, grabbing his sword last and ensuring it was sheathed properly, resting his hand on the hilt, ready to respond to any danger. Before leaving, he spotted the gifted necklace offered to him in the village. He grabbed it and threw it over his neck, tweaking it until it rested easily around his neck.

The fire had long since died down, leaving only burning embers throbbing in the centre of the circle. A familiar dark, lithe form hunched on the edge of the camp, creeping away from the circle and closer to the bridge.

'Ife,' Aleister hissed, flashing his eyes wildly at the mage as she glanced over her shoulder. She pressed a long, slender finger against her painted lips and beckoned for him to follow. 'What are you doing?' he asked as he caught up with her, keeping close and following her gaze towards the bridge.

'Something is wrong,' was all she said, shaking her head with a look of concern.

'I'm gonna need more than that. What is wrong?'

'I feel something. When I had a hold on my magic, I used to be able to sense danger at times. It would set me on edge moments before an attack. More than once it saved my life, and the lives of others. Feeling it now after so long without my magic, I feel it important to listen to my heart and check for any sign of danger.'

The sound of steel clashing snapped Aleister to attention, his eyes darting towards the Gods' Bridge and the source of the commotion.

'Where are the scouts?' he asked, racing towards the bridge and feeling a twist in his stomach.

'On the bridge…' Ife answered with a curse.

'Of course they are.'

Ife blew the small horn swinging around her neck, waking the rest of the camp instantly.

Aleister heard the cries and bustle of the warriors behind him preparing for battle but he couldn't let that distract him now. Ahead of him, he could see the movement of numerous figures crossing over the bridge and heading his way.

'How many?' he heard Ife ask to his left as he drew his blade and readied himself for blood. He tried to count but there were too many. Too many for them to hold off at least. But running wasn't an option now. Nowhere to hide.

'Too many,' he answered with a grimace.

'Then we kill as many as we can,' Ife said, voice resigned but full of more steel than the blades of a thousand kingdoms.

They each slowed as they reached the edge of the bridge, glaring at the forces marching forwards. Rows of four marched towards them. They were dressed in dragon-black leather and all held wide, curved swords and black crested shields. Two of the soldiers stepped ahead as the rest halted their march. One had piercing blue eyes and a big, bushy, black beard. His nose twisted in ways that implied more than one broken nose in his life. The other was a short but wicked looking woman. Olive skin, thin, dagger-like eyebrows and dark eyes dancing with malice, looking at Aleister. She licked her lips and winked, unnerving him momentarily.

'Greetings!' the twisted nosed man called out in a clear, loud voice. 'You must be Aleister of the Red Sons. Or formerly, anyway. A pink-skinned bastard frolicking with these Southern savages. Can't be anyone else.'

'And who might you be?' Aleister asked, spitting at the edge of the bridge, barely two paces from the man's dark, muddied boots. 'I like to know the names of those I kill.'

The man smirked and tapped his ally on the arm before pointing at Aleister and laughing. 'See, Ariadne. I told you he would be funny.' He glared at Aleister, the mirth faded from his icy eyes. 'You will not need to know my name, for you shall not be killing me.'

'Humour me,' Aleister spat, glaring at his opponent.

The soldier bowed theatrically and straightened. 'Hugo del Rey. I hope it brings you comfort in your final hours, knowing my name. You may recognise the name of a colleague of mine.'

'I doubt it if he was as boring as you.'

'Funny, funny, I knew you would be funny. But I digress. A friend of mine passed through recently. Jorges Bana. Our master, Lord Manuel was saddened to learn of his passing. We have been sent to ensure that the appropriate people responsible are punished.'

'Then it is best if you head back the other way. Jorges Bana signed his own death warrant. Tell your Lord Manuel that it is best if he stays north of the Gods' Bridge.'

'Or we can send him your head if that works as a clearer message?' Ife added, twirling her ebony daggers with ease. 'Either way, you will leave this land.'

Hugo's face hardened and he pointed his curved sword at Ife. 'You are almost as funny as him. I will take pleasure in your death. Just as I took pleasure in the death of your fool scouts.'

The woman to his right clicked her fingers and two more soldiers stepped forwards, throwing something heavy onto the ground.

The heads of the two scouts.

Aleister fought to keep his cool, knowing what they were trying to do. He heard the whistle of spears spinning in the hands of angry warriors behind him, pleading for revenge. Outnumbered or not, they would make this a bloody day.

'Keep them on the bridge,' he muttered out of the side of his mouth to Ife. 'Their numbers count for nothing there.'

He thought he counted at least thirty of the black-clad warriors but keeping them on the bridge meant keeping them narrow and unable to use the numbers to their advantage. They could at least put up a good fight but most likely would not make it out of the battle alive. No use weeping over it now, of course. Have to do what you can with the cards you're dealt. Aleister knew that. Now was the time to keep his poker face and go on the offensive.

With an animalistic scream, Ife lunged towards the woman, Ariadne. Her ebony daggers slashed wildly, barely caught by the crested shield stabbing up to block its path.

Aleister needed no other encouragement. He made for Hugo but found the soldier fading into the lines of his warriors with a knowing smirk, using them as a shield to block Aleister's route towards him.

Aleister struck the closest soldier three times, twice landing with a thud on the thick shield and the third thrusting past the defence and in between the ribs of the poor bastard. He pulled the blade out and stabbed with an experienced accuracy straight through the man's right eye, ending his pain. There was no time to be happy with the effort, more soldiers stepped forwards to take the place of the fallen.

The usual chaos of battle erupted as the Southern warriors entered the fray, spears jabbing either side of Aleister's shoulders only to be turned away by shields and curved swords. He gripped his sword tight and tried to find a gap through which to attack but the cramped and tightly packed area meant it was too difficult. Manuel's soldiers packed themselves together, creating an almost impenetrable wall and making the task of defeating them even harder.

But Aleister of the Red Sons was not fighting his first battle. And he was infamous for clutching victory from the gaping chasm of defeat. There was always a way. Even if it was one he did not like.

Jumping back, he used the momentary lapse in combat to reach for one of the fallen shields. He pulled it from the gloved hand of a recent corpse and pulled it tight to his shoulder. With a roar, he pressed forward and slammed into the wall of shocked soldiers, keeping his head low and out of sight and danger. The wall split and Aleister saw his chance.

From the corner of his eye, he could see a tornado of movement as Ife jabbed and slashed with those deadly, ebony daggers, arcing a trail of blood through the air. Focusing on the task at hand, he gritted his teeth and tightened his body, lowering his shoulder and placing as much of his frame behind the shield as he could as he charged at the shoulder in front. He shoved the shield into the soldier's right arm, pushing him against his fellow warrior and causing chaos in the unit. One soldier teetered on the edge of the bridge, heels perilously close to going over as he dropped his shield to the watery abyss, arms flailing wildly in an attempt to stay up.

One more push and Aleister succeeded. The soldier screamed in horror as he went over the edge, his scream fading until it abruptly stopped.

Aleister didn't have time to enjoy his success. Seeing their friend fall to a grisly death inspired the soldiers and they pressed together with a roar, pushing forwards with a renewed intensity.

He made to drop back and stumbled, feeling a

sharp punch into his thigh. His skin prickled and he felt suddenly too hot, sweat pouring from his forehead. Strong hands grabbed him and pulled him backwards as he gave a confused look around him. Away from the bridge, as the battle raged on without him, he turned to see Akhona and Felize, concerned expressions on their faces.

'What? What happened?' he asked as Akhona ripped some cloth from his shirt.

He glanced down and cursed as he looked at his leg, blood seeping from a small wound in his thigh. 'Shit!' In the fury of the battle, he hadn't seen it happen, must have been a sword slipped through the madness of bodies that caught him unawares. It wasn't the first wound he had ever received but that didn't make it hurt any less.

'Sit still,' Akhona ordered as he winced and sucked in air through his gritted teeth. She tied the cloth around his leg tightly, staunching the flow of blood.

'I have to go,' Felize said as the Southern warriors started to fall back, unable to stem the charge of soldiers on the bridge.

Aleister grabbed him by the wrist and held tight until the warrior looked him in the eyes. 'Not that way,' he implored. 'Head back, tell Buhle, tell the others. They need to know that there will be a small army waiting for them past the bridge. Lord Manuel's. Buhle will know. As will my sister, and Bathos. We cannot survive if we stay here.' He stared at his new friends, at the tears in their eyes and he could clearly see the conflict raging inside the both of them. A conflict born from the will to fight alongside their brothers and sisters or to do what must be done and alert their people of the dangers ahead.

'This isn't a request,' Aleister said, voice stern and stronger than the stone bridge the black-clad soldiers had now crossed. 'It is a command. Go!'

The two of them left him bleeding on the floor. They were slow at first, looking back at their friends in the heat of battle. Then they accepted what had to be done and raced away, lost to the darkness of the night.

Aleister sat there uselessly as the Southern warriors fell one after the other. Overwhelmed by the greater numbers and strong press of the enemy, they fought valiantly but it was all in vain. The bodies dropped like flies in a bloody mess, the gleaming edge of the curved swords cutting through the defences until only one warrior remained.

Ife.

Aleister stood with some effort, roaring in pain as he placed weight onto his left leg. He hobbled forwards, wanting to be close to her at the end. No one deserved to die alone.

She fought well but there were too many. He saw the fear in her eyes as she caught the butt-end of a spear in the jaw. She twisted and fell to the ground, daggers falling from her hands. Hugo clicked his fingers and two soldiers grabbed her, dragging her across the earth towards one of the trees to the side of the clearing.

Ife's dazed eyes searched for Aleister, her teeth red with blood now dripping down her chin.

With heavy breaths, he followed. Hugo sighed and pointed his way. Two more soldiers split from the group of ten soldiers remaining and made for him.

Shifting all of his weight onto his left leg, Aleister blocked the first strike and stabbed with as much precision as he could manage. The blade sliced one of the soldier's necks, drawing blood and a yelp from the warrior just as the other slammed a shield into Aleister's bad leg.

He fell to the ground with a cry, clutching at his leg

and fighting the urge to vomit. More kicks rained down on him as Hugo's cackle filled the air. The bastard stood over him, smirking and flashing his wild eyes.

'I'll keep you alive long enough to watch the bitch die. Then it's your turn.'

Hugo kicked Aleister's sword away and muttered something to the two soldiers. One of them was still covering his neck with a bloody gloved hand but he seemed unconcerned. The soldiers grabbed Aleister and pulled him close, ensuring that he could see Ife.

The powerful woman yelled and kicked out at her captors, taking one down with an intense fury. Without a weapon, she dropped her knee flush into his face and Aleister heard the crunch of bone. The other soldier panicked, driving his sword straight through the back of her neck and pushing until it pushed out from her the skin at the front of her throat.

Aleister screamed as her eyes turned to him, lifeless and so different to the ones that danced with the light of the stars. Her body slumped, all fight fading from her as the soldier casually placed a filthy boot on her back and kicked, trying to free his weapon from her corpse. He struggled, swearing and moaning with the effort until Hugo stormed over and punched the bastard, taking the blade in his own hand and pulling it free with one strong effort.

'Get rid of the savages' bodies. They will only spread disease and death, as always' Hugo commanded his soldiers as he wiped the blood from the blade and threw it at its owner. 'Get the rope. Aleister of the Red Sons deserves a slow death.'

A punch to the jaw sent the world into a hazy mess and when it came back into focus, Aleister found himself under a wide trunked tree with a low branch easy enough for a rope to be thrown. One of the soldiers swung the rope over the branch and then set to tying the noose around his neck, pulling it tight. They tied his hands behind his back as Hugo ambled over, a wicked, smug smile of victory on his face.

'You fucked up the Heartlands with that bitch of a sister and the big oaf. This is a just death, Aleister. Surely you know this.'

Aleister spat and showed his teeth in a wide smile as the saliva splashed onto Hugo's smug face. 'Go to hells.'

'I will, one day. Save me a seat.'

Aleister felt the rope pulling on his neck, his feet desperately clawing at the ground but to no avail. His eyes felt as though they would pop straight from his skull and his entire body felt as though his blood was boiling as he swung and twisted, writhing to get free as he looked down at the ten laughing and joking soldiers gazing up at him.

Mind playing tricks on him as he struggled for air, he thought he could see a hooded figure dressed in navy blue standing behind them and holding his sword, Soulsbane. Death. It must be Death. There was no other explanation. He thought of Ella and it brought some semblance of comfort to know that he would soon be with her. Then, his thoughts turned to Ariel and Bathos, praying they would survive the war to come and raise his beautiful niece or nephew.

And then Death spoke.

'Which one of you fools dropped this blade?' a flat voice asked, alerting the soldiers to the newcomer.

'Who the fuck is asking?' one of the ten soldiers asked.

Death lowered his hood to display tanned skin and silver hair along with a neatly trimmed silver beard. His stunning eyes studied each of the soldiers in turn, unfazed by the odds. He moved faster than the wind, dagger flying from his hand and ripping through the rope, releasing Aleister and dropping him onto his bad leg with a thump. He cried out in pain as he crashed to the ground coughing, amazed to be alive.

'Istari Vostor. And I'm not going to ask again…'

SOULSBANE

Aleister had never seen anything like it.

The warrior moved faster than his eyes could follow, a blur of motion gliding through the soldiers and attacking with an unnerving accuracy. The glinting point of Soulsbane led the way, leaving trails of blood in the air and on the ground as he stabbed, thrust and slashed with a precision that Aleister had never thought possible. The beautiful, deadly dance scared Aleister as much as it fascinated him. It didn't seem human. How could it be possible that anyone could so perfectly wield a blade in such a way?

As terrifying as it was for him, it was so much worse for the black-clad soldiers under Lord Manuel's rule.

Caught in the amazing warrior's path, they tried to block or dodge but all they could do was gasp and scream as death greeted them all. In moments, only one of them was left standing, trembling in his boots, the smug smile no longer there, instead it had been replaced with shaking lips and skin as pale as the moon.

'I am assuming that you are in charge here,' the deadly swordsman said with a sigh, wiping blood from the sword and sheathing it. 'Is this your blade?'

Hugo shook his head, whimpering. He pointed at Aleister, who still lay on the ground, tied up and coughing.

The swordsman glanced over and nodded. 'And may I ask, whom do you serve?'

'Lord Manuel. His estate is—'

'—I know where his estate is.'

The swordsman reached forwards with incredible speed and stole Hugo's blade from its sheath and slashed the curved blade across his throat, ending the bastard's life in a single moment. The body dropped to the ground and Istari Vostor threw the blade on top of it with a dismissive noise.

'A poor smith made that one. Far too much weight towards the hilt.'

He glanced at Aleister as though he had only just realised that he was still there. He walked over and cut the rope from his wrists and pulled the noose from his neck, allowing him to breathe easily.

'This yours?' the swordsman asked, holding Soulsbane and pointing it at Aleister who nodded, rubbing his sore neck and turning over to cough and spit onto the earth. 'I'll take care of it now.'

Aleister was in no state to argue, but he knew how important the sword was and what had to be done. 'I can't let you do that,' he croaked, rising slowly and staring at Istari who stood just an inch taller than him. 'You don't understand the power of that sword.'

Istari Vostor gave Aleister a patronising glare and pursed his lips, pulling the sword in close and further away from Aleister.

'A sword that can trap the souls of the warriors that it kills. A sword that was created before the Breaking of Takaara by two fuckwits with too much power and not enough brains. A sword that, if we are to stem the flow of Chaos, must be used to kill the four mages who once believed themselves to be Gods. Have I missed anything?'

Aleister choked on his spit and stared at the old warrior for a moment, wondering where the hell he came from. 'I've also used it to cut the odd cake or two in the past.'

Istari sighed, clearly not a funny bone in his body. He turned away and started marching back south, away from the Gods' Bridge.

'Who are you, really?' Aleister called, wincing with the effort thanks to his raw, damaged throat. He chased after the soldier and slowed only when he was able to fall in step beside him. 'And why are you heading this way?

'You may know me as the Sword of Causrea, and I'm going to kill the idiots who made this sword.'

'Woah, woah, woah, woah, woah!' Aleister said stepping in front of Istari and pushing his palms against his chest. He immediately regretting the stupid action.

'Take your hands off me or you will lose them. I will not repeat myself.'

Aleister did exactly as commanded. 'Sorry. Look, you seem to know quite a bit about all of...' he waved his hands around uselessly in the air, '...this. But I've been with them. This sword is the only thing capable of killing the bastard destroying this world. We need to sort that out first before taking down the others. If Osiron is allowed to wreak havoc across Takaara, soon there will be nothing left to save. And that means heading north and shoving this blade deep into their heart.'

'If you take this blade further north and closer to Osiron, then you are walking right into your own doom. This blade is not the only thing that can save us from Chaos. Only a fool would believe such a thing. It can kill the beasts, it can end Osiron, but one person wielding this blade will mean nothing when that dark army arrives to sweep throughout the land. There is another way.'

Aleister could not conceal his confusion. 'Another way? And what way is that?'

'We need magic to combat what Osiron is planning on unleashing in Takaara.'

'But there is no more magic left in the world. Not since that great quake. People are getting sick, people are dying but magic has left, stripped away from this land. Surely you know that?'

'Of course I do, you fool,' Istari growled. 'But there is one way we can get it back, and that means heading south.'

'And doing what? How can we get magic back?'

Istari smirked and winked, tapping the sword that had belonged to Aleister for so long. 'We need to use this sword. And we need to speak to the Gods.'

THE WAY OF THINGS

Dustin Grey thanked the hunched over, frail man dressed in black and white finery as he poured the old soldier a glass of something that Sly definitely enjoyed the scent of. The reddish-brown liquid swirled around in the glass as the soldier sat back and cleared his throat, twisting his wrist and spinning the glass pompously before holding it close to his brilliantly extravagant moustache and taking a sniff. Grey took a sip and gasped with satisfaction.

'Finest whiskey in the north. Do not let the fools in the city claim otherwise,' he said, glaring at Sly, Kiras, and Cray before turning to his manservant. 'Oscar, our new friends should try the Nightshade whiskey. I believe we have enough for a few nights' relaxation.' His smile pushed his red cheeks up as he looked at his three guests again. 'My father always used to say, "Bad times deserve good drink" and I could not agree with him more. The time could not be much worse and so the best drinks are needed. Please, enjoy.'

The withered servant poured three separate drinks

which were accepted gladly. Kiras nodded to the old boy, looking him up and down with concern, obviously wondering if the man was about to drop any second. Cray grunted and grabbed the glass, giving the whiskey a sniff before raising his eyebrows, unable to express how impressed he was. And then Sly winked at Oscar and took his own drink, knocking it back in one go, much to the clear devastation of the general. The liquid burned Sly's mouth and throat, relaxing him as he took in a deep breath and leant back, placing a foot on the dark oak table that separated the former general of Archania from his guests.

'Such a delicacy is meant to be enjoyed over time, my dear boy…' Grey croaked, looking distressed with his moustache twitching nervously.

'Don't worry, Whiskers. I'll take my time with the next one.' Sly held out his glass and grinned at the old servant who looked almost as flustered as his master. 'Top me up, old chum! The second one will go down a treat!'

Grey nodded his acceptance and Oscar filled the glass again before hurrying away, nodding as he left the firelit room and closing the tall, double doors behind him.

'Now that the pleasantries are out of the way, perhaps we can get down to business,' Kiras said, rapping her fingers on the table and looking between Grey and Sly with a glare of impatience. Sly shrugged, suitably admonished. Even Grey did well enough to lower his eyes and mumble an apology before taking another sip of his whiskey.

'Of course, of course,' he mumbled, sitting up and straightening his back. 'I feel that we should add some clarity to our situation before we move onto what we can do pressing forward. As you know, I was recently relieved of my duties as general of the Archanian army, a position I had held for many cycles with great honour and pride. It hurt, of course, but it was the right time for me to leave. My partner had recently died at the hands of that bastard Mason D'Argio and the idiotic, young King Asher had ascended the throne. With Asher's death, Mason has taken charge and the whole kingdom is now under the glare of the Empire of Light.

'These are dark days that we are living in. When we first met, with your leader, Raven Redbeard,' Grey paused respectfully and placed a hand on his heart, 'a good man, though we have stood on different sides of often warring nations – when we first met, I did not trust your kind. The Borderlands have been a thorn in our side for as long as I have been alive, longer even! But now, there is a great darkness sweeping through the land and it is not just Mason and his powerful sister. Creatures of Chaos are killing any in their path. It is time to put our differences aside and work together, for the betterment of both of our people. Of *all* people.'

'Couldn't agree with ya any more, Whiskers,' Sly reluctantly agreed. 'This shit is getting' out of hand and we've seen the bastards up close.' Sly felt his face drop as the memories of the battle flashed unwanted into his head. 'Fought alongside them too. This army is like nothing we've ever seen before. We ain't exactly shy of a bit of blood and violence but this is different.' He held Grey's eyes, making sure the old soldier was paying attention and knew how much he meant it. 'They are wiping everything from this world. Not gonna have anything left if the likes of you and me don't stand up and fight back. But killing the bastards is gonna be tough.'

The wrinkles around Grey's eyes and face seemed to deepen as he sighed and rubbed his forehead, thumb and forefinger pinching at his temples as he groaned. 'Is there anything that you have learnt after standing alongside them? Anything you can say that will help us in the battle to come?'

Sly pitied the wide-eyed and fearful man pleading for anything that could stem the dark tide heading their way. He could only blow out his cheeks and run a nervous hand through his wild hair, sharing worried glances with Kiras and Cray who just sat there with grim faces.

'The kid. He's the only weakness.'

Kiras sat a little straighter in her seat and frowned, turning her full attention to Sly, her whole body tense and on edge.

'What do you mean by that, Sly?'

Sly swallowed, not wanting to continue but knowing that he had to. 'It's the kid who is their weak link. You've seen him, he doesn't like what is going on, or at least he is unsure.'

'Of course he fucking doesn't!' Kiras snapped, hissing through her teeth and holding her hands like claws in front of her. 'He's not the one pulling the strings. He's just a kid! A puppet being dragged along through this whole shitshow.'

'He destroyed Hillheim!' Sly roared, surprised to find himself out of his seat as he slammed his fist on the table, the four glasses vibrating with his rage and frustration. 'Men, women, children. Didn't matter one jot to Arden. He killed Socket and now he's killing anyone who gets in his way. It doesn't matter if he's just a kid anymore, the lives of the rest of us are more important.'

'Do you think we can turn him? Stop him doing whatever is planned?' Grey asked, cautiously adding his thoughts to the argument.

'It's too late for that,' Sly spat. 'He's killed too many…'

'And how many have *we* killed?' Kiras scoffed. 'You stood alongside Barbarians at Hillheim even though you've slaughtered more of their folk than you've taken shits. What's different?'

'Arden is different. *This* is so fucking different, Kiras. How can't you see that?'

'He can be saved,' Kiras said simply.

'You've changed your tune. Wanted to burn the world not so long ago.'

'Anything wrong with that? Maybe I've just seen enough of the flames to know that this world burning ain't gonna do it for me.'

'Then what will?'

'Saving that kid.'

'It's too late,' Sly insisted, unwilling to budge. He'd spent long enough thinking about it on the way from Hillheim. There was no other way. The kid had to die.

'It was too late for Baldor,' Kiras said, angry tears filling her blue eyes. 'It's not too late for him.'

She stood abruptly and stormed out of the room, slamming the door closed behind her and leaving an awkward silence in her wake.

'Well,' Cray said, finally speaking up. 'Glad that's sorted then.'

Sly left Grey's office with a sore head. A mix of too much of that damned whisky and too many maps rolled out by Whiskers with names of places Sly had never heard of and little wooden figures he had no idea the purpose of.

Too many words.

Point Sly in the direction of the enemy or tell him

where to stand and he'll rip through the bastards. Always
felt like these war leaders tried to make complicated
something that weren't complicated. War was easy. Grab
something pointy and kill the others before they kill you.

He went to rest his hand on the banister as he
trudged down the stairs of the massive house and he
misjudged it, almost falling before catching himself.

'You're pissed,' Cray mumbled, a slight curve at the
corner of his lips.

''Course I'm pissed,' Sly agreed darkly, jabbing a
thumb back to the room they had just left. 'Had to listen to
that old fucker rabbit on about formations and numbers
and the lay of the land for Gods know how long. Raven
used to deal with all of this shit. Not for me.'

'It is now, though.'

Sly grunted as they reached the ground floor and
stepped out into the cloudy night. 'Guess so. Don't mean I
have to like it though! Think I'll be drinking even more
from now on.'

''Specially if you have arguments with the girl.'

Sly glared at Cray, suspicious of this line of enquiry.
He tried to give his best simmering growl but the world
seemed to sway for a moment and his head was thumping.
'Nothing to do with the girlie. She's always been a moody
one and we don't always see eye to eye.'

'Have lately though. Haven't seen her this fired up
for a while.'

'Aye. Just about the kid,' Sly sighed, steadying
himself for a moment and leaning against the wall of the
building. He looked out across the estate and dropped to a
squat, breathing in the cool air. 'We always end up back on
the same side. Had some right storming battles with her,
but in the end, we'll stand side-by-side until our time is

done. Just the way of things,' he said with a lazy shrug.

'Just the way of things,' Cray echoed.

They sat there together at the front of the house, each lost in their own thoughts and watching the movements around the estate. Even at this late hour, Sly could see smoke rising from the forge as the smiths worked tirelessly to make more weapons and armour for the growing band of warriors. He could see a distant orange glow that he thought might be a campfire. Some of those who had travelled preferred sleeping out beneath the stars, enjoying the open space as they felt connected to the world around them.

Sly pulled a small flask from the pocket inside his jacket and uncorked it, taking a harsh swig and waiting for the burn to warm him up. He passed it absently to Cray who took the flask and took a drink in silence before handing it back. Sly shook his head and waved away the action, pulling out another flask from the opposite side of his jacket with a chuckle.

'You can never have too many flasks of rum…' he muttered. 'That's what someone once told me.'

They sat and drank. And drank some more.

'You think we're doing the right thing here?' Sly asked after some time had passed and the orange glow in the distance had died down. 'Coming here. Instead of running as far away as fucking possible.'

'No idea, mate,' Cray said. 'But we've seen what that army can do. Doubt there's anywhere we could run to where they couldn't find us. And I'd rather die tall and with my back straight than cowering somewhere I don't recognise. Least this is still north.'

'Aye, it is ain't it?' Sly said, slowing nodding to himself and feeling the rum work its warm magic. 'Some folk have died in worse places. The way Raven died still keeps me awake at night. Didn't deserve that kind of betrayal. I still see Bane's smug face at night and I go to wring his filthy neck. And Baldor. Never met a such a guy. Big, brutal bastard but he had the biggest heart in all the land. The way he died…'

'We all gotta go some way. Don't suppose it matters how.'

'But it *does*,' Sly insisted, feeling the blood rushing around his body and giving him a burst of energy. 'It has to. It's the last thing we do. Gotta mean something.'

'I've seen some right shits spend all their lives being mean cunts to people less than them,' Cray said, sniffing and taking another swig from the flask Sly had given him. His eyes were red and hazy. 'Then, when they knew the end were coming, they'd repent and start yammering on about how they were sorry. Load of horse shit. They were just scared. Pissing themselves because they didn't know what was coming next.

'I think the last moments are the least important. It's all the other times, no matter how short the life may be.'

Sly sniffed and licked his lips, tapping his flask against Cray's lightly. 'How about we have a drink for that son of yours. Gone too soon.'

He saw Cray's throat lurch slightly as he nodded, biting his bottom lip as he did so. 'Aye, that'd be good.'

'To your boy.' They banged the flasks together and shared a drink, gasping as one.

'To the dead – the young and old gone before their time.'

'Gone before their time.'

A horn blared from the battlements and the two

warriors scrambled to their feet, staring out for any sign of danger. They waited as the horn sounded again. Behind them, Dustin Grey came crashing out though the tall doors, a tight night cap on his head and long robes covering his modesty. The old soldier's face was twisted with confusion.

'Two horns?' Sly asked Grey.

The old man stared at him and then towards the front of the estate and the gates that shielded them from the volatile North. 'Allies. More have arrived. We have company…'

COMPANY

Katerina Kane stumbled wearily through the open gate to Dustin Grey's estate. Her feet throbbed, warning her of the blisters to come thanks to the long march from the drowned republic of Causrea. The thousand or so refugees who had survived the earthquake and mountain of water that crushed the beautiful place had dwindled to less than four hundred. Some had fallen to the hardship of the march north. Others had chosen other paths: to the mountains or the quiet villages to the west of the Heartlands. None wished to stay near the coast, the frightening horror of what they had just survived was too raw and fresh in their minds. Kane didn't blame them. She had promised nothing except that she would lead them to others, others who may be able to help them. She had prayed that Grey was still alive, that he was in some kind of condition to defend his home from the horrors threatening Takaara.

And there he was, rushing to greet her as she led the exhausted mass of travellers into the walled estate. He looked like a man who had forgotten how to smile. His face was pale and drawn and he looked as though the recent conflicts had taken its toll on him. His lips twitched as his eyes scanned the travellers, finally sparking to life when they landed on Kane.

'Katerina Kane…' he mumbled, shaking his head and looking as though he were staring at a ghost. His hair was still cut close to the skin, a life of military service was obviously difficult to step away from, though it was whiter than she remembered and the wrinkles around his eyes were clearer than before.

'So this is where you have been hiding out, Dustin,' Kane said with a tired smile, drawing a weak one from the old soldier. 'It is good to see a familiar face.'

'It is good to see a friend…' Grey responded, pulling her in with one surprisingly strong arm and holding her close. She wrapped her arms around him for a brief moment, welcoming the embrace. They had never been the closest of friends and had often been on opposite sides of arguments in the council chambers. But they respected one another at all times, and their shared grief following Tamir's death meant something. 'Where have you been all this time?' he gasped, taking a better look at her as they pushed apart from one another. The masses of men, women and children from Causrea filed past the two of them, following the advice being yelled by one of Grey's soldiers.

Kane waved a hand in a vague direction behind her. 'I have been to the East and back again. But that is not important,' she added as Grey opened his mouth to respond. 'We have marched from Causrea. There was a quake.' She saw the worry in Grey's eyes as the old soldier bit his lip, his brain working with that small piece of information to fill in the rest of the story. Kane nodded wearily, confirming his fears. 'The waves would have swallowed the entire Upper City. Causrea is decimated,

360

fallen beneath the waves in the most part.' She swallowed what felt like a rock in her throat as she finished. 'So many dead, Dustin. So much lost…'

Tears dropped silently from Grey's eyes as he placed his hand around Kane's shoulder, guiding her towards the centre of the estate. She could see that Grey had a larger force than expected. Soldiers dressed in the style of Archania, but dyed black, stood around the battlements and the land inside. Soldiers with loyalty who had stayed with Grey even in his exile. Her heart swelled at the thought. Her eyes swept the land and fell eventually on two ragged warriors peering out at the newcomers. They stood out like Elders in a whorehouse. One stood on the edge of violence, fingers twitched for the axes hanging from his belt. His wild eyes surveyed the incoming force with hunger as his even wilder beard waved in the night's breeze. The other stood almost like a statue. He was motionless, other than his lively eyes darting out from a large, closely shaved head. His huge arms were folded across his chest and a longsword hung easily from his hip.

Borderlanders.

'You've been making some interesting allies, I see,' Kane said with a smirk as she walked with Grey.

He laughed and it sounded honest and true. 'I have learned much since my *forced retirement*,' he said crisply. 'You were right all along, I must admit. The Borderlanders are not *all* bad.'

'I told you that over ten cycles ago…'

'Yes. I am a slow learner, obviously. But I get there in the end.'

Sleep eluded Kane that first night. The rooms provided graciously by Grey were comfortable enough, perhaps a tad too comfortable following their travels but that would not be a concern for much longer. But as comfortable as they were, her thoughts were too insistent and her fears dominated her mind to such an extent that the only reasonable thing for her to do was to admit defeat and go for a walk.

Grey's estate was not completely alien to her. His summer parties celebrating the nation's birth were mostly full of happy memories. She would dread attending them, worrying about the amount of time she would have to spend biting her tongue as the elite of Archania slapped themselves on their backs and shared their numerous in-jokes without ever seeming to try to better the lives of the people living in the United Cities. Thankfully, that time was shorter than expected and the old guard would fade into the night as the sun dipped below the horizon and the parties would continue with a much more interesting crowd. Those honoured throughout the cycle with medals and honours for bravery, valour, and charity were always happy to speak to Kane and share their experiences and most would make a beeline to speak with Braego, wanting to hear tales from the infamous Borderlander who rose to prominence in the land of his people's enemies. Kane would sit there with a glass of wine and smile happily as Braego's familiar tales drifted her way, the shocked looks of excitement and amazement from men and women lost in his stories made it all worth it to her. Even a young Prince Drayke would find a seat and listen to stories that he must have heard dozens of times before.

Good times. Simple times. Though, perhaps she did not realise it back then.

She grabbed a lantern and made her way quietly out of the room provided and crept along the corridor and down the creaking staircase. At the back of the house was the familiar rose gardens that Grey loved so much. They were much the same as she remembered them from the last party. The moonlight gave the gardens a ghostly but romantic glow as she walked along the patterned stone pathway leading towards one of two large buildings at the back of the complex. She took a right and pushed open the heavy, wooden door to one of her favourite rooms in Grey's estate – the weapons room.

A faint orange glow informed her that she wasn't the only one with the idea for a late night walk. She walked into the tall, spacious room filled with weapons from all around Takaara. Halberds from the Heartlands. Spears from the south. Curved blades from the east. Axes and shields from the Borderlands. Swords of all kinds from the United Cities. She had always loved this room.

She walked towards the glowing lantern and couldn't hide her surprise as the light danced across an aged, tired but familiar face.

'Sir Dominic,' she stuttered, surprised to find the old knight awake at such a late hour and down in the weapons room, nonetheless. The knight had often given her the impression that he wanted to be nowhere near any sign of battle or conflict. Though revered and respected in the capital for his exploits in the Northern Wars, Dominic's embellished tales had always sounded like the bold lies of a child out to impress those around him and nothing more. 'What a delight to find you here.' Not exactly the truth but after all of the death and violence, she was actually pleased to see someone she recognised alive and well.

It took a moment for Dominic's eyes to focus on her but when they did, a broad smile widened across his pale face. 'Katerina Kane as I live and breathe! My dear, what a pleasant surprise to see you here,' the knight said with a hearty chuckle. 'It shames me to say that I thought you were one of the many that we had lost in the recent troubles. My heart soars to find that for once I am incorrect in my assumptions.'

'A rarity, indeed,' Kane said, careful to hide the sarcasm from her voice. 'What calls you to the weapons room at such an hour?'

Dominic caressed the gilded hilt of the basket-hilted sword on display in front of him and eyed it like a lover, the affection clear in his glistening eyes. 'I remember heading into battle all those cycles ago. I was a young whippersnapper with all the arrogance and belief of youth. I felt *indestructible*!' he exclaimed with a clenched fist and a glint in his eyes. The light faded and he once more looked like an old soldier, recalling past glories. 'I thought we would win the war in a matter of days, you know?' He chuckled darkly at his folly. 'What a fool.

'I remember that first battle. Have you ever been in a battle, Kat? The blood, the screams, the *smell*. Men and women who I idolised and believed to be the bravest, most honourable fighters in all the world were left weeping in the mud. Those savages tore through our lines at first, decimating the right wing of our unit and forcing us onto the back foot. It was like wandering through the hells. I still see their bloody faces when I close my eyes, even after all these cycles. Some things can numb the pain of course,' he said, pulling out a small flask with a tired wink. 'But nothing keeps them at bay forever, even after all these cycles.'

'I am sorry you had to be a part of that, Dominic. War is a hell all of its own. There are no winners or losers.'

Dominic pulled the sword from the display and gave it a few respectful swings, his eyes never leaving the blade. 'I always wanted a blade like this when I was younger. Dustin had such a beautiful silver one with a dragon hilt made with perfection. Instead, I had the standard longsword and crested shield. Do you know who the first person was that I killed on the battlefield with that plain sword?'

Kane shook her head. 'No, Dominic, I'm afraid I don't.'

The old knight's voice cracked and tears fell softly down his wrinkled face, so different from the man who would shout around the council chambers like a pompous fool and draw all attention to his outstanding arrogance. 'A young soldier, barely eighteen cycles. He was one of ours. A son of a carpenter, I later found out. It was chaos in battle and I panicked when I felt a hand on my shoulder. Believing it to be an enemy, I spun and, filled with fear, I thrust my boring sword into his gut. Worked just as well as any fancy sword, that I can tell you. He died just like the enemy would have. Just like they did in their thousands. No one noticed. I fell with him and held him as he died. My old captain found me there with his pale, lifeless body. Got a medal for bravery for staying with the poor fellow. They thought that he had been killed by some savage and that I had avenged him and then cared for him until the end. I've held that with me all these cycles since. I am a coward, Katerina Kane. Nothing more.'

'Such an action is not rare in battle, Dominic,' Kane insisted. 'Believe me. Battles are fought in panicked states of chaos. Such unfortunate acts happen all the time. You should not have to carry such a burden anymore.'

'But I was commended for it, Katerina. That is what leaves a sour taste in my mouth. I was treated like a hero whilst that young boy was buried in an unmarked grave with hundreds of others. It is shameful. And I have done nothing about it in the time since. A coward.'

Kane grabbed his arm and saw the flicker of Dominic's eye to her hand. He clutched at her hand and sobbed, his body shaking. She realised that this must be the only time she had been able to converse with the knight without smelling stale alcohol on his breath. For the first time in cycles, she was speaking to him whilst he was sober.

'Dominic, can I ask… why are you telling me this now?'

The knight sniffed and released her hand, wiping away his tears and giving a long sigh. 'I have heard what is heading this way. An army of Chaos capable of wiping us from the face of Takaara. There is no escape. Nowhere to run. I cannot flee and hide from the war to come. My back is against the wall and I must face my fears for the first time since those battles in my youth. I'm scared, Kat.' His lined face turned to her, looking like a scared boy, not knowing what to do and turning to adults around him for answers. 'This is the end.'

He ran a hand through his long, greying hair. He was still a beautiful man and even in his despair, Kane could see why the women of Archania still giggled about the old knight and fluttered their lashes as he rode past them. Not her type, but she could see the beauty, at least.

'These are dark times, Sir Dominic. But dark times are also times when heroes rise. You held the gate in a bloody battle alone against over a hundred warriors armed with just a broadsword. I have heard the story a thousand times, usually from your own lips,' she said with a smile and a nudge. 'More heroes will rise in our time of need.'

'Bah!' he scoffed in response. 'Heroes.' He said the word like a curse that tasted foul on his lips. 'There are no such things as heroes. Soldiers are like pigs being fed and then sent to the slaughterhouses. We blindly follow the instructions of men who keep far from the battle, and if we are lucky, then we make it out alive. That day by the gate… I was no hero.' A dark shadow passed over his features, scaring Kane slightly.

'What happened, Dominic? What happened at the gate?'

Sir Dominic's eyes glazed over and took on the look that Kane had seen before, the look of someone lost in the past. 'They had killed so many and I was still grieving for the ally I had killed. I expected death to take me that day. It was the middle of summer and the heat was unbearable. My entire unit fought valiantly but I could see the way things were going. The savages fought as though possessed, ripping through our defences and butchering every one of us. I cowered away from the melee, hiding in a trench full of piss and shit yards away from the gate.

'I could hear the bastards cheering and hailing one another, impressed with their victory. I peered over the trench as an eerie silence fell over the area. All I saw was a group of around ten hooded figures. Strange, considering the heat. The Borderlanders leered at this small group and marched forwards, eager to finish up for the day. I can't tell you exactly what happened next. The robed Archanians raised their hands to the air and then a flash of light blinded me, followed by a mighty wave in the air that knocked me backwards in the trench. When I woke, I stumbled out of the trench to find the bodies of my enemies and those of the ten mages who had sacrificed themselves to save me. I panicked, mages have never been looked on fondly in our city and using powers for the mass killing of any would cause problems. So I picked up a broadsword and stabbed the dead.

'It was Dustin Grey who found me. He helped to bury the dead. Didn't ask any questions though he looked at the robed bodies with a certain suspicion that unnerved me. When more arrived, he told them the tale of how I had fought valiantly and defended the gate, using the funnelled position to hold back a stream of Borderlanders intent on massacre. He covered for me.'

'He is a good man,' Kane gasped, swaying slightly as she struggled to take in this new version of events. 'A better man than most.'

'A truer word has never been spoken. I am scared, Kat. I do not want to die. But I know that there is no hiding like before.'

'That's true. I'm scared too,' Kane admitted. 'There is no hiding. But at least this time, you will be able to stand side-by-side with friends. We live together, or we die together. That is… terrifying. But I also think there is something calming about it. We do not get to choose when and where we die. Death can come at any moment. But at least we get to do it with people we care about. With people who care about us. That has to mean something.'

Dominic sniffed and nodded as he took two deep breaths. 'You are right. I always said you were a smart woman, Katerina Kane.'

'I heard what you have said about me,' Kane laughed before patting the suddenly distressed knight on the arm to calm him down again. 'It is okay. We have had our differences in the past. But now, we fight together. Whatever happens, know that I am here for you.'

'That means more than you know, Kat. It really does.'

'Now go. Get some sleep.'

Kane watched the knight nod in farewell and leave the room, waving a hand in the air as he left. She fell into one of the leather seats at the side of the room and sighed, feeling all of the energy drain from her body. She had held it together for the knight's benefit, but there was no escaping it, she was utterly petrified of the days to come and feared that this truly was the end of them all.

Sly raised an eyebrow at the old man with bloodshot eyes leaving the weapons room. Bit strange to see someone crying after looking at weapons but he had bever understood these odd guys from south of the border. Weak, fragile, sensitive bastards, all of them. Well, most at least. If the sight of a weapon made them cry then they wouldn't last what was to come. Probably wouldn't last anyway in all honesty.

He eased the door open and was shocked to find a woman sitting on one of the chairs in the low light of two lanterns.

'Not interrupting anything am I? A late-night fuck in the weapons room?' Sly said with a smirk. He couldn't think of anything more fitting. Nothing got him going like weapons and battle but it did make the sight of the man leaving in tears even stranger than he thought.

'You Borderlanders are all so *crude*,' the woman replied though she didn't sound too upset by the comment. 'Would it hurt to watch your language for just one night?'

Sly stuck out his bottom lip and shrugged. 'Dunno what that means, so, probably not.' He pulled one of the long, double-headed great axes from the wall and twisted it over in both of his calloused hands, admiring the craftsmanship of the weapon. 'I know what this is though. Good work.' He sniffed the wood and iron of the weapon and sighed with satisfaction. 'A proper Northern weapon, this.'

'Made in a small village north-west of where the Lapret River meets mountains,' the woman replied, bringing a shocked narrowing of Sly's eyes.

'You know this weapon?'

'My… partner did.' The woman stood and walked over to him with a wry smile, running a slow hand over the edge of the glistening weapon. 'He would yammer on about it for hours at a time. Thought it was one of the best weapons to ever be forged and he detested the fact it was hanging up on this wall, bloodless.'

'Sounds about right. He still around?'

'Just bones now, as he would say.'

Sly's eyebrows lifted in surprise as his admiration for the woman grew. 'From the Borderlands… What was his name?'

'Braego.'

'You're shitting me…' Sly chuckled in recognition at the name.

The woman laughed and held out a hand. 'I'm Katerina Kane, or just Kat.'

Sly ignored the hand and clasped her forearm respectfully as the two of them tightened their grip as was expected in the Borderlands. 'Sly Stormson. Of the Raven tribe. Your fella's brother was a close friend until he died.'

'I heard about what happened, and I'm sorry,' Kane said sadly. 'Braego always said how good his brother was. Didn't deserve to die like that.'

'Nah, he didn't. Still, all gotta end up as bones someday. Ain't nothin' gonna stop it so there's no use crying over it.'

Sly took a good look at the woman now. Keen, intelligent eyes. Dark, wavy hair streaked with grey and a certain strength to her frame that said she could handle herself. This wasn't the frail kind of woman he expected from these Southerners.

'So, why is a Borderland warrior of the Raven tribe back this way? I thought the fiasco of the Night of the Flames would have put you off coming back to the United

Cities.'

Sly worked his tongue around his cheek and his teeth, thinking carefully about his answer. 'Borderlands gone to shit. Torvield is a ghost town and that hells-damned army is destroying everything in its path. And that's all without the damn mountains bursting into flame and the earth breaking every damn week. Seemed like a good time to get away.'

'You going to fight against them when they come?'

''Course,' Sly answered, offended at the question. 'Fought alongside the bastards for a bit. Now we can see how it's gonna play out so we're making a stand against them.'

'You think we have a chance?'

'Nah,' Sly said honestly. 'But that don't change the fact that we gotta fight. We're the last of the Borderlands other than the fuckers who are still fighting against Arden. Gotta do something. Might end up as bones in the ground but that's gonna happen anyway. Might as well do it with an axe in hand and a song on my lips.'

Kane's smile grew. A warm, attractive smile. Sly could see why Braego had opted to lower himself for a Southerner.

'He used to say something similar. A weapon in hand and a song in his heart.'

'No better way to go. Better than he got anyway.'

Sly absently rubbed his hands together as he glances around the weapons that covered the walls. Some were up there just for decoration by the looks of it. Old Neres the blacksmith would have burst a lung screaming about the shoddy work of some of the blades. No use in battle. But there was a gem or two amongst the shit. A few weapons Sly could see causing damage in battle.

'You looking for a new weapon?' Kane asked him, keeping an eye on him as he scanned the walls.

'I got my axes,' he replied, patting the two tied to his belt. 'Though I remember someone a long time ago telling me that you can never have too many axes.'

'What about if they're buried in the back of your skull?' the woman asked mischievously.

Sly stopped and licked his lips, loving the question. 'Then, in that case, one is too many.' His eyes fell on the weapon he was looking for and he plucked the thin sword from its hanging and threw it in the air, marvelling at the ease with which Kane caught the hilt of the blade and dropped into a defensive stance. 'That weapon is the one you should use in the battle. Light, but sharp. Speed will be important to fight against Arden's army.'

'A rapier,' Kane said, twisting her wrist and studying the blade with an experienced eye. 'Thank you. Though it is not yours to give.'

Sly scoffed and raised his palms wide, looking around him in disbelief. 'This place will be destroyed in the battle. What use are these weapons if not to kill our enemies? Take it. Or don't. I don't care.'

He grinned as Kane took the sword and spun it around in her hand with skilled ease.

'I will use it, though I may need to practise with it before it feels like a part of me. Are you going to use that battle-axe?'

Sly shook his head. 'Nah. Too big. Just admiring it for a friend. He would have laughed his head off if he saw me wielding this bastard. His hammer was bigger than I was. Shame he's not here now.'

'We're all bones in the end.'

'Aye, though let's try and put that off for as long as possible, eh?' Sly said with a wink.

'Sounds like a plan to me.'

THE BROKEN PRINCE

K ane darted forward and snapped her wooden sword at her opponent, spotting the clear gap in their defence, a gap that she had already found on four separate occasions. The blade hit into her opponent's chest with a thud, bringing a cry from the young warrior who had yet to unsettle her.

'Pick up your sword, Drayke,' she told her son, biting back her disappointment as she saw the lack of fire in his eyes. He kicked the sword away and spun, pulling at his dark hair in frustration.

It had been some time since Kane had trained with wooden blades. Braego had always insisted on steel, claiming that the danger aspect would sharpen her mind and keep her focused on improvement. But Drayke was not ready for that yet. Though he had proven time and time again that he was comfortable with a blade, losing his arm had affected more than just his confidence. He would overcompensate with his movements and allow far too many gaps in his defence. In a true battle, Kane knew that

Drayke would not last long.

'Pick up your sword,' she repeated, calmer this time, understanding that he was already going through hell but also knowing that he needed to improve if he was going to survive the battles to come. 'We must continue our practice.'

'Why?' Drayke hissed through gritted teeth. 'What is the point? I am not going to become an amazing swordsman with one arm. It is pointless.' He winced as a shot of pain ran up the stub of his left arm and to his shoulder. He would have that pain for cycles to come. Though the medics in both Causrea and in Grey's army were able to offer herbs to dull the pain, they admitted it would be impossible to prevent it entirely. It had been yet another burden for her young son to bear.

'It takes time, Drayke. Time and a lot of effort. I have seen soldiers fight fiercely with just the one arm. They did not let their loss keep them from fighting.'

'Well I am obviously not like them, am I?'

'Your father would—'

'I don't give a shit about what my father would or would not do!' Drayke hissed, skin turning a dark shade of red as his chest rose and fell rapidly.

Kane chewed her lip, doing her best not to snap back. This petulant child was not the same as the young man who had always behaved with such dignity and respect. She reminded herself that he had suffered so much loss recently and even the strongest of people would not have made it through such events unscathed. The missing arm told the tale of the battle in Archania. The yellowing bruises on his temple and jaw and the slight limp as he walked over to his sword spoke of the decimation of Causrea.

'I am sorry, Drayke, I really am. But a battle is

coming, and I just want you to be as ready as possible. I wish I could snap my fingers and take this all away from you but I can't. Braego used to say that pain can be the harshest of teachers. I agree with that, but you can still learn from it.'

Drayke picked his sword up with a groan and glared at her. 'And did Braego ever lose an arm? Did you ever lose an arm? I should have died beneath the waves in Causrea with all the others…'

Without thinking, Kane worked on her rage. Whipping her sword up, she slapped the sword from Drayke's grip and reversed the blade's motion, stopping a hair's breadth away from Drayke's jaw. He stood up straight, eyes alert and worried as he stared at the wooden blade next to his face.

'I know that you have been away from Archania playing soldier with the Red Sons for a while now. And I know that you have been through some shit that I would not wish upon my worst enemies. But I know you Drayke, and I know that the disrespectful, moping fool sulking before me is not the real you.' Drayke opened his mouth to speak but thought better against it as Kane took a step closer to him. 'I am here for you to help you in anything that you need, but I'm going to need at least a small amount of effort on your part. You were raised by a great king and queen and you are the blood of one of the bravest and kindest warriors I have ever had the pleasure of knowing. You are better than this, and I *need* you to realise that. I'll give you one hour to think about your attitude. After that, we train again.'

Kane pulled the wooden blade away and chucked it onto the floor before making for the exit to the training room. 'And I will be using a real blade next time. Think about it.'

*

The training room was packed full of warriors when Kane returned a little over an hour later. It didn't take long to find her son. Some of Grey's men and women had recognised their lost prince and were taking the rare opportunity to speak to young Drayke about their lives in Archania. She was pleased to see that her son had a smile on his face, even when asked about his recent injuries.

'An unfortunate incident,' Drayke was saying to his adoring audience. 'But I will continue to fight, I promise you that.'

'Aye,' one of the men was saying, nudging his female companion and turning his adoring eyes back onto the prince. 'I knew you would. Always said that you were the one we needed to rule back in the capital. You brother was a right shit, make no mistake. But folk always spoke well of young Prince Drayke. It's an honour to be her with you, Your Highness.'

'The honour is all mine,' Drayke responded with a winning smile and a graceful bow. 'Now, I believe my trainer is here.'

The group around him shuffled away, eyes going from the prince to Kane and back again. Kane nodded and waved at the Archanians who grinned back, happy to see another of their own. She supposed they were comforting reminders of their homeland and the hope that normality may return.

'I see that you are more yourself,' Kane muttered as she reached her son.

'I may have lost my arm, but it seems that recently I may have lost my senses too. I am sorry.' Drayke breathed long and slow. 'I will do better.'

Kane squeezed his shoulder and nodded. 'I know

377

you will. What I said earlier is true. I am always here for you. Even when you act like a little shit.' They chuckled together and Kane did her best to hide her relief.

Drayke scanned the weapons available, knowing that this time there would be no safety of the wooden blades.

Kane watched, allowing him the time to survey the weapons available.

'The gladius would be a good weapon for you.'

Kane spun and saw a strange man with dark hair in a bun on the top of his head striding over to Drayke.

'Why?' the prince asked as the man reached him and picked up a gladius.

'With one arm, you cannot wield one of the heavier blades. The gladius will allow you to move easily, with some practice. It is still a deadly weapon at close range if used by a skilled swordsman.'

Drayke took the blade and tested the swing, smiling at the weight. 'Thanks, I'll give it a go. What is your name, I don't think I've seen you before?'

'Sanada. I'm not from here, but I did spend some time in Archania recently. You must be the prince. Care to spar? It has been many cycles since I fought with royalty…'

Drayke turned to Kane but she backed away and offered the room for the two of them to train. 'This could be good for you…'

The strange warrior twisted the hilt of a thin blade and drew it slowly from its sheath before holding it in front of his face, closing his eyes and moving his lips in a silent prayer. 'Do not overreach,' he advised Drayke. 'Stay calm and do not panic. Let your opponent come to your and then attack with precision.'

A circle of hushed, excited men and women shuffled around the unusual pair as Sanada and Drayke tested the weight of their weapons, the islander started the slow, graceful dance with his right foot stepping over his left, leading Drayke in the early moments. Drayke mirrored the movement, his eyes flickering from the glistening blade to Sanada's navy boots, the nerves clear on his young face.

Kane bit her lip and focused on her breathing, hoping to steady her beating heart. All eyes were on the two swordsmen as none dared to breathe too loud. Kane thought it would be possible to hear a feather fall to the ground as the crowd held their breath, waiting for the first move.

She was pleased to see her son take the good advice and hold steady, though the sweat dripped from his brow with the effort. She knew it would be testing the eager fighter in him, the confident young man who wanted to take the fight to his opponents. But he stayed strong, taking the slow steps needed to stay opposite Sanada, his blade held high and guarding his chest and neck from any attack.

And then Sanada struck.

A dip of the shoulder and a dart forward caught most of the crowd by surprise, judging by the choral gasp released throughout the room.

Sanada's thin blade danced through the air with unnerving accuracy. Kane raised a hand to her mouth, her heart in her throat as she feared the worst. But Drayke responded admirably. Though not as graceful as his shorter opponent, the young prince snapped his short blade onto Sanada's and shifted to his right, away from the piercing attack.

He steadied himself with a long slow breath and swallowed as his opponent chuckled and whipped the finely forged sword in the air faster and faster before grinning at

Drayke, sticking his tongue out as though he did not have a care in the world.

'A strong block and footwork that proves you are no rookie,' Sanada said, impressed. 'You will need that and more to compensate for your missing limb. Do not focus on the pain or your nerves. Focus on what you want to do and do it. To hesitate will mean death…'

With that last word, Sanada snapped into motion like a snake, diving forwards with that beautiful emerald sword. This time he unleashed a flurry of attacks. Low, high, low.

Kane cheered with the crowd as Drayke dropped back, diverting the first two strikes.

But he could do nothing about the third. His legs bucked as the flat of the blade slapped against his thigh, dropping him to a knee as he grunted with pain and embarrassment. A frustrated sigh told Kane that her son had wanted more, expected more of himself.

'That blade must become a part of you, moving with the ease of water streaming from a fountain but as strong as a mountain in the storm,' Sanada advised as the crowd cheered for the injured prince, offering him encouragement.

Kane balled her fists and muttered to herself. 'Come on, Drayke. You can do this.' The islander was clearly the more sophisticated and experienced warrior. His speed and ease with the sword were frightening and she wondered for a dreamy moment what it would have been like to see the strength and guile of Braego faced against this short but confident swordsman. That would have been one for the ages. People from all around Takaara would have paid good coin to witness such a fight and they would have spoken about it in the inns and taverns for cycles to come. Her thoughts switched to Istari Vostor, a man she had grown to care for deeply, strange though he was, and she felt a spasm of guilt as she decided that he would have destroyed either one of them in single combat. Hells, even against them both in a two-on-one situation wouldn't have made the Sword of Causrea bat an eyelid. The way he had ended the battle with the Red Sons and the Empire's forces had been the stuff of legend. She doubted any other than those who were there would ever believe such a tale.

Her attention snapped back to the fight in front of her as Drayke stood, emboldened by the support around him from his fellow Archanians, all wanting him to defeat this upstart outsider. She noticed only one man standing silent and watching the fight. A tall, blonde warrior who she believed to be a Barbarian judging by his colossal frame. The warrior watched the fight with an impassive face, lips tight together.

The swords clanged and Drayke moved with an increased energy, the dance of blades picking up the pace and intensity. He dropped back, allowing Sanada to edge closer with a flurry of strikes, blocking and parrying each strike with a pained and worried look on his face as he allowed his opponent to control the bout.

Sanada's blade described a beautiful but deadly arc, starting high and dropping low, edging dangerously close to Drayke's cheek but its path was diverted at the last moment by the sudden whip of the prince's sword snapping up. A shocked and awed collective gasp escaped the transfixed crowd, all heavily invested in the strange but majestic fight unfolding before their eyes. Kane punched a fist in the air and cheered through her gritted teeth at the defence of her son, pleased to see him move with the clarity and grace of his youth. She could see the gleam in Drayke's eyes as his confidence grew. With each block, he seemed re-energised. His footwork was light and purposeful. His bladework neat and tight, each movement careful and precise. She spotted the narrowing of his brow as he stepped forward, finally comfortable to take the fight to Sanada.

He jabbed, sliced, and thrust his sword towards his sparring partner, feet dancing elegantly forwards as he twisted his body to give Sanada less of a focus point for his own attacks. The islander took the shift in momentum well, dropping back and falling into the role of defender as his thin sword clanged with each block, the smug smirk no longer on his face. Instead it had been replaced by what Kane thought were lines of worry as Drayke pressed the advantage.

'Come on Drayke! You've got him!'

'That's it, Prince Drayke!'

'For the United Cities!'

The crowd whooped and hollered, all smiling and cheering for their prince, enjoying the sudden confidence shooting through his frame as he began to lead the deadly dance of swords, finally comfortable with his own body and the shorter blade in hand.

Drayke darted forwards, hoping to land the winning strike, eyes lighting with victory.

And Sanada dropped low and twisted under the attack, leaping up at the last moment as he rammed his shoulder into Drayke's, knocking him to the floor. Sanada watched with a smirk as the gladius slid across the floor of the training room. He stood beside the fallen and clearly frustrated young prince as the noise in the room seemed to be sucked away in an instant.

Kane sighed and shook her head. He had seemed so close to victory!

'A good fight. You should be proud.' Sanada tapped the edge of his blade to Drayke's neck and then slid it away in its scabbard. He held out his hand which Drayke

382

took after a moment's hesitation. 'Keep practising. Every day, as much as you can. You learn fast,' he said once Drayke was back on his feet.

The blonde Barbarian Kane had seen watching earlier was now standing beside them, the gladius looking like a dagger in his huge hand. 'I've yet to see anyone beat him, even with both arms. A good fight, little man.'

Drayke nodded and took the offered sword, clearly fighting back his frustration over the loss. 'Thank you. That is the best I have felt in some time. At least since…'

'Yes,' Sanada stepped in. 'But that is the past. Focus on the present and you will change your future.'

'Good advice,' Kane agreed, joining the three warriors as the crowd began to disperse. Though disappointed with the outcome, the men and women in the training room still called out their praise to the young prince as they left the room, pleased to see his skill and determination. 'They were proud to see their prince fight in such a way. One arm or two, that was a heck of a sparring session.'

A thin smile found Drayke's face at last as he finally digested what had happened. 'I thought I had you for a moment.'

'You almost did,' Sanada admitted. 'But training for years in a palace is different to growing up in the fury of the Blood Islands. Any sign of weakness is jumped on and beaten away. If that doesn't work, the rocks at the bottom of the Shinakawa Cliffs are the only option. A watery grave filled with the corpses of those unfortunate enough to not meet the high standards of my people.'

'Sounds like an interesting place…' Drayke scoffed, his surprise apparent.

Sanada shrugged. 'There is a beauty to the islands.

But we are not known as the most welcoming of people.'

'Not many people are nowadays,' Kane added.

'True,' the Barbarian said. 'That is the way of things.'

'So it is, Sigurd, my friend,' Sanada said grimly, glancing around to find that it was just the four of them left in the training room. 'It has been an honour to fight a prince. I would offer my services to train more often, but it seems that true battle is not so far away now. We wish you both luck in the war to come.'

The Blood Islander gave a stiff bow and strode away, followed closely by his Barbarian friend.

'How do you feel?' Kane asked Drayke as he wiped the sweat from his face and sat down on one of the chairs around the edge of the room. He collapsed into it and rolled his head from shoulder to shoulder, moaning with the cracking sounds of his neck.

'I feel more alive than I have since this happened,' he said with a nod towards his missing arm. 'I may be broken, but that doesn't mean I'm finished. I'll fight in this war, and whatever happens, my people will know that they had a prince who was willing to give his everything to save them.'

'That is the boy I watched grow up. That is the boy who makes his family proud,' Kane said with a lump in her throat, blinking away the tears.

'Now,' Drayke said with a sigh, 'I sure could use a drink. And a bath. I care not for the order.'

The smile on his face was warm and from the heart. A smile that Kane had seen Braego wear so often over the cycles. He may be broken but he was her son. And he was ready to fight.

THE BEGINNING OF THE END

Arden had never been this far east before. His life had been one of sheltered ignorance, spent entirely in the icy tundra of the north of Takaara – a harsh environment of Barbarians and bastards; a place where one wrong look could get you killed. Hardened men and women shaped by the snowy, cold climate of the Borderlands had warned Arden that it was a place where life was a struggle and one where nowhere else could compare. Looking around at the endless sand dunes and feeling the unrelenting heat of the afternoon sun, Arden thought that maybe they had been wrong. Here was a place that could claim to be the toughest in the world. Here was a place that the Gods had chosen to test the spirit of men.

And here was the place that Osiron's forces had laid to waste.

Smoke still drifted lazily upwards, creating a dark haze that blocked the light from the sky. Arden strolled through the ashes and the bloodied bodies: through the ruins of the crumbling stone buildings that had only recently been a part of one of the most affluent cities in all Takaara.

Osiron had told Arden tales of the city of Mughabir; a nation ruled by a greedy, arrogant Sultan who ruled with an iron fist. A man who fought against his neighbouring nation not because of any difference of ideology, but because he grew envious of the growing nation casting a shadow over his own. Arden had argued about the reasoning of picking a fight with Darakeche when the nation stood against the Empire of Light, the greatest power in Takaara and an empire who would stop at nothing to end Osiron and Arden's path to the betterment of the world.

'Remember, child, our path is not one against the Empire of Light. This is no single battle against an army where good seeks victory over evil,' Osiron had explained. 'We need not look for allies. Instead, we seek to wipe the plague of the living from this land and start a world where injustice and evil no longer exist. Such petty squabbles between the tribes of man should not deter us from our destined path. We know what must be done, though the way is full of pain and suffering.'

'Aren't there any who would flock to our call? Any who would listen to what we have to say?' Arden had wondered out loud.

Osiron shook their head sadly, face filled with regret and pity. 'This land is full of petty fools who crave the various vices of man. They preach of piety and goodness in the day but seek the shelter of faze dens and whorehouses at night. There are none worth saving, child.'

Some still sat in the streets, haunted expressions staring into the void as Arden passed them silently. There were no more tears and cries of grief. What was left was an emptiness; a horrible vacuum of nothing where those who had survived the devastation had grown exhausted from the death and loss of loved ones and were now waiting in that painful window of time where they did not know what would come next. To stay clinging to the past would bring nothing but more suffering but to move forwards would bring nothing but guilt and the burden to live for more than just themselves.

The thought brought a pang to his chest and he felt his cheeks grow red as he wondered if there were any who would grieve for him when he was gone. When Socket's blade thrust into his back, was there anyone who actually cared for him? Was there anyone who gave a shit if he vanished from the face of the world?

He knew the answer, and that darkened his mood further as he wandered into the shadow of an orange tree, marvelling that the tree had somehow managed to survive amongst all the destruction and chaos.

'Darakeche has fallen. The Shield in the East is broken. But the Empire of Light is free to prepare their forces and make a stand against us,' Arden said out loud as he took one of the oranges and held it in his palm, rolling a thumb over its strange skin. Such things did not grow where he came from. 'Where do we go next?'

Osiron's voice rang clear in his mind, as though they were standing next to Arden in the shadow of the tree. 'Darakeche is no more. The South awakens from its slumber as King Zeekial gathers his forces. The East is fractured but still strong with the Empress waiting to play her hand. And the North cracks with infighting as Mason D'Argio crushes opponents to the Light. We are nearing the end of days, the time when Chaos rules and a world anew will be forged in the fires of the Final War. Takaara is ready to fall…'

'And what of Causrea, the water republic you spoke of ruled by the Council of Ten?' Arden asked, recalling an old conversation with Osiron. 'And the Heartlands.'

'The Heartlands are doing what they always do. Fighting in their clans and treading over the bodies of friends and allies in order to climb higher in that pit of despair.' Osiron's voice dripped with disgust as they spoke of the infamous centre of Takaara. Even Arden had heard of the madness of that part of the world when listening to old men sharing tales over campfires in the forests of the Borderlands. 'And as for Causrea…' An edge of humour returned to Osiron's voice as they mentioned the coastal republic. 'Perhaps it is better if I show you. It seems Takaara herself is on our side…'

The orange dropped from his grip as Arden felt a now familiar otherworldly pull, the wind whipping around him and driving the world before him from view. No more grief. No more bodies. Just an endless darkness with the hint of dancing blue lights on the horizon. He closed his eyes and allowed the pull to guide him on his journey, allowing Osiron's power to take him to the other side of the world, away from the East and into the far West, just south of the United Cities.

The wind stopped its howling and Arden felt it time to open his eyes. The heat was less oppressive here. He welcomed the slight burn on his forearms and the back of his neck as he stared out at a turquoise sea from the high vantage point of the cliffs. It was a beautiful sight as the turquoise sea met the light blue of the horizon, untainted by clouds. It took a moment for him to see why he had been brought here. But then he peered down at the lines of white displaying the breaking of the waves against the coast.

A wide bridge had been broken in half, its support

beams broken low to the beach below. Arden's eyes were drawn to the rubble and debris floating near the coastline, scattered with what looked like the bodies of the dead. Arden raised a hand to his open mouth with the shocked and sudden realisation that *this* was the Republic of Causrea. Floating beams and debris could be seen all along the coast, the remains of what had once been a beautiful coastal nation that even the cynical travellers of the Borderlands had spoken of with misty eyes and golden tongues.

'A place built by the Gods to show us what true beauty really is…' was how one merchant had described Causrea to Arden. 'Built above the calm waters of the golden coast, the Republic is the one place other than the Borderlands that captured my heart.'

That beauty was now mixed with the devastation of the sunken city.

'What happened here?' he asked, casting a surprised glance over the scene. This wasn't the work of Chaos forces. This was something else.

'Takaara is crying out in pain. The quakes come now with more regularity. The last one brought with it waves taller than the mountains of the Far North. The first onslaught destroyed much of what we know as Causrea, though some were able to escape to both north and south. But they will be dealt with, as will all others. The second and third waves crushed what was left, decimating this bastion of arrogance. The Council of Ten ruled with a belief that they were better than all others. They could interfere in the events of other nations and twist things to their own gain. Their deaths will not bring a tear to my eyes.'

Arden wondered if here were any deaths that would bring a tear to their eyes. The brief moment passed, shook away and cleared with a reenergised focus to do what had to be done.

'So what happens next?' Arden asked, balling his fists and taking a deep breath.

'Mason D'Argio believes himself a God. He marches towards a group of Northern refugees cowering alongside your old friends behind walls that will not prevent us from succeeding with our plan. I suggest we show them exactly what we are capable of. Two birds with one stone, as your people often say.'

'Sly, Kiras…' Arden muttered, rubbing his knuckles and licking his cracked lips. He nodded slowly, steeling himself to the idea of fighting his old allies. 'You saw what I did with Socket. I won't hold back. Mason, Sly, Kiras… no one will stop us now, Osiron. Takaara is ready to be cleansed. No more pain. No more suffering. That is what we promised one another.'

'And that is how it shall be, my young ally. You will pass their walls and show them what the Prince of Chaos is truly capable of.'

Arden took a last look down at the bloated corpses littering the golden sands of the coast. The remains of Causrea spoiled what would have otherwise been one of the most beautiful vistas he had laid eyes on in all his life – and afterlife. How many more such places would need to be spoiled before they could thrive once more and begin to regain some of the natural beauty that Takaara once had? Would they have to tear down the sick and plague-ridden towns and cities brick by damned brick?

He looked up into the stunning blue sky and watched as the birds circled overhead, following their daily patterns with an ease and a freedom that he envied.

'We can watch as Mason's army fights with the bastards in the North, those traitors. Let them devour one another. We can be as the crows, waiting carefully and when the time comes, we will feast on the pieces that are left after the battle.'

Osiron's smile stretched out to their ears in Arden's mind, delighted with the words of their protégé. 'Half of our forces can head north to wipe out those who survive. The other half can head south, ready to meet what scum the Boy King has managed to muster. Our time is nearly at hand. A new world awaits.'

STICK OR TWIST

'That blade needs to head north,' Buhle argued through clenched teeth, struggling to keep her voice down as the army halted for rest. As expected, she had not taken too well to seeing Aleister return without the rest of his scouting party and with nothing but an old man to back up his story. 'You know this. The king commanded that you head north to the Great War. Coming back is folly. Surely even in your sun-addled pink head you are able to understand that…?'

Aleister gave Istari Vostor a quick glance before answering the stern Buhle. 'There's another way to win. Another way we can get out of this sorry mess alive. And that means keeping the sword down here and keeping our army south of the border. The Heartlands will be nothing but a distraction as we pass it now; we must let our enemies come to us and use what we have available. Focus on our strengths above all.'

'And what exactly does that mean?' Buhle asked, eyebrow raised and clearly not suckered into Aleister's words.

'Use the blood of the sacrificed. Speak to a God,' Istari stated quite simply.

Aleister had to grin, however nervously, as he spotted the smile creep onto Buhle's incredulous face. The usually grim warrior burst into loud chuckling, alerting those nearby as they cast curious glances their way.

'Speak to a God? You have lost your mind, old man.' She turned to Aleister and slapped him on the chest. 'And you too. I should not laugh as the situation is clearly dire, but what else can I do? My only other option is to ram a spear into your feeble mind.'

Istari shrugged. 'An option, true. But I have not lost my mind. I am just more knowledgeable than you. And that is not something to be ashamed of. Most people are.'

The incredulous look shifted to one of confused annoyance so Aleister decided that now was the appropriate time to jump in before things escalated further. 'Look, Buhle. I know I'm asking a lot, but you need to trust me. This could save so many lives. Zeek will agree, I know he will.'

The skilled warrior sighed and rolled her eyes. 'You better be right, pink man. I am putting my neck on the line for you. We will keep several warriors on the border in case there is any sign of attack from Lord Manuel's growing army of misfits from the Heartlands. Other than that, we will edge backwards. You can head to the city and speak to Zeek. Though, I doubt he will be pleased…'

'I feel like you've made us march out here for no reason,' Ariel said with a tilt of her head as she reached the two of them, the towering figure of Bathos just behind her. 'You sure the king will be pleased about marching right back where we started?'

'Pleased has nothing to do with it,' Aleister explained, ready for that particular argument. 'The decisions we make will echo through time. I'm not here to please the king; I'm here to make sure as many people survive this shit as possible.'

'As long as I'm invited into that little conversation, I'm happy,' his sister said with a wink.

'You trust this old guy?' Bathos asked, keeping a suspicious eye on Istari as the warrior peered off into the distance some way from them. His cloak rippled in the soft wind, his arms folded as he surveyed the army at a standstill on the plains. 'Big decision to make on the whim of a stranger.'

Aleister absently bit his nails as he followed his friend's gaze. He shrugged and smacked his gums at last, recalling what he had seen with the warriors from the Heartlands. 'That guy saved my live. And I've never seen anyone move the way he did. You should have seen him Bathos… like the wind with the edge of a blade cutting through anything it blows past. And he knew about Soulsbane.'

Buhle clicked her tongue against her teeth and sighed. 'Well, the king will want to speak to him then. I will keep a small force here to ward off any threat from the Heartlands and send messages to the city if any dare to head this way. I will tell the other leaders to head back to Ad-Alum.' Buhle flashed her dark eyes in Aleister's direction. 'I will blame you for this.'

Aleister smirked and flicked his eyebrows up and down mischievously. 'I'd expect nothing less.'

*

'I must admit, when the messenger informed me that you were heading back to the city, I was both alarmed and frustrated. When she said that you have an idea for how to save my people, that turned to shock and scepticism. Tell me, Aleister, why have you forced my people to disobey my orders?'

Aleister had always thought himself a man of confidence, unlikely to wither under a stern interrogation. But when the Boy King's youthful but stern expression shot his way, he had to admit that he suddenly felt like a small boy being scolded for disobeying a parent's orders. He looked over his shoulder for his usual support but Ariel had not been allowed access into the king's war chamber. Instead, Zeek had been insistent that only Aleister be allowed access to the room.

'We were attacked by members of Lord Manuel's army. Manuel is a noble and former soldier from one of the many failed states in the centre of Takaara. It seems he has amassed quite the following and their forces were seeking revenge for their defeat at the hands of Buhle and her forces when first we entered your kingdom,' Aleister explained. 'They killed all of our scouting party, including Ife, though she fought valiantly.' His mouth ran dry and as he hesitated, the dark events flashing unwilling into his mind. 'I barely escaped. But I was saved by a stranger, an old man with lightning speed and expert swordsmanship. If I hadn't seen such skill with my own eyes, I would have thought such a thing madness.'

Zeek frowned at the description, a dark shadow passing over his cool features. 'Who is this stranger?'

Aleister jumped and twisted as the door slammed open behind him. A very distressed looking guard stumbled into the room, stammering an apology as he chased a hooded figure strolling with all the casual grace of someone who owned the place.

'I am sorry, Your Majesty,' the guard moaned. 'He

would not listen to me…'

The old warrior flicked his head, dropping the hood and allowing the lanterns' light onto his scarred faze, knowing eyes piercing the king as though he were assessing the man before him and ignoring the fact that he had just stormed into the war chamber of the most powerful man in all of the southern hemisphere.

But it was Zeek's expression that captivated Aleister. The king's jaw slackened, eyes widening as they fell on the warrior rudely interrupting their closed meeting. The shock left after a moment, eyes turning to the still whimpering and apologetic guard.

'No matter, brother. Leave us. Istari Vostor is an old friend, isn't that right?' The warm words did nothing to melt the icy tone of the king's voice as his glare returned to the intruder who met the gaze with a wry smile.

'Friend? I have killed people I care for more than you, *Your Majesty*. But perhaps it is best if this lackey leaves. It is time for the adults to have a conversation.'

The flicker of fear that flashed across Zeek's eyes was not missed by Aleister following the swordsman's comment. 'Leave us.'

Aleister made to follow the comically rushed guard from the room but Istari's hand shot out and grabbed him by the shoulder. 'You stay. You will need to hear this.'

Aleister glanced over his shoulder at the king but Zeek merely offered the slightest of nods in agreement.

'Take a seat, this could be a long night.'

The heat of the room had nothing to do with the tropical climate of the city. Aleister dug a finger under his collar and pulled his shirt from his sweat-drenched skin, shifting in his cushioned seat and trying for what felt like the hundredth time to get comfortable. Sitting between the two men, his eyes darted from one to the other, attempting to identify how long they had both gone without blinking as they stared unmoving at each other.

He coughed and shifted again, pushing himself higher in the seat and blowing out his cheeks. He drummed his fingers on the dark, circular wooden table between them and looked from the king to the swordsman and back again. Eventually, he gave up, dropping his eyes as the glares of both men shifted his way and landed on those tapping fingers.

'Look, I know that we have some real weird tension in the room right now, but there's a battle heading this way and we could all use the time to prepare for the shit heading our way. The two of you staring at each other for hours isn't gonna help anyone. Agreed?'

Both sets of eyes stared daggers his way but finally they relented. Zeek sat back in his seat and Istari mimicked the action, licking his lips and offering the slightest of nods.

'The boy is right. Osiron will know you have prepared for battle. They will be sending a force this way as we speak. That is certain,' Istari claimed.

'Then why are you here and not sitting on your farm in Causrea or holing up in the desert like you used to love to do?' Zeek snapped with a grimace.

'Would it have been better if I created my own cult in the jungle and made people die for me? Or maybe I could have forged a weapon capable of killing the Gods and tearing Takaara into tiny pieces? Are either of those options preferable to the decisions that I have made throughout my life, Your Majesty?'

Aleister rubbed his neck nervously, only looking

briefly at Zeek as the king bit his lips, trembling with fury at the accusations.

'You could have prevented this,' Zeek hissed through gritted teeth, 'You could have stopped Mason. You could have found Osiron's Guardian. Instead, you chose to pass the time watching the sun set on a dying world.'

'I chose to not make things any worse than you already had. I chose to keep the hells away from the madness that the four of you birthed all those cycles ago.'

'Then why are you here now? Suddenly grown a conscience and want to save the world?'

'I want to ensure that there is a place left for those who survive what is to come. I do not care if I am one of them. But I cannot sit back and watch Takaara crumble into dust and fall to shadow.' Istari blasted back.

'How very honourable of you…'

Aleister had heard enough. He slammed his fist on the table and glared at the two of them. 'That's enough!' he roared, frustrated with them both. 'You are powerful, grown men. This isn't the time for petty arguments and old grievances. Any day now, we will be fighting for not just our lives, but the lives of all the peoples of Takaara. We *do not* have the time to squabble amongst ourselves. Whatever shit the two of you have going on, bury it now as deep as you can and don't let it surface until this mess is dealt with. Now isn't the time.' He breathed heavily, eyes darted between the two scolded men. One, the most powerful man in the South. The other, the deadliest man he had ever seen with a blade. Both looked like the scolded little boys Aleister had felt like only moments before. 'Are we agreed?'

Nods and mumbled apologies came from the two of them, much to Aleister's great relief. 'So, what can we do to stop this madness?'

Istari sighed and relaxed in his seat as he rubbed at the dark shadow of his beard. 'Osiron will send their army this way sooner or later. They know that to rule Takaara, there are two people with the power to stop them. One sits in this room opposite me, the other sits on a throne in the East and is readying her own forces. However, there is a way to stop them, or at least a way to give them a fight worthy of the annals of history.'

'And how do we do that?' Zeek asked.

'That *blood* you have been acquiring from your subjects,' Istari said with disgust. 'And that sword the boy has been carrying around as though it were some cheap antique. Use the two and we can have a conversation that will change the fate of Takaara.'

'A conversation with who?' Zeek frowned.

Istari smirked, a hint of humour on his face. 'A conversation with a God.'

Four of the five players around the table showed signs of nerves. Bathos had sweat dripping in such a large volume that it had pooled onto the dark wood of the table and splashed onto the leaflet the warrior had earlier been reading about weapons from the Crooked Isles. Harish's eyes roamed around the table, flicking from one player to the next and then back down at the selection of cards shaking in his hands. Every now and then the poor man would give a startled little chuckle and switch around the order of the cards before tutting and shaking his head again. Ariel twisted her mouth around as she studied her own hand, weighing up the various possibilities before offering a long, slow sigh. Aleister felt his leg twitching, banging his knee up with such force that he grunted and groaned in pain as it hit the underside of the table, catching the frame and forcing a string of expletives from his mouth and a nerve-easing round of laughter from the others.

Only Akhona seemed completely at ease.

The young Southerner had taken to the game of Four Kings with a startling ease that Aleister had to admit brought with it a large amount of envy. For two days she had played the game after his short tuition and she had yet to be humiliated. In fact, she had won almost half of the games she had taken part in. She bore no sign of nerves, peering across her cards with a steady, calculating eye, oblivious to the weariness of her companions as they fought to win their honour back, and the large amount of coin and items she had procured from them over the two days.

'Twist,' she said after some thought, much to the despair of the room. Aleister flicked a card her way and grimaced as he saw the spark of joy on her face.

'How…' he muttered, shaking his head and releasing an incredulous laugh. At first he had assumed it to be the infamous "beginner's luck" that players loved to speak of so much, especially experienced players who found themselves losing to newcomers, but now he wasn't so sure. He hadn't seen a player take to the game with such ease since Katerina Kane had given Braego a short lesson that was followed by a string of victories for the Borderlander that had many in the Upper City circle of nobility questioning the methods of the weapons master. There had been no cheating involved though, Aleister was certain of that; Braego was too bound to his honour for such a thing in a petty game played by what he called "weird little Southerners". No, the Borderland warrior just seemed to take to the game like a bird to flight and that was the way of things sometimes. No use moaning about it.

Akona dropped one card onto the table and picked another, chuckling darkly as she did so.

'Four kings…' she said, sticking her tongue out and dragging the numerous coins from the centre of the table towards her. She ignored the groans of despair ringing out from her opponents, chuckling with glee as Bathos, Harish, Ariel and Aleister threw their own cards in front of them with a multitude of curses and sighs.

'Luck!' Akhona said with a laugh, 'That's what you called it yesterday, Aleister.'

'I'd call it something entirely different today,' Aleister responded with a groan, rubbing his temples with forefinger and thumb, unable to comprehend how she had won yet another game. 'Luck is fleeting. What you have is a bloody curse!'

'Doesn't feel like a curse to me,' Akhona said with a laugh as the others scraped their chair back and began to leave the room, offering begrudging congratulations and farewells.

Soon, only Aleister was left in the room with the cheerful, young woman, smiling as he watched her collect her winnings.

'It won't last long you know,' he said with a wry smile.

'Well, I might quit while I'm ahead then,' Akhona answered with a wink.

'Too right,' Aleister said, clearing his throat and ambling towards her. He licked his dry lips and sniffed, grimacing as he struggled to get the word out. 'Felize,' he said eventually, feeling like a bastard as he saw his new friend's face drop at the name of her good friend. 'How is he?'

It had been a while since he had seen Felize. The wound had festered, as they tend to do after long periods without the proper care and attention they required. The last time he had laid eyes on the injured warrior, the prospects had not been good.

'We should go see him,' Akhona suggested. 'He would be grateful to see you.'

The makeshift infirmary was a small room filled with low beds either side of a wide aisle. Cut off from prying eyes with the use of large white sheets, the sides of the room blocked the patients' suffering from any member of the public passing through. Akhona led Aleister down the aisle, greeting the nurses and medics treating the various patients with a knowing glance and nod.

The smile of familiarity left her face as she reached the end of the corridor and pulled back the white sheet to her right. Aleister followed with caution, breathing heavily as Akhona pulled the sheet to its original position as he walked past her and stood beside the white bed on the other side of the boundary.

Felize lay on the bed with eyes half closed. He barely acknowledged Aleister walking up beside him and resting a hand on his forehead. His hot skin was clammy with sweat and Aleister pulled away with a frown.

'He has a fever,' Aleister stated simply, recognising the symptoms of a man in fever following a battle. He had seen it often enough.

'Of course he has a fever,' Akhona scolded. She pulled the sheets away and revealed a sickening wound, a bloody stump where the warrior's leg had once lay. Aleister jerked back and covered his mouth and nose at the sight of the horrific injury, averting his gaze as the guilt ate away at him.

'Akhona…' he muttered apologetically. Futile, but necessary.

'It is not your fault,' she said, her own gaze leading away from the missing limb and finding Felize's weary face. She caressed his cheek and bent down beside him, closely watching the steady rise and fall of his chest. 'We know the risks of battle. We were part of the scouting party. We left with more than most of those who were with you. We have to see the chink of light in the shadow, otherwise we would always live in despair.'

Wise words for one so young.

'I'm sorry. I should have been more vigilant.'

'There was nothing you could do. They were waiting for us and that was it. We wanted to fight with something much more dangerous. They snuck up on us when we least expected it and that was it. No use beating ourselves up over it. Felize would say that.'

Aleister watched as the wounded warrior shifted uncomfortably on the bed and groaned, spasming slightly and making odd noises. He had seen it before, the after-effects of a harsh battle. He called for a medic and stood, shifting out the way as the medic rushed over to check the man. Akhona continued to hold his hand, offering what support she could, even if the injured soldier could not feel it.

'He knows I am here,' Akhona said, nodding to herself as though she had heard what was inside of Aleister's head. 'He knows that we are fighting for him.'

Aleister's response hung in the air as a commotion behind him interrupted the conversation. A clatter of something being knocked over followed by shouts and angry words shared between a plethora of individuals filled the air. One voice in particular made Aleister groan.

'Aleister of the Red Sons, I believe they call you,' Istari Vostor said as he managed to make his way past the angry guards and medics and reach them by the bedside of their fallen friend. The old warrior gave a quick glance at the sleeping patient before turning his stern glare on Aleister.

'What seems to be the problem?'

'Your scouts came back. Looks like battle is coming this way.'

Aleister frowned. 'Osiron?'

'Nothing that bad,' Istari replied with a wink. 'Bastards from the Heartlands. You ready to fight that scum Manuel's army?'

Aleister chewed his cheek and gave a determined nod. 'Let's give that fucker a taste of his own medicine.'

'Sounds good to me…'

THE QUIET MOMENTS

The news delivered from the messenger wasn't surprising to anyone in the room. Former General Grey stood still with the letter in hand, his moustache twitching slightly. Sir Dominic shrunk back into the shadows, glass in hand as he raised his brows and had a swift drink. The scruffy Borderlands warrior, Sly, just pushed a grubby thumb against one of his nostrils and sniffed out harshly, letting fly a jet of green slime onto the dark wooden floorboards. He scratched his ragged beard and rubbed his hands together, looking at each one of them in the room.

'Well, looks like that's that then?' Sly said with a wink. 'They'll be here tomorrow. Gotta admit, I've wanted to take a swipe at that cunt Mason for some time now. The fire-worshipping bastard ain't gonna make it out of here alive if he brings his forces here. We'll be ready for him…'

Grey thanked the messenger who saluted and turned from the room without another word. He sighed and leaned against the tall window that looked out across the Eastern Sea as a harsh wind whipped the waves against the coast. 'Osiron is the endgame for all of us. Mason will be an appetiser and we need to make sure we are alive and ready for the main course.'

'And how are we supposed to do that?' Dominic asked, voice rising to an unusually high pitch as he sloshed the whiskey around the glass in his hand. His cheeks were a as pink as a summer sunset and there was a manic look in his eyes. 'Those who witnessed the destruction of our homeland tell the tale with a glassy-eyed look that speaks volumes. Mason or Osiron, we are doomed either way…'

Sly groaned and ambled over to the knight of the United Cities. Kane thought about stepping in between the two men but she hadn't the energy. Better to just watch and see how things played out. She would jump in if it got messy. At least that's how she explained it to herself.

'You're a knight, right?' Sly asked, his voice low and menacingly quiet. He sniffed and pulled on Dominic's jacket, straightening both sides and brushing some dust from the breast pocket. Dominic nodded nervously, lips trembling.

'Well,' Sly continued, 'that means you must have done something very honourable and brave. 'Cause I doubt that your king would give them away for doing shit all.' The blood drained from the knight's face, turning him an odd shade of grey. Sly grabbed the man's drink and downed the whiskey in one gulp, breathing out long and slow, right into the knight's face when he finished. 'Tastes weak. I'm not a fan of weak.' He threw the glass onto the ground, smashing it into tiny pieces. Kane muttered a curse but Grey didn't even turn to look over at the two warriors. Dominic looked as though he may have pissed himself.

'I get the message,' the knight mumbled.

'My message?' Sly growled. 'My message is that if

we are weak, then we all die. You are a knight, I'm expecting you to stand at the front line and set the example. Die with honour if you have to old man, but don't stand in the shadows as less experienced men and women give their lives. Else I'll come hunting for ya myself... understand?'

Dominic nodded and Sly released the man's jacket.

'I think it best if I go and prepare myself for the battle,' Dominic muttered rather sheepishly.

'You go do that big fella,' Sly smirked, allowing the knight to pass and hurry from the room with the briefest of nods towards Kane. She nodded back and closed the door behind him.

'And what exactly did that accomplish?' she asked once she was sure Dominic had left.

Sly shrugged. 'Bit of fun for me. Also, fuckers like that need to be reminded about the need for a backbone. We don't need limp bastards with what we are about to do.'

'And what are we about to do?' Grey asked, his voice flat and tired. He turned from the window to look at them both, seeming older than Kane had ever seen him. The lines around his eyes were more prominent, the weariness in his movements clear to the naked eye. 'In the fight against Mason's warriors we will be outnumbered. In the fight against Osiron's forces we will be outnumbered even more.'

Sly stuck his tongue out the corner of his mouth and stepped forwards to look at the large map of Takaara on the table. He peered down at it with a frown, eyes falling on the Borderlands. 'In the war between our people, there were times when we outnumbered your kind. We were bloodthirsty and experienced warriors. How did you defeat us?'

Grey joined Sly at the table as Kane watched on.

He stared down at the map and twisted the edge of his moustache, lost in thought. 'We were outnumbered. And yes, your men and women knew battle perhaps more than any other army we had faced. Our forces were mainly peasants and unruly young nobles, not trained very well and liable to flee at the sight of blood. Yet we still won...'

'How? Kane asked, pressing her own hands onto the table and raising her eyebrows at the two men.

'We used the terrain. Location is vital in battle.'

'And here we are, surrounded by walls, the sea to the west, and warriors willing to defend this estate to the death as we sit on top of a hill. You'd have to be a dumb fuck to think we don't have some kind of advantage. Play it right and we can hold off an army ten times our size for weeks,' Sly insisted.

Kane looked up into Grey's eyes and it was as though the years seemed to drift away, the lines no longer as noticeable. He had a spring in his step as he twisted back towards the window and gazed out across his home.

'Call all of our forces to the main yard in one hour. I think I have an idea...'

'Mason's army should be here by sundown tomorrow. Are we going to have enough time to sort things out?' Kane asked with a tilt of her head.

Grey chuckled and rubbed his hands together. 'We can do it. I will meet you and the leaders of each unit in the drawing room at midnight. I pray that this is not the last night we may speak together but battles are anything but predictable. It would be apt if we were to have one last drink together, even with Sir Dominic...'

Kane nodded. 'Midnight it is.'

She left the room, followed by the smiling Borderlander.

'One day from battle,' Sly said with wild eyes flashing at her. 'Really gets the juices going, don't it?'

Kane rolled her eyes. 'Don't get any mad ideas Borderlander. I know your kind.'

'You *love* our kind,' Sly snorted with laughter. 'In another world, you would have been one of us. I can see the fire in your eyes and passion in your heart. You wish you were a Borderlander. You would have loved it.'

Kane kept silent. She didn't need to say anything. She knew he was right.

Kane slouched in the leather seat and groaned. The clock in the corner struck midnight with twelve chimes as she shuffled in her seat, trying to ignore the many aches and pains from the days digging. It had all gone well, she hoped, at least. Grey had been more animated than she had seen him in quite some time and the men and women living in their new home had worked to the bone as they fought to follow Grey's clear instructions. Now it was time to rest and recover her strength ready for the battle she knew was near at hand.

The curtains were closed in the long, narrow room. The only light came from the candles burning on the sconces hanging from the walls beside paintings of old kings and queens of the United Cities. Paintings with stern faces and questioning eyes that always seemed to follow you around the room and find you wanting.

Kane almost openly laughed as she looked around at the other men and women standing or sitting in the drawing room of Grey's estate. Such a motley bunch of broken and weary warriors had never before been seen in Takaara, or at least that was what she thought.

Sly sat with his two allies from the Borderlands, a

wild woman with intelligent eyes and a silent, brooding man whose face spoke of death. The blonde Barbarian from the training room stood with Sanada in hushed talk, his eyes darting suspiciously towards the trio of Borderlanders to his right every now and then. That blood feud was older than the rivers of Takaara if the stories were true. The only times she had seen Braego speak with venomous disdain had been when he spoke of those mighty warriors who live to the north of the border tribes.

Abhia strolled casually around, taking in the strange, foreign room with eyes wide open in wonder. It brought a smile to Kane's face to see the young woman staying positive after all she had just come through.

Dustin Grey sat at the head of the long, dark table, lost in conversation with Drayke. From what she could hear, the two Archanians were deep into a conversation recalling a time when King Mikkael had broken a priceless sceptre and attempted to have it replaced with a cheap version from a costume shop from the Upper City market. The ruse had worked for a time until the queen had discovered the old sceptre hidden beneath their bed and had it sent away to a woman she trusted on the edge of the Heartlands to have it fixed. Kane remembered Mikkael telling the story. He had kept the cheap copy, preferring its lightness compared to the ancient, heavy sceptre that his father had passed down to him.

Kane's eyes turned to the sound of a door creaking open from a side room. An old, withered male with a bald pate and warm, squinting eyes crept into the room with the aid of a walking stick. The man waved to Grey and the prince before turning his eyes to Kane, a broad smile widening on his face. Kane shot up and dragged a chair beside hers, offering it to him as he finally reached her.

'I hate to say this Lord Balen, but I thought you

were no longer amongst us,' Kane chuckled darkly as the old council member fell into the seat.

'I presume you mean that I had finally passed from the land of the living to join our ancestors in the realms beyond ours,' the old fellow croaked with a soft laugh of his own.

'Something like that,' Kane agreed.

'Though many have met untimely ends recently, it seems the Gods still have a path for me to tread. Or crawl along. I am not exactly the quickest of men in my current state.' His face darkened and he sighed. 'Though, I must say, I would give my life for any of the poor souls killed in the devastation of Archania. My heart goes out to any who die in such a horrid away. May the Gods be kinder in the battles to come.'

'In my experience, the Gods are rarely kind where battles are concerned.'

'Yet, you still live,' Balen reminded her, his eyes twinkling in the candlelight. 'And our bright, young prince still lives.'

'With a limb missing.'

'A horrible injury but perhaps necessary for him. Often we must lose something in order to grow. The Gods know what they are doing. Dark times are there for us to appreciate the light, this is yet another example and we are the unfortunate fools tasked with getting through it.'

'I hope you are right, Balen. I really do.'

Grey tapped his fingernails against a glass and stood, drawing all eyes in his direction. He cleared his throat loudly and smiled around the room. 'Firstly, I would just like to thank each and every one of you for joining me here tonight. You have worked tirelessly today and we have another big day ahead of us. But I also feel that it is

important that we meet, all of us together in this room so
that we may share a drink as one team standing together.
We do not know what tomorrow will bring, so we must
make sure that tonight has joy and hope, and friendship.'

The whole room raised glasses and jugs to the
former general and he joined them in the common salute.

'We have brave men and women in this room from
all of Takaara. The Borderlands,' he nodded to Sly, Kiras,
and Cray in the corner and they all smiled and winked to
the eyes turning to them. 'And we have a Barbarian with a
Blood Islander,' Sanada and Sigurd waved to acknowledge
Grey's words. 'Abhia, from the Empire to the East,'
Abhia's cheeks turned red as she nodded her own greeting
to the others. 'And men and women I am proud to call
Archanians.' Kane gave him a soft smile and Balen tapped
his cane on the wooden boards three times.

'Some of the warriors in this room have stood on
opposite sides in the past. There are long running feuds that
have filled our blood with hate over the cycles. The fact that
we stand together today ignoring such petty but powerful
rivalries is a testament to the strength of character in the
room and the threat that we face. The whole of Takaara is
united in the face of our enemies. I look around this room
and my chest swells with pride.' Grey battered his chest
with a fist and growled. 'Our differences are put to one side.
Now we focus on what makes us the same, what pulls us
together. We all want to see a world where we can love,
fight, and be free to make our choices. Mason and Osiron
are against this type of world. They wish to trap us in their
iron fist and crush the will from every single citizen of
Takaara. However things pan out in the battles to come, we
must fight against them. Even at the cost of our lives.' The
room fell deadly silent as Grey raised his glass once more.
'So let us drink for being together, drink for those whom
we have lost, and drink in the hope that light may shine on

the world we fight for.'

'Hear, hear!' Balen croaked beside Kane, banging his can once again. They all drank and Grey sat back into his seat, the silence suffocating in the room.

'It is strange, don't you think…' All eyes fell on Sir Dominic as the knight spoke, glassy-eyed and red-cheeked. 'The way life can seem to pass you by; fleeting moments that speed past faster than a blink of an eye. Then, when you stand at the edge of your life, glancing over the side of that cliff called death, everything just,' he held his palms up and froze, 'stops. It is as though one has a final chance to look around and take in the smells, the sounds, the beauty of the world.' Dominic shook his head and sighed long and hard. 'Mayhap it is just the bleating of an old, tired goat heading out for a last stroll in the sun, but I must say, it is an honour to stand beside not just my kinsmen, but great warriors, great *people*, from around Takaara. If this truly is to be the last night of my privileged life, then I am honoured to spend it with each of you.' Dominic smirked, a bit more life returning to his old face. 'Even the Borderlanders…'

The room shook with the laughter of all the men and women, sharing in the dark mirth of the knight – Sly loudest of all.

'Gotta say,' the warrior said once the laughter had died down, 'I always thought I'd die shoulder to shoulder with my brothers and sisters from the Borderlands as we killed as many bastard Barbarians or Southerners as possible.' He tilted his head and shrugged at the blonde Barbarian frowning in his direction, offering a silent and reluctant apology. 'This ain't the way I thought it would be. Still, I can think of worse ways to go.'

'It is said that the Gods often work in ways we cannot understand,' the Barbarian Sigurd chimed in. 'My path has taken me far from my home and almost back again. I may not understand what path I am on, but I trust it enough to follow it with faith.'

Kane shifted in her seat uncomfortably at that last comment, unable to bite her tongue. 'Faith, she scoffed. 'What an absurd concept!' A mix of curious and annoyed faces shot her way, encouraging her to explain her outburst. 'I was raised to trust in the Gods, to have *faith*. Everything happened for a reason, or at least that was the mantra rolled out whenever the shit seemed to fly in my direction. Now, I just feel it is a blind comfort to soothe folk who feel disgruntled. For cycles I praised the Gods whenever something good happened in my life, and when something went wrong, I was told that this is all part of some celestial plan, a path set before me that I could not stray from. I watched good men and women die too soon. I saw cities burn and fall. I watched innocent people, young and old, burn due to the will of a mad preacher.' Kane could feel Grey's eyes burning into her as she referenced Tamir's execution. 'If this is all part of the Gods' plan, then it is a shitty plan.

'I have faith. But not in the Gods, not in some intangible being watching over us. I have faith in each of you. I have faith in the people of Takaara. When the time comes, I know that we will stand as one to fight back the darkness heading our way. Win or lose, that is my faith.'

Prince Drayke stood, rolling his shoulder awkwardly and glancing down at where his arm should be. 'My life had always been one of doing not what was right, but what I was told to do. Being royal can be suffocating, though I do understand it is a privileged position compared to other paths in life. Faith, in my opinion, can be just as suffocating. It is time we move away from the Gods of old. We are in charge of our own destiny. It is in each other that we must have faith.

'Mason D'Argio has poisoned my city and burned it to the ground. From those ashes, we must rise as something different, something unique. We must no longer hide behind walls and look on each other with distrust.' Drayke glared around the room, eyes boring into the people from all over Takaara. 'We must unite as brothers and sisters of the same world, a people bonded in blood and suffering who understand the importance of standing side-by-side. Looking around this room, I see the potential of Takaara. I see the potential of what we can accomplish when we sweep aside the petty arguments of the past and look at one another with fresh eyes. We need to focus on what makes us the same, and not what makes us different.'

Sly stood with a groan and rocked from side to side, stretching over his hips with a wince. 'Well, there's some beautiful words. Time for me to do something similar to all of you, take a fucking piss.' He chuckled at his own humour, ignoring the smiling groans emanating from those around him. Cray had the hint of a smile at the corner of his mouth as his ally left the room; Kiras just rolled her eyes and snorted.

'Is he always like this?' Kane asked them with a grin, jabbing a finger at the door Sly had left open.

'Honestly, no,' Kiras said, a shocked look on her tired features. She leant a bit closer to Kane as she answered. 'Usually he's much more of a bastard. He's on his best behaviour tonight. Haven't seen him like this in all the time I've known him. He's even making friends.'

It was Cray's turn to chuckle now.

'What's up with you?' Kiras asked her Borderlands companion.

'Sly making friends,' the warrior answered. 'If ever there is ever a sign for the end of days, that is it.'

415

THE WARRIORS OF THE NORTH

'Form up! Ready for battle! Form up!' The shouts flew along the lines of nervous soldiers like an eagle swopping across the sky. Kane caught Dustin Grey's eye as the former general rode his horse between the columns of soldiers all saluting him as he passed.

Grey was decked out in his finest armour. His silver armour glistened in the low-light of morning and his specially made battle helm stood out with its horse-hair plume dyed a navy blue to match the cloak flowing down and covering the back of his beast. He held his spear with ease, spinning it in his right hand in a display of strength as he greeted the soldiers either side of him, giving them all a stern look that spoke volumes in regard to his confidence. He was not some old soldier waiting to die; he was here to fight and defend his land and that was what he was expecting them all to do. The nervous glances between the men and women lining up with their shields in hand and sweat-soaked brows turned to grim looks of determination. They had a leader worth fighting for; a man who had given a rallying cry at the darkest of times and brought together an army willing to face chaos itself. If they were to die today, they would do it giving their last breath for the soldiers at their side, fighting to defend innocence and hope.

Kane's chest burst with pride. She had once though Grey to be just like the other pompous old men whom she used to share the council chamber with. They would moan and preen, getting into petty arguments with one another and always missing out on the obvious dangers before them. But she had never doubted the man's courage. Dustin Grey was not a man of words and waiting. He was a man carved for battle and the greatest one of his lifetime stood before him, and he was ready.

'Katerina Kane,' Grey said with a slight incline of his head.

'General Grey,' Kane answered, using his former title. She liked the way his lips widened at the word.

'A general for one more battle. The final battle.'

'Might not be the final one. There's always hope.' Kane reached up and squeezed the gloved hand of the soldier. He gave her a small smile and, ensuring that he was looking directly at her, she said, 'Tamir would be so proud of what you are doing. Whatever happens after death, he will be looking on and watching with love and pride in his dear heart.'

Grey pursed his lips together, clearly fighting back tears as he squeezed Kane's hand gently. 'It has been an honour to call you a friend, Katerina Kane. I pray that this is not the last sunrise we share, though if it is, there is no one else that I would wish to fight beside.'

Kane loosened her grip and let his hand slip through her fingers. She watched with a lump building in her throat as he rode away, guiding his horse towards the gate at the front of his estate, towards the approaching army wishing to wipe them all from the face of Takaara.

A young soldier to her left leant closer to her, questioning eyes worried as they found hers. 'Captain, Mason's army is almost here. Shall I signal for the archers to line the eastern wall and ready for battle?'

Captain. A title Grey had bestowed on those close to him who would be leading their own units in the battle. She had an Archanian force full of young but well-trained men and women to lead. They would be looking to her for instruction in the madness of what was about to begin. That thought brought a cold chill down her spine like the slithering of a snake. Men and women would die if she put a foot wrong. Men and women would die if she did everything right, too, she supposed. It was a battle, and that meant death.

'Yes,' she finally said, sniffing and clearing her throat. 'Yes, prepare for battle.'

Sly gripped the stone wall and leant over the edge, wanting to get as close as possible to the thousands of warriors heading his way. He glared at the marching army, white banners trimmed with golds held high, and wondered if he would be able to piss on one of them too. They were outnumbered by a force that was most likely better-trained and more experienced. The odds were clearly against them.

And Sly couldn't wait for the bastards to arrive.

'Lean over any further and you will fall to your death,' Kiras warned him, not for the first time. 'You want the songs to be about some fool who fell over a wall before the first blood had been spilled?'

'I ain't falling over nothing!' Sly spat back, rocking back and forth with excitement. 'But can't you feel it in your bones? This battle is the one. The one battle that will be sung about for cycles to come. This is bigger than Redbeard's Battle of the White Peaks. Bigger than Logan's Charge of the Damned. This is fucking history and I'm gonna be a part of it.' He licked his lips and then breathed in through his gritted teeth. A young soldier, long hair tied up in a horse like tail at the back of his head walked past and offered them a shield for the battle.

Sly frowned at him incredulously but Kiras took a more diplomatic approach.

'Got twin blades, a shield just gets in the way,' she said with a wink.

Cray grunted and held out his hand, taking the round shield without a word and testing its weight on his left arm.

'Since when did you start using a shield?' Sly asked, his voice rising in his confusion.

Cray shrugged. 'Since I saw thousands of bastards heading towards me with bows and arrows.'

There was a logic to it, Sly had to admit. Still, he had his trusted axes and they would be all he needed to weave a trail of blood.

'Would be good if Socket was here,' Kiras said wistfully. 'He would stay up here and pick off hundreds of the enemy. I miss having an archer to call upon.' She glanced down the row of nervous soldiers with their bows slung over their shoulders as they waiting for the enemy to come within range. 'These youngsters are too green. They'll be nothing but bones before too long.'

'Aye,' Sly agreed. 'The old archer would show 'em

419

how it's done. Shame we don't have Raven and Baldor too. And Arlo. We've fought alongside some hardened bastards in our time, that's for sure. Could do with the lot of them here today.'

'But they ain't here,' Cray added grimly. 'Just us.'

'Aye,' Kiras said with a sigh. 'So let's not die, eh? Enough of us are bones now, how about the three of us keep breathing?'

'Sounds good to me.'

'Me too.'

'Captain Stormson.' Sly jerked back in shock at the odd title and glared at the saluting Archanian soldier standing there staring at him. 'The forces from the Borderlands are ready and waiting your command.'

Sly shook his head and held out a hand to stop anything further from being said. 'Firstly, I ain't a captain. Chief will do. Secondly, why they waiting for me?'

The soldier's face scrunched up in confusion as she glanced between the three Borderland warriors. 'Well… they said that they will only follow your commands. Captain Kiras, Captain Cray, and Cap— erm… *Chief* Stormson. They are ready and waiting.'

Sly rolled his eyes and ignored Kiras stifling her laughter. Even Cray had that shadow of a smile on his stony face. 'Best not keep them waiting then, eh? Time for battle.'

The eyes of every Borderland refugee from Hillheim and beyond gawked at the three of them, waiting for something. Sly felt hot under his collar and pull nervously at the edge of his shirt, tearing it away from his sweaty skin.

'Why they looking at us like that?' he muttered to Kiras, frowning.

'Raven's dead. Saul's dead. Bane's dead. Herick is a fucking bastard. Who else they gonna look to?'

Grey's smiths and armourers had worked tirelessly to get as much gear as possible to those who had come for support, but there was only so much time and resources and so the bunch of grim faces before him were dressed in a mismatch of clothing and armour. Some just in rags and torn clothing. Others in helms that did not quite fit. Some had shields, others swords or spears. But all looked at him. Looked and waited.

Sly groaned and cursed under breath before launching himself onto one of the small, stone walls that circled the animals' pen. It gave him a slight height advantage and allowed him to look out at the sea of faces that all turned to him in anticipation. Never had been one for nerves before a battle but suddenly he found his stomach churning every which way and his mind going blank like an unbloodied axe. Some of the faces looking back at him were the grimmest, hardest faces he had seen in Hillheim. Others looked like beardless youngsters too green for the red business that would be needed today. But that didn't matter now. If you could hold a weapon, you could fight today and that was that.

Oddly, he found himself pleased to see Cray and Kiras pull themselves up and sit on the wall either side of him, both giving him a reassuring nod before turning to face the crowd themselves.

'Folk of the North!' he bellowed into the wind finally. 'Borderlanders, whether you are from Hillheim or Torvield or even further afield. I ain't one for big speeches usually. The battlefield ain't a place for talking but it seems we got a bit of time before the blood flows so what's the harm?' The sea of faces grinned at him and he puffed out his chest, breathing long before continuing. 'Some of you fancy calling me Chief now. I ain't got a problem with that. There's been better chiefs before me, I know 'cause I fought for a couple, and I'm sure they'll be better ones after me. But it don't matter who is chief now. What matters is that we stand as one today and fight until our very last breaths. I've never seen folk fight as viciously or as determined as those from the Borderlands, and today gives us a chance to prove that to the bastards all around us, even the ones we fight beside!' A great cheer went up at this. 'The Redbeards used to always talk about when the time comes, we will all be nothing but bones. That may be right,' Sly scratched his chin and nodded slowly, 'but we ain't gonna lie down and let some bastards destroy us today. One day we will be bones, but we fight to make sure that it is not this day!' The roar of the crowd brought curious glances from the other units of soldiers standing proudly around them – men and women of the United Cities. All turned to listen to the words of the ragged Borderlander with the wild beard and wilder eyes.

'I've seen this Mason D'Argio and his soldiers before. They are the reason Raven Redbeard isn't standing here giving you this speech. They are the reason that Baldor died away from his homeland and his people. They are the reason that we fled our homes and stand here today in defiance against an army that will outnumber us.

'But I look around today and I see some hardened bastards willing to cut through dozens of these monsters from the East,' he roared. He pointed to his right and down at Kiras. 'Kiras is known as the deadliest woman in the North, a warrior to be feared by any who stand in the way of her twin blades.' He turned to the man to his left and grinned. 'Cray here was once of Saul's tribe. I can personally attest to the strength and speed this brute possesses and I have the literal scars to prove it.' Cray shrugged and smiled at the reference to their fight in Archania as Sly turned back to the increasingly excited crowd. 'When you look into the whites of the eyes of your enemy today, know that we three will be right there beside you, picking you up when you fall, giving you a kick up the arse when you get too scared, roaring alongside you when you stab the fuckers through the heart. And so will Raven, so will Socket, so will Baldor, so will Reaver, so will all of the ancestors of our people. Because we *are* the Borderlands. And though we are not standing in our home today, we are standing here defending it, defending who we are and what we want to become.

'This battle might well be the last one our people fight. I ain't planning on that and neither should any of you. But if it is to be the last roar of the Borderlands, then let's make sure we give them all the hells and drown this land in blood!' he yelled to a mighty cheer. 'Give the survivors something to sing about in the future, a song of the hardest, grimmest bastards Takaara has ever seen. A song of the brutal Borderlands and its fighting people who never rolled over. A people who fought to the last breath and killed enough to feed the crows for a generation. I ain't gonna stand here and ask you to fight for me, or her,' he jabbed a thumb to Kiras, 'or him,' he pointed at Cray. 'Nope. I'm asking you to fight for yerselves. For those you care for. Our enemy stands at the gates, folk of the Borderlands, how about we show them what the fuck we do with unwanted guests?'

Sly almost fell from the wall, such was the force of the wave of noise greeting that final question. Nothing could be made out, just a visceral, animalistic roar of people walking the line of life and death.

'For the Borderlands!' Kiras roared, standing tall beside him.

'For the Borderlands,' Cray echoed, raising his shield high.

Sly felt his chest rising and falling in waves as he nodded out at the screaming horde repeating the chant.

'For the Borderlands!' they screamed back.

'For Stormson!'

'For the North!'

'Kill the bastards!'

Sly lowered himself from the wall, almost in a trance as he walked through the crowds of chanting people. They rushed towards him as he made his way through them, feeling their hands touching him for some sign of comfort or some other superstitious bullshit. For once, he didn't care. They wanted this. They needed this. He glared wildly, lost in a battle-lust as he breathed like a bull. His people called out to him and reached for him and he smiled like a beast at them, showing them that their leader was ready for anything, ready for war. One warrior grabbed Sly and pressed his forehead to his own, both shaking with a need for blood. Sly roared at him and crushed his head against him, drawing blood instantly. The crowd roared as Sly released the dazed warrior. He felt the warm blood drip down his face and he wiped it on the back of his hand before licking it away. He laughed maniacally and turned, finding himself in the centre of the Borderland warriors. Strong hands clutched at him and pushed him upwards, holding him high above the crowd. He could see Kiras and Cray still standing on the stone wall. Cray began smashing his sword against his shield in a rhythmic beat that all other warriors took up.

The crowd guided Sly back to the wall where he took his place beside his friends. The rhythmic boom grew as the Archanians joined in with their Borderland neighbours, crashing weapons against shields or stomping their boots against the earth. He looked towards the gate and made a quick decision, one that he knew would have a great impact on the proceedings.

'Let's take the fight to 'em,' he said, expecting Kiras or Cray to scoff at the decision and plead with him against such madness.

'Right y'are chief,' Kiras said with a mock salute. Cray nodded and jumped from the wall.

Sly hid his surprise as the order was followed instantly. He left the wall with the others and led his people towards the gate, parting the sea of Archanians standing their way. The soldiers stared at the Borderlanders, people they had once called savages and scum, with teary eyes, all continuing their beating of the shields and earth as the warriors passed by.

'Weren't expecting you to do it,' Sly admitted to Kiras as he stood beside her.

'Well, that was a decent speech,' she said to him. 'Everyone of us is ready to die for this. And like you said, we're some of the hardest bastards around. No use letting the soft Southerners do the hard work.'

Sly grinned and let a low growl escape from his chest as he pulled his axes free.

Cray nudged his elbow and smirked. 'So Chief, what's the plan?'

Sly chuckled and looked at Kiras.

She didn't even roll her eyes this time as the gate opened and they looked out at the imperious army standing in their way. 'Same as always. Kill the fuckers.'

'Aye,' Sly agreed. 'Kill the fuckers.'

The old general sat on his horse turned to Sly as the soldiers approached the gate. He gave Sly an odd look, half-amused and half-confused.

'Stormson, what exactly are you planning on

doing?' he asked, keeping his voice low so that only they could hear.

'Look, Whiskers,' Sly said, drawing a familiar roll of the eyes. 'We've got this. I know the plan, and we're the best ones to start things off. Get things all warmed up if ya know what I mean?' he said with a wink.

To his credit, Grey took a deep breath and didn't fight against it. 'When you march out to face them, you know the risks. I just want you to know that you do it with the support of each and every one of us. You are not just a Borderlander now, Sly Stormson. You're a Northerner.'

Sly chuckled and patted his hand against Grey's horse, scratching the beast's neck. 'We've always been Northerners, Grey. It's you guys who are still under review. Just make sure you head out when you are supposed to. Need to do this before it gets too light. Darkness is our mistress this morning. We know what to do.'

THE BATTLE FOR THE NORTH

'Guess this is it,' Cray said, completely deadpan as usual, as though facing a deadly force that outnumbered them an insane amount was nothing more unusual than waking up to find that the sun had risen. There was no need for Sly to answer. They all knew this was it. Even as the embers of dawn began to burn in the east, the Borderland warriors stood together and stared at the army dressed in white and gritted their teeth and squeezed their weapons, bristling with rage and probably a fair amount of fear. Sly wouldn't be surprised if a few of them shit themselves in the coming moments but that was what it was like in the heat of battle. Hard enough controlling your fear without having to control your bowels too.

'We all know what we are doing,' Sly muttered to Cray and Kiras as they marched alongside him. He gave a glance towards the bushes far to his right and left, hoping that the plan would work as the others had suggested it would. He'd seen similar strategies pay off before, just wasn't sure if the Easterners would fall for it.

He stepped carefully over the concealed wooden planks covered in mud and grass and anything else the workers had hastily used the night before. It took a moment to realise that he had been holding his breath. Now, he released it in one long sigh and cursed to himself.

'We got this, Chief,' Kiras said, reassuring him after noticing his clear nerves with the plan. He sniffed and tightened his frame, snapping his back up and reminding himself that he had a whole group of soldiers looking towards him for inspiration.

'I know,' he replied, stopping his march as a soldier on horseback broke from the silent and still force of the Empire and rode towards them with a tall, white standard held high in the gentle blow of the wind.

'Warriors of the North,' the messenger greeted them as he reached the three Borderlanders, his tanned skin glistening with a nervous sweat as he looked down from his steed. 'Mason D'Argio, brother of the Empress of the Empire of Light and Supreme Ruler of the United Cities of Archania requests your immediate surrender. If you swear fealty, he will ensure that you are treated well and offered land close to your homes. A tribute to the One God will be sent for weekly to prove your loyalty but other than that, no harm shall befall you.'

Sly raised an eyebrow and placed his hands on his hips, turning to look at Kiras and her stony look and then to Cray who had hardly seemed to notice the words of the Eastern messenger. Finally, he spun to look at the grim faces of the Hillheim refugees who had travelled south after watching the destruction of their homeland. They had already lost so much. Each of them tightened those stern looks on their faces and nodded grimly towards him in defiance.

'That's a tempting offer right there…' Sly said, pointedly stroking his beard and nodding as he gazed up at the man who had the hint of a smile on his face now, white teeth gleaming. 'What's the other option?'

The smile slipped from the messenger's face to be replaced by a mask of contempt. 'Then we shall erase your kind from the face of Takaara and raze this place to the ground…'

Sly frowned and pinched the bridge of his nose as though thinking was becoming too painful for him. He relaxed and gave that infamous bloody yellow grin of his as he pulled his axes free from their straps. 'You know what? I think I like the sound of that option. I would tell you to pass a message on to your coward of a master but there would be one problem with that…'

'And what problem would that be?' the messenger asked with scorn soaking his question as he made to turn away and head back to his people.

Sly raised an axe above his head and winked. 'You'd need to be breathing…'

The arrow carved its beautiful and deadly path through the air and pierced the messenger's neck in an instant. The man's eyes popped wide open but his body hadn't the energy to even raise his hands to the fatal wound. Instead, as his horse whinnied and spun away, the rider fell to the mud and twitched. Sly stepped forward with a grimace and smacked the horse on the backside, ensuring it would run away from the battle. No point in harming the animal. He grabbed his axe tightly as the cries of both sets of soldiers built to a deafening crescendo, the cheers of the North and the agonised and disgusted screams of the East. The messenger's head came off at the third attempt. Three heavy swings of the axe. Blood dripped onto the standard that had fallen into the mud beside its owner and was now soaked red. He raised the head and held it towards the Empire's forces, daring them to come and seek revenge.

They took the bait like foolish fish in a river.

'That's step one sorted,' he growled and licked his lips, still holding the bloody head high.

'What was step one again?' Kiras asked, falling into a defensive stance as trumpets blared ahead of her and the cavalry rushed forwards.

'Piss 'em off,' Cray answered, wrapping his shield tightly to his body.

Kiras tilted her head and sucked her teeth for a moment. 'Yeah. You did that alright. Step one accomplished. What was step two?'

Sly winked. 'Fall back.'

The rush of the cavalry was a sight to behold; the intense determination of the experienced soldiers urging their horses forwards with weapons in hand that glistened in the rising sun. Sly peered up at the sheet of grey clouds that threatened to block the light of a new day from those prepared to never see such a sight ever again. Again, he eyed the oncoming rush of warriors and horses and allowed himself a little smile as peered across to the bushes that ran along the edge of the forest either side of the impromptu battlefield.

'It's a good plan,' he said, scratching the scar on his chin. 'I suppose it's time…'

He raised a bloody axe and just about caught the whip of rope pulled by the waiting groups of Hillheim survivors in hiding. The wooden planks snapped away just as the first wave of cavalry reached what was now a wide and deadly trench. The men and women of the North had done their job admirably, tiring as it had been.

The thunder of hooves was joined by the shocked screams of the fallen as the horses fell in agony with their riders into the pits. Riders leaning low to press their mounts forwards now pulled back with a horrible shriek. They crashed into one another and another row of soldiers fell into the wide dark holes as a horn sounded behind Sly. The signal.

Sly roared, his throat nearly ripping apart with the effort as he raced forwards, leading the lines of Hillheim survivors and allies of the North. Arrows tore through the dull sky and found their marks amongst the panicked soldiers who had ridden expecting an easy fight and found themselves lost amongst chaos. From the bushes, Sly could see swathes of men and women led by Sanada and Sigurd heading towards the cavalry who were now caught in a no man's land between the trench and their own people. Sly ignored the acts of the others and became focused on his own path. Leaping down into the trench, he screamed with all his hatred and anger, allowing the old battle-lust to take over.

His axes weaved a deadly path of red as he finished off two flailing soldiers in quick succession. Another lay beside her stricken horse, ankle bent at an unnatural angle. He growled and made for her but a shadow dropped beside him and slashed cleanly across the terrified woman's throat with the edge of a thin blade. Kiras turned to Sly with a dark look that warned that she meant business.

'Kill 'em all,' he said to her as an agonised wail sounded behind him. He turned in time to see Cray smash the edge of his shield into the skull of a rushing Easterner, smashing the man back against the wall following a crack that could be heard throughout the whole of the trench, even as others dropped in and started their own gruesome work. Cray raised the shield and brought it down hard again between the eyes, ending any possibility for revenge.

'I guess shields ain't so bad after all…' Sly admitted, impressed with Cray's work.

'Ain't so bad,' Cray echoed with a sneer as he stepped over the bloody corpse to stand next to Sly. 'We ready?'

Sly gave Kiras a cursory look. The deadly warrior gave him a short nod and fled farther down the trench to the western edge of the tunnel. Sly winked at Cray and rushed after her as Cray blew into the horn. He could hear the cries of battle and the shouts of the leaders doing their best to keep some manner of control amongst the chaos; almost impossible in Sly's mind. You can plan a fight as best you can but in the end, one stray punch or slipped blade and all hells break loose. That's when you find out who is up for the fight. That's when you find out who can thrive in the bloody madness.

The tunnel grew darker as it snaked to the south, this section still covered by the planks, leaving the dozens of Hillheim survivors who had been brave enough to drop into the trench in almost complete darkness. Sly could almost hear the beating of his own heart as he kept on close behind Kiras, listening for Cray's thudding footsteps behind him. A harsh whistle sounded somewhere in front and he stopped at the signal, waiting patiently as his body shook, ready for the fight.

Though he could hardly see anything before him, he trusted that his fellow warriors were close, and all listening carefully and waiting.

'This is it,' he said, voice shaking with excitement. 'We pop up and slaughter those bastards and then it's up to the rest of them. Gonna be tough to make it out of this alive, but the world is going to shit anyway. Better to take some of these fuckers with us, eh?'

He smiled at the chuckling around him and began the count down from three…

'Three, two, one… Now!' Kane cried, urging her unit towards the western edge of the battle where the trench and Sanada and Sigurd's forces had pushed the Empire's forces to. Her soldiers responded with fervour, racing into the heat of battle with abandon. Spears struck shields and flesh. Swords slashed wildly, and arrows flew through the sky, blocking out the dim light that crept through the clouds momentarily.

A cloud of dust filled the line of the battlefield where the soldiers had fallen into Grey's ingenious pit. He had claimed that first blood was a vital part of a battle and this shock would certainly enable them to claim first blood. Grey had then warned them of what would follow. A battle is long and bloody and the shock will only last for so long. Sooner or later they would reorganise and focus. And when that happened, they would all need to be ready.

The Empire's forces were already pulling themselves together, reassessing the battlefield and shifting to the west, away from the now open pit in their way of reaching Grey's estate. The Hillheim survivors had torn through what remained of the cavalry who had not fallen for the trap. They had wrought blood and death amongst the poor animals and the trained soldiers caught between the pit and the rest of the invading force. It had been difficult to ignore the screams of the dying but she knew that it was what had to be done. Battles are won atop fields of blood and not tears of the weak. She knew that.

Kane snatched at her sword, wondering, not for the first time, if this was really the place for her. But from the corner of her eye, she could see the determined faces of the soldiers who had wanted her there with them, soldiers who took courage in knowing that she was a part of this. She would not scream or roar like the others. She would not raise her sword into the air. She would not kill in the name of any Gods. For if there were Gods, they were as useful as a kick to the nuts, as her dear Braego would say. The memory brought a flash of a smile to her face as she neared the enemy, shining as white as her smile in such splendid armour.

Her sword thrust through the young man's stomach and she pulled wildly, opening a gap wide enough for his gut to fall out onto the ground. Katerina Kane staggered back as her allies rushed past her with victorious cries. She turned and fell to her knees, vomiting and vulnerable.

She closed her eyes and saw the face of a beautiful young woman with dazzling emerald eyes and hair as black as a raven. She used her blade to push against the earth and push to her feet, stumbling slightly as she turned. Her mouth opened wide in useless horror as a spear arced her way. It seemed as though she would soon be meeting the Gods, as useless as they may be.

A sword whipped past and diverted the attack at the last moment, pushing it past her shoulder before twisting towards the attacker and driving with unnerving speed through the soldier's neck. Blood gushed wildly as the spear dropped with a thud.

'About time I saved you. Try not to make this a habit though, eh Mother?'

Kane's shock turned to joy as she grabbed her son by the back of his neck and pulled him in for a tight but brief hug. She pushed Drayke away and grabbed her sword with a renewed energy. Storming ahead of her son, she tore into the line of white-cloaked soldiers and used all that she had been taught in a life surrounded by great fighters. She kicked dust up into the eyes of the enemy and feigned right before snapping to the left. Her sword danced in the low dawn light and carved a deadly path through the enemy's lines, streaks of blood following her wherever she went.

A horn blew loud. Two short, sharp bursts. She gazed over towards the waiting enemy forces to her right and her smile grew wider. With a great roar, Sly and two dozen of his best warriors leapt from their dark hiding place and found themselves in the midst of the Empire's infantry. The wild haired bastard was just about visible from where Kane was standing but she could hear his squeals of delight as his axes ripped through the defences of the shocked unit. They didn't know what to do. They backed away, panic fuelling their every move.

'It's working,' she muttered to herself.

'It's working,' Sly shouted with glee as another of the bastards dropped to the ground, lovely white cloak now soaked in a dark red. 'It's fucking working.'

'You sound surprised,' Kiras responded, kicking the legs of one soldier before casually decapitating him with a crossing of her twin blades.

Sly shrugged and kept moving. 'Didn't think the bastards had it in 'em. Might even say I owe old Whiskers a drink.'

He ducked a vicious sweep of a halberd and rose with all his might, ramming his shoulder into his opponent's gut with enough force to knock them both to the ground. Sly reacted faster, his elbow battering the man's nose deep into his skull with three hard hits. He pushed himself from the still body with a chuckle, admiring his bloody work.

Then he felt a sharp pain lance through his calf.

'Shit!' he growled, hobbling and glancing down to see an arrow stuck in his leg. He dropped to the ground and assessed the damage before furiously gazing up and searching for the culprit. 'Trees! Archers in the trees!' he roared in warning.

Instantly, Cray stood over him, shield guarding them both as Kiras finished off her latest victim with a flourish and returned to them.

'Fucking arrows,' Cray grunted, knocked back slightly by the force of one of the bastards hitting his shield.

'Aye,' Sly agreed as he attempted to pull the bastard from his leg. It wasn't too deep, but it would hurt like the hells. 'Fucking arrows.'

Kiras dropped beside him without a word and scanned the damage. She sighed and pulled a small, sharp dagger from her belt. 'Hold still. You might wanna bite down on something…'

Sly winked, 'Ah, foreplay, you know just how I like it…' He continued to chuckle at his joke even as the woman punched him in the ribs, not gently either. He coughed but accepted the hit. Worth it. 'Just get on with it,' he instructed, his breathing growing in intensity as he realised what she was about to do.

Her dagger cut through the wooden shaft of the arrow but kept the arrowhead in to stem the flow of blood wishing to escape. He growled and gritted his teeth, arching his head back and squeezing his eyes tightly shut.

'That's for always being a cunt,' Kiras laughed as she checked the wound. 'Needs cleaning but don't exactly have time for that.' The arrows continued their path from the trees, taking down more of their own side than the

Northern forces. 'Bastards are killing their own kind…'

'Don't think they give two shits as long as they eventually get to us.' Sly stared up at Kiras and tapped her on the arm softly. 'Things ain't looking too good, girlie.'

'In all honesty, have they ever looked good?' Kiras snorted.

Sly cocked his head to the side and allowed himself a dark smile. 'Probably not. Still, it's been good fighting alongside ya, both of ya,' he added louder so that Cray could hear. 'Might as well go out with bloody weapons in hand and a pile of bodies beneath us.'

He accepted Kiras's support to get to his feet, cursing to himself as he struggled to put weight onto his right foot. Gripping his axes one last time, he stared into the faces of the enemy soldiers closing in on them like wolves with their prey.

A rolling thunder sounded and Sly looked up to the grey skies, expecting to find the Gods' wrath pouring down on them.

Then he saw movement out of the corner of his eye.

An avalanche of horses rushed past them and swept away the advancing Easterners. The horses turned as the lead soldier held an arm high and, for a brief moment, Sly caught the face of the moustachioed man with his shining helmet and long spear.

'Whiskers…' he muttered with an incredulous shake of the head.

'Come on,' Kiras said, pulling his arm around her shoulders. 'We have to fall back.'

For once, Sly wasn't going to argue.

Kane wasn't going to argue with the horns blaring as a signal for the retreat. She yelled at the fighters around her to drop back, opening a gap for the injured to be dragged towards the relative safety of the walls of Grey's estate. Shields snapped together as a group of injured Northerners were pulled and staggered to safety. She wasn't too surprised to see a familiar face hobbling amongst the bloodied and battered faces. Sly looked paler than usual and he favoured his left foot as he was half carried by Kiras away from the battle, his grim face a mixture of pain and frustration.

'I could still take 'em, even on one leg…' he was grumbling to anyone who would listen.

'I know you could, big man,' Kiras said, holding back her mirth to protect her friend's dignity. 'Best to get behind those walls for a change now though.'

There was no argument to that. Even the battle obsessed warriors realised that the tide of the fight had turned and they needed to regroup. The Empire's forces had collected their wits and were now turning what had been a shocking retreat into a steady press, held back only by the bravery of Grey's cavalry.

Now in full retreat, she supported the slower members of her unit, encouraging them with strong words and a slap on the back as they raced towards the walls. Mason's forces cared not for the retreat, they continued their steady march, battling with Grey's mounted warriors and cutting their way past. Another horn echoed throughout the land and Kane breathed a sigh of relief to see Grey signal for the retreat of his brave warriors. The old soldier pulled his mount away from the fight and, for a brief moment, his eyes seemed to lock onto hers.

Her smile faded as movement just past him on the edge of the trees drew her attention. A silver-haired man with hatred in his eyes and a coat of armour that glistened bone-white like dragon scales stood with a longbow in hand and a hateful sneer etched on his face that made Kane's stomach give a sickening lurch.

Time seemed to stand still as the arrow shot through the air. She could see the determination on Dustin Grey's face to get his men and women to safety. She could see the mud flicked up by the horses' hooves as they were urged back to the estate and away from the arrows and spears and swords of the enemy.

The arrow connected with Grey's back with a thud, throwing him from his horse as Kane staggered slightly, the world suddenly catching up in a single moment. Forgetting the retreat, she bolted towards her fallen friend.

More arrows whistled past but they could have been leaves dropping from the tress for all she cared. Her eyes fixed on the unmoving body of Dustin Grey as his horse sped away terrified, leaving its rider to his fate. Kane slid to the ground and pulled Grey's head up and looked into his dazed eyes.

'Dustin? Dustin, it's me. It's Kat.'

The soldier tried to focus his eyes on her, waving a gloved hand up towards her face. She clutched at it tightly and pressed it to her face. Blood had begun to pool around the corner of the man's lips and he was paler than the moon. He managed a weak smile before coughing, spraying blood everywhere.

'Kat,' he croaked, 'it is good to see you one last time. Tamir was with you at the end, it is good that I am as well. I am off to see him at last.'

'Dustin…' Kane said, the growing lump in her throat making it more difficult to speak by the second.

'No more words,' he said, before another coughing

fit. 'Grab me my sword, please, Katerina. If I am to die here, then I will die as a warrior.'

Kane pulled the great sword from his belt and placed it into his hand where he clutched it tight to his chest.

'One last request. Help me to my feet.' Kane carefully pulled him to his feet and watched as he held his sword high in the air as the first drops of rain started to fall. Slowly at first, then increasing in speed until the sound of the rain could be heard as a continuous thump against the shining armour of the enemy marching their way. Grey glared at Mason who had replaced his bow with a long, thin, curved, golden sword. The preacher had death in his eyes and a shadow on his heart as he marched towards them. Kane made to step forward but Grey pushed her with all the strength he had out of the way.

'This is my fight, Kat. My last stand. Go back to the others, close the gate and prepare for the siege. My people need leaders, I will not have them lose two in one morning. This demon has come for me and me alone. The Gods are watching and I shall not fail them and deprive them of their entertainment.'

She pressed her face to his and planted a kiss on his cheek, a final action of farewell.

'You are a true leader, Dustin Grey. A man Archania can be proud of. A man all Takaara can be proud of.'

Dustin Grey puffed out his chest, ignoring whatever great pain his battered body was having to endure as he nodded the goodbye, lips pressed tightly together. Kane backed away, tears filling her eyes as he silently urged her to leave him. She left, but she could not tear her eyes away. He deserved a witness, here at the end, for all that he had done.

Mason D'Argio stopped just a few paces from the dying soldier, tilting his head and surveying the former general with a look of distaste and disappointment. 'You have some clever tricks, old man. But your time has come. It is a shame we are not burning you like your old friend, Lord Tamir.'

'It is a shame that we didn't chop you up into little pieces and feed you to the crows when you first stepped foot in the North,' Grey snapped, blood flying from his mouth as he staggered forwards.

Mason wasted no time. His sword thrust straight into Grey's heart, ending the soldier's life instantly. He didn't even look at the brave man he had just killed. Instead, he chose to stare straight past as Grey's body slumped onto him. Stared straight into Kane's furious eyes.

'I will kill you, you fucking bastard. I promise you that on all of the Gods both old and new. I will kill you,' she muttered to the darkening world as the rain lashed around her. The last think she saw as the gate closed was Mason D'Argio's smirk as Grey's body hit the wet earth.

MONSTERS

The Southern warriors knew the jungles of their land better than Aleister knew himself. They faded into the shadows and crept between the bushes whilst making less noise than the dead. Some jumped from branch to branch along the canopy of trees shielding them from the heat of the midday sun but, still, each leap brought only the barest of thumps as their bare feet landed on the wood of the trees and then they were off and out of sight, causing Aleister to wonder if they had ever been there at all. The steady creeping march of the army was unnerving for him, even though he stood amongst them as a friend and ally, trying to do his best to copy their movements and blend in with his surroundings. He thought for a moment what it would be like to be on the other side and shuddered. Akhona had insisted on painting his face with dark mud to hide the sun's glare from his pale skin and ensure that he could at least make some kind of effort in making himself one with the jungle. The last thing they wanted was for his pink skin to give their position away as they reached Lord Manuel's soldiers.

Instinctively, he glanced around for his sister and Bathos. They were much farther back than he, willing to bring up the rear and fall upon the enemy once the battle started. Bathos's huge frame and milky arms would be too easy for the enemy to find. Ariel had insisted that she stay beside him and so they were back in the darkest edge of the jungle, waiting for the signal.

A shout of alarm rose ahead of Aleister and he dropped to a crouch, eyes searching for the disturbance. The bushes rustled with the increased movement of the warriors around him as he hesitated, unsure whether to break cover to reach the source of the disturbance.

'Shit,' he cursed and breathed in through gritted teeth, torn between staying in the shadows and racing out with sword drawn ready for battle. 'Fuck it.' He leapt from the bushes and onto the dusty path, rushing towards where he assumed the shout had come from. He darted through the trees, dodging one narrowly and landing roughly into something else entirely. Something else that seemed to make a grunting, moaning noise before it fell to the ground with Aleister on top.

Aleister shook his head and for a short moment, he stared into the surprised eyes lined with black paint. Realising that he had landed on the enemy, he slammed his head as fast and as hard as he could into the still shocked man's face and then pushed a hand up, clutching at his scraggly red beard and pushing his jaw chin up whilst scrambling for his sword which had fallen just out of reach. The Heartlands' warrior growled with the exertion and did the only thing he could, bringing his knee up to catch Aleister on the ribs. It wasn't a clean hit but it didn't need to be. Aleister grunted as he felt the air rush from him and he rolled over involuntarily, allowing a moment for the bearded man to roll free.

Aleister scrambled across the dusty ground and gratefully clutched at his sword. He turned, blade leading the way and expecting to find the Heartlands' warrior ready for the fight.

Instead, he found a body on the ground with an arrow sticking out of his throat. Blood pooled around the body, eyes wide open and ready for the Gods.

'You really should be more careful, brother,' Ariel whispered, nearly giving Aleister a heart attack as she pulled up silently beside him. Bathos just grinned behind her.

'Nearly shit myself!' Aleister barked in a low voice. 'Did you really need to creep up on me?'

She shrugged. 'If I can do it then so can they. Let that be a lesson to you.'

Aleister raised his eyebrows and nodded, biting his lip for a moment. 'So that's how it is? Using my own lessons against me?'

'Only when you need it,' Bathos said with a wink.

'Which is most of the time,' Ariel added.

'Seriously, it's like hanging out with laughing hyenas with you two around.'

Aleister crept from between the trees and dropped once more into a crouch as he spotted a group of light-skinned warriors huddled together as they nervously strolled through the jungle. Their heavy, black armour would usually be a benefit to them, but in the heat of the jungle, it was stifling and some had taken off their helms and one had even chosen to wander through the jungle with his bare torso on display, sweat glistening on his skin.

He thought about jumping out and using the advantage of striking a surprised opponent to end the fight as quickly as he could. But he didn't have the chance. It seemed he wasn't the only one with such an idea.

Shocked yelps filled the jungle as four warriors dropped from the canopy and landed on the shoulders of the invaders, taking them down and thrusting spears through their flesh in a flash, ending their lives with no chance of them fighting back. Aleister left his place behind the trees with Ariel and Bathos and met with the four victors as they wiped the blood from their spears.

'I was just about to do that you know…' he said with a smile.

The Southerners grinned back as they spotted the necklace around his throat. They shared a knowing glance before a tall, muscular woman responded to him. 'Your fight is to come, as is the fight for all of the Chosen. The weaves of fate continue to shape your path. Do not worry. There will be blood enough for you. Come.'

They followed the warriors through the trees, struggling to keep up as they darted and weaved through the clusters of trunks and branches. Aleister wondered how they knew the jungle so well, it wasn't like the forests of his homeland where paths were reasonably clear and, at any point, he could stop and listen for the sound of the river to guide him. This jungle was purposefully hostile and confusing, ensuring that its protection was only available for those who called it home.

As he raced after his guides, he could sense more than see the dark shadows flitting through the bushes and flying through the jungle either side of him. The Southerners prided themselves on never suffering an invasion and they knew that they had the knowledge and strength to drive out these unwelcome fools.

Finally, the light grew brighter as the tightness of the trees lessened and the heat of the sun blazed through. Aleister felt the sweat pool around his pits and his breath grew more ragged with each step as the heat started to get to him. He looked for his sister and Bathos and saw that they were growing fatigued with the speed, their faces a dark pink as their cheeks blew hard for each breath. At last they broke through the trees and found themselves in a large clearing in the centre of the jungle with no sign of shade.

He stopped running and paused to catch his breath, frowning as his eyes locked on the hundreds of black-clad warriors waiting for them, swords drawn and grim, stony expressions on their faces. A black standard waved in the warm breeze, displaying a white tower with black sword upon it.

'Finally,' a bronze-toned man with a bushy black beard and broken smile called out to them, 'we can stand and fight like men instead of skulking around in the shadows like cowards.'

'Lord Manuel, I presume,' Aleister called back. 'I've heard quite a bit about you.'

Manuel's face twitched slightly as he slowly licked his lips through a gap in his yellow teeth. 'Introductions are not necessary for the three dogs of the Red Sons.' His wild eyes landed on the three of them and stayed fixed. 'Aleister, Ariel, and Bathos. Are you proud of how you destroyed the peace of the Heartlands? Are you proud of the countless innocents you killed or left to starve in the filthy streets? Some in the Heartlands call me a tyrant,' he pointed directly at Aleister and then shifted his finger to Ariel and Bathos, 'but I am nothing compared to you three monsters. Three demons escaped from the bonds of the hells beneath us and sent to ravage Takara until nothing is left. You claim to protect people. You claim to save people. You claim to be righteous.' Manuel spat on the ground and gave them a look of complete disgust and hate. 'You are a plague. And I will cleanse this world of you and your kind.'

Aleister worked hard to ignore the uncomfortable looks shot in his direction. Instead, he focused on the army glaring at him with their deadly weapons in hand and eager gleams in their eyes. Distractions now would prove to be fatal. He had seen that too many times before. The battles of the past had taught him much, sharpened him into the warrior standing calmly before this dread force and he knew that he would need all his strength and resilience to make it through this one.

'Lies spat through a forked tongue of deceit,' he mocked. 'You have entered a land that does not welcome you, Lord Manuel. I suggest you place your tail between your legs and scurry back to the hole you came from. There is nothing but death waiting for you here.'

Manual accepted the shining, black nasal helmet offered to him and placed it over his head, his sparkling eyes gazing out from either side of the iron bar blocking his nose. 'Death follows you like a bad stench. So be it.'

The clearing wasn't large. It was big enough and wide enough for the two sets of warriors to glare at each other either side of a narrow piece of land that ran between them – an area that both armies hesitated to cross. The first to step foot forwards into that no man's land would invite attack and all hells would break loose. Once the battle started, neither side would be able to leave until all were dead before them.

Aleister promised that he would not be one of them.

He drew his sword and held it high, the sun shining against the metal and casting a blinding light for all to see. A low thumping sounded to his left and he curiously watched as a gap opened up between the rows of warriors, allowing passage for a man dressed in green plate armour with a traditional, colourful gown covering it loosely and hanging from one shoulder. The man's wise eyes landed on Aleister and he tapped a finger to his heart as they did so.

'It is my time to speak now, Aleister, ally of the Southern Kingdoms.' King Solomus spoke with clarity and the tone of a man befitting his station. Aleister had no idea how the man had managed to travel with the army without his knowing but he was pleased to see the king there now, standing amongst his people and holding a unique five-bladed spear in his tight grip.

'Invaders have stepped foot in your land, Warriors of the South,' King Solomus cried to his people in the common tongue so that the opposing forces could hear him and understand his words. 'How shall we respond?'

'UKAFA!' came the cry from the warriors around him as the three captains stepped forwards, ready to lead the charge.

'UKAFA!'

'UKAFA!'

'UKAFA!'

Aleister listened to the chant and felt his blood rush in excitement for the battle. He turned as the chanting continued and caught his sister's eye.

'This will be bloodier than anything we have done before,' he warned Ariel, raising his eyebrows to Bathos beside her as the warriors slammed their spears into the ground, their chanting growing louder. 'Rush back to the king. Tell him to do what we discussed. Take the sword. I won't need it here. Istari knows what to do.'

Ariel looked for a moment as though she wanted to argue, her whole body tensed and ready for the fight. Bathos's huge hand came up and rested on her shoulder and then all of the fight seemed to drain away from her. She nodded and took the sword, offering Aleister her own which he gladly accepted.

'You will fight to your very last breath,' she said, her stern words almost a command. 'And we will see one another again.'

Aleister kissed his sister on the forehead and clasped Bathos's forearm in the usual farewell of the soldier.

The two of them ran away, Ariel pausing only to share one last look with her anxious brother doing his best to hold himself together.

Once they were out of sight, he breathed long and slow, trying to slow his racing heart. 'What is it that they are chanting?' he asked the soldier beside him.

She grinned and gave a knowing wink. 'Death. You asked us how we respond to invaders. And we answer with death.'

And so death arrived.

Aleister joined with the first charge, caught up in the rush across no man's land and slamming into the first wave of warriors standing tall against them, black shields high to block the advance. A few spears and sword thrusts made it through to strike at the enemy but soon the Southerners dropped back to regroup, assessing the damage on both sides. It was a preliminary strike, meant to warn the other side and boost morale for the attackers.

Aleister only saw a few of the native warriors down as they dropped farther back. Others had some minor injuries but nothing that would prevent them from joining with the second charge. Solomus seemed alive and well, his spear bloodied and his face grim and set for battle. The king roared and raised the spear high into the air, showing the blood for all to see. Then he led the charge forwards once more and his people followed.

The crash against Manuel's forces was thunderous.

Takaara seemed to rumble with the force of the impact. A few of the Heartlands' warriors buckled under the pressure, falling back with screams of distress as the southern soldiers knocked them onto their backs and leaped through the gaps opening in the shield wall. Shouts and roars of battle sounded from both sides as leaders struggled to get their instructions to their men and women as the chaos of battle erupted around them. With gaps opening in both lines of soldiers, the blood began to flow and pour onto the dry ground. Aleister spotted Solomus screaming and stabbing his strange spear through the stomach of an unfortunate soldier, pulling it away and tearing the guts along with it. A spear whipped past his own face and pulled his attention back to his own predicament. Scolding himself for allowing a moment of weakness, he snapped his blade up and drove the spear away, using the chance to stab his sword through the attacking soldier's shoulder and driving him back. He used the chance to refocus and take a step back, assessing his own situation.

Aleister took a breath and stepped forwards into the crush of the battle. Block, shift, snap, stab. The repetition broke down the defence of the warriors standing in his way. A beardless young man, likely in one of his first battles, rushed foolishly towards Aleister, roaring in the heat of battle, his eyes clearly showing the fear he felt inside.

It was easy for Aleister to dodge the blade coming his way. There was no need to even block it. He stepped inside the attack and thrust his own sword deep into the heart of the youth. He watched as the light faded from the soldier's eyes. He thought for a moment if the boy had any family and if they would be waiting for him somewhere in the Heartlands. Another family left to worry and fret until

450

the day came when they were told that their son, or their brother would not be making it home to them. He shook the pointless thought from his mind and pulled the sword from the limp body, allowing the corpse to drop before stepping over it and towards his next victim.

With each break in the battle between deadly strikes, Aleister allowed himself a moment to search for Lord Manuel. Killing the leader would cripple such a force. He had always been taught to cut the head off the snake in any battle and this would be no different. This wasn't an army brought together for a love of its people or a passionate ruler. They followed Manuel's coin and feared the wrath of the tyrant. With a bit of luck, killing Manuel would end the fight in an instant. He searched frantically, stopping only to dodge the spears and swords heading his way and to swing and slash with his own weapon, pushing back the advance of the Heartland warriors.

In his frantic search, his eyes locked on Solomus as the king, covered in blood and sweat, lurched forward, spear in hand. A shield thumped against the king's head, cracking off his skull and halting his march forwards. Dazed, the king fell back into his shocked soldiers who froze at the sign of the king falling. Aleister rushed towards him, barging past his allies to reach the falling king.

A spear beat him to it.

The bloodied piercing point of the spear stabbed through the king's chest and drove him to the ground. Aleister screamed in denial as a crowd of Southerners roared forwards and stabbed, slashed, and stomped on the culprit, avenging their king in moments and leaving the unfortunate bastard a bloody pulp at their feet. The Heartland warriors spotted the change in mood of their enemies and pulled their shields tight together once again, retreating cautiously back with worried glances to the men and women down their line.

The Southerners pulled Solomus back and created a barrier preventing any more harm. Aleister wondered if it would be too late.

Reaching the king, he knelt and saw that the soldiers were struggling to staunch the flow of blood. They had relieved him of his armour and were pressing a bloodied cloth against the open wound, trying desperately to staunch the wound and keep their king alive.

It didn't look good.

Aleister watched as Solomus struggled for breath. Wheezy, rasping noises escaped his throat as his eyelids fluttered like the wings of a butterfly. He took the king's hand and grabbed it tightly, pleased to feel the old man's fingers wrap around his own, however lightly.

The warriors surrounding the king exchanged fearful looks with Aleister, clearly aware that it did not look good for the wounded king.

Solomus coughed, blood escaping his lips and splattering his gown. He opened his eyes and pressed his free hand against the blood soaking his skin. He pushed a bloody hand against Aleister's face and nodded, before doing the same to the other warriors around him.

'Blood as a sacrifice holds power,' he croaked, breaking into another coughing fit. 'We know this. We have seen this. This is not the end of our people. The Chosen will stand as one and fight back the darkness. Halale womelale is how we say it down here. Take strength my beautiful people.'

A death rattle escaped the king as the warriors bowed their heads in respect and offered their silent prayers. Aleister closed the eyelids to cover his vacant, unseeing eyes and took a slow breath before thanking the king for what he had done.

'Now is not the time to grieve,' Aleister said, getting to his feet. 'Have two warriors take the body clear of the battlefield and the rest of us fight on. We have lost a leader today, that does not mean we have lost the battle.'

Lord Manuel, a man who had fought in the Heartlands all his life, stood waiting at the front of his line for Aleister. He stepped forwards with a smirk as he spun the sword with casual ease in his right hand, eyes never leaving him as he called out.

'Come, young boy. Time to test your swordsmanship against a professional. You are not facing poor, untrained soldiers now. You are facing a proven warrior, one who wishes to see a monster die.'

They met sword to sword as the rest of the soldiers melted together once more, smashing against each other in a chaotic dance of death. Aleister focused entirely on the infuriatingly calm Lord Manuel, watching the swift, easy movements of the leader as he twisted to the side and slashed high. Aleister diverted the path of the sword with his own and jumped back, readying himself for the next attack.

Manuel rushed forwards and Aleister stumbled as his boots hit against one of the many corpses littering the clearing. Catching himself, Aleister managed to raise his sword in time, knocking the strike high before rolled to his left to escape the next attack.

Aleister cursed as the next attack scored a line of blood across his forearm. He held onto his blade and regained his balance, biting his lip in frustration as Manuel burst into laughter.

'It is amazing to see the infamous Aleister Soulsbane falter in such a way. The legend it seems, is greater than the reality.'

Aleister was slow in the relentless heat and Manuel was growing in confidence. His footwork was near perfect and his strikes almost flawless. Annoyed and feeling the anger rise, Aleister gritted his teeth and went on the attack. He slashed and stabbed with precision but each blow was pushed aside as Manuel took his turn on the defence, dropping back carefully and watching the attacks with those dark eyes.

Manuel screamed something as he pushed forwards again but it became lost in the general roar of the battle.

Ignoring the burning pain on his forearm, Aleister blocked a thrust and rolled forwards. He leapt up right beneath Manuel's guard and stabbed his sword straight through the ribs.

Aleister's face was inches from Manuel's. He watched the confident smirk fade to a shocked look of denial, head shaking from side to side with increasing tempo as he started to realise what had happened. Aleister twisted his blade and Manuel grunted in pain, tears welling in his eyes. He pushed the bastard away and ripped his sword free with a squelch and a fountain of blood.

The body dropped to the ground with a thud and Aleister rocked back, the exhaustion of the battle crushing him like a wave against the rocks. He dropped to a knee, sword helping to support his body up as the world swayed before him. He barely noticed the warriors rushing towards him with frightened looks on their faces. He glanced down at the feeling of wet blood and spotted a wound close to his shoulder where Manuel's sword must have caught him as he dealt his final blow.

'Shit...' he muttered, heaving a deep breath and feeling hot as the hells.

Aleister closed his eyes as comforting hands grabbed him and pulled him away. He thought he heard a rumble of thunder somewhere but couldn't work out how close it was. His body seemed to shake as he heard shocked and frightened cries break out around him. Opening his eyes, he locked onto Akhona's face.

'Gods help us…' she said, covering her mouth with a hand as her tear-filled eyes stared off into the distance.

Aleister managed to raise his head and look out into the jungle behind the Heartlands warriors who had turned their backs on the Southerners and were backing away from the tall trees, losing all sense of order.

'They have arrived,' he heard Akhona say to the other soldiers. 'Monsters of Chaos. We must leave.'

ESCAPE THE DARKNESS

Once dragged to his feet, Aleister's teeth slammed together as he stumbled through the jungle. The vibrant greens, purples, yellows, and reds of the jungle rolled into one as he tried his best to follow the retreating Southerners as they raced back to the city. The pain shooting through his chest and the aching that pretty much covered his entire body made him long for a hit of faze, anything to numb the pain. He could see Akhona in front of him; her anxious looks over her shoulder darted to Aleister's slow stumbling escape and then past his own shoulder onto something that made the blood drain from her face and her eyes widen in horror. Even in the rumble of hundreds of feet thumping against the ground he could hear the soft whimper that escaped her lips.

For a moment, he contemplated taking a look of his own but the way Akhona's face had dropped decided the matter for him. Whatever it was chasing them, it was not something that he wanted to lay eyes on. These stoic, brave warriors who had trained their entire lives for this battle were fleeing in terror and that was enough for him.

Ignoring the searing pain, he gritted his teeth and pushed on, fighting to keep up with Akhona. She reached out and, not gently, pulled him past her, taking a place behind him and watching his back. On instinct, he turned to gaze upon the woman risking everything for his safety. In the blink of an eye, he regretted that decision.

Behind the retreating Southern forces, Aleister saw the wave of Heartland warriors following them, many of whom had dropped their weapons or unclasped the buckles of their armour in an attempt to give them an edge in the race away from the dark cloud hot on their own heels. His mouth turned dryer than the desert of Akram as his eyes caught a glimpse of dark warriors with decaying flesh bounding through the trees with hungry gleams in their eyes. One of the fleeing warriors fell to the floor with a shriek and the dark cloud engulfed him, their coarse weapons ripping and tearing flesh with ease.

That was all he needed to see. That was far too much for him to see.

Aleister picked up the pace, racing forwards as fast as his weary legs could carry him. The pain was nothing to him now. A mere shadow of what may be when compared with the rampaging horde heading his way.

'Come on!' he cried to Akhona, praying that she would be wise and use her energy to save herself. 'Leave me!'

Akhona joined him at his side and gave the briefest of shakes of her head as she kept pace with him.

The screams of the Heartland warriors grew, rising to an ear-splitting crescendo as the dark mass swept through them, devouring the remaining soldiers. It allowed a brief reprieve for the Southerners, a moment that brought with it guilt and shame as they allowed the deaths of the other warriors to fuel their own escape from the horrors of Chaos.

War was a strange thing, Aleister thought. Moments earlier, the Southern army had stood against the Heartland forces with one intention, to destroy them and kill each and every one of them for stepping onto their land. No though, they found themselves nauseous and consumed with guilt as they glanced over their shoulders and witnessed the horrified looks on the faces of those same men and women who now fell to the darkness.

The enemy of my enemy is my friend. Paesus had once written that. Or some other bastard who had been lucky enough to survive a war to be able to write about it in safety somewhere else. In minutes, the Heartland warriors had gone from sneering, bloody enemies to offering the South a chance at survival.

The screams died down and Aleister's heart sank like a stone in the sea. The lack of screams did not mean anything good. It meant that the fiends of Chaos were done with their starter and were ready to move onto the main course. Against his better judgement, he risked another glance and breathed a momentary sigh of relief. The massacre of the Heartland warriors had offered a moment's respite to aid in their escape. The gap between the invading Chaos warriors and Aleister had grown considerably. But he would not let that allow him to drop his guard; if anything it gave him a renewed energy to urge himself forwards and to reach the city.

The blasts of a horn burst through the trees and he frowned as he caught sight of some of the fleeing warriors drag their feet in the earth and spin, spears, shields, and swords all facing Chaos He turned to Akhona and saw that she had done the same and was now facing the darkness of the trees in the direction of the Chaos force.

He grabbed for her arm but she brushed him off and waved him away.

'Go!' she said, jolting her head towards the city. 'This is not your stand, Aleister.'

'And it is not yours,' he argued, pleading for her to go with him. 'Staying here means only death.'

'Staying here means others will survive, others who may be able to stop this darkness,' Akhona answered calmly. 'You know how I feel about sacrifice for the betterment of Takaara. I do not need to explain myself. Go.'

Reluctantly, Aleister turned away, cursing himself for leaving the brave warriors to stand and fight as he turned back towards the relative safety of Ad-Alum. He had just jumped over the bubbling stream when he heard a rhythmic beating of swords against shields followed by one, long, low and familiar blast of a horn.

His face scrunched up in confusion as he wondered if his exhausted mind was playing tricks on him. The madness of the battle, the loss of blood, the running through the hot jungle, any of these could have led to hallucinations and a confusion in his mind. Perhaps this was just another moment of weakness. Perhaps his mind was offering him something wondrous to hold onto before he breathed in his final breath.

And then he saw them.

Just a few at first. Then dozens. Hundreds. Even more.

Men and women cloaked in red stood with the warriors of the South, facing off into the darkness and readying themselves for the battle to come. Their stern faces were painted black and red in varying designs, but all bore the symbol that he himself had designed, the symbol of the Red Sons.

'Saving you and your friends is fast becoming exhausting, my friend.'

Despite the seriousness of the situation, Aleister's lips curled into a huge grin as he spotted Zaina walking towards him. He wanted to ask her a million things but couldn't land on the right words. Eventually, he ended up with just the useless greeting of, 'Why are you here?'

'Nice to see you alive too, Al.' Zaina brought him in for a hug with her right arm and he pulled her close, her red ponytail almost whipping him on his cheek.

'Where are the others?' he asked, looking around for any sign of Ben, for any sign of Adnan.

Zaina's face dropped. 'Not many of us left. Got some catching up to do. But this ain't the place to do it.'

'I have to agree with the beautiful woman, Aleister,' a familiar voice called out from the trees. 'And by the looks of that wound, we need to get you to another place, too…'

Jaxsin Mortella glided between the warriors standing tall, blowing kisses and winking at the Southerners who returned his gestures with mild looks of confusion as the lithe, tricorn wearing warrior placed his muddied boots on the ground one step at a time before reaching his old friend. He had barely aged in the cycles since Aleister had last seen him. The wily man still had that mischievous glint in his eye and dangerous aura around him.

'Jax…'

His old ally twisted the thin moustache that dropped either side of his chin and licked his thin lips. He swept his black tricorn from his head and gave a small bow before rising with a flourish.

'My dear boy, Aleister. I thought you were dead. Close, I see, but not yet food for the crows. My job seems to be to get you away from the monstrosities. The city is near. I will aid in your escape.'

Aleister gave Zaina a concerned look before facing Jaxsin again. 'And Zaina is coming with us, right?'

The red-haired woman smiled softly and shook her head. 'We need to stand strong to keep these bastards at bay at least for a little while. Listen to those around you, Aleister. You are injured and we are not. Go.'

Her tone left no room for manoeuvre. Aleister bit his lip and fought back his retort as he stared into her stern but understanding gaze. She knew how this would be eating him up inside. But she also knew that he had the sense to follow the order.

'Come, boss,' Jax said, offering his arm as support. 'Time to go.'

Aleister watched Zaina stand tall next to Akhona as the Red Sons took their place beside the Southern force. Backs straight. Weapons in hand. Eyes facing the darkness. They would fight to last warrior. He knew that. And it brought a pain in his chest that he thought would tear him apart.

'Time to go.'

Ad-Alum was bedlam. Soldiers marched to their posts as civilians locked up their homes and boarded their windows. Aleister stumbled past the city walls with a grimace, helped by a concerned Jax who supported his weight with one arm and then passed him over to a worried looking Ariel.

'Brother…' she muttered, eyes falling on the nasty wound. She took a swift look at Jaxsin and her eyes widened in surprise but there would be time for that. 'We

461

need a medic.'

'Just needs cleaning and stitching,' Aleister said through heavy breaths. 'Nothing more. I can clean it on the way. We must get to Istari and Zeekial. They are coming…' Ariel's face told him that she didn't need any further guidance to understand what he meant.

Together, Ariel and Jax managed to drag Aleister through the city and towards the great temple. The guards at the entrance recognised them and gave a short salute before parting, eyes focused on Jaxsin until Ariel informed them that he was with them. One of the guards nodded and the other turned to follow them as they hurried into the temple.

Aleister managed the stairs down to the lower level on his own, refusing the support of his friends but wincing with every step on the stone path.

'I can do it,' he snapped at his sister as she attempted help. Instantly he regretted it and decided to change the subject. 'Where is Bathos?'

'Lined with the soldiers,' Ariel answered, unable to keep the fear from shaking her voice. 'He didn't want to sit around and twiddle his thumbs.'

'It is good to know that none of you have changed,' Jaxsin said with a warm laugh that did not suit the mood. 'All fight,' he said with a balled fist.

'The Red Sons,' Ariel said, finally asking the question she had held back since her eyes had landed on the old warrior. 'What happened to them?'

'Many died in the battle for Archania against Mason D'Argio. Most of the others died in the demon wave that covered Causrea. The rest decided to head here and find our old bosses. Things couldn't get much worse so why the hells not? We'd heard rumours that the South weren't too bad and that you were fighting. The Red Sons were strong and whole with you in charge – seemed like a good enough idea at the time.'

'And now?' Aleister asked darkly.

Jax shrugged and snorted. 'My dear Aleister, I feel that everything is a bad idea in these times. One merely has to go for a piss and they can be sure that the wind will push it right back into their face.'

There was no arguing with that.

'And Zaina is in charge now?'

'We had Prince Drayke in charge for a moment following Adnan's untimely passing… I briefly flirted with the idea of being leader but it was a fleeting moment of insanity,' Jaxsin said with a sigh. 'Zaina is loved by our people. She has been there longer than me. She was the correct choice.'

Aleister nodded in agreement. 'She is strong.' He paused and attempted to process Jax's words. 'Prince Drayke? Of Archania?'

Jax flashed a smirk and raised his eyebrows. 'It has been an odd cycle or so… even for us lot. It has made me long for the days when we slept in the desert and plotted our way into that winter ball in Arakh. Those were the days…'

The overwhelming scent of iron filled Aleister's nostrils as he stumbled into the cavernous room. The light of the candles around the room and the deep red pool of blood in its centre gave the room an ominous glow.

'I have been to a few parties similar in life,' Jaxsin laughed to himself, scanning the room with his piercing eyes. 'But this is something dark and special indeed. The only surprise is that everyone seems to be clothed…'

Istari Vostor marched over, leaving King Zeekial and standing barely an inch away from Jax, eyes filled with a furious fire.

'I know you… what in the circle of the world do you think you are doing here?' he snapped, voice low and threatening.

Aleister placed a hand between them and gently pushed Jax back, who happily obliged, though that familiar smirk was still etched on his face.

'Istari, this is my friend, Jaxsin Mortella.'

'I know who he is,' Istari snapped. 'He beheaded his friend to seize power. He cannot be trusted.'

The guard who had followed them from the entrance placed the sharp end of his spear against Jaxsin's neck as the warrior raised his palms up in surrender, the smirk turning into a shamed smile.

'A simple misunderstanding,' he said as Aleister turned a questioning gaze his way. '*I* was not looking for power. It was the prince. I was merely an instrument being played like so many. Without my part, everything would have ended in a much darker way.'

'Darker than the slaughter of your people in Archania?'

'If you remember, old man, I argued for the continuing effort in the East but not an attack against the Empire or anything to do with the North. If my plan had been followed, many of my people would be alive today.'

King Zeekial spoke with the other rulers sitting on the stone seats at the side of the room before nodding and strolling over. He placed a gentle hand on Istari's shoulder. Aleister noticed the way Istari's eyes flashed to the unwanted touch before the old warrior breathed heavily and backed away.

'Now is not the time for fights to break out amongst us. Aleister, you are here, and that can mean only one thing,' the king said. 'Chaos is coming to my city.' He glanced over to King Milani and Queen Cebisa who both wore grim looks on their regal faces. 'We have planned for many eventualities in this fight. Istari Vostor has offered one which is drastic and distressing but may be the best course of action if we are to save our people.'

'It is the best option, my friend.' Aleister jumped as Harish crept from the shadows, his face pale as though the blood had fled from his body. 'Though I feel it is right that the Archanian is the one to wield the blade.'

The eyes of the entire room fell on Aleister and he felt suddenly exposed, lost in a labyrinth with everyone watching him.

Istari drew Soulsbane and spun it effortlessly in his hand, offering the hilt of the blade to him.

Aleister took the blade and sighed in relief, welcoming the familiar feel of the weapon. His breathing steadied and he felt whole again, as though he had spent the past few days with a piece of him missing, like losing a limb.

Harish stepped up to Aleister with a sad smile that placed him on edge, waiting for something to happen but wanting with all of his being for it to be stopped. Harish placed a hand on Aleister's good shoulder and grinned as the edge of Soulsbane pressed against his bare torso.

'Do not worry, Aleister of the Red Sons. You are Chosen. And this is what you have been chosen for...'

Before Aleister could say anything, Harish pressed forwards whilst pulling Aleister closer to him in a tight embrace. There was no preventing the blade from thrusting straight through the thin man's chest. He cried in alarm as Harish's eyes widened first in shock and then softly closed, his face taking on a look of quiet contentment.

Jax and Ariel leapt away in surprise, both releasing squeals of horror. The others just watched impassively, fully aware of what would happen.

Istari stepped towards Aleister and pulled Harish away. Blood stained the blade as Istari held the lifeless body, blood seeping across his chest and down his body. He raised the still form of Harish and marched over to the pool. Kneeling, he gently placed the body into the blood, pushing it down so that the red liquid covered him completely.

'What the fuck have you done?' Aleister said, his heart racing as he finally found his voice. Ariel's hand rested on his arm as she too watched on in horror.

'What had to be done,' Zeekial muttered. The Boy King of the Southern Kingdoms allowed a single tear to fall down his cheek before turning to Aleister and wrapping his hands around the hilt of Soulsbane. 'Forgive me.'

Aleister felt the king's hand force his own to guide the blade so that the point of Soulsbane stabbed through his neck, spraying blood everywhere. Just as before, Istari was there to catch the body, turning with it calmly. He placed the body into the pool in the same way he had Harish.

Aleister shook in horror with what had been done as sweat pooled around his skin. He searched for some kind of understanding but nothing jumped out at him. The remaining King and Queen of the Southern Kingdoms just sat beside one another, holding hands and bowing their heads in mourning.

'Why?' was the only word Aleister could breathe out past his quivering lips.

Istari stood, covered in the blood of the two

victims. He cleared his throat and sniffed before finding something irritating on his jacket and cutting away the thread hanging from his cuff. He looked up at Aleister with a calm gaze as though nothing out of the ordinary had just happened.

'There is a power in blood, one that must be unlocked if we are to survive. The blood of the four mages who nearly brought this world to its knees will mean so much more. Their sacrifice will mean our survival.' Istari waited and scratched the growing beard on his chin as if irritated. 'Though we will need permission for what we are doing.' Aleister spotted the sister blade to his own hanging from Istari's left hip. The warrior drew the weapon and glanced at its black blade with reverence.

'Permission from who?' Aleister asked.

'From the only one who can allow what we are about to do,' Istari answered. 'Permission from a God.'

He rammed the black blade straight into Aleister's heart without a moment's hesitation.

Aleister choked in shock and felt the world turn as screams filled the room. He frowned as the world seemed to move in stages, its flow interrupted by the horror of what had just transpired. He could see both Jaxsin and the guard holding his sister back as he fell into Istari's waiting arms. Then he felt the warmth of blood swarm around him.

A shadow appeared in the blurry light, looking down at him.

'Are you sure this is the only way?' a distant voiced seemed to ask.

'I am sure Elena. There is no other path to take. It is this, or the destruction of all Takaara.'

'Then let it be done. I believe I am next.'

'Yes, Empress…'

Then Aleister closed his eyes, believing it would be for the last time.

THE COURAGE OF COWARDS

The dark bat-like wings of dread wrapped around Katerina Kane as she dropped back with the remaining soldiers of the North. The weight of losing Dustin Grey pressed against her as though she were carrying a boulder on her shoulders. Her slumped, grieving form was not appropriate for the weary and nervous warriors looking towards her now for some form of inspiration. She straightened her back and forced her head high as the rain lashed down against her. She marched through the muddy puddles and offered words of encouragement and slaps on the backs of those she passed, plastering a smile onto her face and feeling slightly better as they returned the look with smiles of their own, pleased to see that with Grey gone, they still had someone they could trust at the top to lead the line.

'Hold your head high, soldier,' she said to one weary-looking youth sitting with slumped shoulders on one of the long benches in the estate. He looked up with dazed eyes and shook his head as if trying to pull himself together. 'The first battle is over. Now we dig in and fight to protect

469

our home. We are soldiers of the North and we do not give up without a darned good fight!'

The youth twisted his face into one of stern annoyance at those words and nodded angrily. 'You're right, Captain,' he growled. 'This is our home! We will fight to the bitter end!'

'That's the spirit, lad!' Kane said, doing her best Dustin Grey impression before marching past the young soldier and allowing the smile to fall from her face. She surveyed the estate and puffed out her cheeks. The archers lined the battlements, looking out for any sign of movement from Mason's forces. Each unit had dropped back farther behind the walls and now waited with their captains and chiefs for any instructions. Those unable to fight – the elderly, sick, children – were walled up inside the larger buildings towards the rear of the estate along with a few warriors sworn to protect them to the last. There were tunnels leading out under the walls to the west that would allow some to escape in small boats onto the sea and off towards Norland if needed. It was a last resort, but one that Kane honestly felt would be needed as the battle continued, else it would just be a bloody massacre.

'Kat…' a low voice called to her right. She turned and smiled weakly at Sir Dominic. Th knight was dressed in his finest armour and wore a grim look on his face that was threatening the idea of him actually fighting in the battle. 'I did not see Dustin return through the gate…'

Kane swallowed the lump in her throat and paused whilst the pit of her stomach twisted as though filled with dozens of angry snakes writhing around inside her. 'I'm sorry Dominic. Dustin Grey gave his life defending his people. He fought bravely and with honour.'

Dominic's face dropped and he gave a grim nod, his lip quivering in his grief as he fought back the inevitable tears. It was strange seeing the usually pompous and arrogant knight wear such an honest mask of grief and sorrow. She found herself once again feeling sorry for the old warrior.

'He was a good man. A great man,' the knight said, voice cracking with emotion. 'His death is a loss for all of Takaara.' The knight took a deep breath and scratched his chin slowly, eyes off towards the gate. 'Kat, I am ready for this last battle. I will stand at the front and be there when they get through the gate, as we both know they soon will. I will make Dustin proud.'

Kane pushed the hair from her eyes and grabbed Dominic's chin softly, turning his face so that he was looking into her eyes. 'Sir Dominic. There are many scared and confused people waiting back in Grey's home who don't know whether they will see tomorrow. Those people need someone strong and brave to protect them. If you want to fight with honour and make Dustin Grey proud, I suggest keeping from the front line and instead focusing your efforts on making sure those people are protected until the very end.'

The old soldier thought about it for a moment, forehead creased in concentration before nodding. 'Yes… they will need someone willing to put their life on the line when the time comes.' He looked into Kane's eyes and she could see how grateful he was for the suggestion. 'Thank you, Katerina Kane. Once again, your wisdom shines through. I will be back at the house protecting those who cannot protect themselves.'

'A good idea, Dominic.'

They clasped forearms in the Northern tradition and she watched him march away, a spring in his step.

Many of the soldiers who had not fought in the first skirmish were looking at the injured and bloodied warriors who had with nervous eyes. Kane took her time and wove her way across to each of the unbloodied units, giving them strength with what words she had left. The captains and chiefs echoed her words and followed her lead, raising spirits and filling their soldiers with the battle-lust needed to survive.

'I could head out and speak to him, to Mason D'Argio.' Kane shook her head as Abhia walked towards her, biting on one of the green apples she had procured from somewhere nearby. 'I am of the Empire. It has been a while since Mason was in our city but I know his sister. Perhaps he will speak to me and I can make him listen.'

'I'm sorry Abhia but I would not risk you in such a way. Mason is not a normal man. You should have seen him…' Kane shuddered as she recalled his piercing eyes before ending Grey's life. 'Words will accomplish nothing now. It is too late for that.'

'A shame. There will be an ocean of blood spilled in this battle. If there was a way to stop it with words, we could save so many.'

'If only it were that simple,' Kane sighed. 'Dominic is heading back with the injured to Grey's main house. Reckon you could keep an eye on him and make sure he is okay?'

'I can do that,' Abhia replied, whipping out two curved daggers and spinning them dramatically.

'You'll be fighting your own people.'

'I follow the Empress. Her aim is to save Takaara. Mason has taken things too far. If that means I have to fight soldiers from my country, then that is what I will do.'

A loud bang from the south of the estate broke the conversation. Kane saw the soldiers on the walls tense and ready their bows, all aimed to the front walls past the gate.

Another thump echoed around the estate and the captains cried out to their units.

'Stand fast! Hold your position!'

'How long until they plough through?' Kane tilted her head and saw Kiras standing beside her.

'Won't take them long.' The first wave of arrows loosed and the screams of the Easterners filled the air. But still the thudding of the battering ram continued. 'The gate will act as a funnel and we should then be able to hold them at bay for some time…'

'That is good.'

Kane looked out of the corner of her eye at the Borderland warrior. She had some bruises and was covered in blood though Kane couldn't tell if it was her own or her enemies'. She had an icy look on her face and frowned towards the noise at the gate.

'Where is Sly? I saw him take a hit?'

'Cray has dragged him to the back of the line to get the wound cleaned. No point making it through the battle only to die from a damned infection. Seen it happen too many times before.'

'He better get it cleaned up fast – looks like we're gonna be needing him soon…'

Kane marched away, pushing her way to the front, sword in her hand in the hope that it would help calm her nerves. Each bang against the gate brought with it ripples along the puddles growing every second with the torrential rain. It was as though Takaara itself knew what was going to happen and it was crying out in pain. Kane reached the gate and stood at the front of the line, steeling herself for the battle and for what she felt would be the last moments of her life.

'Look after the person standing at your shoulder,' she cried to through the pouring rain. 'We stand together. We fight together. This is our home, and we will make it a hell for any who come through that gate…'

Arden watched the battering ram hitting against the wood with a mixture of impatience and curiosity. He had a sudden urge to reach out for his bow and loose a few arrows into the crowd of Easterners attempting to break through the gate and advance into the northern compound. Or maybe he would aim for the archers twitching on the wall, bows shaking in their wet hands. The weather would make things more difficult for sure, but that was the test of a true archer. Socket always used to tell him that. An archer's job in the Borderlands with the chaotic weather was that much more difficult. But it bred better archers. Hardy archers capable of fighting in any condition.

It hurt to think of his old mentor. He pushed the bittersweet feeling down into the pit of his stomach and prayed it would stay there. There wasn't time for such thoughts and feelings. Not here. Not now. Osiron was keeping an eye on the efforts in the South. Arden had been trusted to make sure the North would fall. By the fall of the sun, or what little sun was available in the North, most of Takaara would have been cleansed. Or at least that was the plan.

He watched the Easterners preparing for battle and he felt a need to pour out his frustration and his anger. He couldn't just sit there and wait, watching the two armies tear one another apart. Instead, he needed to prove that his forces were the dominant ones in Takaara. They would usher in a new age for the world, one which would cleanse the old of the plague of humanity.

'My prince, shall we wait?'

Arden looked behind him and thought for a moment as he stared at his commander. The soldier scratched at the open wound on his throat, a reminder of what had sent him to this place of existence.

'We have waited long enough,' Arden answered, his heart thumping against his chest. 'Show them who we are. Show them what we are capable of...'

The ground shook, nearly knocking Kane off her feet. Others fell to the ground in cries of shock and anguish. The battering of the gate had stopped and only the sound of the rain hitting against the metal armour of the soldiers could be heard as the world seemed to hold its breath. Kane didn't hesitate. She rushed up the stone steps and pushed past archers to make it to the top of the wall. Gazing out across the open field, she saw the cause for the disturbance. Mason's forces had turned their back to the wall and the gate. Instead, they were looking out with fear towards a dark mass of warriors rolling in from the east.

'Holy shit...' she muttered, rubbing at her eyes and trying to work out what she was seeing. Hundreds of monstrous soldiers swarmed towards the Eastern soldiers. The rumbling of the world continued as their boots smashed against the ground and the soldiers around Kane looked on in horror.

They turned their attention to the Eastern forces below them. Some were beating against the walls and wailing, crying out for the gate to be opened, to get some kind of protection from the Chaos heading their way. Kane stared into the eyes of the panicked men and women as they looked up to the battlements in horror, pleading for help. She scanned the battlefield and locked eyes with Mason. The preacher had lost the air of arrogance that she knew so well. He now looked up at her stone-faced and resigned to his fate.

'Let us in! Please!'

'Let us in!'

'They are monsters! Let us in!'

One of the guards turned to Kane and frowned. 'What do we do? General Grey isn't here...'

Kane took a moment to think about what the former general would have done. She didn't need to think long. 'Open the gates. Let them in.'

'We spend hundreds of lives fighting the bastards and now we are just letting them in without any hesitation?'

The question from Kiras was an expected one. 'We can either stand together against the Chaos or we can die fighting two battles against armies that are stronger than us. This is the only option we have available where our deaths are not guaranteed,' Kane said, hoping that it made some kind of sense.

'Just keep an eye on your back, I don't trust these Easterners and I certainly don't trust that preacher...' Kiras spat on the ground as Mason made his way over to them.

'Katerina Kane,' Mason D'Argio said curtly.

'If there is any trouble, I will kill you myself,' Kane threatened with an icy glare.

'We seem to have enough on our plates without causing more trouble for ourselves. Once we defend this...' He looked around the place with his lips curled and a face that made it seem as though there was a bad smell just under his nose. '... *lovely* place.'

'This is Dustin Grey's home,' Kane reminded him.

'Yes. Well it *was* his home...'

She took a deep breath and let the jibe slide, her fingers twitching for the hilt of her blade. 'Keep your soldiers at the front by the gate. Fall too far back and you will feel the tips of our blades.'

'How brave of you…'

'How kind of us…'

Mason swept away and clicked his fingers, summoning a whole host of soldiers who followed him towards the roar of the warriors of Chaos at the gate. It wouldn't be long until they made it through. For better or worse, the fate of Takaara was about to be decided.

'Why we waiting all the way back here?' Sly snarled, pushing the medic away with a growl.

'You needed that cleaned up,' Cray answered and pointed at the wounds stinging Sly's shoulder and calf.

'Had worse. Let's go fight.'

'You'll get your fight.'

'Those bastard Easterners are inside the walls with their backs to us,' Sly said licking his lips and chuckling. 'Think about how many of the fuckers we could kill…'

Cray rolled his eyes. 'Got worse things to think about now.'

The humour was swept away from Sly like a leaf on a winter wind. 'The kid… He'll be here.'

'Aye.'

'Won't be the first time I've stood opposite folk I know in battle. Just the way of things. Survive long enough and it's bound to happen. Shit, I remember Raven putting the blade through Brogen the Mad cycles ago and those two were mates for longer than the kid's been alive. These things just happen don't they?' He realised that he was just chatting shit now, trying to convince himself about how normal it all was. But it wasn't normal. None of it was. Arden had been betrayed and killed and yet he had come back with a dark army to seek revenge. He liked the kid but now he would be trying to kill him. No two ways about it.

Cray frowned and put Sly on alert as the ground wobbled.

'You feel that too?'

Cray nodded slowly, looking with concern at the puddles near the eastern wall.

'The tunnels,' Sly spat. 'Blow the horn to warn the others. They're coming through the fucking tunnels!'

Cray blew the horn as Sly raced to the wall, shouting for the unit closest to him to follow. They did so without any argument, trusting him and pulling their weapons free in an instant.

The ground erupted like a volcano as mud and earth blew all around them. The stone wall gave way, bits of the wall flying through the air with some crashing into unfortunate soldiers and ending their battle before it had even begun.

Sly made for the hole and roared, axes raised high as he saw the first warriors creeping out of the ground. His axe slammed into the first warrior, cracking into his skull and battering him back into the hole. The other soldiers around him felt heartened to see that the terrifying enemy could be beaten. Their spears thrust into the glowing flesh of the invaders and their shields diverted the first wave of attacks as they led the charge.

Sly felt the rush of battle take over, throwing the pain from his shoulder to the back of his mind, somewhere to be forgotten for the moment at least. His axes danced in all directions, carving their way through the strange warriors and blocking strikes that would have ended his life and sent him to the Hall of Ancestors.

One sword beat his defence as he swung wildly but another blade snuck in and blocked the strike before delivering a swift attack that beat the enemy back into the hells it came from. Sly grunted his thanks to Cray but there was no time for anything more as the swarm of enemies continue to come.

'We can't let a single one get past us!' Sly called to his soldiers. 'If they do, they will have a free shot at Grey's house. The poor bastards huddled in there don't stand a chance. Beat them back! Send them to the hells and keep them there!' he roared as the blood soaked Takaara.

He took a breath to steady himself and gripped his axes tight enough for his hands to turn white with the effort. He stared into the mass of demonic warriors heading their way and, for a moment, he thought he may have felt a trickle of fear fall down his spine. Growling, he shook it away and stared at the closest bastard to him, visualising the different ways he could tear his opponent apart.

'Come on you fuckers!'

Kane's arms ached but there was no time to rest. Each swing of the sword brought with it a grimace of pain as she fought against the stream of warriors still pouring through the gate. The horror of seeing the decaying and wounded warriors swarm past the walls had passed, replaced with the horror of what felt like inevitable death as the demonic men and women cleared out the first shield wall and wreaked havoc amongst the trained units of soldiers hoping to stand fast against the mass of Chaos. Easterners and Northerners stood together as one, fighting shoulder-to-shoulder in an effort to defend every inch of land available. But there was only so much they could do. The Chaos army seemed to be never ending and they shook off attacks that would have felled even the hardiest of warriors. Only a clean strike to the neck, head or heart seemed to produce the desire results and even then, there were barely seconds left until another bastard would take their place, snarling and frothing from their mouths and launching themselves at any sign of flesh and blood.

Her sword lanced through the neck of her latest victim. With a great pull, she ripped out its throat and fell back as her sword buried itself into the ground, bringing with it a shower of blood and gore. She paused, leaning against her blade as her chest rose and fell in heavy breaths.

Kane looked back and swore under her breath. Pockets of the enemy had made it past the wall using the tunnels built cycles before. Two units of Borderlanders were fighting furiously to keep the new threat from Grey's main house and away from the vulnerable people hidden inside.

'Fall back!' she cried, hoping that someone was listening. 'Fall back!'

A horn blasted again and she sighed with relief as two more units fell back towards the main house to support the Borderlanders. Kane stumbled back to support the rear but each step felt as though she was dragging a body through quicksand. She stumbled and her cheek hit against the ground, splashing into a puddle and spraying dirty water all over her. She spat and winced, turning onto her back just in time to see the snarling face of her death looming over her, axe high in the air as two decaying hands made to swing it straight into her skull.

Kane would have loved to say that she was brave enough to face her death with eyes wide open and the knowledge that she had fought as best she could in the defence of others. But she squirmed and shut her eyes, praying it would be a quick death.

The sound of metal on metal forced her eyes open just in time for her to see a thin sword slice into her attacker's neck. Her saviour pulled the sword free just as another blade finished the job.

'Teamwork. Saves lives.' Kane looked up to see Sanada and Drayke grinning at one another. Sigurd joined them, offering a hand to Kane and pulling her easily to her feet. The three warriors were covered in the blood and filth of battle but each were smiling as though they were having the time of their lives.

'Thank you,' she said to the three of them between ragged breaths as her heart beat so fast that her head started to ache. 'Thought that was it for a moment.'

'No need for thanks,' Sanada said, wiping his blade on his trousers. 'I am sure there will be more than enough opportunities to return the favour.' He nodded to Sigurd and the two warriors leaped away across the bodies scattered across the muddy battlefield. Drayke waited beside her.

'Are you okay?' he asked, concern lining his face.

Kane waved his concern away with her free hand. 'I'm fine.' She saw the disbelieving look on his face and rolled her eyes. 'Or as fine as anyone can be when fighting against demonic armies sent from the bowels of hell.' She was glad to see him smile at that. 'Go with them. They are your best chance for survival.'

Drayke shook his head. 'No. I'll stay with you.'

Kane butted her head gently against his as his father used to do to her. 'Go. I will be fine.'

Reluctantly, Drayke nodded and tore himself away to run after the two warriors. Kane blew out her cheeks, relieved that her son would be fighting with those experienced warriors. She trudged on herself, making for the house where it looked as though some of the enemy had finally made it past the Borderlanders' blockade.

She stabbed at the wave of enemies still pouring from the holes that had opened up inside the grounds. Just a few lines of warriors now stood to prevent them from overwhelming the house. Kane took the leg from one warrior and rushed past, leaving the job unfinished with a curse. She hoped that another soldier could step in and finish that one off but time was now of the essence. She blasted through the half open door to the main house and bounded along the corridor, taking the stairs three at a time. Her throat burned as she struggled to get the air she needed for her effort but there wasn't even time to worry about that. The sounds of a fight echoed down the hallways and she rushed towards it, hoping that she would not be too late.

The sound of footsteps followed her so she picked up her pace, knowing that any distraction would mean more of the Chaos warriors reaching her and ending it all.

She whirled around a corner and found herself at a chokepoint filled with fighting. With a roar, she disregarded the aches and pains and threw herself against the backs of the enemy. They tumbled to the ground as she pushed herself up and stabbed wildly. She staggered through the door and screamed, aiming her sword right into the face of a shorter woman caked in blood and holding her bloody daggers high.

'Abhia!' Kane screeched, lowering her sword.

'Katerina,' Abhia wheezed. 'You are still alive. That is good. And I see that you have noticed that the enemy has found their way inside...'

'How are the others?' Kane asked, searching the

empty room.

'They are safe. That old knight led them to the weapons room and said that he would protect them with his life. One of the tunnels runs from that room. I have told them to go if they hear the slightest sound of battle. I presume they are already on their way under the wall.'

'Then we need to give them as much time as we can,' Kane said, her words falling like an avalanche in the empty room. Abhia's bloody and sweat-drenched face told her that she knew what that meant. 'There is only one entrance to the weapons room. We must ensure that none are allowed to pass.'

Abhia nodded slowly and pulled her dark robe to the side, revealing a slowly bleeding wound to her ribs. 'I might as well use what time I have left to look after others.'

Kane rushed to her side and knelt beside her, studying the wound with increasing sadness. It was deep and wide. They could cover it but there was no certainty that she would survive.

'Then let's stand together. One last time.'

'I wish we could have spent more time together, you and I,' Abhia said sadly. 'I have grown fond of you, despite your strange ways.'

'We still have some time together, my sister. Perhaps we were brought together for a reason,' Kane replied with a tearful smile.

'Ah,' Abhia's chuckle transitioned into a hacking cough. 'You sound like a follower of the Gods now, Katerina Kane.'

'Well, if they are real, let us pray that they are watching over us now.'

Kane helped Abhia down to the weapons room as

the sounds of battle grew closer. They reached the corridor just as a body slammed through the wall beside them and took Abhia off her feet. The corridor filled with bodies flailing and the screams of the dying. The Chaos warriors looked different now. Their skin looked burned with an orange glow beneath the charred darkness and long claws stretched out from their skeletal hands. They ripped and tore at the Borderland warriors, blood and flesh flying freely.

Kane grabbed Abhia and dragged her into the weapons room. She shut the door behind them and fell back onto the wooden floorboards.

'Kat?' a voice called out from the shadows.

She looked over her shoulder to see Sir Dominic rushing to support her. He helped her to her feet and then lifted Abhia up and placed her onto one of the seats at the edge of the room.

'My hero,' Abhia said weakly, hand pressed to her ribs.

'I am no hero, my lady. Just a man trying to hide his cowardice.'

'That's what being a hero is,' Abhia said, her face draining of blood as she raised a hand and brushed her fingers against Dominic's cheek. 'Doing things even when you're scared because you know it is right.'

'Dominic,' Kane interrupted, 'where are the others?'

The knight motioned to the back of the room. 'They are all down in the tunnels. I made sure they had enough fighters with them and then promised to stay behind and guard the entrance. All of the injured, the children, the elderly. All have managed to escape this madness.'

Kane felt her chest burst with pride as she saw the way the old knight beamed with joy that he had played a part in saving lives. 'Well done, Sir Dominic. They owe you their lives.'

'I owe them so much more, Lady Katerina. So much more.'

A crash of broken glass sounded close by and drew their attention. Abhia stood gingerly to her feet, helped by Dominic.

'They are coming,' Kane said, not fighting against the weariness in her voice. They all knew it would be a battle to survive as long as possible. Such a foe meant that they would only stand for so long. 'We need to give the others enough time to reach the boats. That means we stand here and fight to the bitter end.'

She took a breath and pointed her sword towards the door, waiting for the incoming onslaught.

'No.' Kane looked over to Abhia, unsure if she had heard the woman correctly. 'It means that I can stand and fight. You are needed out there. Grey is dead. They need someone to rally them for the final stand. Otherwise, Mason will be the one they follow. I know what he is like when there is a vacuum of power…'

Kane shook her head but even Dominic was agreeing with it. 'I am sorry Katerina Kane. This is where I must stand on the other side of the argument to you. Leave us here to fight. We will protect those who are fleeing to safety. You must help the others.'

Before she could answer, the door burst open with a splintering of wood and broken glass. Dominic lurched forwards without hesitation and drove his sword into the face of the demon heading towards him. With a scream, he pulled the blade free and stabbed it through the heart of the

485

next attacker before backing away and giving her one last tearful look.

'Go!' he cried as he glanced down at three scratches on his forearm bleeding freely. He grimaced and spun, his chest heaving as he stood there defiantly. 'We will finish up here.'

Abhia squeezed Kane's hand and joined the knight, bloodied daggers out and ready for the next attack.

Sensing her hesitation, Dominic turned and grabbed Kane by the shoulders, bending slightly so that his tearful eyes met hers. His voice was low and quiet. 'Katerina Kane. You are going to go now. And you will survive this. I know that. It has been more than an honour to be able to call you a friend, even if that is just a recent turn of events. I know that I have been a fool, but I hope that in these last few moons, you know how much it means to me to call you a friend. Now, as your friend, I must command you to leave. Things are about to get bloody.' He kissed her on the forehead and smiled one last smile.

Kane grabbed his hand as he made to turn away, the shouts and screams growing in the open doorway. Abhia took down another of the soldiers hoping to make it into the room.

'You are more than a knight, Sir Dominic. You are a hero of Archania. And the whole world will know it one day,' Kane said as the tears fell down her cheeks.

'I am a coward, Kat. I know this. But today, for one brief moment, I am something more. And that is enough. Take the tunnel, turn the first left and take the ladder up to the garden. Continue the fight, Captain.'

Dominic didn't wait for a response. He spun and roared into battle beside Abhia, fending off the horde of warriors attempting to break through.

There was nothing more Kane could do. If she stayed, the three of them would die together. A pointless sacrifice in the hope of honour on her part. But if she did as her friends had asked her, she could make this all worthwhile.

The tunnel was dark and damp, but she followed Dominic's instructions. Even the grey light of the stormy day in the garden was blinding as she rose from the depths.

She covered her eyes instinctively and allowed a moment for them to adjust to the sudden light. When they at last focused, she found herself in Dustin's Grey's garden, watching Mason D'Argio pull a dagger across the throat of a soldier dressed in the armour of the Empire. His pupils were a blood red.

'Ah, you see my brothers and sisters,' he said to a circle of his followers who all stared at Kane. 'The God of Light delivers. We have another sacrifice to support our cause…'

THE BROKEN GODS

The warmth of the blood soothed him for a moment. Then he woke and thrashed around, his mind unable to come to terms with what had just happened.

Aleister remembered Istari driving the blade through him and throwing him into the vat of blood along with Zeek and Harish. He rushed up above the blood and took a deep breath, pulling as much air into his lungs as possible.

Then he realised that he wasn't thrashing in a pool of blood anymore, he was standing in a dimly lit corridor. He stumbled along the dark corridor, his legs not following the instructions he was trying to give. He coughed and raised his arms as he fell into the wall to his right, holding himself up as he struggled to acclimatise to the new surroundings. There was a green glow to the world around him, a faint light that seemed to show him the direction he needed to follow. Her trudged forward, following the dim light without thinking twice, knowing for some reason that this was what was expected of him.

Aleister's head pounded and he pressed a hand to

his forehead in an effort to ease the thumping pain he felt. It did nothing but he hadn't expected much. Instead, he shook his head and carried himself forwards through the low light, hoping to find some escape from the dark despairing gloom that had descended around him.

He recalled the distorted words before he had felt the strange embrace of the blood and darkness. Something about an Empress…

He fought to hold onto those words but they fell through his mind like water through his fingers. He steadied himself, glancing around to better understand his current predicament. His mind felt like it was full of a fog, every time he thought he had a grasp on something, it would escape his clutch at the last moment. He roared in frustration and battered his fist on the wall beside him. The action brought a moment of hesitation as he watched the wall shift and mould around the push of his fist before snapping back into place as he pulled his hand away.

Aleister followed the corridor with a frown etched on his face, fighting against the ringing in his ears and the pounding in his head as he stumbled towards the green light at the end of the corridor. Reaching it, he took a deep breath and tentatively pushed out a hand towards the light, a glowing orb that seemed to pulse with its own heartbeat.

Aleister screamed as his entire being lurched forwards into the green and he felt his body dragged towards the light and ripped into a million different pieces. He screamed and closed his eyes as every piece of him felt like shattering into tiny pieces and threatened to shoot all over the ream as they tried to pull in a million different directions. He fought back, trying his best to hold onto himself but feeling it was a futile battle. Time passed but he knew not how long. All he felt was the agonising pain of his body tearing apart in the green void. Aleister prayed for death, wanting an end to the seemingly endless suffering.

And then it stopped.

He lurched forwards and fell onto a cold, hard ground. His fall echoed across the dark abyss. Green flares popped up one after another either side of him, lighting a path before him as he scrambled onto his feet and frowned off into the distance. He didn't recognise any smell. He didn't see anything familiar. He could not hear anything but the low thrum of inaudible whispers growing in volume around him.

Shaking the voices away, he followed the lit path, not knowing what would greet him at the end.

'You come for judgement, purveyor of violence...'

'The blood you spill has built a pathway to the undead...'

'You should not have come here, killer...'

'The end of everything is upon us, another cycle of darkness awaits...'

'Flee! Flee and save yourself!'

'There is nothing more to do but listen to the Gods... only they know what is possible now...'

'He is Chosen... he can stand before them...'

'But will he be allowed to leave?'

The voices whirled around in his head as one voice, smashing together in a way that made it difficult for him to decipher the words bouncing around. He looked around and found that he wasn't in a corridor anymore. Instead, he was walking along a stony pathway between two tall cliffs as thunder and lightning blasted around the air above. Rain poured from the heavens but not a drop seemed to hit Aleister as he followed the green lights that flashed up sporadically along his pathway.

The lights grew in intensity and Aleister shirked back as he saw rows upon rows of gruesome soldiers glaring at him from either side of the path. They growled and grasped their various weapons with deadly intent but none moved past the green light as he continued his walk through the storm.

'You killed them. You killed all of them.'

'Vengeance. That is all they ask for. Vengeance for the lives you ended in the hope of doing something for your friends. In the hope of becoming a warrior of legend.'

'You wanted to be something more than the street urchin you were seen to be by others... how many lives were lost in the pursuit of something more?'

'I did what I thought was right,' Aleister snapped at the voices. 'I did what I had to to make this world a better place.'

'Ask the thousands who have died if the world is a better place without them. Ask their families and their friends...'

Frustrated, Aleister scratched at his face and pushed forwards, choosing to ignore the voices burrowing their way into his already thumping mind.

'We will all be judged at the end of days. You will be found wanting, Aleister of the Red Sons.'

A wind whipped up around him and pushed him forwards. He teetered on the edge of darkness, arms flailing uselessly as he rocked back onto his heels as the voices laughed at his poor efforts on the edge of nothing. And then he fell.

He fell for some time, his screams making no sound as he raced towards whatever was waiting for him at the bottom of nothing.

After some time, his fear faded and a wave of

tranquillity washed over him. By the time his fall ended, he felt ready for death to embrace him. But that was not his fate.

'Rise, Aleister of the Red Sons, and look upon the remaining Gods of your people. An ocean of despair may ride over you, but this is not the end, not yet, anyway. Rise and glance upon that which is more than you can comprehend…'

Aleister glanced up as he levelled his breathing. A green haze filled the air but he could see well enough to picture two tall thrones that rose almost to the dark clouds hovering above as green lightning flashed, followed by the roar of thunder.

A circle of warriors dressed in the Southern armour stood staring at the two thrones and the two colossal beings sat on them. They watched Aleister's every movement with black eyes that somehow sparkled in the green light. Long golden robes lined with black like the night sky ran down to the floor and their bald pates glistened in the green haze.

'Where am I?' Aleister asked, looking up at the two monstrosities. He pushed through the circle of Chosen and noticed that they each had golden pupils staring up at the two giants seated on the thrones, their eyes not even glancing his way. It was as if he was not there.

'Aleister of the Red Sons.' The voice boomed around the open space and shot through Aleister's entire being as he walked towards the giants. Neither had moved their lips but he knew that one of them had spoken. 'You are called to be here at the end of everything. But at the start of something new.'

'And what exactly does that mean?' He called up through the pouring rain, wanting answers now more than ever. 'And who in the hells are you?'

They looked at one another and Aleister could almost see a wry smile shared between them.

'We go by many names. Some of our number have passed on but we remain here to witness the end of Takaara.'

Aleister laughed in disbelief but he knew who they were. 'The Gods of Takaara. Two of The Four…'

'Eight, there were. In the beginning. Though your people were crude and in a state of being unable to comprehend what we were in the early stages of Takaara's life. The Four was the name given to us once the use of magic had drained four of our number and threatened this world created for the humans gifted this land.'

'Eight?' Aleister repeated, shaking his head. 'There were eight Gods?' His head swam as his mind tried to comprehend the fact that he was speaking to two Gods of Takaara. Perhaps he really was dead and this was the last hallucination before his mortal coil ceased to exist. A last test before deciding where his spirit laid to rest. He thought of Ella and prayed that he would see her again, at least one last time.

'In the beginning we allowed a small group to use magic, though we knew that it drained us of our life force and in doing so damaged Takaara. There was time, we thought, nothing would be irreparably damaged.' One of the Gods sighed and lowered their head. 'We could not foresee the damage it would do to ourselves and the world around us. At first, the damage was barely measurable. In time, your kind pulled more of the fabric of the world around them. They craved more power and took from the land and nature and then dragged the very life from the eight of us. Four withered away over the centuries. Two left for new worlds and the hope of a longer existence. Our kind are not eternal, but the two of us decided to stay and be here for the end of days, waiting to guide those who were left in the hope that we could salvage... *something.*'

'So Takaara is dying...' Aleister said, his shoulders slumped in defeat.

'It is almost dead. A lost cause. There is no power left in Takaara. It is dying and ready to rest.' The God speaking frowned, the first action of pure emotion Aleister had seen and it frightened him to the core, sending shivers down his spine. 'There were some who hastened the end of the world, knowing that their greed would be the downfall of others.'

A green light sparked to Aleister's right and he saw Zeekial and Harish tied up against a stone wall, their mouths gagged as they squirmed against their tight bonds. A woman stood beside them, one hand pressed against her throat as though she were trying to speak but no words would come.

'Your friends brought a darkness upon the land we created. They tore the energy from the Gods, from the world around them, knowing full well that it was to gift themselves a power that none could fight against. In their greed, in their despicable actions, they trapped their friend who they knew would fight against them. They created a world of their own where even the dead could not rest, a place full of despair and regret. They tormented the very fabric of reality in the hope of eternal life and they were not ready to deal with the consequences. They created a being of Chaos and Darkness that Takaara was not able to handle. Now there are three beings on Takaara capable of ending it all and it is all because of their greed – Mason D'Argio, Arden Leifhand, and Osiron Shadowsight all wish to rule what is before them. We wish to stop them, and we believe that we can...'

'There is another way to offer hope to those

fighting against the darkness gripping the world of Takaara,' the other God added. 'Our last threads of energy will give the people of Takaara enough energy to fight against those who wish to decimate all we have built. A last roll of the dice and a chance to use our magic to fight against those who wish to in darkness and blood.'

Aleister thought of Ella and wondered how she would feel if offered the final chance at hope, a last ditch effort to allow magic to overcome the darkness threatening the people of Takaara,

'What can I do to help?' Aleister asked wearily.

One of the Gods waved a hand and the gags disappeared from the mouths of the two captives.

'Aleister! Don't listen to them, they are weasels, figments of your mind sent by Osiron to play you against us!' Zeekial screeched, his face wild and furious. Harish just stared, mouth working furiously but his eyes almost unseeing.

Aleister turned and spotted a dark shadow drifting towards them. It was a black-cloaked being with an odd mask covering their face that had crooked, bloody antlers creeping from the crown.

'I listened to every word…' the newcomer said, facing Zeekial and Harish; their faces seemed to drain of all the blood they had and Zeek fell silent. 'You sent me there on purpose, a prison to lock me in because you were afraid of what I was capable of…'

Zeek shook his head and scrunched his face in anger. 'You don't believe this shit! We took you in when no one else would, Osiron. When they mocked you and laughed at you? When they wanted to kill you. Who was there?'

The antler mask tilted to the side as Osiron stepped

closer. 'You were always there for me. You used my blood for some of your tests. You scolded me for the tests I attempted on my own. You hit me one time. Elena was the voice of reason, she took pity on me.' They turned to the silent, distressed woman with pity. 'But the two of you were using me. You knew what I was capable of and you were scared...'

'Come on!' Zeek roared. 'We moulded you, Osiron.'

'No. You abused me. You used my own power to crate your Guardians so that you would not die, and then you used it to trap me in a world where I could not escape.'

'Zeek, Harish, is this true?' Elena had regained her voice. Her hand was against her chest now and she peered at the two captives beside her with a look crossed between sadness and rage. 'I can't believe it... Osiron came to us for help!'

'And brought the eyes of everyone else upon us!' Zeek snapped. 'They wanted them dead and they chose us. Osiron's power was too great and they could not control it. So I stepped in. Used it for the greater good.'

'I am so sorry Osiron...' Harish muttered, unable to look at his old friend. 'We were wrong. So wrong.'

Osiron took their mask off and their form seemed to shrink from a tall, skeletal figure into a small, young person with tears in their dark eyes. 'I came to you for help when I needed it the most. You said that you would always protect me. Instead, you used me and created your little Guardians. You locked me in a prison of the dead and filled it with others who struggled to pass on. Do you honestly know what that felt like? Do you know the grief, the torment, the pain that I and others have had to suffer because of you?'

496

There was no pity in Zeek's eyes now. The Boy King only wore a mask of cold hatred. 'We could have been Gods. We sucked the life from the very Gods before us and yet you would still cry about the people bothering you in Takaara, or Elena would moan that we were becoming the very thing we detested. You were both too weak. That is why Harish and I acted as we did. We were the ones with guts to carry out what had to be done.'

A single tear ran down Osiron's cheek before they morphed back into the tall, foreboding figure that had arrived earlier. 'Takaara is mine. Your dreams are over. But mine will bear fruit. Goodbye, old friends…'

With that, the so-called God of Chaos disappeared in a purple fog, leaving a rage filled Zeekial behind.

'Takaara bleeds and is struggling to take in its last breaths,' one of the Gods said, their voice weary and tired. 'The only chance for the people of Takaara to survive lies in taking the last threads of energy available from Gods and those who wished to be Gods. But for us to die, two more must take our place. A balance must be restored and given new life. There must always be a God of Life, and one of Death. They must replace the Light and the Dark. The Chaos and the Order. This is the only way for Takaara to survive.'

Zeekial stepped towards the towering Gods with a smirk on his face that made Aleister want to slap it off.

'Replace the pair of you? That is what Harish and I have been planning over the generations since the Breaking of Takaara. We are more ready than anyone in existence. Tell us what we must do, and we will do it. Your time is over, our time is just beginning.'

'I am afraid… that we have chosen another…'

His eyes opened to the odd green haze which had replaced the usual purple and blue he had grown accustomed to. His body ached as he pulled himself up from the ground and stumbled towards the light. There was no hesitancy in his actions, he knew where he had to go though he didn't know how he knew. The air was thick as he struggled for breath but he fought through the pain to find himself somehow in an open enclosure along with a circle of frowning Southern warriors, each holding spears in his direction. He took another breath and raised an eyebrow as all of the spears were raised as one, deciding that he was no threat.

The circle shifted as one and allowed a gap for him to enter. He strode through with a smirk and nodded at the closest warrior he passed but gained no reaction in response. Finally, he found himself standing with four others in the shadow of two towering beings the size of mountains. The colossal beings stared down with blank expressions but showed no sign of shock that he had appeared.

He looked over at the others: a livid Southerner fighting to hold back his rage; a brown-skinned frail man who he thought he recognised from somewhere with the look of defeat painted on his scrawny features; a beautiful woman with intelligent eyes and a shrewd face, and a Northerner with a familiar frown.

'Hate to crash the party, but in my defence, I've no idea how I even got here. I'm supposed to be dead…'

'Cypher Zellin,' one of the strange beings uttered with a voice like the harsh mountains of the North, 'you are here to take my place. You have a role to play yet.'

Cypher stuck out his tongue for a moment and chuckled. 'A role, for me?' he asked, pointing at his chest and staring around at the others who all seemed equally as bemused as he was. 'And what role might that be?'

'You, will be the God of Death.'

Cypher's smile dropped for a moment as he let those words sink in. The God of Death. The surprised looks from the others warmed his soul as he glanced up at the towering figures and nodded his acceptance, all words seeming insubstantial at this point. An ebony blade appeared in his hand, its weight comfortable as he lifted it, knowing exactly what he needed to do.

The angry bastard was the first to go. The blade ripped through his chest and Cypher watched with glee as the body crumpled into green dust that faded and was carried off by a swift breeze. He twisted the blade in his hand and whistled, feeling a renewed energy surge through his body, a new life. The frail looking man fell to his knees, eyes closed as his lips buzzed with a quiet prayer. Cypher made it quick. There was no need for anything more.

It was the woman's turn next.

'Stop,' she commanded in a voice that informed him that she was used to giving orders and having them followed. She held her hand out, silently requesting the blade. 'I have earned the right to do this myself.'

Cypher shrugged and smiled. What was it to him? He was a God.

She thrust the blade straight up into her chest and twisted. Her eyes went glassy and lost their spark that Cypher had found so intriguing. She slumped to the ground and faded away just like the other two. Cypher retrieved the blade and turned to face the remaining man.

'Cypher Zellin,' the man said with a scowl. 'Torturer. Murderer. Turncoat. Coward.'

Cypher scrunched up his face and bit his lip. 'And now you can add God to the list of names people have for me…'

'You can't let this rat hold any kind of power,' the man called up to the Gods sitting patiently. 'I have seen his work. He is a monster.'

'He is a necessary tool in the survival of Takaara. He will shepherd the dead to their rightful place. He will ensure that there are no souls left to wander aimlessly or be trapped in realms where they will fester and grow malevolent.'

Aleister sighed. 'Then what of the other? Who is to be the balance to *this*… God of Death?'

'You are.'

BALANCE

Arden stumbled on the muddy ground and frowned. He should not be stumbling. He hadn't stumbled in quite some time. He felt his heart beat faster and tried to steady himself as he marched through the warriors fighting to their last breaths. He clutched the long, bloodied dagger in his hand and gritted his teeth, passing the odd moment off as just a trick of his mind and nothing more. He wasn't like all the rest. He was a Prince of Chaos and he was here to rule.

As soldiers roared and raced towards him, he sighed and whipped the dagger easily across their flesh, opening deadly wounds and spilling blood that sank into the earth at his feet. He pushed forwards as the bodies piled up, searching for Mason D'Argio.

A crack of lightning ripped the sky and thunder echoed all around him. The weather of Takaara had always been volatile. But there was something different about this. The sky shimmered and took on a green haze as Arden inched closer to the tall building that his soldiers were tearing apart with ease. Ignoring the strange sight, he made for the stone path leading to the garden around the back of the house, feeling a strong pull of magic guiding him.

Mason stood with a group of soldiers and a pile of bloody bodies. The blood had stained the beautiful stone of the garden and created a grim sight as Arden entered the enclosure. The preacher was holding a struggling woman by her hair. His eyes flared red and he stared at the woman with a sick kind of hunger etched on his face, teeth bared like a wolf waiting to devour its prey.

'You are the preacher who tainted Archania...'

Mason's glare turned to Arden. He dropped the woman with a thud to the floor and stood up tall, eyes running over Arden as though weighing up a prize.

'And you are the boy who would be king... you have the power I crave, though you do not know how to use it.'

'I am the Prince of Chaos,' Arden exclaimed angrily. 'I know the power I wield. And I know how to use it.'

'Cute,' the preacher smirked like a teacher toying with an arrogant student. 'You are happy being a prince when you should be a God. My sister taught me about the power your kind can wield. I ripped the rest of the information from that weasel Harish in the dungeons of Archania. I will enjoy tearing the power from you...'

'And I will enjoy sending the pieces of your soul across the hells.'

Mason took a step forwards and then the blood seemed to drain from his face. 'Your eyes... golden. It cannot be...'

The preacher squealed in pain and looked down in shock to see the point of a dagger sticking out from his chest.

Always keep a dagger in your boot. Just in case.

Braego's words rushed back to her as Katerina Kane jabbed the short dagger through the back of her foe and pushed with all her strength until she felt the blade pop out of his chest. She had not the energy to pull the weapon free. Instead, she kicked him to the ground in an unceremonious slump and fell back, breathing heavily.

Crawling forward, she leant over the shocked face of Mason D'Argio and stabbed. Once. Twice. Three times. Four times. She lost count and just kept pressing the blade into his flesh, the squelching thud becoming rhythmic until the tears began to flow down her cheeks.

She glanced up to see the pale hooded man who had argued with Mason walk towards her. He stopped in front of the body on the ground and looked down at Kane. She could see the gold of his pupils staring down and it reminded her of Ella.

'Your pupils are golden…' she muttered at the wonder.

'But that must mean that I'm…' Arden felt a punch in his back that took the breath from his body. It took him all the way back to the time when he stood in the snow with Socket.

'Mortal…' Sly's voice whispered into his ear as he pulled the axe from his back.

Arden reached around and winced as he felt the wet blood dripping from the wound. He turned to see Sly staring at him, tears falling down his cheeks and lost in the pouring rain.

'I'm sorry, kid. I wish it hadn't ended like this.'

'But… I'm the Prince of Chaos,' Arden whimpered, his chest heaving with sobs at he glanced at his blood covered hand. He looked up at the strange green sky and shook his head, knowing that something had gone wrong. He lowered his gaze and looked into Sly's eyes which were full of sadness. He had always seen the warrior as a hardened man willing to do anything for his people. But he had also helped Arden in the beginning, in his own way of course. He wished he could go back and change everything. But it was too late for that. Various paths that he could have taken flashed before him in an instant. A thousand different visions of lives he could have lived. Now, all would fade to nothing. 'Finish it, my friend.'

The axe split his skull. There was no pain.

Sly pulled his axe free and knelt next to Arden's body. His body burned with the aches and pains of the battle but that was pushed to the back of his mind as he gazed down at the wet body of Arden Leifhand. His face was a mess, thanks to the strike of the axe across his skull. It was a clean hit. He wouldn't have felt any pain. Sly felt an exhaustion incomparable to anything he had ever felt before, a weariness brought on not just from the physical exertions but the mental ones too. He was tired. Too tired for it all.

'Sly… time to go,' Kane muttered, grabbing him beneath his arm and dragging him to his feet.

'No, we can't leave him next to that bastard,' Sly argued as he stared down with horror at Arden's body beside the corpse of Mason D'Argio. 'It ain't right…'

'No way around that right now.' Sly followed Kane's eyes and glared at the marching Eastern soldiers. Their shock had turned to fury once it had sunk in that their leader was dead. Sly gripped his axes, wanting to take out his rage and sadness on the soldiers standing before him.

'Not now!' Kane warned, this time more forcefully. She pulled him away and he relented, hobbling away back to the battlefield. Horns blared and confusion covered the battle. Arden's army had disappeared from the battlefield, leaving a green dust suffocating the air. But the fight was not over. Mason's forces had turned once again on the Northern warriors and were doing their best to take the estate. Another horn blared and Sly looked across the many fires and slaughter.

A familiar warrior held a hammer high as he led the Barbarian horde forwards, clearing out Mason's remaining forces with glee, blood splattered across his tall, scarred frame.

'Who is that?' Kane asked, eyes widening at the destruction.

'Ragnar the Bloody,' Sly answered with a tired smile. 'Chief of the Barbarians.'

Sly wasn't going to watch any longer. He ignored the pain screaming from his body and raced from Kane with his axes in hand. If this was to be the end, he would make it a glorious one for the ages.

His axes sang as they whistled through the downpour of rain, whipping left and right, up and down and always finding their targets. He saw Kiras and Cray fighting with renewed vigour, their faces covered in blood that could be their own but most likely would be that of their enemies. The green haze gave the battle an otherworldly feel and Sly wondered if he was fighting in one of the hells beneath Takaara and that he was already dead, resigned to fight for all eternity.

A sword flashed his way and he made to parry the blow but he was too slow, too tired. The edge of the blade cut into his forearm and he grunted in pain before dragging his other axe wildly and catching the attacker on the neck. A lucky strike but luck was everything in battles like this. He pulled back, assessing the wound, which was thankfully a shallow one, though the blood was dripping from the cut.

'Getting slow, old man!' Kiras chuckled, falling in beside him after taking the knees from one soldier and slashing her swords across one another to relieve the man of his head. 'Time to pack up.'

'Aye,' Sly agreed. 'Looks like it.'

Kiras frowned at him and gave him a searching look. 'What's happened?'

'The kid,' Sly choked, forcing down the lump in his throat as he replayed the axe finding its mark in the young man's skull. 'I killed him.'

Kiras paused, rocking back and forth for a moment before deflecting an incoming attack and forcing the attacker back. Cray jumped in and finished the job, allowing them some space as the Barbarians tore through with their fresh wave and took apart the Eastern forces. A horn filled the air and Sly was relieved to see the enemy fall back in retreat. Victory was at last at hand...

'You had to. You saw what he was capable of,' Kiras said to Sly in the hope of soothing him. 'Had to be done.' Her voice turned stern and uncompromising. 'Just the way of things.'

'Aye,' Sly said, agreeing but not feeling any better for it. 'Aye.'

A heavy hand fell on his shoulder and Cray gave it a squeeze. 'You did what had to be done, brother. Had to be done. Saved a lot of folk, my family included.'

Sly nodded and allowed the big man to pull him close for a brief hug before pushing away.

He walked through the scattered, tired men and women of the North and offered them weak smiles. Kiras was better. She skipped through the blood and filth and spoke of victory and a battle for the ages. She was the one who brought smiles to the faces of the weary and drained. She was the one who offered an energy for those who needed it most.

Sly reached Sanada who sat against a wall, the large body of his Barbarian friend lifeless against his lap.

'He fought bravely,' Sanada said, his voice as lifeless as Sigurd's body. 'He will dine with his ancestors. They will raise a jug to his valour and bravery.'

Sly sat beside the islander and nodded. 'Songs will ring out in the halls of his ancestors. A death in battle is one not to be sneered out. It is all we ask for in our line of work.'

Sanada's glassy eyes just looked out across the destruction as he stroked his friend's cheek softly.

Sly sat beside him for a while until he noticed that Kane was walking over to him along with her one-armed son whose face was pale and ghostly. She was covered in the filth and muck of battle. 'Something has happened away from here. The forces of Chaos did not just disappear for no reason…'

*

Aleister stood at the top of the Gods' Falls and allowed himself a moment to appreciate the beauty of the land as the red sun hung high in the sky. Beautiful. The light glistened against the water and filled the air with a warm orange glow. A pale figure stood alone on the edge of the

Falls, admiring the view of the South.

'I spent much of my youth craving an escape from this world,' Osiron said as Aleister took his place beside them. 'Thought myself a coward for not being able to end my own life. Then I found Elena, Zeek, and Harish. They were so kind to me. They showed me what it meant to have friends and gave me meaning. For the first time, I wanted to live and seek out new places and see beauty such as this.' They turned to Aleister with a sad look on their pale face. 'All I ever wanted was to belong, to have people around me who cared for me, who wanted me to be happy. I thought I had that. But they were using me to become Gods. They trapped me in that dark world and filled the place with the dead. My anger, my rage twisted those souls into things who wanted nothing but revenge for their enslavement. All souls need rest. They need Gods who can ease their passing. That is all. I felt nothing but pain in that place. I suffered along with every soul there. That is why I wanted to change things. That is why I wanted to start anew.'

'But many would have suffered if you had succeeded,' Aleister argued. 'There are good people in this world. Good people who deserve better.'

Osiron sighed. 'Perhaps. You are lucky to know them. I have known nothing but traitors and bastards.' They frowned and paused for a moment. 'Arden was a good, kind soul. If I regret anything, it is leading him astray. He had goodness in his heart and looked for the kindness in others. I hope he finds peace in the afterlife. I never wanted power, you know. I just wanted a normal life. To have power is to have a responsibility to others that can be a burden if not dealt with properly. You are to be the God of Life – a balance to Death and hope to all Takaara. I hope you are able to bear that burden of responsibility. They will pray to you and you cannot listen to them all. They will love you, hate you, worship you, turn their backs on you, and you must take it all in your stride. I wish you luck. You will need it.'

Osiron twisted and fell back, dropping from the edge of the cliff and falling towards the jagged rocks at the bottom of the Falls. A green light erupted as their body met the base of the Falls, flowing up and following the dance of the wind.

Aleister took one last look out across the beauty of Takaara, tears silently falling down his face. He thought of his sister and her unborn child. Aleister would never lie eyes on them or see them grow. Bathos would take care of them, his large friend had a heart bigger than his colossal frame and he would go to the ends of Takaara to ensure they lived a good life. The thought calmed him as he asked his best friend and his sister for their forgiveness. They would not hear him, but he knew that they would understand, some day. Finally, he thought of Ella and wondered if she was at rest at last. She had wanted a better world free of prejudice. Perhaps she would have that now. He closed his eyes and prayed that he would do the world justice. He prayed that he would be better in death than he had been in life.

THE UNFORGOTTEN

The snows seemed particularly harsh this winter. Worse than the past few cycles anyway. Sly pulled his jacket tight around him and raised his hood to keep the deadly cold wind from biting his skin. His boots crunched into the mounds of snow as he made his way up the hill, smiling at the frozen river and recalling marching in the opposite direction with Arden and Bane over a cycle and a half ago. Time really did seem to fly. He winced as the old wound in his shoulder played up as it liked to do more often than he liked recently. Still, he couldn't complain, others hadn't been so lucky.

He trudged past the circle of stones that had been erected a cycle earlier. He placed a cold hand against one of the towering stones and offered a silent prayer to the dead. Locals had taken to calling the stones The Unforgotten. He liked the name. They represented the dead who had given their lives for Takaara in the Final War as it was now known. He thought Raven would have appreciated that. Baldor too. Socket would have just scoffed and waved it off as some dumb thing the living did to make themselves feel less guilty for surviving. But Sly liked it. He enjoyed being reminded of his old friends. Raven. Baldor. Socket. Frida. Arden. Thinking of the kid always brought a pain to his chest but it passed sooner now. Time may fly liked the crow but it also healed.

'Taking your time.' Sly turned to see Cray leaning against one of the stones. His beard had been left to grow for over a cycle and a half and was now liberally streaked with grey and tied in a tail like that of a pony.

'Not in any rush are we? The ale won't go off any time soon.'

Cray laughed. He did more of that lately.

'How's the little one? And the wife?'

'All good. Complaining as much as usual. Glad to be out the house and free from tidying it in all honesty,' Cray said with warm smile that told Sly he was only half-joking.

'Aye.'

'They would like you to stop by. The wife always says that there is a space for you in our home.'

'Appreciate the offer, but I'll be spending time sorting out Cagen's place. You should all come up once its ready again. I won't be serving the piss that old bastard used to give us!'

'I'll be there.'

The two of them walked together as brothers into the main town of Torvield in silence, comfortable with one another. Only a few of the townsfolk were out. Too cold for that. The few that were offered wide smiles and waves which were returned. Raven would have enjoyed seeing the place like this. A Barbarian strode past, not even wearing shirt, snow covering his dark beard as he saluted Sly and

Cray.

'Morning, big man,' Sly said with a nod before making for the Great Hall.

He barged the door open with his shoulder and then pushed it back once Cray had followed him inside. The howl of the wind lessened and he could already feel the heat coming from the large fire in the centre of the room. He lowered his hood and took his jacket off, shaking the excess snow from himself and running a hand through his long hair.

Ignoring those sitting on either side of the long table, he marched straight up to the throne covered in bear fur and smiled warmly at the Chief of the North.

'Sorry we are a bit late, Chief' he muttered as the chief stood and embraced him. He offered her a kiss on the cheek and pressed his forehead against hers.

'You are always on time, my friend,' Kiras replied. She pulled him tightly in and whispered into his ear so that only he could hear her, 'And stop calling me chief…'

'Sorry, Chief,' Sly smirked before pulling away and taking an empty seat alongside the others.

Ragnar the Bloody slapped a hand on Sly's shoulder and welcomed him with warm eyes and a full cup of ale which Sly gratefully accepted. The others around the table nodded and saluted with smiles on their faces. Katerina Kane of Archania. Zaina of the Red Sons. Buhle of the Southern Kingdoms. Ambassador Matthias of the Free Nation of Norland. Sara Guidice of New Causrea. Powerful people coming together to make sure that Takaara would never again face the perils it had just had to face.

'Well,' Kiras said, clearing her throat and standing as she spoke. 'Welcome to my humble home of Torvield. It is good to see you all again. The last half-cycle has been relatively calm, which I think we are all pleased and relieved about.' The smattering of laughter informed her that it had been a relief. 'No gods or demons to fight, thankfully. Just trade disputes and annoyed farmers up here. And the constant battle against the damned snow… but things are looking up, at least. Matthias, what news is there in Norland?'

The scrawny fellow stood with a scrape of his chair on the stone and pushed his glasses up before coughing nervously. 'Chief Kiras, thank you once again for the invitation to Torvield. The people of Norland are enjoying freedom from the United Cities. There has been a recent spate of attacks on former church building from a group calling themselves The Cult of Death.' Matthias sighed and took his glasses away from his face and pinched the bridge of his nose before continuing. 'A nuisance and nothing more. They wear broken plague masks and appear to just revel in the chaos they bring. It is being handled.'

Kiras nodded in her seat and rolled her tongue over her gums thoughtfully. 'Good. Well, if you require any help, just say the word. Ragnar, how are the Barbarians settling in?'

'All good, Chief,' Ragnar said with a huge grin. 'We love life in the North and under your guidance, my people feel at home once more. There have been a few drunken quarrels but that is the way of our people. It is all forgotten with the rise of the sun.'

'And Buhle, how are things in the South?'

The dark-skinned warrior rolled her eyes and gave a sigh. 'How long do we have?' she chuckled darkly. 'The kingdoms are divided. Queen Cebisa has threatened war with Milani and Bthanda over what is to be done with Zakaria. King Solomus's death only worsened the tensions in the region. We are a broken people, still grieving over our fallen king and the horrors of the war. The shock will pass. We are still stationing soldiers near the Heartlands but that situation has calmed of late. The region is more settled than I have seen it in many cycles.'

'That is good news,' Kiras replied, looking tired and weary with the information. 'And Sara?'

Sly sat up straight as the beautiful woman swept her long blonde hair over her shoulder and stood. 'Construction on New Causrea is going well. We have had many flock to our aid and though the work is hard, it is helping to give renewed life to those displaced by the war. A new council has been chosen and the city is starting to grow and fill with life. The situation in the East with my father is slightly less hopeful. Istari is king-regent but he is not built for leading. He is a fighter who wishes to live alone.'

Katerina Kane snickered at this, failing to hide her action by suddenly downing the wine in front of her. The thought of the grumpy warrior having to deal with the petty disputes of the people would never fail to make her laugh.

Sara just smiled wickedly and gave her a wink. 'A vote will be held with suitable candidates. The Red Sons have been helping with the rebuilding of Darakeche,' she said with a nod towards the red-haired Zaina who waved a hand her way. 'Many arguments broke out but we expected this. It will take some time before that area is stable once more.'

'And Kat, how are things in Archania and Starik?'

Kane shrugged and blew out her cheeks. 'Drayke has decided to move away from the royal model. A council of chosen peers will lead the two nations. He is helping to oversee the development. There is an air of uncertainty but promise also. Danil leads the army and is training the soldiers daily just in case any unpleasantness occurs.'

'Excellent,' Kiras said heavily. 'Well, I think that will do for now. The taverns are open and I can almost smell the meat from here. Perhaps a break and then we can meet this evening.'

The sound of multiple chairs scraping across the floor erupted as the men and women left their seats and made for the door. The howling of the wind grew as they left one by one, leaving only Sly and Ragnar in their seats. Cray stood in the shadows with arms folded as usual, keeping an eye on his chief as she greeted Zaina with a wink and a gentle kiss on the lips. The two of them had been close since their last meeting.

'I'll meet you in a bit,' Kiras said to the red-haired leader of the Red Sons. She winked and smacked her on her arse as she turned away.

'You two seem happy,' Sly said when the door shut.

Kiras smiled and picked up a bone from the table and waved it at the great, lazy, black dog sleeping by the fire. Instantly, it shot up and bounded across the stone to its master. 'We have fun together.

Sly watched happily as the dog took the bone and then nudged Sly's leg in greeting, tail wagging frantically. 'Who's a good boy?' He patted the dog's head and knelt beside it, giving it a big hug. 'You been good, Baldor?' The big dog's eyes were full of an easy joy as it dropped to the ground on its belly and gazed around at the humans left.

'Think I did okay?' Kiras asked, her eyes full of concern. 'I still think one of you should be seated here.'

Ragnar shook his head. 'We would just breed more war and more blood. Our people love you. They respect you. You are the right person to lead.'

Sly agreed. 'Don't think men are cut out to lead

anyway. Also, I'm too pretty to lead. You're the brains.'

'Speaking of pretty,' Ragnar said with a conspiratorial wink, 'I think I will go and speak with that Buhle… what a woman! Such beauty and fire!' The Barbarian laughed and left the room, leaving just Sly, Kiras, and Cray.

Cray walked closer to them, playing with his long beard.

'Got anything for us to do before the next meeting, Chief?' he asked Kiras.

She chewed her cheek for a moment before answering. 'Heard there's been a couple group of fools out in the woods attacking Barbarians heading south.'

Sly felt the old fires burning inside at her words. 'And what would you like us to do about it?'

Kiras gave them both a wide smile and leant down to scratch behind Baldor's ears. 'Kill the fuckers.'

Sly and Cray grinned at one another like lucky boys on their name day.

'Aye, we could do that…'

Katerina Kane felt the wind in her hair as she urged her horse on, racing as fast as she could in the bright light of the winter sun. She pushed forwards up the hill and only slowed down once she found the familiar tree that brought back a wave of memories. Jumping from her horse, she gave the beast a scratch and an apple which it accepted happily as Kane left it and walked over to the bare tree, slightly out of breath.

'Do you come here often?' Matthias asked as he tied his own horse up. 'I know this was one of Ella's favourite spots. You can see all of Archania.'

Kane looked out across the snow-covered lands with a smile. 'I don't come often enough. It reminds me of her. A bittersweet feeling.'

'Whenever I am in Archania, I always feel as though she will just turn up out of the shadows with that beautiful smile of hers,' Matthias said with a dark laugh. He looked exhausted. Dark bags hung under his eyes and there were grey hairs streaked on the sides of his head. 'That's why I stay in Norland. It's quiet. Free from those painful memories. Every time I tried to do something good, I seemed to make things worse. Ella and the mages. The plague. I feel life on an island away from it all is good for me.'

'You look tired, Matthias.'

'Don't sleep much when I'm back here. I see her in my dreams.'

Kane grabbed his hand and squeezed as they looked down from Hangman's Hill and out across Archania. 'There is good in you, Matthias. Do not beat yourself up. The past is the past.'

Matthias nodded slowly and squeezed her hand in return before changing the conversation. 'And where are you off to now?'

'I have been meaning to visit Bathos, Ariel, and the twins for the past few moons. I have an open invitation to join them in the Southern sun.'

'How are they doing down south?'

'Good,' Kane replied, unable to keep a smile from her face as she thought of the little ones. 'Two babies are a good distraction from the pain of Aleister's death. From the letters Ariel is writing, they already have Bathos wrapped around their little fingers.'

'That is good,' Matthias said with a grin of his own.

517

'Are you travelling alone?'

'No,' Kane replied, spotting her companions riding up the hill and waving. 'In fact, here they are, right on time.'

Matthias gave her a hug and said farewell, leaving Kane on the hill to wait for her companions to make it up the tricky path.

'Why couldn't you have met us at the bottom of the hill?' Istari Vostor grumbled as he jumped from his mount. He sighed and strolled over to Kane, hugging her and giving her a soft kiss on her cheek.

'Good to see you too…' Kane said, cheeks burning slightly.

'I still can't believe you're leaving to go journeying to the Southern Kingdoms…' Sara said from her own horse, shaking her head but smiling at her father.

'The East has survived without me for countless cycles. It can last a moon or two,' Istari snapped back as he helped Kane onto her horse. 'If it cannot, then I am afraid that it will not survive for much longer. Anyway, you were the who said that I need to get out more…'

Istari and Sara continued their bickering as they rode down the hill but Kane waited on her mount and surveyed her home from on high.

Tears fell freely down her face as she smiled, lost in memories both good and bad. Silently she said farewell to all her friends and promised that they would never be forgotten.

'We will meet again, one day,' she whispered to the wind before blowing a kiss to the land and urging her horse forwards. She had a strange feeling that someone was watching over her and listening to her final farewell.

She patted her horse on its neck and smiled. 'Come

on girl. Time to go.'

THE END

Acknowledgements

So that's it. The end of the trilogy. Writing that it is a bittersweet experience doesn't quite touch the vast, overwhelming feelings I have regarding the end of *The Broken Gods.* The story started out titled Blood of the Heretic, an absolute mess of a novel with far too many POV characters and too much plot but with a few golden nuggets nesting amongst the filth. Rachel Rowlands first helped me to see what I had to cut way and supported me by shining a light on the things I had done well that were worth keeping and without her, I wouldn't have been able to write *Flames of Rebellion.*

I have fallen in love with the characters over the years of having them in my head – I've enjoyed watching them grow (and killing them off) and nothing makes me happier than when I hear that those characters have found a place in the hearts of the readers around the world who have bought my books. It is an honour to have such an impact and I hope for many more such moments.

Thanks to Jon Oliver who has managed to pick out the numerous mistakes I managed to make over the three books as I tried to find time day and night to write the trilogy even through the strangest of times on a global scale. It is very much appreciated and it has been a pleasure to work together.

To Mars Dorian for the awesome covers across the trilogy. I have always looked forward to seeing the artwork as they progressed from drafts to the finished piece so thank you very much.

To my family and friends who have bought my books and supported me throughout this journey, you are all amazing. Thanks to Dom, Jon, Luke, Pete, and Dave who brought a smile to my face as they messaged me day or night when they reached a significant event in the stories – I loved hearing of your reactions on something that would have taken me so much effort to write the year or so before. You make all the hard work worth it.

And to Sarah and Kiwi. It may take until the end of days for you to read my books but your support is what allows me to write and that is more important than anything I could ever ask for.

The writing community on Twitter and the Super Relaxed Fantasy Club. It has been a pleasure to meet such great authors such as G R Matthews, Steve McHugh, Adrian Selby, RJ Barker, and many more. The random writing and book chats I have had since the world started to open back up have helped with my own development as a writer and long may that continue.

To Adrian and the amazing folk at Grimdark Magazine for allowing me to write for them and get some of the numerous thoughts out of my busy head and onto their website – your support has been incredible and it is great to be a part of such a hard-working and caring team.

And lastly, and most importantly, to you – the reader. Without you, I'm just some madman with odd ideas whirring around my head that somehow find their way onto the pages. Being a self-published author is hard work. Thanks for every book you have bought, every review you have left (good or bad), and every message you have sent. The hours are long but I love it.

Thank you for everything.

Aaron S. Jones

Printed in Great Britain
by Amazon

76140973R00314